Twisted Fates

The Xun Ove Series: Book 3
Step Across The Barrier

James William Peercy

James W. P.
11/29/15

TWISTED FATES Copyright © 2015 James William Peercy

Line By Lion Publications
4641 E. Mahalasville Rd.
Morgantown 46160

www.linebylion.com

ISBN: 978-1-940938-66-0

ACKNOWLEDGMENTS

I wish to express sincere appreciation to family and friends. In particular: Claudette Peercy for putting up with me when I've said, "Come look at this..."; Clifford and Dianne Peercy who never set limitations on what I could become; Brian Miller and Darrell Miller with whom I used to swap stories and dreams as we rode to school on the bus; Elizabeth Mendoza whose excellence in photography is equal to her personality and friendship; Arash Mahboubi for reading and commenting (to the point of asking, 'When is the next one?); Alan Martin for all his detailed and careful evaluation; and Jose Jimenez for the ability to take a description and create artwork. Thanks to K.A. DaVur and Three Fates Press for all the hard work.

To all of you, highest commendations.

CHAPTER 1

The trumpet rocked the city.

"Hear ye, hear ye! Attend to the queen!"

With a fury of racing feet, elves throughout the kingdom rushed toward the palace. Queen Freya had called a royal assembly. No elf would dare ignore the summons. Thank God Jonna was no elf.

With a deft hand, he grasped the handle to his and Elfleda's abode, opened it slightly, and slipped in. The solid oak doors muffled the proclamation and gave him a great excuse should someone catch him sneaking away. Not that it mattered. He knew the reason for the announcement.

"Where ya going?" Bob the Pixie flashed into existence. A small pixie bag swung from his dark leather belt. His dark green pants and shirt brightened briefly as the light faded from the transition. He adjusted the maroon feather in his green cap, folded his arms, and crossed his maroon-colored boots.

Sometimes, Jonna thought the pixie had placed a tracking device on him. "None of your business." He stepped faster in an effort to lose the pixie, but Bob would have none of that. The pixie floated along beside him and matched his speed. "Bob, leave me be!"

"Getting the jitters, I see."

"I am not."

"Then why are you heading toward the closet?"

Jonna stopped before he slammed into the closet doors. His gaze followed their intricate twists and turns. Interlaced into the design, the elven symbol of eternity, a lemniscate, stared back at him. He spun to the left, huffed, and hurried on. "Because it is right by my bedroom."

"You should be heading toward the palace."

"Bob, they don't need me there."

Elfleda stepped from the bedroom, caught his arm, and lovingly turned him around. "Yes, they do." In her hand lay the sheathed Rune Blade of Knowledge on a leather belt. She fastened it over his shoulder and back. "And you need this, too."

"The presentation is tomorrow!"

"But the edict is today. My mother won't be happy if you miss it."

"Your mother is too caught up in formality. All I want is peace and quiet." His eyes brightened. "We should go on a picnic!"

"After the presentation, I'll have the bag ready." Elfleda's eyes twinkled. "Until then, we must fulfill our obligations. We are royalty after all."

"*You* are royalty. I'm just a human who lost his way."

Her eyes narrowed. "You don't mean that, do you?"

Jonna cringed. Life at the palace wasn't all it was cracked up to be. Saving the kingdom had been one thing, but day-to-day royal responsibilities were monotonous.

Flashes of light erupted from the side of the hall, causing everyone to blink. In the corner, a small green chameleon directed two fireflies, while a dragonfly floated in the middle of them. The wings of the dragonfly amplified the fireflies' light as they flickered past. Their actions created an upside down image on a parchment. The chameleon traced the image.

Jonna sighed. "We even have paparazzi sneaking in!"

"You mean lizarazzi." Bob grinned. "Papas have nothing to do with it."

"Lizarazzi or paparazzi, they are all the same!"

"Actually--" Bob glanced at the chameleon with a smile.

Flashes went off. The lizard reached for another sheet and started to draw furiously.

"--although related, a camera and *camera obscura* are not the same. While a camera, used by the paparazzi, came from the idea of the camera obscura, camera obscura, used by the lizarazzi, means dark chamber."

Jonna turned his head away as another flash ignited. "Bob!"

"Bob's right." Elfleda guided Jonna toward the exit. "Now, smile."

The two huge abode doors swung open. Outside, lining both sides of the tree-supported walkway, a regiment of elf warriors snapped to attention. The plastic smile Jonna had become accustomed to materialized on his face despite Elfleda's sincere one and Bob's pixie grin. The three walked forward exactly as they had practiced.

"Wait a minute." Jonna tried to break loose. "Where's Elpis?"

Elfleda's arm remained firmly in his. "You know where Elpis is. The Queen has a special task planned for her."

"But I don't want--"

The tip of Elfleda's finger pressed against his lips. The tingling of her touch calmed him. Despite the desire not to go, his body did relax. Jitters--Bob had used that word. If he did have jitters, it was with good cause.

His duel with the giant had been a huge success. Not only that, but it had resulted in him replacing the fellow as the Queen's Champion. Jonna should have known something was up when later he found out the giant had been relieved to lose. It made him leery about the title they so graciously would bestow upon him the next day: *Protector of the Realm.*

The elves marched beside them. Wind rustled through the leaves. They passed over bridges as woven baskets lifted others from below by means of the spiderweb ropes. Elvish lords and ladies had come at the queen's behest.

The cool breath of autumn whipped at his clothes as the palace loomed closer. Two guards heaved back the tall, ivory doors of the palace and allowed them to pass through.

An entourage awaited them, not that they didn't already have one. Elven lords and ladies stood at the sides dressed in bright colors of yellow, orange, and gold. With their shoulders back and their spines straight, their superior stares tried to daunt Jonna and his companions.

The attire of the elvish upper class established their stations. Each lord and lady wore their traditional clan weapon. A certain noble caught Jonna's attention with his silvery eyes.

The elves bowed as Jonna passed, that is, all except for two couples: Lord Ilbryn with Lady Lyeecia, and Lord Tanyl with Lady Mylaela. The first pair was husband and wife; the second pair was lord and betrothed. While the choice to bow had not been required, not to do so showed disrespect.

Jonna ignored them. Thankfully, Elfleda's head had been turned the other way. Bob's feather whipped in the wind as he twisted about.

The corridor in front broadened as they stepped from the hall into the main throne room. The glistening chairs of state for the king and queen sparkled with gems of green, blue, and yellow. At the top of each throne lay a clear embedded diamond.

At first a mere whisper, a song drifted upon the wind. It flowed from chamber to chamber until it filled the throne room. With familiarity, it tickled the edges of his mind.

"Wisdom of a thousand suns gathered now in glory. Wielding from our daughters gone: strength, life, and boree. Bring the scroll of names before; witness what will be. The time has come to mark the names of those who will the throne to see."

In a burst of dazzling light, Queen Freya shimmered into view. In her hand was a unicorn chalice. Remnants of magic danced away as the light dwindled by degrees.

A page approached the throne. In his hands lay a red velvet cloth decorated with the elven symbol of eternity. Embroidered in gold, the sacred symbol glimmered as the cloth slid off a leather-encircled scroll.

A tree had been stamped into the wax seal of the leather. With a wave of the queen's hand, the scroll opened itself.

A shaft of light came from above to touch Queen Freya's chalice. Over it--in golden prickles of flame--a feathered quill formed. She nodded to Jonna and Elfleda. "The forest agrees. You are invited to sign the scroll."

The magic engulfed them. The hairs on Jonna's arms stood as he and Elfleda bathed in the warm glow. As the queen extended the quill, Jonna nodded toward Elfleda. Elfleda's fingers grasped it.

The scroll hovered in the air. The closer the quill came, the brighter its tip shined. With deft strokes, the quill flowed over the scroll's surface as the writing of golden light cooled to the color of black.

Elfleda's signature appeared followed by the date of the signing. She turned toward Jonna with beautiful, bright eyes. "Your turn, my love."

He reached for the quill. Though his fingers touched its smooth surface, the image of four quills blurred before his eyes. The world took on a distorted, rainbow tint that swirled around him. The Queen's eyes grew wide. Elfleda's eyebrows rose. Bob shot away from Jonna as if thrown by an unseen force.

Elves on all sides shuffled away from the couple as dancing glitters of light spun. On the floor, the elven sign of infinity glowed with bright, white light.

As the quill touched the scroll, a ping sounded. What had he just done? How had he broken the laws of majik this time?

His eyes grew large. He watched a blurred image of his own hand sign his name. As the date appeared, he felt the world slide sideways.

CHAPTER 2

Linen touched Jonna's fingertips. He remembered the cabin they had come to stay in and felt the breeze of an open window. However, when he opened his eyes, the linen became silk, and the bed lay in their elven abode.

A raven dropped to the window and stepped cautiously over the sheathed Rune Blade of Knowledge. The bird eyed him warily as it jumped from the sill to the dresser. Its feet dodged Elfleda's sparkling jewels of diamonds, emeralds, and rubies. Though notorious for stealing shiny objects in Jonna's world, the ravens of the elven forest had completely different manners.

It turned toward him and spoke, "Find the hill that mountain-borne, lies past lakes and snakes the thorn. When you seek what you will find, then you'll know the right of mind."

With a flurry of wings, the bird launched toward him. Only by pressing into the bed did he avoid its talons. It whipped a tight curve and skirted the walls of the room. As it neared the wall hook where Väinämö's amulet hung, the bird snatched it and soared toward the window.

Jonna launched from the bed, grabbed a pillow, and hurled it at the raven. The bird whisked the other way.

The bedroom door opened, and Bob floated in. "So, are we better?"

"Bob, stop that bird. He's taking my amulet!"

The pixie dodged to avoid a midair collision. "Ravens don't steal."

"Catch him!"

With a burst of speed, Bob soared after the bird. It ducked and weaved to avoid the pixie's grasp. Jonna rushed to the windows and closed them one by one. As he reached the last, he heard a ping and felt himself slide sideways. A baby cried. The bird slipped by into the forest green.

~

Linen touched Jonna's fingertips. He remembered the cabin they had come to stay in and felt the breeze of an open window. However, when he opened his eyes, the linen became silk, and the bed lay in their elven abode. His eyes widened. He had done this before.

A raven dropped to the window and stepped cautiously over the sheathed Rune Blade of Knowledge. The bird eyed him warily as it jumped from the sill to the dresser. Its tiny claws tapped on the maple wood top as it avoided Elfleda's sparkling jewelry composed of diamonds, emeralds, and rubies. Though notorious for stealing shiny objects in his world, the ravens of the elven forest had completely different manners.

It turned toward him and cocked its head. "Find the hill that mountain- borne, lies past lakes and snakes the thorn. When you seek what you will find, then you'll know the right of mind."

The raven launched from the dresser toward the amulet Väinämö had given him, but this time Jonna knew its goal. His hands forced the silk cover up, enclosed the bird, and snagged it.

Bob came through the bedroom door. "So, are we better?"

"Get me something to tie this up!"

"What?"

"I've caught a raven. Get me twine. He was going to take my amulet!"

"Ravens don't steal."

"This one does."

Bob whisked toward a curtain, removed its cord, and brought

it to Jonna. As Jonna struggled to hold the silk and tie it up, one side opened, and the raven darted out.

"Bob!"

The pixie turned. The raven swooped by him. Bob spun around. "Where'd he go?"

In one smooth curve, the bird caught the amulet and headed for the window.

Jonna leaped to his feet, grabbed, and missed. The raven flew into the forest green. A baby cried, a ping sounded, and Jonna slid sideways.

~

Linen touched his fingertips. He remembered the cabin they had come to stay in and felt the breeze of an open window. However, when he opened his eyes, the linen became silk, and the bed lay in their elven abode. This time, the raven sat on Jonna's chest and eyed him closely.

"Find the hill that mountain-borne, lies past lakes and snakes the thorn. When you seek what you will find, then you'll know the right of mind."

It launched from his chest as its claws punched downward. It swept around the room, grabbed Väinämö's amulet, and soared out the window.

Bob came through the bedroom door. "So, are we better?"

Jonna folded back the silk sheet to see small punctures on his skin. With three dots toward the top and one beneath, a single claw mark had been left. The bleeding didn't last long.

Bob stared at him. "What is going on?"

Jonna's eyes rose from the wounds. "That's what I would like to know."

"Well," the pixie hovered over the side of the bed, "let me rephrase that. Other than you collapsing at the signing of the Elvish Scroll of Legend and being carried to your home--" He looked down at Jonna's wounds. "--What else is going on?"

"I collapsed?"

Bob nodded. "Right to the floor. You fainted."

"I don't faint, Bob."

"I mean, I understand the pressure. It's quite an honor to sign the scroll. No power given is without--"

"Bob."

"--responsibility. And with your abrupt insertion into an elven society--"

"Bob."

"--it is perfectly acceptable for a person to--"

"Bob!"

Bob turned toward him with a pixie grin. "Yes?"

"I don't faint."

"Well, something happened."

Jonna glanced at his wounds and grabbed his clothes from off a chair. "It certainly did." He pulled on his pants and shoes and then buckled his belt. His gaze dropped to his chest. "I need to tend these claw punctures before I put on a shirt. After that, we need to find out what's going on."

Almundena walked into the room. "By *we*, you mean *us*?"

Jonna's jaw dropped. The last time he had seen her, she had implied she didn't want to see him again.

Merriment filled her eyes. "You act like you've seen a ghost."

"You told me--" The spell cast by dark magic whispered within him, and he could feel the draw toward her. "--You told me you were leaving."

She arched an eyebrow. "When did I say that?"

"Right after we defeated the Dark Mages." His head felt strange, and he shook himself. "Not that I wouldn't welcome your help."

"Are you feeling okay?" She came forward and placed a hand on his head. "You don't have a fever, but perhaps you need to lie down?"

Her soft touch drew him, and he found himself wanting to hold that hand. He resisted. "No."

"I should think not." She smiled brightly. "You know where that got us last time."

Bob grinned. "Worse than young pixies, you are!"

Jonna swallowed. "Uh, no. Where did that get us?"

She touched her stomach gently with a loving look in her eyes.

Jonna stepped back. He found it hard to breathe. He had only been with Elfleda, not Almundena. Elfleda was his wife.

"What's wrong, love?" She came closer and touched his cheek as her eyebrows narrowed. "You don't look very well."

"I--I--" He backed toward the window. The air had become thick like water. His lungs labored to breathe. "Where is Elfleda?"

Almundena's eyes dropped as a grim line took away the smile. "Don't you remember? She died in the arena before you could save her."

That wasn't right. It could not be true. His back touched the outside wall, and his fingers stopped on the window sill. Something bumped against his hand and fell from the window.

Despite the draw he had toward Almundena, his heart tore. The words came out in a whisper. "That's not possible."

Bob floated toward him. "It's true. The strain overcame her. By the time we got there, she lay at the edge of death. I watched her take your hand and Almundena's, place them together, and wish you both a long life."

"And Elpis, where is she?"

Bob wrinkled his brow. "Who is Elpis?"

The cool window sill felt unreal under his fingers. If he didn't leave this room immediately, his heart would shred again. With a turn, he faced the window. Green leaves waved back and forth on boughs all around them. It helped, and the thick air thinned. His lungs breathed in deeply and released slowly. He turned back toward the room. Alfgia's face stared at him. "What's wrong, love?"

Jonna jumped backwards as a column of light waved before his eyes. The image of Alfgia, the beautiful dark elf princess, blurred to become Almundena once more. Almundena reached out to catch hold of him, but he fell from her fingers. Her voice rose, "Bob!"

Beneath him lay the Rune Blade of Knowledge caught at the end a large branch. He must have bumped the sword off the window sill. Leaves and branches slapped at him as he grabbed hold of the sheath's leather strap. It was the only thing close enough to hold his weight. The strap bowed the branch that held it and slipped off.

His body dropped backwards. The elvish abode shrank from him. As he closed his eyes, he saw the Eye of Aldrick broken into a million pieces. He flipped over, stared down, and plunged into the darkness.

~

His thumping heart brought to attention the ground beneath his fingers. His back and chest stung. Jonna squinted and gradually opened his eyes. Above him lay a canvas of foliage spread out across the sky. Beneath him, a cushioned mattress of grass lay; he could feel the blades on his back. How far had he fallen?

"Awake already?" A deep voice rose from his right.

Jonna fought to move his arms but could not. A long rope had been wrapped around him multiple times. "Who are you?"

The huge head of a green dragon stared down at him. The dragon grinned. "Humans make tasty morsels but need to be plumped up."

A bubbling cauldron with red flickering flame caught his attention as sparks shot off the wood under it. "Are you going to eat me?" He turned his head and caught sight of the Rune Blade of Knowledge, still in its sheath, lying three feet away.

"Well--" The dragon studied him. "While I do enjoy a nice treat upon occasion, I don't think your magic would be palatable."

"What?"

"Your magic." The dragon's eyes grew. "You do know about magic?"

Jonna nodded.

"Well then, I don't have to explain myself, do I?"

"Why is my magic not *palatable*?"

The dragon rubbed its chin. "That is an excellent question. Perhaps we should ask a mage."

"That wouldn't be Väinämö, would it?"

"Vä-who?"

"Of course not." Jonna stared. "Why should a dragon know one of the greatest mages in the elven forest?"

"Elven forest?" The dragon extended its lower lip. "These forests do not belong to the elves. The elves only live in the trees."

"Okay, let's go with that. Whose forest is this?"

The dragon chuckled. "You should know better than I." He hooked a claw under one of the ropes that wrapped Jonna's middle and lifted him into the air. Jonna's body bent in an arc. Though not painful, it certainly wasn't comfortable. "Did you not sign the Elvish Scroll of Legend?"

Jonna's mind clicked. "No one owns the forest; it belongs to all." He stared at the dragon. "You know who I am?"

"Of course, and I would suggest we head away from here, before I do have to eat a few other creatures. *Those beings* have no qualms with digesting your magic."

"So the cauldron isn't yours?"

The dragon shook its head.

"My sword. Don't forget my sword!"

The green dragon glanced at the forest floor. "That tiny piece of metal?"

"That sword defeated the dark mage Cassus. It has earned respect."

A snicker formed on the dragon's face. "You think so?" It raised Jonna to its mouth.

"Hey!"

The creature stopped. "Yes?"

"Don't eat me!"

A bellowing laugh escaped into the forest as the dragon held

Jonna up. Its hot breath made Jonna grimace. The huge mouth opened wide as the dragon lowered Jonna toward its bottom jaw. A single tooth snagged part of the rope. The rope sliced, and Jonna fell. The dragon caught him and lowered him to his feet. "There, isn't that better? Now you can carry your own *respectable* sword."

Jonna wiggled free of the rest of the coils, picked up the Rune Blade of Knowledge, and strapped it over his back. It stung. Without a shirt, the leather touched his scratches. At least he had put on his shoes and pants. He turned toward the dragon. "Well, so long. Thanks for the help." With a turn, he headed the opposite direction.

A large green tail descended in front of him.

"Or not." The tail slid toward him, and he quickly reversed.

"I'd be a poor host, indeed, to let you walk into danger. This way will let you observe their camp."

"Camp?" Jonna walked beside the dragon as they moved to the right. The ground rose, though not steeply. To the left, off in the distance, he caught the view of a river meandering through the trees. "Large camp? Small camp? Where are the baskets that rise up to the elven city?"

They stopped on an outcropping that overlooked the valley. A stream branched into three parts to run across it in snake-like directions. The dragon nodded. "Look."

Round huts with wooden sticks and grass dotted the valley as huge trees loomed up from the valley floor. Most of the huts had conical, peaked roofs and were gathered in units of four to five. "Who are they?"

"Vulkodlaks. They have ventured from their valley to hunt. They have keen senses. If you came from the elven city, then you must pass through their camp to return."

"That doesn't look too difficult." He studied the landscape. "Logs have been placed over streams as bridges, and if the vulkodlaks are there, they must be asleep."

The dragon eyed him. "The eye seldom sees what the mind does not know is there." It pointed. "Look closely."

Jonna concentrated on the areas around the huts. Shapes emerged. The wooden sticks he thought as part of the landscape were beings with two arms and two legs. They were draped in clothing of grass that had been woven together as a type of camouflage. "Why did they take me to begin with?"

"You were to be offered to their god."

"You implied I was to be eaten."

The dragon nodded. "That is part of the ritual."

"Thanks for getting me out of there."

"I do have another suggestion."

"And that is?"

The green dragon vanished. From its place rose a raven that flapped its wings and hovered in front of him. "Find the hill that mountain-borne, lies past lakes and snakes the thorn. When you seek what you will find, then you'll know the right of mind." It launched up toward the branches and disappeared into the sky.

Jonna's voice chased after it. "Who are you?"

CHAPTER 3

The words came out louder than expected. A low growl rose from the valley as multiple voices intertwined. Growl? A shiver shot up Jonna's spine as his body rotated to look. The brown sticks twisted toward him. They bounded over branches, past rocks, and shifted through the tall grass on all fours.

Jonna bolted in the opposite direction as his heart thumped in his chest. He leaped small ditches, jumped from rise to rise, and plowed through underbrush. Large tree trunks, like skyscrapers, blocked his path. He zigzagged between them.

The smell of wet dog struck his nose; it came in various flavors. Bushes rustled behind him as his pursuers gained ground. Sweat trickled down his face. Only one possibility came to mind to throw them off his scent.

The river approached. His feet rushed toward the bank, leaped into the air, and dropped into the cool frothing water.

The tremendous splash swept downstream faster than he could run. He joined the flotsam of branches that rushed with the current.

A howl went up from the bank behind. A chorus of voices joined in. Fur and sometimes human-like faces appeared from the shadows of the foliage. They leaped along the bank as they matched his speed. His arms and legs fought with great strokes across the river's current.

The bank inched toward him. Plants and tree limbs hung over the water. The water shot him downstream. Something bumped his leg. Sticks, gathered around him, pushed away at his touch.

Large rocks appeared. Behind them, a swirl of water spun. The swirl countered the flow of the river and slowed his speed as he shifted closer.

Tree limbs came within Jonna's reach. The bump hit his leg again.

A howl shot up from behind. Vulkodlaks tested the far bank, hunting a way across. However, they would not dive into the water.

With a lunge, Jonna grabbed hold of a branch. As he pulled himself up, something seized his leg. His muscles tensed as his gaze swung downward.

A tentacle wrapped around his ankle. It jerked him toward the swirl of water. Horror filled him. His lungs labored. Despite his soaked hair, sweat trickled down the sides of his face.

Hand over hand, he struggled to go higher as the tentacle stretched, and the branch bent. With a subtle crack, the tree limb jerked again. Either that or a bone had been broken.

As his grip slipped, he threw one arm around the branch, freed the rune blade from its sheath, and swung it downward. Green goo shot out as the blade bit true. The tentacle severed, the pressure released, and Jonna shot up into the air.

"Jonna!" Bob's pixie body slammed into him.

Jonna paused, slowed his rise, and then tumbled into the swirling pool.

It spun him around. Dizziness took him. His knuckles turned white to keep the rune blade in his hand as the funnel sucked him down. When the funnel became too small for his body, it spun him out under the water.

The air vanished. Fish swam around him, plants waved attached to rocks, and a creature lay on the bottom in pain. He kicked his feet toward the surface and felt the catch of the current above his head.

A song, distant, called to him, and his eyes dropped down to the creature at the bottom. Where her feet should be, a fish-like tail waved gently in the water. Her flowing hair and curvaceous figure said this had to be a nixie.

Jonna sheathed his blade and swam toward her, caught by the power of the song. She cringed at his touch though her eyes beckoned for help. His arms wrapped around her and lifted her from the bottom. As his feet prepared to jump for the surface, the gentle movement of her hand pointed toward a cave. There, the whirlpool spun down to a small funnel and touched the cave's side.

He needed air, not a cave; the added exertion had almost used it up. His pulse quickened. With a shake of his head, he pushed upward and found his feet could not leave the bottom.

Eyes wide, he looked back to her. Her left hand touched his back with gentle assurance, and her right pointed toward the cave. Chest muscles tensed as he fought not to open his mouth. With a reluctant nod, he followed her instructions.

Agony gripped each stride he took. The air in his lungs became toxic. The fish took on eerie shapes he had never seen.

At the cave's mouth, he staggered, steadied himself with his shoulder, and scrapped his skin against the rough surface. Blood flowed freely as his eyes looked in. Her grip tightened upon him, and she pointed. Light reflected from the top of the water inside the cave. Air lay a few feet away.

His legs pushed, fought for each step, until his head broke the surface. He exhaled, inhaled, and let labored lungs breathe as he collapsed on the slanted bank.

The nixie sobbed with her head on his shoulder. As his mind cleared, his eyes focused on the cave.

Golden light in various shades danced around the room. Sparkling, uncut gems of sapphire and green glittered in the light. In the center of the cave lay a pool lit white from a brightness deep within. A circle of silks sat against one wall shaped like a nest.

Liquid touched his fingers. From a gash in the nixie's side ran a stream of green ooze. "Did the creature hurt you?"

The nixie shook violently. It took all he could to hold her still. When she stopped, he used a smooth clear crystal for her pillow.

"I'll be right back."

His legs wobbled. The lack of air had been harder on him than he thought. In one of the cave's walls stood a small opening. The whirlpool touched the outside surface of the cave and allowed air to filter in. What excess water came with it created a waterfall that vanished down another hole.

Silks of greens and blues made up the bed-like nest. A cloth mural hung upon the wall behind it. It showed rivers and trees as nixies frolicked in the water. Not surprisingly, a group of human males watched on the banks.

From the nest, he chose a shorter cloth, brought it back to the nixie, and tied it around her. "Maybe that will help the bleeding."

Her eyes opened to stare up at him. Her blue irises were stunning. In a low, forlorn voice, she whispered, "There is but one way to heal me. You must enter the pool of light."

"What will that do?"

She groaned; her face contorted in pain. Concerned, he leaned near her. As she grasped his hand, hers felt cool like the water of the river. "Please!"

"Pool of light?" He swallowed. On his first experience with a wood sprite, the wood sprite had tried to change him into a tree. According to Sir Verity, an elvish noble of the realm who had saved him, only by knowing a magical being's name could that being not have control over a person. "Tell me your name."

The nixie's eyes opened wide. The beauty of them caught him. "I would not put you under that obligation."

Her answer puzzled him. It did not match what he had learned, yet he dared not proceed without it. "I must know."

"Very well," she smiled. "I am known as Aroha, nixie of the river Shi Me. I am honored, great prince."

"Then you know who I am?"

Aroha gave a single nod. "I do."

The words came with such complete trust, Jonna felt ashamed that he had asked her name.

Her hand extended once more to touch his, but this time it

felt different. No longer the cool of the river, the flesh felt warm to the touch. "Fear not. Go to the pool of light."

As her hand slid gently from his, he made his way to the pool. The closer he came, the more it glowed. Using one hand to cover his eyes, he dropped into the water.

It didn't feel like water. His arms smoothly kept him afloat. The warmth from it filled his body and opened his mind. Ideas, places, and people came to awareness. His body knew the drifting of the underground currents. Slack-jawed, he understood their nature and paths.

The river mapped out before him. He saw every twist and turn. Shallow or deep, the aromas and textures filled his mind. Even the contents of the pool made sense. The source of the lighted pool was a crystal powered with magic.

Jonna dived down with both eyes closed. He didn't need to see it. The stirring of the magic drew him into the depths. At the bottom lay the crystal carved in the shape of a beautiful nixie. Not knowing what else to do, he reached out and touched it.

A ping occurred, but he did not slide sideways. His mind opened to somewhere else. From far away, Aroha called for him. He felt her thoughts, touched her heart, and rose to help with her pain.

As he surfaced, his body glowed like the pool. Light radiated from him in all directions, and a sense of belonging to the water filled him. An invisible tether drew him to her side. "This may hurt."

The light around him leaped toward her; both jerked at the jolt. A comforting peace followed, and the brightness faded.

Where the wrap lay tied about her body, a glow issued from the wound. It gained in brightness and then tapered off. He exhaled, undid the silk wrap, and ran his fingers over the smooth, seamless flesh. She giggled.

With a grin, he touched her hair. "What happened?"

She rose toward him and kissed him gently. "As you have

sacrificed for me, so I give to you." Her hand moved over his shoulder; the damage vanished. Each place she rubbed, the flesh became new.

His body relaxed as pains he had ignored vanished. The tree fall, the scratches, the overtaxed muscles and limbs, the soreness of his hands from gripping the tree limb, all faded except for the raven's punctures.

She tried three times, but the punctures would not go away. Her eyebrows crossed. "I don't understand."

His hand overlapped hers. "It doesn't matter. You have helped me greatly. Thank you."

A burst of color glistened along her lower body. Her fin vanished. Smooth, long legs appeared followed by a fish-scale skirt. As she rose demurely, the action accented her long legs and figure. "Do you like it?"

The shimmer of the skirt's colors danced in the light. "It is beautiful."

Her face blushed as a smile formed. Her eyes sparkled at him. "It is time for me to fill my nest."

"Nest?" Jonna glanced at the silk covers by the wall. "Is that for--children?" He looked closer at the mural. For the first time, he spotted smaller nix and nixies playing in the water.

"But of course," her smile broadened. "You know my name. You touched our god. The wisdom of the waters came. For humans who would do this task, a special place will come at last."

Hoots and hollers echoed from the whirlpool. Bob rode through the waterfall, flipped over twice, and finally slowed to a stop in the air. "What a ride! Wow! No wonder you stayed down here." His voice cutoff as his head jerked toward Aroha. "You're a nixie?"

She gave a single nod.

His gaze snapped to Jonna. "You're a human?"

Jonna nodded though the question sounded strange. "You know I am."

Bob's eyes widened. "Uh, Jonna? You didn't, uh, *do* anything, did you?"

A frown crossed Jonna's face. "*Do* what, Bob?"

"I mean, like--" Bob bit his lip. "--play in a pool--" The pixie nodded his head toward Aroha. "--with anyone?"

"No playing," Jonna assured. "Aroha lay dying, and we healed each other."

"So you--shared magic?" Bob bit his lip again. "Was it--blissful?"

Aroha nodded enthusiastically. Jonna stared at him. "What type of question is that, Bob?"

"Oh, uh, nothing." In the air, Bob frowned as he paced back and forth. "A little free mixing of magic, I suppose, shouldn't hurt much." The pixie gritted his teeth. "The side effects should be minimal."

Jonna's eyebrows furrowed. "What do you mean?"

The pixie sighed and swallowed. "I'm sure it will wear off in due time."

Jonna glanced at Aroha. "What are you taking about?"

"If you start wanting raw salmon, just *ignore* the feeling."

The eyebrows on Jonna rose. "Are you saying I've turned into a fish?"

"Not a fish." Aroha slipped behind and put her arms around him in a tight hug. "A nix." She kissed him lightly on his shoulder. Sensuous pleasure flowed, and instinctively, his hand drew to hers.

"No." His hand shook as his mind fought against the desire. Both hands turned to fists as his body trembled. Lungs labored and eyes closed. He held that position until the shaking stopped and a measure of control returned. Gently, he separated from the pressure of her body. "I am married. I cannot do this." As he pulled away, his knees dropped to the ground. Pain ripped through him. Every nerve felt on fire. Only by gripping his hands together could he keep from coiling into a ball.

Her sympathetic eyes gazed lovingly at him. "You are no

longer mortal. You are not confined to the surface laws. The spirits of the river gods have placed a brand upon your soul."

"But, I know your name," he gasped. His will fought the pleasure that drew him and the pain that pushed from behind.

With a beautiful smile, she nodded. "A gift you asked of your own free will."

His voice wavered as the desire within intensified. "Bob?"

The pixie cleared his throat and leaned in. "That only works on sprites."

"What?"

"Didn't Sir Verity tell you?"

"No!" Jonna half-shouted as he tried to lean away.

She brought him closer and held him. "There now, my love. Doesn't that feel better?"

"Yes," he breathed in relief. "But it's not supposed to."

"Give it time. All will be well."

"Bob! By all the pixie magic you have, help me!"

Bob stabbed his hand into his pouch and pulled out a fistful of pixie dust. "Release him!"

Aroha eyed him intently. "And what will you do with that, little man? Perhaps you would swim in the pool as well?" Behind Bob, where the lake entered the cave, the waters stirred. Long green tentacles reached for him.

"Bob! Behind you!"

The pixie spun around. He dodged left and right as the appendages tried to grab him.

"You see--" She looked lovingly down at Jonna. "We nixies can alter our form from our mer-bodies to take on various shapes. When I saw the courage by which you fought my hold, my heart fell in love."

A tentacle slapped Bob. He tumbled toward a wall, but his momentum played out before he struck it. With pursed lips, he glared at the dancing limbs, reached into his pouch, and brought up his fist. "You asked for it!"

Pixie dust flashed to glisten in the golden light. The dust absorbed the light, grew, and separated. A billion sparkles zeroed in on the tentacles. The appendages stopped moving, frozen in place. The creature below the water thrashed, but its limbs would not move. In a blaze of brilliance, the tentacles vanished.

Aroha clung tighter to Jonna. "What did you do?"

"I--I--" Bob pointed at water. "Turned her back into her nixie shape!"

Aroha exhaled, and her grip relaxed. "You may be worthy of a swim after all."

Bob's eyebrows narrowed. "I have my own shape-shifter, thank you very much! Come to think of it, what's the big deal, Jonna? Do you honestly think Almundena will be jealous over a fish?"

"Not fish," Aroha stomped her foot, "nixie." She bent down to Jonna and kissed him lovingly. "We will make beautiful nixies together."

By the entrance, soft, brown hair hit the lake water's surface as another nixie appeared. Her eyes widened as a human hand rose from behind, grabbed her by the hair, and wrenched her head back. Dark hair appeared beside the second nixie. The face of Almundena stared at them all. "*Calipso Monstratum!*"

Aroha hurled backwards, struck the mural on the wall, and dropped unconscious into her nest. Jonna's passions drove him to follow, but Bob grabbed him by the ear and slapped pixie dust on his head. "Stay."

"Get him out of here!" Almundena pointed toward the water. "I'll finish this one." The nixie squirmed. She wrenched back the nixie's head. It whimpered. "I'll teach your kind not to play with married men!"

Jonna struggled, but Bob's magic held firm. The pixie looked at Almundena and asked, "Where do we regroup?"

"Go inland, due east from here, away from the river. I've a camp set up with a magic circle to protect it."

"Gotcha." Bob forced Jonna toward the entrance.

The moment Jonna's feet touched the water, his legs, pants, and shoes merged together. Fish scales grew. He stumbled and fell toward the lake.

Bob's eyes opened wide. "Uh, Almundena?"

Almundena struggled to keep hold of the nixie. "Hurry!"

Bob dove. He pulled Jonna after him through the underwater entrance.

Jonna's eyes widened as his head dropped below the surface. Though he held his breath, his lungs continued to breathe. When he opened his mouth, the water tasted sweeter than air. A smile lit his face, the water enhanced his strength, and the spell Bob held him with shattered. He spun around and headed for Aroha's cave.

Bob seized his tail and struggled to hold him back.

Jonna turned to grab him, but his hands shook as his mind refused to carry through.

The pixie's words bubbled through the water, "That's right, Jonna. Fight it! It's only a spell. The feelings are not real."

Despite the bubbles, Jonna heard the words loud and clear. Conflicting emotions tore at his insides. His head tried to explode. Aroha's call tormented his mind as his own will fought back. A single name formed within; only she could help him. "Naida Perdita, I need you."

A ripple hit the water as his call surged out. It gathered energy from the whirlpool's eddy, picked up momentum, and raced down the waterways. Fish scattered, bottom dwellers burrowed, and water plants strained against the pressure of the flow. Instead of an answer, the tow reversed. It distorted the whirlpool and altered the speed of the river.

A wave, larger than the others, raced toward him. As the momentum slowed, it dropped beneath the river's surface. The lithe, transparent body of Naida distorted the view of the water. Where the light streamed from the surface, it bent around her delicate figure. She extended her translucent hands toward him. "I am here, Jonna McCambel."

His body shook. "Help me!"

The water sprite nodded smoothly as her long hair waved in slow motion. Her right index finger pressed toward his forehead. It glowed brightly as it penetrated an unseen force, passed through, and touched him softly. "I cannot break this magic, but I can diminish its call. Let division be within your mind--a wall to muffle the call of her kind. So let your soul that's trapped receive--until there is no more a need."

Relief flooded through him. His face relaxed. The shaking stopped. For the first time since swimming in the pool, his mind could focus on something other than Aroha. "Thank you, Naida. You are a godsend!"

"I am a sprite, my lord, not to be confused with a river god." She leaned toward him and whispered, "They get quite jealous." A beautiful smile crossed her lips. "It was my pleasure." She slipped back, curtsied, and faded from view.

"Bob, to the camp."

The pixie eyed him cautiously. "How do I know that it's *really* you? For all I know, you could have called Naida under false pretense and made a grand show just to--"

Jonna huffed. "Bob."

"Alright, you don't have to get ugly." He released the fin, waved toward the surface, and grinned. "This way, my lord."

CHAPTER 4

With a swish of his tail, Jonna swept toward the surface. The water ran down his face as he burst through and leaped into the air. Droplets spun off as his body curved, angled down, and slipped beneath the waves.

A wide grin spread across his face. Free of the nixie's hold, he felt the pulse of the water as it brought life to all that lived. With a flip to the right and a twist to the left, he spun, shifted, and settled to float on the surface. Though his tail barely moved, it easily kept him still despite the river's current and the whirlpool that had reverted to full strength.

Bob huffed from the bank. "Any time you're ready." Water dripped from the pixie's hair and clothes. Only the bag of pixie dust remained dry.

The smile slid from Jonna's face. "Sorry, I guess the nix part of me still has influence." His tail swished him closer. "How do I get my legs back?"

Bob scratched his head; more water drained down his arm. He shook it off. "You're asking me?"

"You are a pixie."

"And you're part nix. How should I know?"

The eyebrows on Jonna's face rose. "Pix--nix. They are similar."

"Oh, don't you go there. Similar words don't have similar--" He noticed the smug smile on Jonna's face. "Two can play at that game. I'm the trickster, remember?"

A chuckle left Jonna's lips as he studied the bank. He slid forward until his fingers could squish the mud in the shallow water.

TWISTED FATES

Bob tapped his chin. "Well, when did the nixie get her legs?"

The vision of Aroha lying helpless stirred Jonna's heart. "Aroha--" He sighed and rolled over in the water. The blue sky shifted as the tree leaves swayed above him. "Why did I leave you?"

"Jonna?"

His head shook, and his thoughts cleared. He flipped back over and used his hands to pull closer. "Good, I'm good." With a deep breath, he touched dry land; the dirt helped him focus. "After the pool of light is when she--" He swallowed. "--she." His eyes looked into the distance. "To stroke her hair and touch her face, I long to gaze upon her grace. The call of love is strong within. I must now go to--"

Bob flew near and slapped him on the side of the head. "Come on, man. Focus!"

"Focus. Yes!" Jonna stared at the embankment determined to fight the enticement of the water. "Must go forward." His tail struck the bottom. His body flipped onto the bank. The sun's warmth sent a tingle through his fin. As his tail started to dry, the scales faded in color. "It's working!"

Bob grabbed one of Jonna's hands and pulled him further up the bank. Bit by bit, the fin became shoes, the tail turned to pants, and the belt took shape around his waist.

He rose to wobbly legs. His stomach grumbled. "It's like I ran a marathon. Flipping a tail takes a lot out of a nix." With a glance at the river, he spotted a fish as it leaped into the air to catch a fly. The clarity of the view surprised him.

"Hold up there. We've a camp to find, remember?" Bob flew behind Jonna and pushed.

Jonna's legs moved reluctantly. "You're right. The camp."

A deep, feral growl came from the other side of the river. A shiver went up Jonna's spine. He could feel the creature slip from the shadows to tap a paw against the water's surface. Ripples sent out warnings to the water creatures that lived near. His brow wrinkled. "They're trying to find a way across. We need to hurry."

With a glance back, he saw the front of a vulkodlak as it stepped back into the shadows. "Bob?"

"Yes, Jonna?"

His legs stopped resisting. "Since you know the way, perhaps you would like to lead?"

Bob stopped pushing and flew to the front with a grin. "Good idea. Due east from the water cave should be right about there."

He pointed toward the right, slightly off the path they took. To get there, they would have to go down a gully, cross a creek, and catch the trail on the other side.

As they hurried down the gully, the gurgle of the creek made Jonna think of the river. His throat became parched. The sun's heat seemed to bear down upon him like a desert though in reality it trickled through the trees. Sweat formed on his sideburns as he thought of sliding through the cool water.

"Focus!" His thoughts concentrated on the path they took. As they crossed the creek, his feet stayed safely on the stones. Relief flooded through him as they reached the trail on the other side.

The symptoms abated. It was all in his head, literally. Whatever magic Aroha had used, could be fought by thought.

As they stepped from the trees into a small clearing, the enchanted circle glowed. Within its protective field, a fire pit burned. Around the fire pit sat a stack of wood and a yurt.

A bucket of water caught Jonna's attention. His skin felt terribly dry. The desire for the water drew him, yet he hated the fact it held control.

He stepped forward and hit the protective barrier around the camp. His fingers touched it lightly. Without a second thought, he spoke, "Hove."

A ping sounded. The forest vanished. He stood in the arena of the Dark Mages writhing in pain. His knees dropped to the ground as his chin touched his chest. With teeth clenched, the agony drained slowly away.

A hand touched his shoulder. A young voice spoke, "Are you okay?"

He jumped and caught the eyes of a lad who stared down at him. As the pain faded, he took deep breaths. "Where am I?"

"Forest Lost, or what's left of it. Once the Dark Mages were defeated, not many stayed in the city."

Jonna's eyes opened wide. "Where did they go?"

"Other places, I guess. With no magic to protect the walls, creatures of the forest invaded. Many were killed."

In a whisper, Jonna spoke, "Nature reclaimed its own."

"What was that?"

Jonna shook his head. "Why are you here?"

The boy shrugged. "With the bridge and heavy doors, it offers better protection than the outer city. We set up this camp. I was scouting for others when I found you. Who are you?"

"Jonna McCambel."

A ping resonated across the arena. His body slid sideways.

~

"Jonna?" Bob slapped him until he opened his eyes.

"Bob?" His lungs sucked in air. The enchanted circle lay around him. The trees stared down. A blue sky showed in glimpses as the leaves waved in the wind. "Bob--" Jonna panted. His fingers dug into the soil as his eyes focused on the pixie. His voice dropped, "Something's not right."

The pixie gazed down at him. "You're speaking in riddles. Ever since you signed the scroll--"

"The scroll." Jonna glanced toward the fire and spoke to himself. "No, not the scroll--the raven. I have to find the place in his riddle."

"Right now, I think you should rest." Bob stared at him as he nodded slowly. "And I need to talk to Almundena."

"Don't you see?" Jonna shook his head. "Elfleda didn't die. Almundena and I were never meant to be."

Bob backed up. "We really should bring in another authority on this."

"Who do you suggest?"

"How about--"

"And don't say Almundena."

"She's your wife!"

Jonna winced as a sharp pain went through his head. "No. I mean, yes." His head shook. "In this version she is, but it was not before." His eyes begged Bob to understand. "It's a conundrum."

"A-come-on who?"

The pain moved into his forehead. He rubbed his temples. "A conundrum. A puzzle, a challenge, a problem."

Bob sighed with relief. "Why didn't you just say so? We use corundum to sand wood. Pixies are good at it."

Jonna sat up. "Bob, did you hear what I said?"

"Jonna, I see your lips moving but nothing makes sense." The pixie leaned closer. "Say that again?"

"It's a conundrum. A puzzle, a challenge, or--"

Bob held up his hand. "Never fear. I'll be right back!" He zipped off toward the river. "And don't leave!"

"Where are you going?" Jonna exhaled. He flopped back and stared at the top of the trees. As he did, his hand touched the bucket of water.

The ripples produced called to him. Its sweetness teased his mind. His right hand reached up, drawn to the top where it lapped the sides. Aroha came to mind.

His hand wrenched away in a tight fist and shook as he held it to his chest. "I will not. My will is stronger than magic."

On the wind, a voice came, "Indeed?"

Before him, a ray of light descended between the leaves of green. It touched the ground with dazzling brightness and formed a miniature sparkle that circled toward the sky. As the sparkle rose, hooves took shape. Legs, a body, and a horse's mane appeared. In a final brush of paint, a single, twisted, white horn formed.

A voice soothed his shaking hand. "Are you stronger than magic?"

He gawked. The unicorn glowed before him with its beautiful white skin. "I--I know you."

It pranced within the enchanted circle and gave a nod of approval. "As well you should. I talk to you in your dreams."

"Who are you?"

Its shiny black eyes turned toward him. "I am life and death. I am the birth that is and will be. I circle in the heart of all, and keep the secrets that should not be free."

"You are the quill that signs the Scroll of Legend." The memories flowed back: the unicorn chalice, the ping, and the sliding sideways.

"I am known by many names."

"Why are you here?"

The unicorn blinked. "Did you not issue a challenge?"

"I challenged no man."

The unicorn neighed. "Well said, for I am not mortal. Did you not say your will is stronger than magic?"

"I--" Jonna rose slowly to sit as he stared up at the unicorn. His voice became hard. "Would that frighten you?"

The unicorn shook its mane. Sparkles of light flew into the air. "The question you want to ask is *why do I frighten you?*"

The pain in his head returned. Jonna rubbed his temples. "I am not afraid. However, I do not like to be controlled."

"And thus the reason you fear me."

Jonna stared. The unicorn watched amused with those dark, shiny eyes. "I am not your enemy, Jonna. I am your friend."

Growls erupted from the river. The ground rumbled. Almundena and Bob raced into sight as Jonna turned.

Bob hollered first. "They're coming! Run!"

Large wolves with thick, regal-looking fur galloped after them. Trampled foliage bent. With huge leaps, the vulkodlaks gained ground behind the pair.

The pixie zipped forward, curved toward the enchanted circle, and smashed into its invisible wall. He bounced back. "Jonna!"

Almundena raced up to the enchantment's edge. "Open the circle!"

This made no sense. If Almundena had created the circle, why couldn't she open it? Jonna turned to the unicorn. "You did this."

"No," the unicorn shook its head. "You did."

The spell--it had to be the spell he used to enter. "Hove!" He rose and pressed toward them but slammed into the wall. "Why isn't it working?" He struck it with his fist. "What is going on?"

"It is your fear that keeps the wall intact."

"I am *not* afraid."

"Prove it." The unicorn nodded. "Open a portal."

The wolves rushed closer. Bob beat upon the wall. Almundena's face held terror, and from a far distance away, Jonna heard the cry of a baby. *The Sight* hit him as facts slid together. In this realm, Almundena was pregnant with his child. Was the baby crying out to him? Did it know they would be killed?

"No!"

Anger swelled within him. A vision of the dark mage's arena formed. Above it hung the Eye of Aldrick as it fed upon his power. The hilt of Rune Blade of Knowledge touched his hand as he reached behind his neck.

"Jonna," the unicorn cautioned, "this is not the way."

His voice hardened. "Then show me another."

The tip of the rune blade arced through the air and struck the enchanted wall. Power lashed out in a pinpoint of light as he traced the outline of a door. When the outline finished, he stabbed the sword forward. The piece he had cut flew out from the circle right into the horde behind his friends.

Wolves toppled. Some howled. Angry jaws bared their teeth. Those behind slammed into those in front. The horde slowed to a trot, but advanced nonetheless. Almundena and Bob stared.

"Get behind me!" Jonna stepped out with the rune blade held before him. He stared at the vulkodlaks. "Who will be the first to die?" His lungs heaved in anger. His eyes showed a tint of red.

The vulkodlaks stopped, and silence dropped. A guttural growl issued from somewhere in the middle. One by one, wolves slid right and left until a path opened. In the center of the path stepped the largest of the wolves; its eyes glowed silver in the light.

Jonna nodded toward it. "Will you be the one?"

A wolfish grin crossed its face as it rose up off all fours and walked upright toward him. "I am Conall, heir apparent to the kingdom of Ylva. What dishonor have we done to thee?" Conall eyed the rune blade and sniffed the air.

"Why do you prey upon my friends?"

"It is the law of the forest. We may eat what we find during the autumn hunt before we return to our winter home."

"These are off the list."

The wolf stared at him. The debate to attack weighed in its eyes. It blinked. "Your weapon is elven, but your odor says human. Might you not be the new prince of the elves?"

"I am."

It bowed its head with a calculating stare but did not step back. "'twas our mistake, my lord. This is part of the lands we are allowed to hunt by treaty. Had we known they were with you--"

Jonna would not be taken in. "I think you'll find when conscious, I can be a formidable enemy."

"That was not our intention. I will let my people know that you and yours are not to be harmed. We would rather have you as an ally than for dinner, of course." The wolfish grin returned.

"Of course."

Conall bowed again, started to turn away, but then twisted back. "Might I give a suggestion, my lord?"

Jonna's eyes never left him. "You may."

"I suggest an honor guard composed of my finest warriors. It would show our good will and apologize for our indiscretion."

Almundena stepped up behind Jonna. Though she shivered against him, she whispered, "It is the diplomatic thing to do."

He whispered back, "They just tried to eat you. All three of you!"

Her hand took his. Despite the lack of the elven tingle, he could feel the love in her touch. She placed his hand on her belly. The life within her reached out though she was not even showing. "They are allies until proven enemies. There are many who would see harm come to you."

"I don't need a protector."

The unicorn's head appeared beside him. "Do you not?"

"Bob? What about you?"

"My vote's with the others, although--" The pixie took in the horde before them. "I wouldn't turn my back."

Jonna sheathed his blade though his eyes stayed wary. "It would be an honor, Prince Conall."

"Excellent!" The smile that shined uncovered all his sharp teeth. His paw waved, and five subordinate werewolves came forward. Though not quite as large as Conall, they were very close in size. "I present these to my lord and place them under your command." He motioned toward the left and continued toward the right. "Jasna, Vytautas, Gerulf, Limbik, and Esti." A gleam showed in Esti's eye as he finished with her. Her gaze never left Jonna. The first and the last were female. The rest were male. "These represent the five houses of our realm and are all members of the royal household. They are yours until you release them." Conall bowed. "A gift to the new prince."

The idea of the Trojan Horse came to Jonna's mind, but he did not show it on his face. "Thank you, Prince Conall."

"It is my pleasure. And now, we must be off. The autumn hunting season stirs the blood more than most." With a wave of his paw, the horde slipped back the way they had come.

Jasna came forward. She snapped to attention within four feet of Jonna. "Your orders, my lord?"

Half-circled by five vulkodlaks and with the rune blade sheathed, the odds of surviving a surprise attack were not good. In his gut, such large, dangerous creatures this close unnerved him. However, Jonna met the werewolf's gaze without a flinch. "How do you protect the pack?"

Jasna's head turned sideways. "We stay together. We patrol in pairs."

"Then that is what I ask. The camp is protected except for the entrance. You shall guard the entry."

"It will be done." Jasna curved toward the others.

Jonna did not listen to the exchange, but caught sight of Vytautas and Gerulf as they headed off into the forest. Jasna, Limbik, and Esti remained to guard the entry.

Bob dropped next to his ear. "It this wise? Letting them go off means we don't know where they are."

Jonna headed toward the center of the camp. With a purpose, he avoided looking at the bucket of water. "You're in an enchanted circle, Bob. What more do you need?"

"Jonna, vulkodlaks are not known to be the most honorable of creatures."

"Then why did you agree with the others?"

"To refuse the prince would be like spitting in his face."

"So what are you complaining about?"

They reached the yurt in the circle's center.

Almundena grasped his arm. "We need to talk--inside."

"Sure."

The animal hide door pushed easily back to reveal elven beds set on the east and west walls. Rugs decorated the floor with two chairs against the north. An elven woodstove stood in the center.

"When you said camp, I thought sleeping bags and a stick tent. This is luxury. How did you do this?"

"With the help of a few elven mages," Almundena grinned but the grin stopped as she thought on his words. She squinted at him. "Why would you sleep in a bag?"

"It's a type of--bag you sleep in. Maybe I can show you some time." Or not--the nearest store was out of the question.

She pushed him toward a chair. "Sit down."

"Whoa! What's going on?"

Her face heated up. "How could you?"

35

"How could I do what?"

"That nixie!"

Jonna's eyes opened wide. "It wasn't my fault."

"So you just stumbled into her lair, had a casual swim in her pool, and thought I wouldn't find about it?"

"Hold it right there." Jonna stood up. "I saw a creature dying after being sucked down into a whirlpool. I didn't know her plan."

Bob slipped forward. "It's even worse. He asked her name."

Her breath inhaled sharply. "You did what?"

Jonna gritted his teeth. "Bob, you're not helping."

Her eyes grew wide. "You *asked* her name?"

His eyebrows rose. "Sir Verity told me--"

"That only works on sprites!" She threw up her hands.

His voice deepened, "I know that--now." He stepped toward her. "You don't think I would purposely choose to--to woo with another female. I'm not even supposed to be married to you."

Almundena gawked dumbstruck. "You don't want to be married to me?" Tears welled in her eyes and slid down her cheeks.

"No, no. You don't understand. I didn't realize Elfleda--"

He reached out to her, but she turned her back to him. "You're still in love with her."

"She was my wife!"

"And who am I, the errand girl? The fall back? Did you love me at all?"

The pressure in his head built. Jonna's eyes snapped tightly shut as his open hands formed fists. The fists shook until every part of his body trembled. "Almundena, something's not right." His body slid sideways and collapsed to the floor.

The leather hide pushed in as the unicorn's head appeared. "Jonna, fighting it only makes it worse."

Jonna's teeth chattered as every nerve felt on fire. "F-f-fighting what?"

"The magic, of course."

With large eyes, Almundena dropped to his side. "Bob, what's he saying?"

"How should I know? That's why I came to get you!"

She touched his forehead. "It doesn't feel like a fever."

Bob whizzed through the facts. The pixie finished, "Oh, and the nixie's name was Aroha."

The shaking gradually stopped. In the distance, Jonna heard the distraught cries of Aroha in her cave. "Have no fear," he whispered. "I am not far away." The calls softened, and he felt a glow come from somewhere else. His lips became dry--his throat parched. "Water," he croaked.

CHAPTER 5

"Did he say water?" The unicorn stepped back as Bob dashed for the door. The pixie's tiny body punched the leather hide and knocked it out of the way. A moment later, he slammed back through carrying the bucket of water as it sloshed. "Here!"

Almundena found a ladle, dipped it, and placed it to Jonna's lips.

Aroha's call grew as the liquid trickled down his throat. In his mind, Naida's voice rose as her rhyming spell countered it.

Gradually, his dry throat abated, and clarity returned. The world had not only changed, but the details he remembered had weaved into a new existence. And yet, the flicker of truth remained. Why could he remember when others did not? Could he be causing further damage by denying his current reality?

Jonna swallowed. Before the dark mage's spell, he had been drawn to Almundena. Had Elfleda blessed the marriage as Bob had said, he had no doubt events could have turned this way. It explained the truth he fought to deny. He stared up at Almundena.

Tears started down her face. "I love you. I just don't understand this."

He sighed as the cool water soothed the fire. Though Aroha's voice called, each time he succeeded in controlling it, his will became stronger. "In my world, they call it hormones. When females become pregnant, they are prone to emotional highs and lows. It is perfectly normal. I should have remembered it earlier."

Bob scratched his chin. "What do *ore moans* have to do with pregnant females?" His eyebrows abruptly rose. "Oh, I get it. I've heard some dwarfs say that the caves moan right before they strike a new vein!"

"Not ore moans, Bob, I said hormones."

Almundena's lips pursed. "In any case, we have to break Aroha's spell."

At the nixie's name, he could sense her. Though less sharply, his nix part still longed to hold her close. "If you don't mind, let's not mention her name until we do. I'm working at it, but--"

"Oh, I'm so sorry!" She leaned forward and kissed him on the forehead. Her voice growled. "Just don't go near that river."

He laughed. It helped. "Believe me, the river is the last place I want to go." With a breath, his eyes switched between her and Bob. "How do we break the spell?"

An image materialized in the yurt. A table with a chair hung in the air. In the chair sat a mage's robe and cloak. A hat floated about six inches over the top of the robe. An unsure voice questioned, "Hello? Knock, knock. Is anyone there?"

Jonna tried to rise but could not. "Water," he croaked.

Bob floated closer to touch the image. His hand passed through.

Almundena dipped the ladle again, moved protectively closer to Jonna, and held it to his lips. As it flowed down his throat, his strength returned.

The empty robe shifted. "Water who?"

The voice and empty clothes reminded Jonna of a certain mage. He grinned. "What-are-ya doing in our yurt, Väinämö?"

"Who is this? I'm supposed to be contacting Jonna, not some jester. This is a private line!"

"I am Jonna."

"What?"

"I am Jonna and you're in our yurt!"

"Then why can't I see you? And why do I see women's clothes walking around by themselves?" The empty sleeve pointed at them. "Hm, there's a tiny pixie set floating in the air, and a pair of pants rising from the floor."

Jonna's head shook. "You are responsible for your own magic."

"Am I?" The chair scooted back. The robe stood up and bumped the table as it shifted around the desk. "Remember, I don't flirt with sprites!"

"If *only* that was the problem."

Bob nudged Jonna. "Well, actually, nixies and sprites do have a common branch--"

"Bob."

"Nixie? Sprites?" Väinämö shook his head. "Where are you?"

"The best that I can figure out, east of the elven forest."

"There is no elven forest. The forest belongs--"

"To everyone." Jonna rolled his eyes. "I know, I know. Have you heard of the river Shi Me?"

"Shi Me, a river? Let me check my maps." The floating robe vanished from sight and returned with a large book. It thudded down on the desk. Dust billowed as Väinämö opened up the cover. It continued to puff while he flipped the pages. An empty sleeve waved away the dust. The sleeve stopped on a page. "You're not far from the elven city."

"That's what I've been trying to *tell* you."

"But Jonna, it's the Vulkodlaks hunting season, and they are scheduled for that part of the forest. It is not a safe time to be playing in the woods."

"Been there, done that, and I was not playing." A howl came from outside the tent. Two others joined in. "We are now allies."

"Vulkodlaks have no allies, especially during the hunt. The blood lust is too great--among other things."

Almundena shivered. "It was necessary. I know of the treaty. They leave their valley each autumn and return before winter with food supplies. Settlements are off limits, as well as, posted lands."

"The treaty was designed to keep things like this--like you being in the middle of their hunt--from happening." Väinämö huffed. "Get back to the city as soon as possible, preferably during the day." The image shifted sideways like an analog television that had lost its signal. "Wait! Don't go!"

Jonna stared at him. "We aren't doing anything."

"Watch out for the--"

The image faded. As it did, a white horn moved back the hide flap to the yurt. "Something's happening outside the circle."

Jonna rose to his feet and pushed through the opening. The sun dropped toward the horizon. How long had they been in the yurt? He turned toward Almundena with Väinämö's warning in his ears. "Can we make it back to the city?"

"Not before nightfall. Without the river to cross, we'd have a chance, but with it?" She shook her head.

"Then we stay." His eyes drifted to the unicorn. "What did you see?"

The unicorn gave a slight smile. "In the darkest regions, eyes and flutters. Movement there will bring near others."

Had the unicorn cast a spell? Jonna watched him closely. "I am not impressed. Many poets I know can do the same."

"Ah," the unicorn neighed, "but can they do this?" It shook its mane. Golden sparkles leaped in various directions, but instead of vanishing, they spun away through the enchanted circle. Each one spread apart and hung at the edge of the clearing around them.

Eyes glowed from the shadows. The fluttering of wings met their ears. The tiny sparkles winked out.

Jasna's voice held urgency. "Fall back into the magic barrier!"

Esti and Limbik obeyed. Jasna never took her eyes from the forest as she backed in. All three howled.

Jonna approached.

A growl issued from Limbik before Limbik and Esti turned to see him. Esti sniffed. Limbik huffed, "Human."

"What's happening?"

Jasna shifted position. "We are being hunted."

"By what?"

"That's what I'm determining, my lord." A flicker in the shadows drew her attention. She sniffed the air. "It reminds me of--"

41

"Then, it's not Prince Conall?"

Limbik growled with scorn. "We are honorable, my lord, despite what others may say."

"Despite the blood lust?" Jonna spotted another flicker, but the shape could not be made out.

Esti laid a paw on Limbik. "It is ignorance, my brother, nothing more. Let it go."

Jonna looked from one to the other. "If I have insulted, I meant no disrespect. These are questions I must ask."

Jasna spoke without turning; her eyes followed another shadow. "If I may speak candidly, my lord."

"Please do."

"They are questions of ignorance and fear. They are questions that imply malice. Our kind would not attack us."

Limbik turned toward him with ears straight and eyes glaring. "You should not be here."

Jonna stared back. "Granted, but we are and can do nothing else for the night."

Esti watched him. The sparkle returned to her eye. "You are not offended by our demeanor?"

"Since you are honest with me, I will be honest with you. You are the first of the vulkodlaks I have encountered. Despite my former impression," he grinned, "I do appreciate your honesty."

At a flutter, Limbik's head darted toward the right. Worry filled his voice. "For our brothers, we should howl again."

Jasna nodded and all three joined in chorus. The bushes shook in front. Two shadows bolted from the darkness. Vytautas and Gerulf raced toward them. Something tagged Vytautas from behind, and the vulkodlak yelped. Gerulf slid sideways, scrambled to get his feet under him, and charged back toward Vytautas. Razor sharp teeth glistened in the remaining light as Gerulf chomped down upon something the others could not see.

Black ooze dripped down the wolf's fangs as two shadows dropped. Vytautas limped a step, saw Gerulf in danger, and turned back.

Limbik started forward, but Jasna caught him. "Our duty is to the task at hand. We all knew the risk."

"But Jasna--" A tear ran down Esti's face. "They will not survive."

A shadow attached itself to Gerulf's shoulder. A howl of agony filled the air. Vytautas caught the creature in his jaws and ripped. Ooze splattered across the forest floor. A frenzy of shadows erupted above them.

The white unicorn came up from behind. "Jonna, you must help them, but you cannot use magic."

Jonna's head ached as he struggled to focus on the battle. "All this time you tell me magic is my friend, and now you say I can't use it?" His eyes narrowed at the unicorn, and he pointed. "You know what these shadow creatures are."

The unicorn nodded.

"And you're not going to tell me, are you?"

The unicorn's mane shook. "There is no time." It nodded toward the two vulkodlaks. Vytautas snapped as Gerulf spun. The shadows closed in.

Jonna darted past Jasna's paw that held Limbik back. As he left the entry, his hand pulled the Rune Blade of Knowledge from its sheath. "No magic," he growled. "I hope this qualifies!"

Jasna blinked in shock. "Follow him! Keep close quarters!" The three vulkodlaks leaped after Jonna as he raced toward Vytautas and Gerulf. Paws struck, heads turned, and jaws snapped. The shadow creatures launched into the fray.

The rune blade slashed as it moved. The shadows caught in its wake dropped to the ground in pieces. Some collided as they swooped in. They felt its sting as they were sliced and fell apart.

This wasn't working. The frenzy of the creatures grew faster than Jonna and his companions could kill them. Hundreds had launched from the forest, and the trees rustled with more. With a glance toward the camp, Jonna saw that the shadows inched closer to the enchanted circle.

The sword glowed, and a musical hum emitted from its blade. Jonna's hands felt a heat grow. A change in the fray erupted. The shadow creatures that had been drawn to the enchanted circle now drew toward him. They began to chitter.

Vytautas and Gerulf slashed but were no longer the objects of the attack. Jasna, Limbik, and Esti spread out around Jonna and with sharp, white teeth snatched the shadows from the air. Jonna stood in the center. The great rune blade arced as it divided the creatures asunder. Despite the pile that rose at their feet, the shadows' numbers grew. He shouted above the tumult, "Get Vytautas and Gerulf to the camp. I'll draw their attention." A glance at the camp caught Almundena and Bob rushing toward him.

Jasna growled. "You are the assigned liege. We will not abandon you." With a snap, she caught one of the shadows in her teeth, bit it in half, and spit it out. "If only they were tasty!"

Jonna chuckled despite the swing of the rune blade. Thankfully, he didn't have to bite the creatures himself. "I can't even imagine that!"

A grin formed on Jasna's face between slashes and bites. Limbik chuckled, too. As the laughter hit them all, the battle shifted.

"I am your liege," Jonna finally got out. "Do as I ask. I will hold these."

She glanced toward him with a turn of her head. Her eyes bore into him as she snapped another shadow, crunched, and spit it out. "Pull back!"

The roar of the shadows rose above him. They drew toward his blade. The vulkodlaks worked toward the entrance.

Almundena slowed at the wolves' withdrawal and tried to get in close, but the shadows created a barrier. "What is going on?" She spun toward the circle as anger flooded her face. "Come back! Fight!"

Bob tossed pixie dust into the air. "*Hectora!*" The shadows sped up. Their strikes came closer to Jonna with every flyby.

"Bob! What did you do?"

To keep from being caught, the pixie ducked and swooped. "It was supposed to hold them still!"

The words the unicorn had spoken echoed in his brain. His sword had drawn them from the others. "No magic from anyone except me! Give them no magic!"

Almundena twisted and stopped as her hands rose. "Why?"

"Don't you see? They are drawn to magic. They--" *The Sight*, that ability to know the unknowable, flashed into his brain. "They feed on magic." An idea formed. "Almundena, remove the enchanted circle!"

"But we'll be defenseless!"

"Remove it, or we'll be dead!"

She swung toward the circle, placed her hands in the air, and chanted.

The pixie ducked and weaved through the barrier to Jonna's shoulder. Bob managed to stay beside his ear. "Without magic, we have nothing to fight with. We can't leave you alone!"

"In order for this to work, it must be." Sweat trickled down the sides of his face as he swung. "Go, my friend."

Bob crossed his arms. "No."

"Go. I must do this alone for it to work!"

A tear formed in Bob's eye.

"Please, protect Almundena!"

Bob swooped away. Some of the shadows shifted toward Almundena as she focused on her spell. Using his body as a bullet, Bob slammed into the shadows and shot through their icky hides. Ooze spun from him as he turned from one to another. His tiny hands cleared his face while he zipped in low arcs around her.

The enchanted circle faded. As it did, the shadows swooped toward Jonna. Bob nailed them. Almundena turned, picked up a thick branch, and swung at the barrier the shadows had formed.

Jonna's voice rose from the other side. "Stay here. I'll be back." The glow of the rune blade grew brighter in Jonna's hands. The shadows' chitter rose to a shrill.

"No magic!" Almundena screamed in terror. "You said no magic!"

With so many of the shadows around, the last rays of the sun darkened. Despite the warmth of the rune blade, Jonna's body shivered. He could feel their hunger, and should one strike upon his skin--

His head jerked to the right as he felt a flicker brush his arm. The shadows closed in.

They attacked from all directions. The rune blade could not fend them off. They slapped against his bare back and chest with greedy bites.

Jonna gasped; he had to get them off. The rune blade sliced in an arc as he surged into the edge of the forest.

Flora tripped him. Leaves and branches slapped him. The terrain rose and fell in unexpected twists. Almundena's voice faded into the distance.

All light vanished. At every turn, the shadows struck. The pain in his limbs intensified until the rune blade tumbled from his hands. The glow of the blade stopped as he collapsed to his knees. The smell of wet dog met his nose, but he could not tell its direction.

His ears caught the gurgle of a tiny brook. On hands and knees, he crawled forward, still being struck by the flutters. The song of Aroha met his ears, and he fell toward the water.

Shrieks launched away from him. The pitch-black darkness became a dull glow. At the horizon, as the sun set, a moon had risen to take its place. A graceful, female voice soothed, "Aren't you a little far from the river?"

A water sprite sat on a rock as she combed her long, dark green hair. Her startling white fishbone comb glistened in the moonlight.

Relief flooded through him. He looked down at his body to see his fin had returned. "They're gone."

"Of course they're gone," the sprite smiled. "Magic contrary to their purpose always upsets them."

"They only feast on certain types of magic?"

"You didn't know that?" She flicked some water toward him with a playful laugh.

The water soothed him. His fin stretched out as he lay upon his back in the shallows. Despite the wounds inflicted by the shadows, the sweetness of the stream fed his soul. Though different from the river, it nonetheless felt great. "Thank you for sharing your stream, and no, I did not know that."

"Shame on you. Someone has neglected their schooling." Her body slipped into the water and smoothly glided toward him. "Perhaps we should remedy that."

She floated from the deeper waters to move beside him in the shallows and traced her fingers up his arm. Her touch made his fin quiver. "You are hurt badly. Let me help you." As she bent toward him, her hair tumbled to his chest. Her lips touched his with loving embrace.

The nix part responded. Like peas in a pod, the nix and water sprites did have a common branch. Between the pain of the bites, the relief of the water, and the gentleness of her touch, his nix-self almost gave in.

"No, I cannot." His chest heaved as he mind fought against it.

The sprite pulled back with woeful eyes. "Would you not be healed?"

"Please, wonderful sprite, if you would heal me, I must be left in peace."

A growl came from the edge of the forest and the water sprite faded from sight. As Jonna looked up, two red eyes glowed back at him from the forest shadows. The wet dog smell returned but with a subtle difference.

"Esti." A smile broke across Jonna's face. "You followed?"

The she wolf slipped out of the darkness and sniffed. Her nose wrinkled in puzzlement. "It is I, my lord. We are out hunting for you." Her eyes briefly darted to his fin. "I will keep your secret."

"That's not exactly what I would call it, but thank you."

"And yet, it saved your life." A sparkle appeared in her eye. "Is that not worth the price?"

Aroha's call met his inner ear. He could feel her through the water. Despite the plea to remain where he lay, Jonna flipped over onto the bank. Though not as fast as during the day, the scales dried out and fell away to reveal his legs, belt, pants, and shoes. He contemplated Esti's last question, and his voice hardened. "I would have found another way."

Her head nodded slowly as she studied the wounds on his torso. "You are hurt, my lord." Her brow creased though the sparkle remained in her eye. "We should see to these immediately." Her paw touched his chest; he cringed. "They are already infected."

In a slow, methodical fashion, he rose to his feet. Without the water next to his skin, he felt weak. The reflection of moonlight upon his blade caught his eye. "I'll be fine."

His hand picked up the sword. It weighed heavy on his arm. With aching muscles, he sheathed the blade. The weight dragged down upon his back.

"You will not." Esti's gaze met his. "Unless I help you." Her round, dark eyes waited for him to concede.

"You're serious?"

She grinned. "I am, my lord. That is my secret."

Jasna and Limbik rounded a tree. Esti backed up, the grin faded, and she went silent.

Jasna's gaze went from Jonna to Esti; urgency filled her voice. "We must hurry to the camp. If these are the creatures I think they are, they will return. Follow me."

She turned quickly and took the lead. Jonna hurried to follow. Limbik and Esti brought up the rear.

They rushed in silence until Jonna asked, "What are they?"

With a fixed stare, she whispered, "If I am correct, they are the *itzall*: dread beings sent to purge souls whom the gods have chosen for death." Her eyes drifted to him. "None of ours has done this; it must be yours."

The words of Tlyme, one of the three Norse fates, came back to him, *Though the gods would use you as a tool, they will find you gone before you go*. Did this mean he was going to die? His mind refused to believe it. No god determined his fate. No prophecy predicted his future. He changed the subject.

"I take it--" Jonna pushed through the low hanging branches as Jasna ducked under. "--Vytautas and Gerulf made it to the camp?"

The she wolf nodded as she noted what he did. Her voice rose slightly, "They guard closer to the center now that the enchanted circle is gone. They will be diligent."

"Are they okay?"

Jasna glanced at him with a wrinkled muzzle. "Why are you concerned?"

He ducked a branch to walk closer to her side. Each step became harder though he forced himself on. "You already know that answer."

"Our kinds are different. They do not care for one another. Humans and werewolves cannot coexist together."

He drew a breath to help focus. "Believe it or not, I think they can."

She caught his eye and swung her head forward again just in time to avoid a tree. Her voice rose. "There are those of us who believe as you do--that equality for all can be had." Her voice dropped to almost a growl. "I am not one of them. Do you not see the difference? We eat your kind."

"And yet, you are here."

"By our *own* mandate."

"The choice is yours to stay."

Leaves rustled in the silence. Jonna's footsteps were louder than the paws of the wolves. She did not face him. "You would release us?"

"I do not hold you, even now." His face felt hot.

"Knowing the peril you face?" A wolfish grin spread. "For

once the bargain is ended, there is nothing to say we may not hunt you, too."

"You are honorable, Jasna, you and all your companions. Why else would I seek to save your lives?" Sweat dripped from the side of his face.

The vegetation broke to reveal the clearing. Tracks led from the edges into the camp. As they approached, Vytautas and Gerulf rose from where they watched and sniffed the air. The unicorn looked in their direction. Jonna's head throbbed. Almundena burst from the leather hide opening followed by Bob. As Jonna reached the fire pit, she threw her arms around him.

"Your skin is clammy and hot." With her hands still upon him, she stepped back with a frown. "Something invades your body."

The unicorn moved closer. Its eyes studied Jonna's. "Indeed. The venom of the shadows is surging through your veins."

Esti trod forward with a gleam in her eye. "I can cure him."

"No," Jasna blocked her. "You cannot do this. He is not one of ours."

"He has given his life to save our brothers!" Esti's words cowered all except for Jasna. "Is he not worthy?"

Almundena stood in front of Jonna with her hands ready. "Girls, I don't know what you're talking about, but I will not let you hurt my husband."

"No magic," Jonna gasped before a wave of nausea hit him. The unicorn shifted to catch his weight. Jonna clung to the horse's side. "Thank you."

"I told you we were friends."

He hung there taking deep breaths as the world spun around him. The breeze through the trees grew louder. The moon's brightness cast a golden hue. In the distance, he heard a flutter. "They're coming." With a struggle, he stood straight as Jasna's details about the itzall played in his mind. "Everyone into the yurt."

Jasna stared at him. "Your dwelling will not save you."

She was right; only one thing could be done. "Go to safety. It is my order. Take Almundena and Bob as well. Once that is accomplished, you are released--you, and all your friends. I will meet the itzall."

Limbik gaped followed by the others. Only Jasna's eyes narrowed. "You cannot release us that way. We were assigned to guard you!"

"You are to obey. What is the penalty for a vulkodlak's disobedience?"

Her head rose higher as her lips curled back. "Do as he says."

"No." Almundena turned toward Jonna. "I will not leave you." Her hands caught his arm. "We can leave through magic. We can find a way!"

Bob dropped between them. "Don't you see? It is the very magic we possess that the shadows feed upon. Unless you can wield another weapon, all we will do is draw them to attack."

Jonna touched Almundena's face. "With the sword, I can get their attention. Everyone else can escape."

Her face turned to stone. "You can't make me leave."

His hand laid gently on her stomach. "For the child's sake, I can ask."

A tear ran down her cheek as she stared into his eyes. "That's not fair."

"You are all I have left." His thoughts went to Elfleda, Elpis, and his unborn child from the other reality. They were gone. Something had happened, and he had lost them. Now, he could lose another family.

His heart trembled. As his arms encircled her tightly, he whispered in her ear. "I don't want to lose you, too."

The single tear turned into many, fell from her cheeks, and cascaded down his chest. He fought back his own and gently pulled her arms from around him. His eyes caught hers and gave a single nod.

She turned away. Surrounded by the vulkodlaks, Bob and

Almundena headed off toward the river--back toward the city of the elves. He watched them go until the forest swallowed them up.

"You should go, too." He threw a look at the unicorn. "It's not going to be pretty." Branches shook not far from where his friends had gone, but nothing else materialized. The shadows' hunger clung to him. He could feel their presence though they were too far away to be the cause of the disturbance. *The Sight* hit him. They were coming this way fast.

The unicorn snorted. "They're drawn to you, not me."

Jonna chuckled. "Thanks for reminding me." A noise came from the right. "Should we check that?" He moved toward it, only to hear something move at top speed through the bush. "Those aren't shadows."

The unicorn tilted its head. "No, they don't sound like it."

"But the shadows are getting too close to wander off. If they are after me, I don't want them finding any others." He stepped backwards toward the center of camp.

"Mind if I hang around?"

"I take it they don't like your magic, either?"

"It does give them a rather distasteful feel."

"What are they?"

"A creation, Jonna, from the very source of magic. They attack and destroy when the balance is upset."

Silence dropped. Jonna's voice fell to a whisper. "Majik's antibodies tailored to destroy me because I've cracked the Partitions of Majik." He stared. "Am I really that dangerous?"

The unicorn nodded. "Unfortunately, you are correct. You have not been rejected Jonna, but there is a proper way to use magic. You have fractured the fabric of its existence, and altered what was meant to be."

Jonna's thoughts went to the ones he had lost, and he whispered, "Is there hope? Can I get them back?"

The dark eyes of the unicorn stayed steady. "There is always hope."

Determination filled Jonna's voice. "How do I fight them?"

The unicorn winked. "That is the *start* of a good question."

Jonna's eyebrows knitted together. His eyes grew as *The Sight* struck again. "Don't dwell upon the symptoms. Address the cause?" He met the unicorn's gaze. "How do I do that when the shadows keep attacking?"

Wing flutters brushed the treetops. Dark shapes descended.

The unicorn nodded toward the trees. "Incoming."

"Thanks. I got that." Antibodies? How could he fight an antibody designed to take him out? Despite the weakness, he spun toward the yurt. The conversation had given him an idea. As the leather hide knocked back, his eyes did not adjust quickly enough. His foot tripped over a pole lying across the floor.

Down he dropped. The breath slammed out of him along with his reserve strength. As he gasped for air, the fluttering came closer. His eyes centered on the water bucket Bob had left sitting on the ground next to the chairs at the north wall.

He tried to rise. Every muscle in his body complained. The flutters struck the yurt's outside. The canvas shook.

A female voice surprised him. "Jonna, let me help." It was softer than its wolfish version but nonetheless recognizable. "Esti?" His eyes sought but could not spot her. There was no time for hide and seek.

"We came back to help. Limbik and I overheard your conversation with Jasna. She was right. There are those who believe as you do."

The flutters struck the yurt. Jonna struggled toward the water. "I don't think this is the time unless, perhaps, you want to hand me that bucket?"

"It is exactly the time, don't you see?" A woman wearing a blue silk robe stepped from the shadows. Her long brown curly hair bounced against her shoulders. "It is perfect. The wait is over."

"What wait?" He shook his head as the flutters struck closer to the door. "I would *love* to continue this chat, but first I must have that water!"

A man dressed similar to Esti slipped from the shadows. With short dark hair, his muscular build pressed the limits of his robe. "You don't the need water." Using a deft hand, he picked up the bucket.

"What is going on?"

Esti came closer with a smile on her lips. "You were infected by the bites. Vytautas and Gerulf were not. Did you ever wonder why?"

CHAPTER 6

"No, I haven't had a lot time to wonder." Jonna glanced at Limbik holding the bucket of water. "Be careful with that!" A stirring swept the top of the yurt as something tried to lift up the cover. "Come on, guys. Please!"

Esti helped him to his feet. With a firm hand, she led him to a bed.

"Esti, I appreciate--"

She placed a finger to his lips, and his voice refused to continue. His eyes widened.

"This will only hurt a little. Some experience a slight memory loss, but it will come back."

Jonna tried to struggle but his limbs would not respond. His lungs labored against the weakness, and his face flushed in anger.

In desperation, his mind reached out. The rune blade sang in response. Though he could not reach it, its energy crackled in small bursts of light.

Tent walls bounced from right to left as a surge of flutters struck the outside. The vulkodlak's eyes shined as she gazed into his.

Limbik growled, "Esti, now!"

The depths of Esti's eyes drew him in. His body leaned toward her. Time slowed as nothing else mattered.

"That's right, come to me. Touch my inward soul."

The fluttering missed the hide door by inches as the shadows struck the yurt's outer wall. Limbik's voice rose, "Esti!"

"He's almost there," she whispered in ecstasy. Her chest rose. "I feel him almost there."

The crackle of energy around Jonna waited for his command. He heard the shadows attack--like the sound from a distant sea.

In his mind, a void appeared, darker than the blackness around it. It drew him in, offering safety and warmth.

Within the darkness lay a single speck of light. As he watched, he became the light surrounded by a sea of alien magic. It covered his essence like the amniotic fluid covers an embryo in a womb, and he knew he was about to be reborn.

The hide door ripped back. Dark shadows swung through the opening and spun in a circle within the yurt.

Esti leaned forward and whispered, "He is ready." She licked her lips, leaned further, and sank her front teeth into his shoulder.

A geyser of power erupted as the alien magic and his own combined in a swirl. The embryo launched from the darkness into the light.

Jonna's eyes were blinded. He felt a woman lying in his arms as a blood-curdling scream came from his left. As the brightness faded, the yurt ripped apart.

The shadows fled from him and the unconscious lady he held in his arms. He stood slowly and carried her out of the yurt.

A scream cried out behind him. The shadows roared within. He placed the woman on the ground beside the fire pit. Who was she? Who was he? The knowledge sat there but he could not reach it.

Another scream bellowed. A whimper followed it. He turned to the yurt and went through the hide door.

Shadows shrieked by him. As he approached, others fought to escape through the walls. They clawed and bit the wooden supports in a frantic attempt to flee.

A bucket lay on its side. The tent's rugs absorbed its contents. In a tattered silk robe, next to the bucket, lay a man with dark hair. His body did not move.

Jonna picked him up. The man weighed nothing. The wounds from a thousand bites showed red upon the man's skin.

Outside the yurt, Jonna put him beside the unconscious female. He stared at both. Something had occurred, and he had played a part.

"Jonna?" A unicorn stepped nearer to him. "Are you okay?"

Jonna turned to stare at the unicorn. "Who are you?"

"A friend," the unicorn neighed softly. "You don't remember?"

"No." The past teased him as it flaunted just out of reach. "Why can't I remember?"

"Why, indeed?" The unicorn eyed the two on the ground.

A wisp of memory peeked out. "Did they do something to me?"

"Shouldn't *you* know?"

Jonna stared blankly at the forest. "I should, yes. I should know." He heard a baby cry but could not tell its direction. The smell of a river wafted toward him from the left. He glanced down at the two people beside the fire. "Will they be safe?"

The unicorn raised one eyebrow. "Interesting."

"What?"

"Even without your memory, your basic nature comes through. I shall note that down for later."

The call of the water became stronger in Jonna. Something there could heal him, but he could not leave until he knew these two would be okay. Urgency filled his voice, "Will they be safe?"

The unicorn nodded. "I have made arrangements."

Jonna abruptly started toward the smell of the water.

The unicorn trotted beside him. "Are we leaving?"

The urgency grew. "Yes."

They crossed the clearing and pressed into the dark forest. "And where are we going?"

Despite the darkness, Jonna's eyes could see various shades of gray vividly. This was not normal. As the wind changed, the smells overwhelmed his senses so that he could not find the way. "Home."

"And where is that?"

Jonna's head tilted as he stared. "I want to go home."

"Jonna?"

Panic grew as the disorientation continued. He observed the world through a different creature's perspective. No, not different; it was a mixture of more than one. "Yes?"

"Where is that?"

Jonna gazed out at the forest; nothing felt familiar. Pictures wandered into his mind, but the moment he snatched at them, they fled. "Surely, if you are my friend, you know."

"I have been to many homes. Shall I show you some of them?"

Jonna clung to his words. They helped to steady his thoughts. Though the images still fled, they grew sharper. "All right."

The unicorn bent low. "Climb upon my back, and I will show what you do lack."

Jonna slipped onto the unicorn. Its soft hair gave little to hold on to. "Is this correct?" His fingers knotted into the unicorn's mane.

The unicorn neighed softly, "You're doing fine. Shall we be off?"

A headache pierced through him. He rubbed his temples. "Of course."

With a shake of its head, fairylike sparkles danced away from the unicorn's mane. The glimmers flew to the front and created a long path into the sky. The unicorn trotted up the path.

Pictures twisted around them. As Jonna gazed from side to side, glimpses of his memory came into focus. Names twirled just out of reach. Faces appeared. Places he had seen waved in front of eyes. "Tacoma, Washington, I know that place."

"Is it home?"

Jonna shook his head. "I can't tell."

"Then, we should continue."

A palace appeared tall in the trees. A cabin flashed through his vision. A cave dropped down into the earth with a city lit by glowing fungi. "There. I remember that."

"You want to go there?"

Jonna blinked. "I think--I do."

"Very well."

The pathway descended into the darkness. Narrow rock sides blocked their way, but the unicorn passed through as if none of this existed. It dropped into a huge cavern in the earth.

Light glowed up in various colors brightening the city below. Luminescent fungi decorated the walls and roofs of the buildings. Elves walked in the streets. The unicorn's hooves clicked upon the stone road as they touched lightly to the ground.

Jonna pointed. "That way, I think." The images became clearer. He remembered a queen and her daughter, a conflict with the humans above, and hope returning to a dark elf city that had stood on the brink of doom. "It feels familiar."

The unicorn walked along. Dark elves gaped. Merchants stepped back. The glow of the unicorn lit the streets brighter than the fungi.

"Hold!" A group of three warriors with gold masks and spears blocked the path. "In the name of Queen Siardna, surrender your weapon."

"Weapon?" Jonna slid off the unicorn's back and stepped closer. "I come in peace."

A spear leveled at his chest. "Your weapon, knave, now!"

The unicorn leaned near. "I think they mean the sword on your back."

"Sword? Back?" Jonna turned his head and caught sight of the hilt. "This one?" As his hand touched the handle, a jolt of magic ripped through him, a ping sounded, and his mind remembered more details. He pulled the blade in reflex.

With a cringe, he twisted sideways as a headache ripped through his skull blurring his vision. An elf's spear stabbed at him, narrowly missing its mark.

The rune blade sliced, severed the end of the spear, and turned to face the other two guards. "Guys--" Jonna tried to focus.

Though his hand held the blade, it moved with a mind of its own. "If you'll give me a minute--"

The first warrior lunged. Jonna met the attack with the flat of his blade and forced his opponent's weapon to the ground. The end of the elf's weapon snapped off. A second elf swung toward Jonna's head. The rune blade dashed upward, and the spear broke over its edge.

The three warriors backed up. Two held the wooden staves of headless spears as the last cast his away, drew a sword, and prepared to attack.

"Wait. Just give me a minute!" In the brief moment they hesitated, the pain eased, and Jonna's vision cleared. The bits of details flowed into a whole thought as the magic of the rune blade washed away the unknown. "She bit me!"

"Who bit you?" The unicorn eyed the dark elves. "They all three look male to me."

"Esti! Why?"

"Because they are about to attack."

Jonna parried a wooden pole and sliced toward another. "Not them--back at the camp." The memory of the two types of magic combining startled him. He recalled seeing in the dark in shades of gray without using pixie sight. On top of that, the way he had picked both Esti and Limbik up made no sense. They had felt weightless. Two of the dark elves remained at the ready while the third searched for an avenue of attack.

The unicorn nudged him. "Are you sure this is home?"

"Home?" Jonna glanced at the buildings around him. "This is the dark elf city." His eyes darted back to the three guards as they advanced. "I brought us here? Why?"

"Hold," a female's voice called before her body rounded the corner. Queen Siardna stepped into sight followed by a troop of dark elves. "That is my question as well. When I was told a human bearing an elvish blade had entered the city by magic, I suspected it was you."

Jonna sheathed his sword, "Adonia Queen Siardna, I meant no trouble."

"Despite your intrusion, you have at least remembered proper manners." Her voice dropped and turned hard. "I have kept my side of the arrangement. Why have you not kept yours?"

The last time Jonna had been here, there had been no conditions. His voice lowered to match hers. "What arrangement?"

"We shall continue this in private." She shifted toward the guards, and her voice rose. "Your life for his, if he is touched. Do you understand?" The commander bowed, and she waved Jonna forward. "Come."

Jonna glanced at the unicorn with eyebrows raised. "This way."

The queen led him to the large palace entrance. Inlayed golden serpents wove around its outer edge. Two guards swung the doors back. As they stepped through, the guards halted. A few feet inside, the queen's gaze locked with Jonna's as her voice dropped once more. "You will wait until *called*." Her voice paused before adding, "Prince Jonna."

Jonna bowed, clearly not missing the venom in her expression.

The dark elves stood at attention. Their gaze ventured neither left nor right, but he could feel the dislike flow from them. Surely he had left on better terms than this? After all, he had helped the queen save her kingdom and aided in the restoration of her magic.

The royal steward approached. "This way, my lord."

Jonna gave a nod and followed. The guards parted to let them pass. A distinctive clunk boomed as the outer doors sealed behind him.

"Jonna," the unicorn bobbed his head toward the left, "I'll wait here in the hall."

Jonna nodded.

"Here, my lord." The dark elf steward motioned toward an arched entrance with carvings of green living things on one side and nocturnal creatures on the other. "I have doubled the guard to keep you safe." With respect, the elf stepped back.

As Jonna passed through, the chamber doors closed with a foreboding clang. The ring echoed in the chamber. As the sound faded, an unnerving silence followed.

This was not the room that Jonna remembered, though it was similar in construction. The glowing red, orange, and yellow fungi brightened the elegant décor, not to comfort, but to intimidate.

Ornately carved seats and benches cast odd, distorted shadows before the queen's dais. Velvet pillows, vases, and pictures sat around the room. The murals that hung upon the walls were familiar, all expect one. It showed a family of three sitting under the trees at a forest's edge. Of the three, he recognized Alfgia, the queen's daughter. Had Alfgia found her mate? She had fallen in love with Jonna before.

The queen sauntered in through a secondary door and glided to her large throne. Fabrics of fluorescent patterns draped over its back though they had not been there on his first visit. Were they there to impress or distract?

Beside the queen's throne stood a second throne and a third, although the third one was much smaller. As the queen sat down, her hands went to the arms of her chair. When her left hand touched the chair, her fingers jumped. With a quick glance, the queen's eyes narrowed at her hand. She rubbed her middle finger with her thumb as she turned her gaze to Jonna. Her voice held an edge. "Be seated."

Jonna bowed and picked the closest bench. An uncomfortable silence fell. The queen scowled thoughtfully as he waited. Though the room had a different feel, something else felt amiss, too. It clicked; he sensed no magic in the queen.

"Why have you returned, Jonna McCambel? Our deal was very clear."

"Deal?" A wry smile emerged. "Arrangement? What is this about?"

Her eyes narrowed. "Don't play games. With a snap of my fingers, a troop of dark elves would gladly disembowel you."

His smile dropped. "I don't understand. We parted on good terms."

The queen arched an eyebrow. "Must I spell it out? For the humans to be free, you agreed to have no communication with my daughter."

Jonna's jaw dropped. "Why would I say that?"

"And now, you are here, and I must placate my daughter. Word is already spreading of your visit. If you had left before it reached her, she would have never forgiven me. But be warned, after this, you will abide by the agreement and never return. Do you understand?"

To his right, a door burst open. Alfgia's faced glowed with delight. As she swept toward him, the colors in the room danced off her jet black hair, highlighting the contours of her face and neck. Beneath the silk-like clothing lay an obvious baby bump that accentuated her shape and beauty. Her voice spoke softly, "Adonii Prince Jonna."

A smile overtook his face. "Adonia Princess Alfgia."

Like a soft flutter on the wind, the princess curtseyed. Her eyes stared into his as she blushed with excitement. "I am with child, my lord. It will be a son!"

A dark elf stepped from the same door. His shoulders and back stayed straight as he looked down over his raised chin. On his chest, the official symbol of the crown hung by a golden chain. The orb of a sun reflected from its surface. It seemed out of place.

A sneer decorated Siardna's lips as her eyes stayed on Jonna. "Adonii Aubron, please meet Prince Jonna of the woodland elves. He has come to pay his respects."

Aubron paused. His eyes narrowed in disdain. "It is about time the woodland elves paid tribute." He slowly approached Jonna and stopped to Alfgia's left.

Alfgia's focus never left Jonna though Aubron firmly took her arm. "I have found my true love. Is it not wonderful?"

Concern swept through him though he hid it with a nod and a

smile. "I am delighted at your good fortune and wish you both the greatest of happiness." He turned to the queen. "I should be going. There is a long journey ahead."

The queen gave assent.

A pout dropped on Alfgia's face. "Why so soon when you have only just arrived? I would ask for but a day."

The queen watched him intently.

Jonna deferred to the queen. "At your consent only, Queen Siardna."

The queen touched her lips. "Perhaps it would be better." Her eyes darted from Jonna to Alfgia. "Yes, I do believe it would. Steward?"

The elf stepped into the throne room through the same door Aubron had used. "I am here, Queen Siardna."

"You will prepare a room in the palace for Prince Jonna."

"Aye, my lady." The steward bowed. "It shall be as you command."

The queen gave a nod, and the royal steward hurried out.

Alfgia pulled her arm from Aubron and took Prince Jonna's hand.

A tingle traveled through Jonna as they touched.

"Thank you." Her eyes sparkled. "Knowing that you have extended your stay means all the world to me. We shall meet at dinner." She shifted back, curtsied, and took Aubron's arm. "Until then, Prince Jonna."

He bowed, curious. "Until then."

Though he maintained his smile, his thoughts flew. That tingle meant only one thing. Was Aubron not her true love? Jonna had told her the last time he was here that nothing could happen between them. He inhaled. What if, in this reality, things had gone quite differently?

He drew a quick breath as the doors to the throne room opened. The steward entered and hastened to stop beside him. "My lord, your room will be ready when we arrive."

He led Jonna from the throne room. The unicorn joined them in the hallway. The elf guided Jonna to the left, passed through a large door, and headed down another hall. Statues of dark elf kings and queens stood at the sides. The name of each one had been engraved on its pedestal.

However, one pedestal did not have a statue. The steward led Jonna to the room beside it. As they passed through the door with the unicorn trailing, the rune blade hummed.

The elf glanced curiously toward Jonna's sword. "These are your quarters, my lord." A long, woven cord hung next to the door. "Should you require anything, simply pull this."

"Am I to stay in my room?"

"It would be wise, my lord, unless escorted." The steward leaned toward him and whispered, "Keep the door locked. Keep your sword ready." He turned on his heels and departed.

Jonna turned to the unicorn. "Why would I bring us here?" The fog that had hidden his memory had washed away. However, the memories did not offer a reason why he had chosen this place.

The unicorn blinked at him. "You brought me, remember?"

The words taunted him as they echoed in the large chamber.

"Maybe--maybe this holds a way back. Maybe it's instinctive."

His eyes took in the room. A lavish elven bed stood near one wall. The wall held a series of intricately carved images. A full-length mirror and a closet with dual doors stood between two of the carvings.

The images went from right to left. They depicted scenes of bright, sunny days on one side which gradually changed to dull, dark ones, only to brighten once again.

Tiny scenes of elven activity lay carved into each image. Peace, war, love, and sadness reflected from the artist's design.

At the top of the carvings, the artist had engraved a horizontal track that started at one side of the room and reached the other. A sword with a green, multifaceted jewel hung from the track.

Jonna approached the images. The rune blade hummed. "Nothing happens by accident. There is a reason for everything."

The unicorn watched intently as he neared the wall. "Indeed."

Jonna's eyebrows crossed. "And why did I hear a baby cry?"

The unicorn lifted one eyebrow. "As you said, there is a reason."

He twisted toward the unicorn. "Did you hear it near the camp?"

The unicorn's silence was answer enough.

"You know what I'm talking about. You know what's going on."

As he turned back toward the wall, his hand lightly touched the flat of the sword that hung upon the track.

A surge of power struck him, and a ping sounded. As images burst into his mind, he slid sideways toward the bed.

CHAPTER 7

Jonna had shifted to another majik partition. He knew it before he opened his eyes, but this time it felt different. Why?

The bedroom door opened. As Jonna rose from the top of the bed, a headache racked his temples. The same steward that had left moments ago approached quickly.

A jeweled sash hung across the dark elf's shoulder. "I beg your pardon, Your Majesty, but the invasion has begun!"

By instinct, Jonna's fingers grasped the sheath of the sword that lay upon the elven bed. As he fastened it to his belt, the green gem glowed in its hilt. An image flashed into his mind: the green-gemmed sword mounted above the carvings on the inlaid track. It was not his to wield. It was not the Rune Blade of Knowledge.

He blinked in confusion. The image faded, uneven clouds of fog closed in over his past memories, and an entire new life filled his head. "Where are they now, Athtar?" Splint mail armor encircled his body. When had that been put on?

"They have entered the caves. They are closing on the city."

The new memories entered his brain as a play he saw for the very first time. He tried to stop the next words yet they came as if preordained. "Show me."

They hurried out of the bedroom door. Though he didn't know why, part of him said no statue should be on the pedestal beside it. However, one did stare back. His own likeness with a sword raised high looked down with eyes that bore into the soul.

Athtar gripped his arm. "Your Majesty, we must hurry!" A rumble echoed in the halls as soldiers rushed down the palace corridors.

The dark elf commander, Lord Aubron, approached. He did *not* give a salute. "We have secured the main tunnel. That will force them to use the smaller." A grim line hit his face. "Your orders?"

"Hold them. Do not initiate first attack."

"If we do not drive them back, once they assemble in their entirety, their numbers could overwhelm us."

Jonna's eyes remained steady. "Hold them."

With pursed lips, the commander gave a nod and hurried off.

Athtar leaned toward him. "They do not like this plan of yours. It is too close to home."

Jonna placed a hand on his shoulder. "Do not fear, my good friend, it will be well."

Would it? His memories were vague. Though the details filled in what was necessary for the moment, the clouds of mist blocked his past at every turn, thinning and thickening of their own volition. New thoughts and feelings jammed his head. Like a script recited from memory, he knew the places and people around him as they occurred, but the play's grand opening had only begun.

With a turn, they stepped into the main hall. The throne room appeared to his left. The doors to the palace loomed closer.

Two guards hurried to remove a great bar and swung out the doors. From the street, a frenzy of voices erupted.

Dark elf children headed toward the safety of deeper caves. Men and women, elven and human, had taken up arms. They prepared to fight house to house.

They were ready, but was he? He started to bite his lip, but stopped the action. Only confidence could be shown for the plan to work. What was the plan? They walked rapidly past side streets and ended at the city square.

Alfgia came up beside him in glowing, golden, splint mail armor. Her eyes sparkled. She never ceased to amaze him. With a spear in one hand and a sword strapped to her side, she stood a model of strength and beauty.

"My lord," her stance stood firm, "we are ready."

"You should be guarding the deeper caves."

"I should be by your side in peace or war." She touched her stomach. "And so should your son."

Did he have a son? Yes, a son would be born, but-- His mind remembered a life with Alfgia. If this was true, why did it feel wrong? The script that played in his head forced him onward.

Jonna's heart fell. "Love, no." Panic struck his insides and threatened to rip them out. "I want you safe!"

"We are a family. Neither I nor your son would choose to live without you." She took his hand. "We will face it together."

The tingle struck him as his hand gripped her smaller one in loving embrace. She could take care of herself. Her agility and training could not be matched. Yet, their enemies knew that as well. Her presence in the battle could play into their hands.

"You know my concern. When it comes to you--"

Her hand released. They stared into each other's eyes as her hand touched his face. "It is under control. I will not leave your side."

"I cannot let you do this."

Fierce defiance filled her eyes. "I choose to do this. It is the right of every dark elf, high-born or low."

"Alfgia, please!"

Athtar touched Jonna's shoulder. "My lord, if I may, you cannot fight generations of tradition no matter how much you wish. It is the pride of every wife to be beside her beloved in war."

Jonna's eyes closed. His heart thumped hard inside his chest. "I just want you safe."

Her lips touched his in gentle caress. "With you, I am."

Their magic mingled. The clouds in his mind became denser and hid something he should see. All he knew was now.

She kissed him fiercely, and he returned it just as intensely. A speck grew in the mist until the speck became the voice of Väinämö. Its volume fluctuated up and down, struck by waves of interference. "Wake up, man. Give me something to find you by!"

James William Peercy

"My lord," Athtar touched him. Jonna jumped.

The kiss broke, and they exhaled. Their cheeks flushed, and both turned toward the street in front.

Jonna cleared his throat and hid his puzzlement over Väinämö's voice. "Thank you, Athtar."

"No, my lord, thank you. It is the love between you both that proved human and dark elf could coexist in harmony."

Additional memories of his life with Alfgia raced into existence. It had not been easy. Old hatreds had produced battle scars for humans and dark elves. However, gradually, both sides had come to an understanding. If they could not live together for the purpose of peace, then the merge had to be done to prevent their extinction in war.

The group moved forward away from the city square and along the streets. He blinked. A cloud-covered memory, held hidden by Alfgia's magic while they kissed, stirred but faded and was replaced. The path they took mirrored the one Jonna had first arrived on many years before.

As the newly built outer walls appeared, dark elf troop formations came into view, and the plan filled his mind. Dark elf mages stood ready upon the towers. These vantage points had been placed in one hundred foot intervals all along the walls.

A square building with a single door guarded one of many accesses to the top of the wall. A guard opened it at their approach. They climbed the circular stairs to the top of the nearest tower.

Jonna's eyes swept over the craftsmanship of so many laborers. The walls were composed of thick embankments with a moat on the outer side. A second moat, more shallow and wide, lay beyond the first covered with mats of fungi. The glow of the dark-gray fungi cast eerie shadows that reflected in the faces of the dark elves that stood upon the walls.

Upon the tower's floor lay an elven rug woven with the symbol of eternity. He remembered that from the palace of the woodland elves so many years ago--before the deceit had been discovered.

70

He stepped toward the front, outer edge of the tower. In the far cavern wall, torches emerged from a small, side cave.

Due to the narrow path from the side cave, humans and woodland elves clad in armor came cautiously down the slope in single file. All upon the wall could see the intruders' weapons held at the ready.

Sir Verity, in charge of the woodland queen's forces; Lord Tanyl, who controlled one of the queen's regions; and Alkae, Andas' father, who had been released by Jonna's intervention from dark elf servitude: emerged from the cave. Andas could not be seen, and memories concerning the reason flooded Jonna's mind. After Alkae had recovered, Andas and his father had fallen into disagreement. Alkae did not like Andas' selection of a dark elf as his wife.

Sir Verity raised his voice as they stopped at the halfway point between the battlements and the cave. A marker had been set equidistant from all embattlements. It would allow them to speak directly to the tower Jonna stood upon without shouting.

"Jonna McCambel, you are called forth to answer for your crime."

Jonna's heart smote him as the past events associated with the crime rolled into his memory like thunder. To fulfill a prophecy, Elfleda, a tyrant, had tried to trick him into marriage. In a quiet voice, he took in all before him and spoke, "*Audio.*"

The spell touched both forces. His voice, though low, spoke clear to all who watched. "The heart chooses, but two must agree. The crime you speak of does not exist. Elfleda chose her own fate."

Alfgia's hand touched his.

"You lie!" Tanyl jabbed his finger toward Jonna's tower. "You lie to cover up that you broke her heart!"

"You cannot break what was never given. You cannot force another to love. I did love Elfleda, but she desired power, not love." As the words left his mouth, they scorched like a flame too hot. He fought back tears before they showed.

"Your marriage was foretold! The glory of the woodland elves was to rise into the heavens. And now you stand with a laugnea of the dark elves." He spat at the ground. "Face your crime, or we will destroy you and your pathetic pets."

Alfgia's hand tightened on his as Jonna's muscles tensed at Tanyl's insult at his wife. Her voice stayed calm as her eyebrows arched. "Do not let them goad you, my love. Their words have no power. Love is its own truth."

Jonna's jaw set. "Our hospitality is at an end, Lord Tanyl. Despite your disrespect, you will be allowed to leave without repercussion for your words or you may stay and suffer the penalty. The choice is yours. *Audio*."

With the last word, the spell toggled off, and a silence dropped across the yard. Men and weapons from the woodland elves continued to filter in through the small cave.

Athtar nodded. "You did well, my lord."

Jonna's eyes narrowed. "He called my wife a prostitute. It is an insult that will not be forgotten."

"Nor should it." Athtar shook his head. "However, perhaps they will they take your gracious invitation and leave."

Alfgia squeezed his hand. A faraway look lay in her eyes. "We must invite them in."

Jonna turned his gaze from the battlefield to her. "Who?"

"We must invite them or we will surely perish." Her round eyes turned toward him. Her hands held her stomach as fear ripped across her face. "It must be so."

"I will not have them in our house to spit upon you."

Tears welled in her eyes. "Jonna, please."

Athtar's eyes darted between them. "There is merit to what she says, my lord. Think wisely on this. While we may, indeed, drive them away, if our destruction is a possible future, we must be cautious."

Her pleading eyes swayed his heart, and Jonna gave a nod. "Send two envoys: one elf, one human." He squeezed her hand. "I pray you're right."

"As you wish." Athtar bowed and whispered to a page. The young girl dashed off. The trio left the tower.

The street swarmed with soldiers. Civilians were in their homes. A foggy glimpse of the first time he had walked toward the palace struck, followed by a not so foggy second. The memories of this existence matched the former one, yet they fought each other in details.

A glimpse of the house beside him showed a different slant. The luminescent glow of the fungi existed in an altered place. As the two memories become one, nausea filled his stomach, and his heart beat wildly.

"You shiver, my lord." Alfgia's grip tightened. "Are you well?"

He gathered his strength. "As well as can be expected when we bring enemies into our home."

The distant look caught her as they approached the palace doors. "They were not meant to be."

The fog in his mind winked open, only to close a second later. "No." His mind shifted through the two different memories. "They were not." He clung to what he had seen. "Save maybe one."

As the doors to the palace drew open, Lord Aubron approached. "We must speak--" His eyes flashed toward Alfgia. "--my lord. Alone."

Athtar bowed slightly and stepped back. "I will prepare for our guests' arrival." The elf hurried off at Jonna's nod.

Jonna swung his gaze toward Aubron but did not stop walking. "There is nothing you can say that does not concern my wife."

Lord Aubron's eyes narrowed into steel. "May I be candid, my lord?"

"By all means."

"You are a fool to let those infidels inside."

Alfgia's eyes snapped into flame. "It was not His Majesty's suggestion, Lord Aubron. It was mine."

Aubron stepped back. "Pardon me, my lady. Had I known--"

Her words were sharp. "You would have said nothing, but thought the same." She growled, "Leave us."

With a curt bow and eyes averted, Aubron hurried from the palace. Even then, the flames still flickered in Alfgia's eyes. "He is insolent and arrogant. I want him replaced."

A slight chuckle escaped Jonna's lips as he gave a polite nod to others that passed. "You were the one that picked him."

They turned and entered the corridor with the statues. Toward the end, her royal chambers lay next to his. "A choice we will soon remedy. I don't understand what I saw in him."

As they stepped within, Jonna closed the door. The fungi glowed in wondrous colors to wash away the shadows in its soft light. "I think it was a consolation prize. What he really wanted was to marry you."

She pressed him toward her bed. At her touch, he fell backwards onto it, and the metallic overlaps of his armor clinked. She grinned. "There was no chance of that."

Jonna stared at the decorative canopy over her bed. "Not even if we hadn't been married?"

Her body dropped beside his, and her armor chimed. "Why would you say that? From the moment I saw you, I knew you were the one."

The fog in his mind shifted. Three memories stabbed through his skull. All displayed a different personality of Queen Siardna. The three varied in intensity but all had one common result. He blinked. "Even though your mother had other designs?"

"She meant well. After you were forced to flee from the woodland elves, she found you and took you in. She would be proud to see us now had the illness not taken her." Alfgia's eyes became distant. "It happened so fast, the healers found no cure."

He drew her back. "I seem to recall finding her in the forest."

Alfgia smiled as his words drove away the sadness. She laughed and rolled on top of him. Their armor chimed together. "How about we walk through our first encounter?" Her eyes

sparkled. "I remember something that even made you blush."
Someone knocked thrice upon the door. With exasperation, she
exhaled, "Come in."

As the door opened, Athtar bowed. "Excuse the interruption,
Your Majesties, but Lord Tanyl, Sir Verity, and Alkae await you in
the throne room." Athtar bowed and closed the door.

With a sigh, she rolled off of him. "Duty calls, my love."

"Not so fast." Jonna pinned her. "After a tease like that, surely
I get something?" He leaned toward her. "A kiss, perhaps?"

"Perhaps." She gazed into his eyes. "Perhaps more."

A tingle went through him as their lips touched. The fog
thickened and intensified. The unity of magic hit so strongly both
pulled back in a gasp.

"When--" Her chest heaved. "--did you learn that?"

His eyes grew large. "I--don't know."

"Of all that's holy, forget the visitors--"

Something tried to stir in the fog. The voice of Väinämö called
again, but he could not make out the words. He put a finger to her
lips. "Duty, remember?"

She narrowed her eyes. "I'll remember."

He rose with a nervous chuckle and helped her to her feet.
"Come love--" Väinämö's voice faded. However, it left a swirl of
fog. As places thinned and thickened, the reality around him felt
unreal. "I want these people gone."

"So do I--especially now." Her hand held his as she guided
him toward the carved images that lined the wall behind her bed.
She pressed three places. One of the full length images slid out to
reveal a secret passage. "Let's take a shortcut."

Jonna followed behind her. The dark passage gave no light,
but his vision didn't waver. As the light dimmed behind him, the
differences in the shades of darkness became easier to see. When
had he learned to do this?

As if by his request, the fog shifted. The memory of two sharp
objects stabbing into his shoulder flashed. How was that possible?
He had never encountered a creature that could do that.

The light went completely dark, and the pixie sight Bob had given him kicked in. That he did remember; Bob had given that ability when he had been cast into Chernobog, the prison city.

"Jonna? Come on!"

His eyes caught her lithe figure with long black hair. It enthralled him. The memories rolled back through his mind. Their merged magic had taken them to places most humans could never attain, even from the very first time they met.

The end approached. Alfgia pressed three different places on the wall, and the barrier slipped forward. A breath of air stirred around them as they stepped into a room behind the thrones. With a debonair poise, they came out a side door and stopped.

From beside the door, a herald stepped forward. "Presenting His Majesty King Jonna and Her Majesty Queen Alfgia. All rise."

Those seated rose. Jonna and Alfgia took their seats.

Lord Tanyl's eyes narrowed though he had risen as well. Perhaps the soldiers around the room had something to do with his compliance.

"If I may speak, Your Majesty?" Sir Verity kept perfect poise.

Jonna gave a nod.

"We seem to be at a stalemate. Why call us to your hall when our army is ready to invade?"

"That is a good question, and one my wife will answer. Had it been my choice--" He eyed them all. "This meeting would not be."

"My lords," Alfgia nodded toward them. "There is an evil in this battle, one that will waste many lives. It is our goal to avoid this. The vision I saw will bring all our deaths."

"Bah." Lord Tanyl shook his head. "You will say anything to stop what is about to happen. There is only one option." A sneer spread across his face. "Let His *Majesty*, Jonna, come with us to answer for his crime. Only then can this be avoided."

Jonna's voice stepped in. "Confrontation or blackmail?"

"Call it as you wish--" Tanyl sneered again. "--my lord."

Alfgia's eyes took on a distant view and opened wide. She grasped Jonna's hand. "We must speak, my lord."

He nodded to her, but addressed them. "We will consider your words."

"Consider quickly," Tanyl glared. "Our patience grows thin." The three rose.

"See them out." Jonna's voice hardened. "If they try anything, kill them."

As the throne room cleared leaving only the guards, Alfgia and Jonna rose, stepped from the dais, and passed into the room behind. Tears streamed down her face.

"We must go with them, together; I have seen it. There is no other way." Terror gripped her face. "If not, the dark elves and woodland elves will cease to be."

Jonna's head twisted toward her. "We cannot trust them; they will kill you and the child. If any must go, it will be I, alone. I will not return."

"No." Her eyes swept over his face. "You will return." She squeezed his hand tightly as her eyes searched for answers in the distance. "Just not here." With a lunge, her arms went around him in a grip of death. "This is wrong, my lord. It was not meant to be."

At her touch, their magic merged. A wind beat at the fog in his mind to expose the memories of what lay lost. Slack-jawed, he whispered, "I--know." With gentle hands, he held her. "Our world is about to change."

The wind became a torrent. His body shook. Pain ripped through his skull as his eyes blurred. The grip he had on Alfgia released as his palms went to his eyes. The eyes blinked back tears as his hands came away.

The image of a desk and chair appeared. Three books, leather bound, sat on one corner. The hollow robe and floating hat hovered in the air. The empty sleeve reached over and picked up a staff. The invisible Väinämö pointed at Jonna with a huff. "Do you know how difficult it is to keep up with you?" He shook the staff at him. "Do you?"

Jonna's vision cleared gradually. "Are you tracking me?"

"Of course, I'm tracking you. How else will we get you back?"

Alfgia blinked in confusion. "Who is this, my lord?" She drew closer to the image and touched it, but her hand passed through. "Is it a vision?"

"Something like that. Some might call it an illusion."

"Illusion?" The mage rapped his staff on the floor. "I'll have you know, young lady, I am an A++ certified mage of the Arts of Majik, thank you very much." He pulled out his license, held it so both could see, and slapped it on the desk. "And you--" The mage's staff pointed at Jonna. "You should be ashamed of yourself!"

"For what?"

"For dabbling in laws you don't understand!"

"I did not dabble," Jonna glared. "I don't even know how I got here."

"Oh, you dabbled," Väinämö pointed at Alfgia's stomach. "In more ways than one."

"I didn't do anything!"

Alfgia glanced toward him with a smile. "Dabbling wasn't the half of it."

Väinämö folded his arms. "The evidence speaks for itself."

"It wasn't me!"

Alfgia stared at him. "My lord, I distinctly recall--" She took his hand.

At her touch, Jonna's face blushed. She had done it again, and he remembered what that tingle meant. When an elf woman chose the one she loved, she could instigate a magic tingle that flowed into her beloved. For those without magic, it was just a tingle, but for those who had magic, unusual things could happen.

The fog that hid his memories shifted; her magic drove them to thicken. However, the strange torrent that had started before ripped through and revealed the truth. Three memories collided: his loving Elfleda alive and well, his loving Elfleda dead and he married to Almundena, and a tyrannical Elfleda alive while he had married Alfgia.

The memories of all three attempted to merge into one, but it was not possible. How could they be real? Which one was? His hand pulled from hers, and the tingle stopped. He stared down at his fingers, unbelieving. The facts became dominant. "I know the truth." He turned to her. "I know this is hard to explain, but--"

The mage cut in. "He's a victim of circumstances."

Jonna nodded, slowly. "Yes, I'm a victim of--no! I am not victim of circumstances! I choose my own destiny!" He glared up at the mage. "My will is stronger than magic!"

"Then you admit to--" The mage stroked his finger. "Shame on you."

"I did no such thing!"

Alfgia cleared her throat. "I beg to differ." She patted her stomach.

Jonna stared at the mage. "What is going on?"

"Magic, my boy, magic."

Her face glowed. "That's what I told him." Her eyes abruptly dropped as sadness filled them. "But it wasn't meant to be, was it?"

Väinämö shook his head. "I'm sorry, my child. It was not, and I'm afraid when things are put right, your past with Jonna may cease to exist."

As tears fell, Alfgia wrapped her arms around herself. "No baby?"

"I'm afraid not."

She looked toward Jonna. "No love returned?"

"I will always love you, Alfgia. No magic can take that away."

She spun around and fled from the room.

Jonna bit back tears. "Why?" He looked at Väinämö. "Why did you have to tell her that?" The unreal memories felt too real.

"It is part of the healing, my boy. Magic must be restored."

"But she would never have known the difference."

"Wouldn't she?" Väinämö tilted his head. "The key is not her, it's you."

"How?"

79

"How should I know? I'm just an A++ certified mage, not a magician." Väinämö grinned.

"Now what?"

"You're about to visited by an old friend." The mage vanished.

CHAPTER 8

A white point of light formed, brightened in intensity, and ripped a slit in the air all the way down to the ground. Hooves clicked on marble. The twisted horn of a unicorn pushed its way through followed by its head and front legs. The front of its body hung in the air without having a back. "Jonna, come."

"No, I can't leave. I have to go with Lord Tanyl and the others."

"Jonna, this is not your reality."

The anguish in Alfgia's face filled his mind. "I can't let her be hurt anymore."

"By choosing our future, we defeat the peril and prevent an alternative past."

Jonna gazed toward him. "What did you say?"

"By choosing our future, we defeat the peril--"

Jonna chimed in with the unicorn. "And prevent an alternative past." He swallowed as Väinämö's words came into his mind. "I'm creating this."

"Now you're getting the idea."

"How?"

"On that, I cannot help you."

"Why?"

The voice of Lord Aubron demanded from the throne room. "Jonna McCambel, what have you done?"

Jonna's voice hardened as he nodded toward the unicorn. "Give me a second." He turned toward the doorway.

The unicorn neighed. "Jonna!"

"I have someone I need to deal with. I'll be right back."

"This is madness. Do you know how long I had to search to find you?"

Jonna stepped from the chamber into the throne room as he called back to the unicorn, "You remind me of a mage I know."

Lord Aubron's eyes glowered. His unsheathed sword lay in his hand as he marched toward Jonna.

Jonna drew his dark elf blade.

"You bring infidels into our city--you and your pathetic human pets, you defile our race by being king, and now you bring doom on us all."

"How long did it take you to make up that list?"

The man shook with fury. "You made me look like a fool in front of Alfgia. I will run your body through and toss it over the walls to the woodland dogs who want it." Aubron lunged.

Jonna dodged to the right as his dark elf sword with the emerald jewel easily parried Aubron's stab. "Your anger makes you sloppy, Aubron. You cannot win this duel." With the unusual strength he had felt after being bitten, he thrust his opponent's blade away. Aubron leaped back with it to maintain his defense as Jonna's own blade sliced a mere hair's breadth from Aubron's throat. With a quick circle, the tip of Jonna's sword focused on the center of Aubron's body. "You would turn on your king?"

Aubron spat. "You are no king. You were never meant to be king. When I poisoned--" His words stopped as his sword struck Jonna's, and he side-stepped in. The jar as the two swords met shook them both. A clang filled the throne room. Aubron feinted toward Jonna's chest, and let his sword arc down in an attempt to sever Jonna's hand at the wrist.

Jonna slipped sideways and angled a strike against Aubron's blade; their swords vibrated again. "When you poisoned who?" With a quick twist, Jonna's point swiped at Aubron' wrist.

The elf jerked back as blood oozed from the cut. With a drop to one knee and head bowed, he tossed his blade. It clanged to the floor. "I was wrong, my lord. You have drawn first blood. What can I do as penitence?"

Jonna eyes narrowed. "How do I know you are telling the truth?"

"By my word, my lord, as a member of royalty--after this day, I will not lift my sword against you again."

Jonna kicked the man's blade to the left. It bumped against the lower step of the dais. "You will call the guards and turn yourself in, or I swear, I will run you through myself. Is that understood?"

Alfgia's soft voice called from behind. He turned to see her tear-stained face. "My lord, forgive me. I know it is the right thing, but the emotions--" Her chest heaved. "--are overwhelming."

He sheathed his sword and moved toward her. "Alfgia, I am the one who must apologize." His hands cupped her face as he stopped in front of her. "I would never have knowingly hurt you."

A flash of light reflected from her armor. The sting of metal pierced his back and extended out the front. Blood oozed where Aubron's sword had stabbed between the overlapping plates. With wide eyes, Jonna fought to turn but a groan escaped his lips; the sword kept him still.

"Pompous dog," Aubron glowered as his hot breath spoke next to Jonna's ear. "We see whose body has been run through!"

Alfgia screamed, "No!" Her hand pulled her sword. "Let him go!"

"So you can watch him die?" Aubron sneered. "Certainly, My Lady."

The sword slid smoothly back as Aubron stepped away; blood flowed more freely. Jonna struggled against the pain as his strength slipped from him. His knees buckled.

Alfgia's hands went to support Jonna as her voice rose, "Guards!" The throne room doors opened as dark elf warriors rushed in. "Call the healers and arrest Lord Aubron!" A single guard rushed out while the others halted in dismay. "Arrest him, now! Or I swear by my mother, you shall not see the end of day!"

Aubron dropped his sword. It clattered to the ground. "I will not resist."

The distant look hit Alfgia's eyes. "Quickly, help His Majesty to the chamber behind the thrones!"

The lead guard, Elaith, stepped forward and took the other side of Jonna. They moved slowly for the chamber door.

As the others shifted to guard Aubron, Aubron laughed. "Do you not see that she's gone mad? The blood on my blade was by her order."

The eyes of the guards shifted from Aubron to Alfgia.

Jonna's vision dimmed as his eyes closed. His heart beat erratically. He could feel his lung filling with blood.

He struggled to fight it. The memory of the healing spell Bob had taught him tickled his mind. However, he dared not try it. He did not know its equivalent in this realm, and to use it could damage the partitions of majik even more.

They reached the door. Elaith glanced at Alfgia. "Your Majesty, would it not make more sense to lay him outside the chamber?"

Jonna could hear horse's hooves; his eyes opened enough to see a slit in the air. Alfgia urged them forward, "Move!"

The guard shifted, but his voice pleaded, "There is only a bench, My Lady. The healers can address him better somewhere else."

"Move, I say!"

Lord Aubron shouted behind them, "Watch her sword!" Elaith slowed. His eyes darted between Jonna and Alfgia.

In a fury, she growled, "Hurry! He must go through the slit!"

The guard's eyes swept the room. He swallowed. "W-what slit, My Lady?"

"Right there!"

Jonna's eyes barely opened. He leaned his head toward hers and whispered, "He cannot see it."

She stared at the spot as her voice calmed. "In a few

moments, a portal will open. He must be at the exact spot when it does. Do you understand?"

The guard's eyebrows rose.

"Humor me, if only until the healers come. Is that too much to ask?"

Elaith shifted and stopped. "My lady, I do not understand. If you send His Majesty through a portal, he will no longer be here. How, then, can they heal him?" His hold relaxed. "I cannot help you do this."

Jonna dipped forward. She struggled to hold him up. His muscles fought to move but were sluggish.

Her voice pleaded, "Hold on, love. It is only a short distance."

"My Lady," Elaith's eyes narrowed, "This is insane."

She lunged forward. Jonna slipped out of the guard's grasp. Jonna's feet tripped as Alfgia struggled with the added weight. Both fell. Their armor clattered against the marble floor. Elaith reached down to help her up, but she growled him back. "Do not touch us!"

In a flash of light, a white, twisted horn pushed though. It brushed the tips of Jonna's fingers. Colors swirled. The room brightened. Jonna found himself slumped beside the bed in the palace of the dark elf's suite.

He gasped as breath filled both lungs. His heart held a steady beat. The armor had vanished. The dark elf sword with the green gem hung in its place on the track along the wall. He had shifted back to the prior reality, but how? If he could do it once, why not again? His eyes steadied on the unicorn. "What happened? Why am I still alive? Why am I still here?"

The unicorn blinked in surprise. "Because you never left?"

"I did leave. I journeyed to another dark elf city and was murdered."

"You fainted to the floor beside the bed."

Jonna's words hardened. "I don't faint."

The unicorn tilted its head. "How else do you explain lying there?"

Jonna pointed up. "I touched that sword--"

"And fainted." The unicorn nodded. It moved closer to Jonna. "Why is that so hard to believe?"

"Because I don't faint!" Jonna huffed. "Didn't you create a portal to find me? Didn't you touch me with your horn?"

"One's horn is rather personal. Are you sure it was me?"

"Of course it was you!"

"Well, if it was, shouldn't I remember it, too?"

Jonna stared. "Yes, you should. Unless--when I passed through the portal, all existence of that reality faded. But if all existence faded, why do I remember?"

"Hypothetically," the unicorn looked toward the ceiling, "if such a thing did occur, then memory would be dependent upon existence. Which means something else connected to you also came through."

"Then why don't you remember?"

"I didn't exist there."

"But you did. You located me and gave me a way back."

The unicorn stared at him. "Was I all there or only partly?"

"What kind of question is that? You walked through the slit and the front half of your body--" Jonna's mouth dropped. "Partly."

The unicorn nodded. "Then, there is the reason. I never completely existed there. Therefore, my reality would not retain those events after it faded." He cocked his head at Jonna. "That is perfectly natural."

Jonna chuckled as his head shook. "Do you know how ridiculous that sounds?" He tossed his hands in the air. "I can't create reality. No one can do that! I even dreamed Väinämö--"

The air waved in front of them. The chair, desk, hollow robe, and empty floating hat appeared. "Drat!" The mage struck the end of his staff against the floor. "Missed again!"

"Missed what?"

"Missed the part where you are not some invisible body making clothes walk around!"

86

"You missed?"

"Of course, I did! The timing has to be precise." The top leather bound book rose from the desk as the empty sleeve neared it. The cover flipped back but no dust billowed.

"Nice touch," Jonna nodded. "You cleaned off your books."

The empty hat tilted toward him. "What?"

"The books--you cleaned off the dust."

The hat tilted toward the book. "Dust? What dust?"

"The dust that comes from the books when you--"

"Hold that thought!" Väinämö slammed the book closed, dropped it on the desk, and threw himself on top. A gale blew in and snatched at his hat. One empty sleeve moved near the edge of the hat while the other clamped tightly to the desk. When the gust abated, the mage exhaled. "Thankfully, that was short. Last time, I chased my books into the next wing."

For the first time, Jonna noticed the hardwood floor. "Where are you?"

"In my library, of course. Where else do you think I study?"

"In the hut in the woods that had to be rebuilt?"

"Bah." Väinämö waved one sleeve as the other adjusted his hat. "That's my vacation home."

"Hold it, you vacation in a hut?"

"You went to a cabin."

Jonna started to answer, stopped, and gave a nod. "You got me there."

"Of course," Väinämö beamed. "I'm the mage, remember? Now, as I was saying, 'Missed!'" The transmission jerked sideways briefly.

"Väinämö, why the wind?"

"Uh-oh!" Väinämö leaned forward and gripped the desk once more. As the gale built up, he hollered over the storm, "What was that?"

Jonna shouted back. "Why the wind?"

His voice rose, "My heating system! The dragon in the

basement gets a little distracted sometimes." The jerk in the transmission grew worse.

"Why is that?"

"He snores." The transmission faded away.

Jonna looked to the unicorn. "He has a dragon in the basement."

The unicorn nodded. "Most mages have one somewhere."

Someone struck the door three times. Jonna thought back and remembered those knocks. "Come in, Athtar."

As the door opened, Athtar peeked around the corner. "My lord?" His eyes became round. "You know my name?"

"Of course, I know your name. You are a good elf, Athtar, and one that can be trusted."

The steward's eyebrows rose. "Thank you, my lord, but I am the bearer of grave news. The queen has taken ill and has asked for you."

"Me?" Jonna studied the floor. "I should think I would be last person she would want."

"My lord, though the queen can at times be trying, it is by her tenacity that our city survived when the springs dried up. It was by yours that the springs were returned. Judge her for her intention to save her people, not the means by which it was done."

So in this world, he had come and restored the springs of life, just like the first time he had ventured into the dark elf city. However, instead of welcoming him, the queen had forbidden him to stay near Alfgia. Why?

Unlike the last reality, he was no longer in a scripted play. Everything he had experienced he could remember, but he knew nothing of what was about to happen next. He gave a nod and looked up. "As always, Athtar, your counsel is well received."

Athtar's eyebrows knitted, but he did not say why. "Thank you, my lord." His hand pointed. "If you would come this way."

As the door opened, they were struck by the volume of voices. Whispers about the queen ran rampant in every hall they passed.

After several turns, they stopped at a grand, dual, carved door. The symbol of the crown lay embedded in the door's header.

The steward nodded to the two guards posted outside. "Lord Jonna has come at the queen's request."

The doors glided slowly outward in response to the guard's firm pull. When they stopped, the steward stepped briskly forward.

Two additional guards, one on each side, stood next to the doorway as they shifted inside the square room. A row of chairs bordered the entire room except where a second door appeared. Above the second door, the symbol of the crown lay upon its header as well, but with a subtle difference; the first letter of the elven alphabet stood beside it. Jonna and the steward moved quickly to the door. Two additional guards met them.

"Lord Jonna has come at the queen's request."

The humor struck Jonna. These guards had already seen that they had gained entrance. Why state the summons a second time?

One of the guards gripped the smaller door and pulled. It swung out slowly as if it had great weight. Once it stopped, they proceeded.

They entered a second square room. A row of chairs went around its border in the same manner. As they advanced toward a third door, the crown's symbol stood beside the second letter in the elven alphabet.

Jonna leaned near his guide. "Athtar, why all the rooms and doors?"

The steward slowed to a stop in the middle of the second room and whispered, "The procedure is by order of the queen. A ward of magic holds each door set by the queen herself. The first ward measured the truth of my words: did the queen ask what I claimed. If not, I would have been removed from service until an inquiry could be held. The second measured the exact nature of the words: did I perform the queen's request. Had I not, I, again, would have been removed from service until an inquiry could be made. The third will check for our intent in relationship to the queen's."

"And if it doesn't match, we will be held until an inquiry can be made?"

Athtar chuckled. "Actually, no. If the queen intends any ill will, we will be killed on the spot."

Jonna swallowed and felt the reassuring pressure of the Rune Blade of Knowledge on his back. "Please define ill will. Is it the '*I don't like you*' kind, or the '*I am going to kill you*' type?"

Athtar grinned. "Never fear, my lord. I have done this many times."

"At this moment, I don't think you understand the relationship between me and the queen."

"Come."

They stopped in front of the guards. The guards' spears leveled at them.

"Lord Jonna has come at the queen's request."

The guards waited. Jonna prepared to reach for his blade. He knew the queen wanted him gone, and one way was as good as another.

One of the guards reached for the door though the spear of the other never wavered. As the doors pulled back, a large canopy bed could be seen. Around it were gathered several healers. The Lady Alfgia and Lord Aubron stood to one side. The queen's personal guards waited on the right.

Jonna spotted Elaith. In this reality, the guard's decorative gems showed him to be in charge of the queen's royal guard; in the other, he was not.

Alfgia rushed toward Jonna. Aubron narrowed his eyes. "My lord," her eyes pleaded with Jonna. "You must help her!"

Jonna blinked as the memory of the other world stabbed through his mind. He had seen this before; he had been here before. From the reality he had just left, it was deja vu.

Alfgia grasped his hand and pulled him through the doorway toward the bed. "Move back. Give Lord Jonna way."

A sigh escaped Jonna's lips as no guard reacted. Maybe there could be peace between them, yet. Lord Aubron scowled as he passed through.

The queen whispered weakly, "Give way."

With a nod, those gathered around pulled back but only enough so Jonna could approach. Concern filled their faces.

Jonna's eyes took in how pale the queen's dark skin had become. "When did this happen?"

The oldest of the healers stepped forward. His hair had a touch of gray. "After your arrival, my lord. The symptoms began soon after." All eyes focused to Jonna.

Queen Siardna waved him closer. Her eyes searched his face, and her voice came as a mere whisper. "Someone has tried to kill me, Jonna. Lord Aubron believes it is you."

"Despite our differences, I would not."

"Find the one responsible."

"Guards--" Aubron snapped his fingers. "--you will take Lord Jonna to the dungeon until this can be sorted."

Alfgia spun toward him. "What are you doing?"

"I am protecting the queen." His eyes narrowed. "And you."

"Jonna would never do this!"

"Your dedication to the human is admirable but immaterial. The evidence I have gathered is clear. However--" He closed his eyes briefly and smiled. "--I will note your objection."

Four of the queen's guards assembled around Jonna. They were led by Elaith. The one in front gave a nod toward the door. His voice held daggers. "This way, my lord."

Jonna mumbled, "*Audio.*" As he shifted to follow, Alfgia turned toward him with raised eyebrows.

"Hold him in the next room." Lord Aubron pointed toward the guard. "I will be there shortly. I will retrieve the set of charges to be presented against Lord Jonna."

As they walked through the main doorway, Athtar and Alfgia followed. The door closed behind them, and they waited.

From a far corner, a passage opened in the wall. Lord Aubron walked out of it carrying a scroll. "Now that we are out of the queen's presence--" Lord Aubron sneered. "Take his weapon."

Alfgia stood between them. "No. Lord Jonna is royalty and will be treated accordingly."

"I am your husband and the queen's counselor. It will be done as *I* say."

Alfgia glared at him.

The rune blade gave a low hum. The elven guards stepped back.

Aubron glowered at them with narrowed eyes. "What is this? Do the dark elves fear a mere sword?" Aubron shoved Alfgia aside.

Jonna twisted. "Don't touch her." The endpoints of four spears leveled at his midsection from all cardinal directions.

A smirk formed on Aubron's face as he stepped between two of the guards. "But of course, Lord Jonna. I will leave that to the bedroom where I will touch her all I wish." His eyes burned. "Give me your weapon."

With a smirk, Jonna held up his hands. "It is yours to take."

The hum strengthened. Aubron stared. As his fingers rose toward it, the rune blade glowed. His eyebrows lifted, his breath labored, and his hand shook against an unseen force. The tips of his fingers glowed red.

The hand jerked away to be held against his chest with a closed fist. "Call the mages. They will clip his magic wings!"

From their presence, a guard hurried. Athtar slid forward. "Lord Aubron, if I may--"

"You may not. How dare you address me until spoken to!"

Athtar nodded in silence. He stepped back beside Alfgia.

Jonna glanced nonchalantly at the guards. "This is awkward." He gave a grin. "I mean, think about it, guys. With a sword like this strapped to my back, I could have cut through all of you and still killed the queen."

They tightened their grip on their spears.

"However, I didn't, did I?" He turned with his back toward

Aubron. Aubron stepped away from the sword. Jonna twisted his head to look over his shoulder. "No sneak attack, this time? Aubron, I am disappointed."

Aubron's eyebrows knitted. "I don't know what you mean."

"Sure you do. If I had to bet, I'd say everyone in here remembers something."

Elaith focused at Jonna.

Alfgia's mouth dropped. "The dream. You had it, too?"

Jonna's eyes caught hers. "It was no dream, my lady. It was very real." He turned toward Aubron. "Would you permit me some leeway, my lord, to speak my mind? At least until the mages come?"

Lord Aubron sneered. "Speak your lie. The truth we already know."

"Indeed." Jonna gave a grin toward the guards. "It occurred to me, when I stood in the queen's chambers, that a connection existed between this reality and a previous one. Mind you, it wasn't intentional, but it happened nonetheless." He turned to Alfgia. "Do you remember?"

Her eyes stared at nothing. "I--do."

"Athtar, you told me that the third door compared our intentions to the queen's, is that not right?"

"It does, my lord."

"And did I not tell you my concerns about this?"

"You did, my lord."

"And yet, I passed through unscathed. If I had conspired to kill the queen, could I have done that?"

Athtar lifted his head. "No, my lord. It would not be possible."

Jonna waved toward the door. "And the queen would agree?"

Athtar nodded.

"Bah," Aubron shook his head. "You have proved nothing."

"Would it hurt if I continue?"

Aubron glanced at the second door. No mages had come through yet. His voice was wary. "Very well."

"So, I said to myself, if the magic sensed no danger from me, and yet, I am accused of the crime, who is right? Either the magic is flawed--" His eyes took in the queen's royal guards. "--or I am not truly guilty."

Aubron huffed. "That is your second offense. No person may accuse the queen of having anything less than perfect magic."

"Which leads me to my next point," Jonna smiled. "When I first arrived, I sensed no magic in the queen."

"Preposterous! Infidel! I will have you struck down!"

Jonna turned to Alfgia. "The queen of the other reality had the magic."

Her face became hard. "He is right."

Aubron turned on her. "How dare you! Guards, you will put Alfgia under custody until we can separate her from this mad human!"

The guards did not move.

"Did you not hear me?"

Elaith turned his spear toward Aubron. "Let Lord Jonna speak."

Jonna nodded toward Elaith. "Thank you." He twisted around to face Aubron. "You brought it all together." He stepped toward the man. "You, who did not walk through the queen's protective door." His feet went forward, again. "You, who hollered out poison." Jonna grabbed Aubron's arm and started to pull. "Let's go see the queen together."

Lord Aubron knocked his hand away. "How dare you touch me!"

"Do it," Elaith prodded him with his spear. "Go see the queen." The other guards shifted their spears from Jonna to Aubron.

"You're all mad! You've all gone crazy! Guards! The royal guards have turned on the queen!"

The third door burst open. From the queen's chamber, her royal guards flowed in. They lined up to form a path down the middle and ignored Lord Aubron's orders. The path led to the queen's chamber door. The second door opened, and the soldiers who stepped in guarded against leaving. No mages had come. Jonna's spell had worked. All involved had heard Aubron.

The queen rose from the bed and stood on the other side with the aid of two healers. "I await your entry, Lord Aubron."

Lord Aubron stammered, "H--He's lying. It's all lies!"

The queen's voice spoke soothingly, "I know. Come to me, and prove it so that all may see. Walk through the doorway."

Aubron took a step forward as Jonna matched him. The elf lord's eyes danced left and right. Sweat trickled down his brow. His chest heaved in panic: another step, another look. With each passing moment, his eyes grew wilder. As he neared the doorway, his hands lashed out, grabbed a spear, and brought it back to launch it at the queen.

The Rune Blade of Knowledge slashed through the shaft of the spear, and Jonna followed with a body slam. Lord Aubron stumbled to the right. Jonna knocked the spear out of Aubron's fist.

"You were dead!" the elf lord screamed at Jonna. "I killed you with my sword!" He backed toward the second doorway.

Jonna pressed him and spoke calmly, "Did you?"

"I did, and I can do it again!" With a ring, the man's sword slid from his scabbard. Metal clanged as the rune blade parried in the air.

"You are pathetic, Aubron." The swords met with a second clang. "You betrayed your race." Jonna drove him back. "You betrayed your wife." Jonna shoved him. "And you attempted to kill your queen."

The rune blade sliced with a mighty blow. The two swords struck in the air. The vibration shook both followed by a metallic crack, and Aubron's sword shattered like glass.

"And you will pay for this!"

CHAPTER 9

Aubron ran backwards, spun around, and met a sword. He gasped as it plunged through his heart. His eyes drifted upward as the blood oozed out. They followed the blade to see Alfgia.

With a grim line across her lips, she met his eyes. "This is for Jonna, this is for my mother, and this is for the kingdom." She jerked the sword out in one smooth motion. "Farewell."

Aubron collapsed and so did Queen Siardna.

Jonna sheathed his blade and hurried toward the queen. "*Audio*." The spell toggled off. "It's poison. Check the left arm of her throne. You will find toxin where the hand lies!" Elaith rushed out followed by two others.

Alfgia appeared beside him. "How did you know?"

"Something pricked her when we met in this reality. In the--" He fought for the right word. "--second reality, Aubron said he had poisoned someone. It all made sense." The healers picked up Siardna and carried her back to the bed. "There is a chance to save her."

"Jonna, I--" The words left Alfgia, and she stared into his eyes. "Was it real?" She reached to touch him but pulled back. "Was any of it real?"

Her words echoed in his mind. Not only had it felt real, but he realized whatever had come back with him had caused everyone to remember. It had changed this reality. How could he explain this?

Elaith rushed back through the door carrying a small clay cup. He moved directly toward the healers. Jonna and Alfgia followed.

One of the healers took the cup and moved off to a corner

table. A small stick dipped in and rose from the container. A dark liquid clung to its end. As the stick hovered above flat bowls, a single drop fell into each. With a mixing rod, the elf healer chanted, "*Ex scientia vera.*"

Puffs of smoke erupted from the dishes. He picked up each and observed the reactions. After a few moments, he selected one jar from many. The healer hurried toward the queen.

Jonna caught the meaning. "Truth," he translated from his own understanding of Latin. "They seek to identify the type of poison."

Alfgia nodded. "Once they know what it is, the selected magic jar creates the antidote." She moved to the bed. Jonna followed.

One healer helped the queen to sit while the other added some of the jar's contents to a small cup of glowing liquid. The queen drank slowly. Her eyes focused on Jonna thoughtfully. Once emptied, a healer took the cup away. The queen waved Alfgia and Jonna forward.

"Why?" She stared into Jonna's eyes. "Despite my effort to keep you away, why have you done this?"

"Done what, Queen Siardna?"

"Why did you save my life?"

He thought over his words. "Because it was the right thing to do."

Her head nodded. "I hope you still feel that way when I have you expelled from my kingdom."

"Mother!"

The queen's head turned toward Alfgia. "Hush, child. I know what is best for the realm. I know what must be done. My magic is restored."

Siardna's eyes cut to Jonna. "You were right. When my magic returned, it allowed us to remember the images of the dream that was not a dream. It altered this existence. You knew I did not have magic. You knew I had refused Lucasta's gift. And yet--" She squinted her eyes. "And yet, there was a time and place when I did accept the wood spirit's aid." A distant look took her eyes. "You have cracked the partitions of majik, Jonna. You must fix what you have changed. And--" Her eyes drifted back to her daughter. "--some things will never be the same."

Her eyes closed as she inhaled the air. Her voice became hard as her eyelids opened. "Elaith."

Elaith stepped forward and bowed. "Yes, my queen?"

"Escort Jonna to the forest. He is to leave here and never return."

Elaith's eyebrows knitted.

"Are you questioning the order?"

"No, my queen."

"Good. Do it, now."

Alfgia grasped Jonna's arm; the magic tingle touched him. "No, mother. This is wrong. You cannot do this." Her grip tightened.

The queen's eyes narrowed. "Are you challenging me?"

"If that is what I must do."

Flames ignited in the queen's eyes. However, all at once they went out. "He must leave, Alfgia. He does not belong here. Surely you can see that?"

Alfgia looked away from Siardna. Her face focused on Jonna. The tingle between them strengthened. "You *did* belong here."

Siardna reached out a hand and touched Alfgia's wrist. "That was a different place and time. This is here and now."

"Not quite." The distant look took Alfgia's eyes. "No, this is not right." Her eyes opened wide. "Our realm is--confused. How can this be?"

The tingle started to probe. He could feel it searching the magic within. His head shook slowly. "I don't understand it, myself."

Her eyes grew brighter. "But it can be reality. I can feel it just as you can feel me. We can make it happen." She turned to face him. "If you wish." Her face glowed as her left hand took his right. "Come to me."

98

The queen's face paled. "Elaith, stop her!"

Elaith lunged forward, but his hand never reached Alfgia. It hung there suspend like a fly caught in amber.

The colorful fungi grew in brightness. The room distorted around them. Jonna could feel the magic inside as both hers and his intertwined.

Two separate heartbeats sounded in their ears followed by a tiny third. The louder the beats, the more in sync they became. A crack sounded--not a ping. A baby cried, and Jonna found himself sliding sideways.

~

Jonna's lungs sucked in air. The dry heat of a bright desert gazed at him curiously. The light beat down on his shirtless chest, its only protection the strap that held the Rune Blade of Knowledge to his back. His skin had already turned red.

A strange growl met his ears. He lay on his back staring up at a bright, blue sky. A voice whispered, "Don't move, or the *caileancoatl* will strike."

His eyes slowly panned around. Above his head, a man stood wearing a turban. Light reflected from the man's bright colored clothes.

To both their rights, a cobra-like creature with a dog head rose. It had a trunk as thick as Jonna's thigh and two-inch front fangs that reflected bright white in the sun. Massive jaws flared as a forked tongue stuck out in Jonna's direction. The growl occurred as it hissed.

Jonna's voice remained low. "I have no intention of moving."

Most of the creature's body lay coiled beneath the part that stood up straight. The man brought to his mouth a *pungi*, a wind instrument made from a gourd, and played. The end of the pungi wove slowly in the air. The head of the caileancoatl followed its dance.

The hiss lessened. The flared jaws decreased their size. The caileancoatl slowly descended toward its coil and rested its head to look the other way.

"You may now, slowly, roll to the left. The serpent is twice my height in length so do take your time."

Jonna's body rolled slowly away. "Is that far enough?"

"It is."

With a gradual rise, he stood to his feet, took another step back, and dusted himself off. The gritty sand fell from his skin. "Thank you."

"It was fortuitous that I found you when I did. Now, come stand with me on the road."

Jonna came toward him.

The man gave a nod. "Had you risen while it sensed you as a threat, you would have surely been bitten. While not deadly, its venom has driven many men mad." The man paused. "May I ask why you lie outside the protection of the city?"

"Which city is that?"

The man focused on Jonna's face. "Do you not know of the kingdom of Mirthra and its capital city of Delicia?"

Jonna shook his head. "I'm afraid not."

The man turned toward the area where Jonna had lain. No footsteps led to the spot. His eyes slowly rose to the sky as his voice became almost a whisper. "The wind is soft today. From which direction did you come?"

Jonna's eyes took in the sand dunes and rock. "I don't really know."

"To where are you headed?"

Jonna shook his head. "I don't know why I'm here."

"I see." The man's mouth remained slightly open as he studied the ever reddening tint of Jonna's skin. Nonchalantly, he offered, "If you have no special place to go, I would accept your company as I travel home. I do not have a ride, but the walk is easy, and my house is close."

A glance at the sand offered Jonna no better choices. "I accept."

"Perhaps a shirt as well to keep you from being scorched by the sun?"

A cringe crossed Jonna's face as he touched his shoulder. Already it felt uncomfortably warm. "That would be an excellent idea."

While the man went to his pack camel and opened a side bag, Jonna took off the strap that held his sword. The man glanced at the lighter skin where the strap had lain. As Jonna dropped the shirt over his head, the white material felt soft and light.

"It is a little snug, but better than a burn. It will help soothe the hot skin." The man nodded.

Jonna hefted his blade and dropped the strap back over his shoulder. "Much better. Thanks."

Both started to walk. The camel trailed behind as the man kept hold of its long reins. A slight wind blew toward them. It carried the faint sound of a baby's cry.

"You live in Delicia?" At the edge of the road, sand had formed in small waves. As his foot lifted from walking in it, grains ran down the sides of the print to fill it in.

"Yes, but only the chosen can live within its inner walls. I am a merchant who dwells on the bridges that lead to the center city. Those who run the city give us protection."

"I don't understand."

"Come and see."

The man turned at a rise in the sand. The sand gave way to hard, dry rock that protruded from the desert. An aura of colors grew denser in the blue sky as a precipice came into view and beyond it a valley.

A blue lake of immense proportions contrasted brightly against the shore's white sand. From the shore, blue, unconnected, monolithic fortifications with yellow trim guarded narrow strips of land. Eight narrow strips extended toward the center like spokes on a bicycle wheel. They matched the eight cardinal points of the compass.

After a short distance, each narrow strip lifted into the air. They gradually rose by larger arches until the far end touched the top of a lone mountain in the center of the lake.

Buildings adorned these strips of land. Roads wove between the buildings. Where the strips touched the top of the mountain, a huge wall made one continuous circle around a city. From the top of the wall glistened various colors of light as the sun struck facets of gems. However, it was the symbol on the fortifications that intrigued Jonna. A glowing orb, that matched the medallion Lord Aubron had worn, decorated their sides.

"Behold, the great oasis city, Delicia."

From the outer fortifications, roads wove off in various directions. In the distance, poles dotted both sides of the roads at equal intervals. Upon the poles hung metal cages.

Jonna nodded. "Impressive. Are their hearts as great as the wealth they portray?"

The man blinked. "Hearts?"

"How do they treat their fellow man?"

The stranger chuckled. "They are gods, my friend, not men. Mankind is a mere tool for their cruel delights. It is the reason we merchants are invited to stay. We provide distraction."

"If that is how they behave, then they are not gods."

With a grin, the man extended a hand. "I like you, my friend. They call me Mumin."

"I am Jonna McCambel."

"That is an unusual name." A distant look touched the stranger's face. "Yes, it is indeed unusual and dangerous. While we may speak freely in the desert, you must be cautious in the city. There are those who would take offense to your words." He glanced at the trail that led down the slope toward one of the fortifications. "It would be wise if you used a different name, too. Outsiders draw attention." His eyes went back to Jonna. "You should go by the name of Mahdi Huri. You will be my cousin come to help me from across the distant sands."

"Won't my appearance give me away?"

"The vastness of this kingdom covers many lands." Mumin shook his head. "That is not a concern." He started forward. Jonna followed.

"If that's so, is a name change really necessary?" Until now, Jonna had never had to hide his identity, and it didn't make sense. "Are they truly that hostile against strangers?"

"You will see."

The road broadened until the firm feel of stone lay under his feet. Metal lined both sides of the road. The sun beat down, but the white shirt kept him cool as his body sweated, and the sunburn that had started faded away. Occasionally, a growl would sound from the other side of the dunes or around large rocks, but none of the caileancoatl approached. For some reason, these creatures had learned to avoid the road.

As they walked, the tall poles came closer. The poles were set into the metal strips along the road. When the wind blew, a stench hit his nose. The cages on the poles were large enough for a man.

At their approach, two flying creatures, the size of large buzzards, launched into the air. In their claws were bones with putrid flesh. Though their wings looked like buzzards, their lion faces appeared disturbingly out of place. The squeal of a cage shrieked as it swung in the wind.

Mumin nodded toward the cages. "Those who died there are the lucky ones. Others were burnt alive by the *ifrits*."

Jonna's eyes opened wide. "Tell me again why you trade here?"

The chuckle returned in Mumin's voice. "The reward is worth the risk."

Where the outer walls of the fortification ceased, between two spokes, access to the water lay unhindered. Though the water lapped the shore, nothing grew within three feet of it, yet the land of the spokes stood green and lush. "What good are fortifications when one could simply take to the water around them?"

"The voices of the gods protect those areas. None would dare to cross."

"Voices of the gods?" The more Jonna thought about this place, the less he liked it. "Maybe I should move on, now."

"Tomorrow, my friend. I would be remiss if I did not offer at least a night's lodging. There is no other city near here before dark."

The dull thud of their shoes on stone gave way to the sound of voices. An outer fortification towered above them. It was made of blue brick trimmed in yellow. As they passed under a massive arch, shops stood on either side.

The clatter of wooden wheels drew Jonna's attention to a line of carts that moved to pass. On them lay the bodies of men. Groans issued from their lips. However, two caught his focus. A gash lay across the head of one; his vacant eyes stared at nothing. The other's leg had been cut off. The rags wrapped around it were drenched in blood.

Jonna's voice whispered, "To the cages?"

Mumin's head nodded.

As they passed through great iron doors used to secure the entrance, the rune blade vibrated on Jonna's back. Images of gods on thrones decorated the doors declaring their right to preside over their subjects. As they reached the inner road, the rune blade's vibration stopped.

The road changed to decorative brick woven in angular patterns. The green around them offered shade and refreshment. Tables and chairs of stone and wood stood outside shops and under trees.

The eyes of many watched curiously as they passed. Only a few appeared to carry weapons. To their right, a street of vendors offered various produce and called to those who traveled.

"That is the market." Mumin pointed. "Our goal is up the road."

The main thoroughfare led them to other retail buildings. Mumin pointed to a whitewashed structure with bright-red terracotta roofing tiles. The arched windows held open shutters. An arched wooden door stood closed. A sign above the door carved in a lighter wood said "Huri's". Mumin tied the camel to a post and guided Jonna in.

The door pushed back to reveal clothes on tables in various sizes and colors. A marble counter stood in front of a hallway that led further into the building. "Kali, I am back."

Kali came through the hallway with her hands on her hips. Her short, black hair existed in miniature curls on her head. With deep, penetrating, dark eyes, she took in Mumin. "And why the delay this time?" She stopped as her mouth dropped open. "You didn't bring a stranger?"

"This is my cousin, Mahdi, from beyond the dunes. For the night, he has stopped by on his journey to Bahman." Mumin winked.

Her eyes narrowed. "I see. For one night?"

Mumin nodded. "Unless, of course, he might give a hand with the clothes? Perhaps he could share a new design, hmm?"

"You know the counsel is watching us." Kali huffed. She turned and disappeared down the hallway.

He leaned near Jonna. "She means no harm. I find strays often."

Jonna chuckled. "So you're a Good Samaritan?"

Mumin's eyebrows rose.

"Do you often help strangers on the road?"

The man chuckled as he led Jonna around the counter and into the hallway. Two doors sat on the right and three on the left. Mumin pointed at the second door on the right. "This will be your room for the night, but come, let me show you the garden."

The hallway ended in a kitchen. The kitchen had a large window that looked out through flora toward the water. A garden with fountains and bridges covered in-between.

The firm strike of a knife on wood met their ears. Kali diced up vegetables, though her cuts sounded overly hard. She ignored them as they approached, but from the corner of his eye, Jonna caught her glance.

They stepped out the back archway, and entered the garden. As they crossed over a small bridge, orange and yellow fish played in the pool below. Mumin kept his voice low as the sound of a fountain echoed around them. "I look for the one who will come." He smiled. "Whether it is you or not, I do not know."

Jonna spotted Kali watching through the window. She immediately turned away. "You're expecting someone?"

The man nodded. "When the time is right." His eyes focused on Jonna.

What did the man want? The wind picked up and the subtle cry of a child met Jonna's ears. Unlike the previous calls, this one sounded closer. "I would think raising children here would be dangerous."

"Children?" Mumin's eyebrows knitted together. "There are no children in Delicia."

Jonna squinted. "Then why do I keep hearing a child's cry?"

"Perhaps it is a trick of the wind." The merchant looked toward the house as Kali's voice rose. She shouted out the window at them. "Mumin, councilman Senka has come to buy some shirts."

"Come, cousin," the merchant smiled. "We must establish who you are so that fewer questions will be asked."

He entered the house quickly as Jonna followed behind. As they stepped up to the marble counter, two men studied Mumin's merchandise. One sorted through the clothes on the tables at the other's prompt.

"You have outdone yourself with the new colors." The man who spoke wore a rich purple cape decorated with a weave of gold at the edges. In one hand, he gripped a staff. The staff held carved runes with a diamond at the top. "Ghulam, I want two of those." The man pointed. "And that one."

Ghulam reached for the third, but as he lifted it up, the staff slapped down on his wrist, and he dropped it.

"Not that one. The one next to it."

Ghulam's hand moved slowly toward the other and touched it with hesitation. "This one, my lord?"

A satisfied smile lit Senka's face. "Yes, that will do nicely." He turned toward Mumin as his hand reached into a small pouch at his waist. From it came two gold coins. These he handed to Ghulam. "Pay Mumin his due."

Ghulam gathered the clothes in one arm, accepted the coins, and started toward the counter. The staff stabbed in front of him, and Ghulam froze.

"What do we say?"

"Yes, my lord."

"Very good." The staff pulled away as Senka looked toward Mumin. "I know the trainers do their best, but proper manners are learned by practice. Don't you think so, Mumin?"

Mumin gave a single nod. "As you wish, my lord."

"See, Ghulam, even the merchant caste knows the process. I will teach you, yet."

Ghulam reached the counter and held out the hand with the coins. Mumin accepted them. "Thank you."

Senka huffed. "How many times must I tell you, Mumin? Thank you is reserved for after-beatings, not politeness. Ghulam is simply doing his assigned task." The man's disgust turned back to a smile. "If it weren't for the exquisite work you do, I would have you punished."

"Yes, my lord."

Senka spotted Jonna eyeing him. "And who is this?" The man's attention briefly cut to something further down the hall. His eyes came back to Jonna.

"My cousin, Mahdi, from beyond the dunes. He stopped by on his way to Bahman."

Senka's eyebrows rose. "Is he a scholar? We've not had a scholar stop by in ages. Has he studied in the arts?"

Mumin averted his eyes. "I was not informed about the reason for his journey."

The man with the staff turned his full attention to Jonna and caught sight of the sword on his back. "Are you a warrior, then?"

"It is only for protection, my lord. Nothing more."

"A merchant?"

"Yes, my lord."

"Nonsense, you carry a sword and do not have the countenance of a scholar or merchant." Senka shook his head. "Only three types of people travel to Bahman: merchants, scholars and warriors. If you are not a merchant or a scholar, you are a warrior. Curious, I've never known a family to have two separate castes in its lineage except by royal decree. I may have to look closer at your family, Mumin."

Mumin bowed without expression for or against. "Yes, my lord."

"Hmm." Senka adjusted his hold on the staff. "I shall have to think on this." His gaze went from Jonna to Mumin. "Why don't you and your wife join us at the dinner tonight? And please, bring along your cousin, Mahdi. I think the other council members would be interested in meeting him as well. Ghulam, come." The man turned heel and headed out the door. The door thudded closed.

Mumin leaned toward Jonna. "I am sorry, my friend. I should have realized the conclusions he would draw. Tonight could be dangerous."

"You don't think he believes the story?"

Mumin's head shook. "He doesn't, and even if I could persuade him with coin, every council member would have to be done the same. That is Delicia's politics."

"Then perhaps it would be best that I left."

"No, that would only make matters worse."

A movement caught Jonna's attention. Kali approached slowly until she knew he saw her and then sped up. Jonna turned back to Mumin. "Is there something I can do?"

"Leave the sword in your bedroom when we go to dinner tonight. Perhaps he will forget the weapon and accept you as a merchant."

Jonna inhaled slowly as uneasiness went through him. "I'm not sure I can do that."

"If he decides you are a warrior, he will expect a demonstration."

"I will consider your words." Jonna nodded politely.

Kali stepped past and quickly crossed toward the front door.

Mumin followed her with his eyes. "Are you leaving, Kali?"

She spoke quickly, "For a moment only. I go to the market." The door closed behind her. They watched her pass in front of the right window and head toward the gate.

Jonna stared after. "Do you trust her?"

"She is my wife."

"But she doesn't agree with your actions."

Mumin put a hand on his shoulder. "Do not let her abruptness be confused with disloyalty. She and I have disagreed on my actions many times."

"If you trust her so much, why speak to me by the fountain in words she could not hear?"

"Mahdi," Mumin removed his hand, "it was not a matter of trust, but of conviction. Not all believe what shall come to pass."

"And what is that?"

Mumin pursed his lips as he stared at the counter's surface. He glanced over at Jonna. "Come."

Down the hallway, through the kitchen, and into the garden both went, but instead of stopping by the fountain, they followed the smaller path toward the lake. A small grove appeared. Inside the grove stood a large rock formation excavated in the shape of a spiral. The tall sides hid their passage as they followed the curved wall in.

The spiral emitted a vibrational aura. Mumin's face brightened. Jonna felt the rune blade hum in response on his back. The nearer the center, the stronger the aura became, and the more the rune blade hummed. The path dead-ended, and they stopped.

"This is our sajjad. Each family in Delicia has their own."

Embedded in the ground were a series of marble tiles in the shape of a rectangle. The tiles were well worn.

"This is where we prostrate ourselves to our gods, but it holds a secondary secret." He reached forward, found a crack, and worked out a piece of the stone. A dark cavity stared back as his hand reached inside and pulled out a book.

The book had a stringed binding, a leather cover, and some form of thick paper. Mumin's eyes brightened as he stared it. "It is the Zaman Dar--given to me by one of the gods who does not believe in the cruelty. Only a few copies exist." He handed it to Jonna.

As the leather cover folded back, Jonna noticed the slant of the writing. "It is written right to left."

Mumin's smile went ear to ear. His head bobbed. "Indeed." His voice quivered in expectation. Can you read it?"

Jonna stared at the unfamiliar letters in a language he had never seen. They jumped and twitched as if alive on the page, but he could not grasp their meaning. "No."

Mumin's face fell. "I thought--" He sighed and shook his head.

"What?"

A sad smile hit Mumin's face. "It is of no concern, my friend. The less you know of these matters, the sooner you will be on your way." He took the book from Jonna, closed it, and placed it back in the dark cavity. The stone worked back into place. "I ask you not to speak of this."

"Of course."

"There are still a few hours before we must meet the council. I must unload the camel. You are free to explore the garden if you wish, but I would caution you about exploring the town."

"I understand."

TWISTED FATES

Mumin bowed slightly and hurried out. The aura Jonna sensed altered its form but did not go away. The hum from the rune blade did not change. Despite the trees' shade, warmth radiated from the spiral formation. Red veins of a mineral ran through the walls. Jonna touched the stone.

An electrical flash arced over him. He dropped to all fours upon the marble tiles. From the rock, a quiet, low voice vibrated. "And who have we here? A stranger come to pray?"

Jonna stared.

"Are you mute? Can you not hear my words?"

Jonna stood slowly. "Who are you?"

"Those are for kneeling, not standing. Please pay attention where you place your feet."

He stepped off the tiles and observed the walls. "I have done as you asked. I would like an answer to my question."

"Petulant, too, I see. Why should I? The privilege is for the Huri clan."

"I was accepted as a Huri clan member."

The walls considered. "You are and you aren't."

Jonna folded his arms. "If you know so much, why don't you know who I am?"

"Why, indeed." The wall gave a soft chuckle. "You are an anomaly to this world. It is a place you do not belong."

"That, we can agree on. I'm trying to find my way home."

"And yet," the wall paused. "There is a purpose for your visit."

"Who are you? Why didn't you speak when Mumin was here?"

The wall's warmth grew. The voice huffed. "Communication with a god is a personal thing."

Jonna's voice changed from annoyed to amused. "One of the gods in the city behind the inner wall?"

"The same."

Jonna laughed. "Then you are no god."

The voice rose to a high pitch. The warmth emitted grew hot. "How dare you! Who do you think you are?"

"Smart enough to know when people are being duped."

Electrical sparks rose across the wall's surface. "I am not like the other gods. I do not agree with their methods. I desire the Time of Change."

"What is--" Jonna shook his head. "Prove it."

"Why should I?"

"Because if you really are a god, you should have nothing to hide. If you really desire this Time of Change, you can prove your good will."

The sparks slowed as the god considered. "Very well, what would you ask of me?"

"Show yourself."

It chuckled. "In what form?"

"You have more than one?"

"But of course. It is a natural part of our godhood. Hmm, I know. It must be a form that is not lethal to you for that would defeat the purpose. I will use one that is more familiar--my human form."

"A wise choice."

"Are you being facetious?"

Jonna chuckled. "Probably."

"I should strike you where you stand for your impudence, but you intrigue me. Very well, I will do as you ask."

Crackles of electricity leaped from wall to wall directly in front of Jonna. They struck together over the marble tiles, and a body formed. The outline of feet, legs, thighs, hips, midriff, and chest took shape. A face and long hair molded as the transparent outline took on color and contour.

Jonna's mouth dropped open. This was a woman he had met in Chernobog. "Artemis?"

CHAPTER 10

He quickly turned around as she appeared without clothes.

"Do you not find this form pleasing?"

"Too much of a memory."

Her eyes widened. "I have never met you before."

"But I have met you," he assured. "And in about the same way."

The eyes narrowed. "How do you know my future name?"

He continued to keep his eyes averted. "What do you mean?"

Her hand touched his shoulder and pulled him into a turn. She glared. "Is that better?" A red silk robe had formed. It clung to her curves.

"Somewhat."

"Answer the question: how do you know my future name?"

"I have--met you--before." He studied her features closer. "Though, I think your complexion is more olive than when we first met."

"I have never met you!"

"Okay."

As her eyebrows rose, she glared at him. "This is a trick."

"Are we not in the northwest kingdom?"

She nodded. "Everyone knows that."

"Is not the king named Dagda?"

"That is well known." Her voice hardened. "What is his future name?"

Jonna swallowed. He had no idea what all this future name stuff was about, or what the king's might be. However, if the turbans, desert, and sand combined with the idea of Alexander the Great and his conquests had anything to do with it, it might be--"Zeus?"

She gawked. "You know his future name."

Jonna sighed with relief. Footsteps approached from behind. As he turned, Mumin dropped to his hands and knees to speak at the ground.

"Oh, great goddess, Arta. Forgive your servant for looking upon your beauty!"

Artemis came forward, reached down, and lifted Mumin's chin. "There is nothing to forgive, sweet Mumin. You have done nothing wrong."

Mumin's eyes darted from Arta toward Jonna. "Why do you not kneel?"

"Why should I kneel to an equal?"

Mumin's eyes bulged. "You are a god, too?"

Artemis smirked.

Jonna shook his head. "Mumin, please get up. There are no gods here."

Artemis slapped him. "How dare you!"

His fingers touched his red cheek. "That feels human to me."

"Mahdi," Mumin pleaded. "Please watch what you say! She must not be disrespected. She supports our cause."

"Thank you, Mumin." She glared at Jonna. "Although I may be more tolerant than others of my kind, I will not permit insolence."

Jonna crossed his arms. "What proof have you given that you are a god, other than appearing in human form and slapping someone? How do I know that wasn't your form to begin with?"

Mumin's eyes enlarged. "My friend, she is a god. One that is benevolent and kind. She means to help our people."

"Mumin, I know this woman. Did you not just agree with me in the desert that they weren't gods?"

Artemis' gaze went to Mumin as she drew in a breath. "You didn't?"

"I meant only those who treat us with cruelty do not deserve that title." Mumin's head shifted toward Artemis. "Not you!"

Artemis crossed her arms. "My father, the king, would never be cruel."

Jonna raised one eyebrow. "But would let others do the job for him? I know the type. I've studied their stories. They are just beings who use their power to control others."

"Stories?" Her eyebrows knitted together. "What stories?"

"Stories from my homeland." No, that wasn't quite right any more. "Stories from the place I was born."

"Enough." She huffed. "This debate is getting us nowhere. Whether you believe I am a god is irrelevant. The fact remains that we must help each other to bring the Time of Change. Mumin would never have brought you here unless he thought you could help."

"He fell from the sky, my goddess. His skin is pale."

"My skin is not pale. It is slightly tan."

Artemis stepped toward him and opened part of his shirt. "Let me see."

"Hold it there, princess." He smacked her hand, and she jerked it back. "I don't like people trying to take off my clothes."

Mumin huffed. "Mahdi!"

"Don't Mahdi me." He pulled his shirt closed. "I know my rights."

Her eyes glared as she rubbed her hand. "You are insolent!"

"You are overbearing!"

Her face flushed. "No one speaks that way to a god!"

Jonna's jaw set. "Go ahead, if you are so powerful. Strike me down."

"Mahdi!" Mumin's voice pleaded. "Do not tempt the gods!"

Ripples of electricity increased along the walls. "I could do it. Do you have so little respect for us that you would challenge all?"

"I know of magic. I have seen the source that powers spirits and men. I have traveled into the depths of the Otherworld. From what Mumin has told me, you are no more than creatures who have abused their power."

Flames leaped into her eyes. The ripples of electricity shot off in great strikes around them. A faraway look took her. "However, I will not destroy you." Her eyes narrowed. "You will be given a chance to understand." An unfriendly smile lit her lips. She raised her hand and held the palm toward him. An eye formed upon the palm. "*Ba-ru-ya.*"

Lightning arced. A torrent of voltage surged. A prickling sensation danced over his skin. Like a great wind, it encircled and lifted him off the ground. Above, dark clouds formed and streaks flashed. A dark vortex opened. His body drew toward it.

His first thought was to counter with the spells he knew, but those spells were not from this land, and he had grown smart enough to know not to use them. The dread of what might happen to further damage the majik partitions stayed foremost in his mind. There had to be another way.

Instead of reacting foolishly, his mind fought to uncover a magical alternative. It did exist; he could feel its presence very close. Magic could be channeled through her. Magic could be channeled through him. Could magic be channeled through his sword? Yes, he had done this once before. His unspoken thoughts merged into one word, 'Protect!'

The sword responded. The vibration grew into a hum, and it stopped his rise. The prickling sensation abated. Winds struck the trees as they swayed back and forth. Not far away, waves in the waters grew in height. Below him, Mumin fled. Only Artemis stood with a shocked expression on her face. He hollered down to her through the air's torrent. "I take it, this is not what you intended?"

Her jaw dropped. "No."

His body settled back to the ground, and the torrent of energy faded. The hum from the sword decreased. The vortex vanished though the dark clouds remained. The clouds mirrored her expression.

She staggered back against the spiral wall. Her shoulders slumped, and her head rested as her eyes grew wide. "Who are you?"

With firm footing beneath and a resolute glare, Jonna advanced.

Her eyes opened wider. Her voice dropped to a whisper, "Have you come to destroy us?"

"No, I want to go home."

Her eyes saw through him. "You speak the truth, yet you are here for a reason. That I know." Her dark eyes drew him in. "Is it Deela?"

The name triggered a memory. She was one of the women who had been chained to the pillars in Chernobog, the prison city. "Deela is here?"

"Then you do know her." Artemis' gaze turned away from him. "She is the one that opened my eyes to the truth." She extended her hand. "Come, not as a prisoner, but as an ally. I will take you to her."

The moment he touched her hand, her legs buckled. His arms caught her before she reached the ground. "What's wrong?" The warmth of the walls faded to almost nothing. The rune blade's vibration did the same.

"I must return to the inner city. Only there can I renew my strength."

His mind clicked. "Is that why the gods do not come out?"

Her gaze hardened, but after a moment, the steel melted away. Her chest labored with each breath. "Yes."

His heart softened as she struggled to breathe. "Will rest help?"

"Some, but I must return."

He lifted her up and followed the spiral toward the exit.

"What are you doing?"

"Mumin assigned me a room in the house. You can rest on a bed."

"No." She struggled against his hold but could not break free. "I must..." Her voice drifted off.

"Resting on cold stone will not help you revive." He stepped out, and she fainted. Panic filled him. "Artemis?" A stone bench sat to one side. He placed her upon it. "Artemis?" His fingers checked her pulse. The slow beat remained steady. Her lungs barely moved. His eyes swept toward the house and caught sight of Mumin staring out the kitchen window. An odd feeling came over him, and he found himself looking up at the sky. The wind whispered in voices just out of hearing.

Mumin hurried toward him. "What are you doing?" His steps slowed as his eyes drifted up. "We are being watched."

"By whom?"

"The gods, and they are angry."

"Help me get her to house."

Mumin gawked at him.

"Mumin, help me, now!"

The man came forward, but each time Jonna coached him to touch her, he recoiled. "I will not touch the goddess."

Jonna huffed, picked her up, and laid her over his shoulder. "Can you at least open the doors?"

The man nodded with eyes wide open. "Perhaps we should place her back into the spiral?"

"Are you going to help or not?" Jonna started up the path.

Mumin hurried in front. "Of course. It's just, you are touching a god!"

The flora slapped at them as they rushed. "She touched you."

They passed the fountain and headed over the bridge. "That was different. It was her choice."

Mumin swung open the door. After passing through the kitchen and down the hallway, they stopped at the room assigned to Jonna.

The door creaked open to reveal a modest bed made up of pillows and covers with woven designs. The most prominent design displayed a round, yellow globe with eight cones extending from it in eight different directions. Two eyes, a nose, and a mouth decorated the globe. It matched Lord Aubron's medallion.

A desk with a drawer stood in one corner. The same symbol on the pillows had been carved into the back of a wooden chair. A shuttered window sat in the outside wall. Light filtered in through the wooden slats.

Jonna laid Arta gently on the bed and pulled a cover over her. "Now, she can rest."

The front door opened and closed. Mumin stepped toward the hallway. He half-shut the bedroom door as he leaned out. "Kali, can you get--"

Mumin's eyebrows narrowed. "Can I help you, my lord?"

Senka's voice met Jonna's ears. "Yes, I think you can. You have lied to me, Mumin, and for the last time."

Jonna glanced at the window. The release for the shutters was on the inside. His fingers fumbled with the rope and let the shutters open.

Light poured in to shine upon the wall. Luckily, the brightness did not hit the doorway. A soft jingle touched his ears.

Mumin held very still. "How have I lied to you, my lord? Did you not like your purchase?"

"A week ago, you told me you had no new designs. Now I find out from Kali that you are preparing to reveal another."

Leaves rustled outside the window. The dark clouds had faded away. However, in the background, the whispers on the wind had grown.

Jonna leaned out the window and looked toward the front of the shop. The back of a shed blocked off his view of the road. It butted up beside the store next to it. The shed door, this side, stood closed.

"You shall be the first to know, my lord, when it is ready. Rest assured."

"I will, won't I? Perhaps sooner than you think."

"My lord?"

A fence stood between Mumin's building and the next. At eight feet high, it kept prying eyes from seeing easily over its top. Though the boards were close together, Jonna caught faint flickers between the tiny gaps as people moved past. The jingle stopped. A tiny piece of roofing tile bounced off the top of the roof to drop beside the window.

"I have decided you will be my personal tailor. You will design your clothes for me, alone. Of course, you will be handsomely paid."

"My lord, I don't know what to say."

"A thank you would be in order."

"Thank you, my lord." Mumin bowed. "The design will be finished right away."

"At my living quarters, of course."

"I don't understand."

"I can't have you live here when a new place has been prepared."

"But, my lord, my tools and cloths?" Mumin extended his hands.

"They will be moved," Senka said with finality. "After the dinner tonight, I will send servants to bring them all."

Mumin pleaded, "This is my home, my lord."

"Not any more. The gods have declared it."

At the words 'gods', Jonna threw a look toward Mumin.

Mumin's jaw dropped, but he did not glance into the room. His voice sank to almost a whisper. "Yes, my lord."

"Walk with me, now. We have much to discuss."

A flick of Mumin's hand told Jonna to stay undetected. "What of my cousin, my lord?"

"Never fear. I have posted guards to inform him."

Jonna slipped closer to the window as Mumin moved out of sight.

"As you say, my lord." His footsteps left the hallway. The front door closed with a thud.

A rope snaked down from the roof top. The knotted end bounced in the window's center. The rune blade hummed.

Jonna's right hand reached back and eased the rune blade from its sheath. He waited. A horn poked down followed by a man's head with reddish-brown skin. He stared at the familiar face. "Lokke?"

A grin spread as Lokke gazed back. "He remembers me!"

"Of course, I remember you." Jonna glanced toward the door and kept his voice low. "What are you doing here?"

The half-demon flipped around and crawled backwards down the rope. A thin layer of chainmail over a tunic shirt adorned his torso with leather pants covering his legs. A small leather pouch swung at his waist. Beside it, a dagger caught the sunlight. "Väinämö sent me." He straightened the backpack on his back.

To the best of Jonna's memory, Lokke had never met Väinämö, other than seeing him in one of those strange visions. "How did you find him?"

"He looked me up. Said something about Bob caught in a multi-magic screwup. Anyway," he beamed, "here I am. Ready to save the day!"

Behind Lokke, the shoulders of a guard rose above the eight foot fence. With eyes bulging, the guard's hands lifted a bow and arrow.

"Lokke?"

"What?"

"Down!"

In one smooth motion, the guard drew back and fired. The arrow sliced the air. Lokke twisted and dropped. Jonna sidestepped as the rune blade arced in front. The arrow bounced off the angled blade and shot toward the opposite wall.

"Lokke!"

"What!"

"Get in here!"

The half-demon leaped through the window as Jonna grabbed the nearest shutter. Three arrows pierced the shutter as it closed.

Footsteps hurried into the hallway. Jonna leaped toward the door, grabbed the handle, and slammed it though he found no lock. "Lokke, close the other shutter!"

The half-demon's hand stuck out and jerked back as another arrow whizzed by. "I can't grab it!"

Jonna's eyes zipped around the room. "They have boxed us in. They know there's no way out. Watch the door." He moved toward Artemis.

"I can't watch the door and close the shutter! Which one do you want?" As he reached for the shutter again, two additional arrows whizzed by. He jerked back and shook his hand. "That was close!"

Jonna shook Artemis. "Wake up! Come on, I need you awake!"

Her eyes fluttered.

"That's it! Come on, open up those beautiful dark eyes!"

Her voice murmured. "You think my eyes are beautiful?"

"Of course, I do. Come on, show them to me!"

The eyelids slowly opened. The dark eyes blinked up at him. "Where am I?" An arrow ripped through the shutter and stabbed into the wall. Her eyes shot open. "What's going on?"

"Someone wants to kill us."

She studied him as she listened. "You can hear their whisperings."

He nodded.

"They know you can. Those outside were sent to destroy you."

She struggled to sit up. "I can't--I can't help us. I am too weak."

The bedroom door jerked partially back while Lokke snatched the open shutter and slammed it home. He tied the two shutters together. "I did it!" An arrow pierced the wood near his head. He leaped away.

"Grab the door!"

"I just fixed the shutters!"

Jonna leaped toward the room's entrance. A guard raised a scimitar to meet the rune blade. Sparks flew as the two struck in the air. Jonna shouted to Artemis, "If you could use a spell, what spell would you use to get us out safely?"

With his free hand, the guard struggled to jerk the door all the way open, but Jonna used his own to hold it firm.

Her eyes took on a distant look. "The same spell I used earlier."

The rune blade feinted. As the guard attempted to block, Jonna slammed a kick to his midriff. The guard collapsed backwards, and Jonna slammed the door. "Where would you go?"

"To the Najwa Miraj."

"What is that?" A scimitar tried to wedge its way between the side post and the door while another hacked at the door.

"Why?"

"I have to know!"

She shook her head. "It is the secret place of ascent."

"Describe it!"

"Why? What does it matter?"

Splinters of wood broke off the door. Gaps appeared. "I'm trying to save our lives!"

"There is a pool in the center of the room. A lattice of woven flowers decorates the right side. A stairwell behind the lattice leads off toward the next floor. The..."

Jonna grabbed every detail and built the picture in his mind as another scimitar jabbed through. He dodged and gripped the door handle tighter as someone tried to rip it from his grasp.

"Is that enough?"

By the handle, a scimitar slipped through a gap. A man's hands grabbed a piece of the door and ripped back. The board snapped.

"It better be." Jonna leaped away, grabbed Lokke's horn, and dove for the bed. Artemis clutched his arm. Focusing, Jonna spoke, "*Ba-ru-ya!*"

A crackle of energy leapt into the room. It bounced from wall to wall until it found them. It touched swords and zapped their holders. The screams of startled guards echoed from the hallway.

Arrows stopped flying. Artemis's grip tightened as the magic vortex built. The torrent of electricity spiraled faster.

The goddess became stronger. "Hold together." She reached forward and grasped Lokke's hand. "The transition will be easier on all."

They rose exactly as Jonna had. The bedroom door jerked open, but the guards who did it cowered back. The vortex completed. It engulfed the room and sucked them in.

Pleasure danced upon Artemis' face. She stretched as the tingles went through her body. Her hand pushed the cover away. It sank through the electrical torrent to drop to the floor. In complete control of her actions, she forced Jonna closer with narrowed eyes. "Who are you?"

Their faces were mere inches apart. She pressed her body against his. "I feel life; the movement of the currents abound. I want more. I need more."

She pressed her lips against his and the torrent no longer went only around them. Energy burst inside his skull. The rune blade hummed and vibrated. He could feel the flow of magic but could not stop its drain. She released Lokke's hand.

Her eyes glowed. They were all Jonna could see. A wall of intense energy struck his body and locked his muscles so he could not pull away. As her arms went around him, her embrace tried to consume him, every piece, as if he was no longer a part of himself. Unable to adjust his grip, Lokke's horn slipped from his grasp.

His heart thudded in his chest. Sweat trickled down his brow. Her eyes held delight as she drew him closer. The crackle of the power flashed in front of his eyes until he could no longer see. The thought struck his brain, "She's feeding off the energy. She's feeding off me!"

"Enough!" On the brink of exhaustion, her hands shook. "No

more. I can't handle any more." With a whimper, she shoved him away.

The torrent burst. The vortex vanished. He found himself in pitch blackness. His mind's eye remembered Esti's bite on his shoulder just before he had been reborn.

She giggled quietly, "*Jan-ros-shan.*"

Illumination sprang up. Mounted in the corners, where the ceiling touched the walls, hung balls of light. Iron protrusions showed from the wall behind each brilliance.

No pool, stairs, or lattice existed. A door sat to Jonna's left. Bows of various types hung from hooks on the walls. Murals were painted between them. Arrows in different quivers draped beneath the bows.

In one corner, an iron post curved up. It split into two handles which pointed in opposite directions, similar to a bicycle's handlebars.

Jonna gulped air. Beside him, Artemis' chest heaved. She gawked at him with round welcoming eyes as her fingers caressed his arm. "Amazing."

He felt soft pillows beneath him, but it did not soothe what he had felt. She had fed off him. She had taken his energy by force.

Every part of him wanted to wrench away from her, but he steadied his will and shifted to conversation. "I take it we aren't in Najwa Miraj?"

"No." She snuggled into his shoulder with a glowing smile. "I chose not to share you. I redirected our destination."

His eyes opened wide as he fought to contain his nervousness. "Share me with whom?"

"The others. You don't think I'm the only female in the inner city? What would I do if they discovered your secret? I could never have you alone again." Her eyes brightened. "I've never felt energy so pure."

"Wait a minute. You're a--succubus that absorbs electricity?"

"What's electricity?"

"The sparks of light that jump from one point to the next. My people call that electricity."

"No, not a succubus, but my kind does absorb this *electricity* as you call it. We generate our own by using the resources of this city and the lake. It is our primary source of life and defense. We extend its protection to the others in exchange for their allegiance, food, and crafts."

His voice remained calm but his anger burned. "You stole it."

"I absorbed what you generated," she purred. Her eyes rolled. "Surely it wasn't painful?"

"You held me against my will. If you want my cooperation, you will never force yourself on me again."

Her eyes flared briefly, but the effects of the blue electricity washed her anger away. She giggled. "Fine. I will never force you, but if you are generating, it is my right to partake."

His eyes narrowed. "Have you done this to others?"

"I suppose we could, although, it would take so many humans, we would starve to death before getting full. You are *different*."

Jonna gave a slow nod. "So, it was chance that you discovered you could feed off of the spell?"

"I suspected I could after your first demonstration in the spiral. I was weak, Mahdi, my love. The power you generated with the spell revived me." She stroked his arm again. "I have never felt such pure, raw power."

With great control, he patted her hand. "Let's not go there." His eyes scanned the room. A frown crossed his face. "Where's Lokke?"

"Somewhere close, I'm sure." She hiccupped. "He'll be safe, never fear." A giggle escaped her lips. She stretched back. "I feel magnificent!"

"What's your definition of safe?"

"Shall I show you?" As she stood up, a crackle of blue light sparked between her fingers. Her face glowed with delight. "Never have I felt such a force." She spun around the room as he stood.

126

"Wow!" She watched the room spin. "So good! So pure!" Her body fell toward him, and he caught her before she landed. "Let's do that again, please!" Her fingers grasped his hands in pure joy. "I'll be good, I promise! Speak the spell, and anything I have is yours, I swear."

His fist tightened. "Artemis--"

"Call me Arta. That is the name they know me by."

"Arta, you are drunk."

Her eyebrows crossed, and she laughed. "Silly, I have taken no alcohol."

"If electricity is your food source, you've had more than your fair share."

She held up her hand and watched the sparks shoot through her fingers. "It's never happened before." She hiccupped and giggled. "But I would love to repeat that." Her head lay against him. "I'm well versed in what humans like to do." A grin spread across her face. "Shall I show you?"

"Arta, look at me."

Her eyes went very round and innocent. "Yes, my lord?"

He shook his head. "No, no, not that way. Focus. We need to find Lokke. Remember?"

Her head nodded. "Anything for you." She rose from his arms, steadied herself, and walked with perfect steps to the door. When she reached it, she turned back. "But tonight, you will give me what I want in return. That's not forcing, is it?" With a giggle, she pulled the door back and stared out. Her face became sober.

"Arta, where have you been? We thought someone had abducted you!"

"I've been," she glanced into the room and winked at Jonna, "busy."

"Busy with the king's business, I hope?"

Her voice became very serious. "But of course, my brother."

Jonna approached the door cautiously and watched the two interact without being fully visible. Arta stepped out of the room and ambled toward her brother. "Dear, sweet, brother Mot. Don't be so serious. Remember what father told us? We've all the time in the world." As she leaned toward him to peck his cheek, a blue arc leaped out and stung him.

He jerked back. "What was that?" His fingers rubbed the cheek gingerly. "What's wrong with you?"

Innocent eyes decorated her face, but she could not hold that expression. She hiccupped. A grin spread as a giggle left her lips.

"Are you drunk?"

"Of course not." Her chin went high. "I do not drink."

He leaned near to sniff her breath. A second blue arc stung him. "Then what is going on?" The eyebrows of her brother crossed as he stared at the door behind her. "Who's in there?"

She chuckled. "I'm not gonna tell." Her eyes brightened. "He's mine."

"Your what?" Mot scowled at the door. "Come out, whoever you are. What have you done to my sister?"

CHAPTER 11

Jonna stepped out of the room and planted both feet evenly. The sword on his back hummed.

"No!" Arta spun toward him and pressed her back against Jonna's chest. "Leave him alone. He is mine!" She pulled Jonna's arms around her. "Leave me, or I will not be merciful." The bluish crackle of energy grew between her fingertips.

Mot focused on the blue sparks, and his voice patronized. "Of course, sister. I would never consider taking away one of your human play things. Have you shown *it* to our father? He may be quite impressed."

Her face beamed. In a haughty voice, she spoke, "I may decide to do that. Yes, perhaps I will." A smile crossed her lips. "Leave us. Mahdi and I have much to discuss."

"Mahdi." A smile crept onto Mot's face as his eyes caught Jonna's. "As you wish, sister." He turned to a side hall and vanished down the corridor.

"There," she grinned at him. "All taken care of."

"And Lokke?"

A pixie grin hit her face. "Oh yes, we can't forget Lokke." Her face swept both directions of the hall. "To the right."

The marble floor alternated red and blue colors in a checkered pattern. Murals depicting many lands decorated the hall walls as they strolled from her room.

Jonna pointed at the heads which adorned the walls. Flames in orange and red had been painted upon the faces. "What are those?"

"Stone ifrit heads; they are the guardians of our realm."

With soulless eyes, the ifrit heads watched. They were spaced at thirty foot intervals down the length of the corridor. Orbs of light, similar to the ones in Arta's room, hung close to the ceiling. Periodically, a door would show on the left or right. Arta would pause, shake her head, and move on.

"What are you looking for?"

Her voice became lofty. "I have many powers." A giggle burst out. "If I know the person I'm looking for, I can detect them."

"So electricity produced by a creature is unique." That made sense to Jonna. "I hadn't thought about that before. It is like a fingerprint."

"A what?"

"You know, if you press your thumb into some oily substance and place it on paper, it leaves a unique design."

Her face brightened. "We shall have to try that." She leaned near him and tilted the direction they had come. "I have oil in my room."

He straightened her up. "Lokke, remember?"

"Yes, Lokke. That's right." She walked a few steps, yawned, and touched the handle of the door beside her. "He should be right in here."

The door swung back. On the walls, geometric shapes at odd angles complimented more infrequent murals. The pictures painted on the murals included green lush landscapes, rolling seas, and beautiful mountains. Statues of men and woman in playful poses decorated various surfaces in the room.

Toward the back, a large bed of pillows and covers sat upon a dais. Greek columns stood at the four corners of the bed. A table with grapes and other fruit sat near, and a woman with long wavy hair filled the room with laughter as she fed Lokke grapes. Around her waist was clasped a golden girdle.

Lokke's eyes grew large as Jonna walked in. "J--"

Jonna cut in; the warning Mumin had given him stuck in his mind. "Mahdi, remember?" His eyebrows rose. "You're okay, I see?"

Lokke swallowed the next grape quickly. "Thank you, love muffin. This is J--Mahdi. The friend I was telling you I had to find." He sighed with relief. "Luckily, he has found me first."

"It is a pleasure to meet you." The woman rose and stylishly drew near Jonna. Her eyes were bright and alluring. "You have done well, sister." She extended her hand to Lokke's friend, the rune blade hummed low, and a question mark crossed her expression. "I am Al-Uzza."

Jonna accepted the hand and gave a nod. "As in Al-Uzza, belonging to the daughter trinity of Allah?"

She flipped her hair over one shoulder and nodded. "The same."

He released the hand. "Yet, Artemis is Arta, great mother of nature, and not one of the trinity. Why?"

Her gaze looked to Arta. "He knows your future name?"

Arta nodded. "I do not know how."

She turned slowly back to Jonna and pursed her full lips. "You speak of Al-Lat and Manat." She shrugged flirtatiously. "They are in the city as well."

Jonna gave a single nod. "I get it. It's pre-Islamic."

Artemis raised her eyebrows. "Pre-is-who?"

"Before Allah was named the one and only god under Muhammad, there were many gods. Muhammad eventually did away with the trinity as well."

Al-Uzza stared. "He wouldn't dare!"

His eyes studied Al-Uzza. "Who? Allah or Muhammad?"

"Either!" She eyed him closely. "Have you heard something you are not telling us?"

"I assume Muhammad is a prophet, but who is Allah?"

Arta leaned toward him. "One of dad's many names."

"But you said his future name was Zeus."

Al-Uzza sucked in her breath accentuating her chest. "You told him dad's future name?"

"No," Arta glared at her. "I would never do that!"

"Then how could he know?"

Artemis' eyebrows crossed as she swayed slightly back and forth. Her face turned toward Jonna. "How *did* you know?"

Jonna watched them closely as both frowned. He pointed at Al-Uzza. "The same way I know your future name is Aphrodite. The golden girdle is a dead giveaway."

Al-Uzza's body stiffened as fear crept across her face. "Only two types of creatures know that. You are either a god yourself--" She checked him up and down. "--or a destroyer of them." She leaned away. "Which are you?"

Her words felt strange to Jonna. A baby cry sounded from somewhere far away, but no one else appeared to hear it. Was he a destroyer of the gods? Did he have that power? "I just want to go home."

Artemis giggled. "I would rather you stay with me."

Al-Uzza stepped closer as she walked demurely around him. "And where is that?" The rune blade gave a faint hum.

"I don't know."

A smile lit Artemis' face. "Then you have no reason to leave." She tugged him toward the door. "We should return to my room."

Al-Uzza reached toward Artemis' free arm. A blue crackle leaped toward her, and she jerked back. "Sister, this could be serious." For the first time, she took a good look at Artemis. "What has happened to you?" Her eyes swept toward Jonna. "What have you done to her? She is--"

"Drunk?" Lokke stepped closer and leaned toward Arta. With wary eyes, Arta inclined away. "But I smell no alcohol. When I was in the Otherworld that was the one thing they had plenty of on all levels. All kinds: vodka, wine, beer--"

Jonna cleared his throat. "Lokke, now is not the time."

"I am not drunk!" She glared at Lokke.

"No." Al-Uzza shook her head. "Not on fermentation, but consumed with--" Her head jerked toward Jonna. "Power." Curiosity crept into her face. "How?" Her head turned toward the metal handle bars that extruded from one corner of the room. They matched the pair at Arta's. Her voice became speculative. "Arta, have you tried to recharge today?"

"Charge up?" Arta giggled. "Why do that when I feel so good?"

"Let me help you." Al-Uzza started to touch her but pulled back as blue tendrils leaped into the air. "Perhaps your new consort would aid us." A slight smile reshaped her sculpted lips. "After all, if he stays, it would certainly be something he should experience." Her eyes drifted to Jonna. "Among other things."

Arta shook her head. "I really don't think--"

"Come." Al-Uzza slipped to the other side of Jonna and slowly reached out until her fingers touched his arm. Nothing crackled toward her. With a firm grip, she led Jonna and Arta toward the device. "I really must insist."

Within ten feet, the rune blade's hum increased. Al-Uzza's eyes searched to locate the source. The hairs on Jonna's arm stirred slowly. The hair on his head rose. Arta's breath quickened as he felt her press against his side. A low moan came from her lips. Al-Uzza reached forward to touch one of the handles, and Arta collapsed.

Blue light leapt from Arta, passed around Jonna, and struck Al-Uzza. It licked the handles of the device as shades of indigo met shades of yellow-orange. Crackles burst around them and created a ball of azure light. It exploded, and all three shot backwards to crash against the floor.

Lokke dashed to Al-Uzza's side. "Love muffin!" He touched her face. "Are you hurt?"

Her eyes fluttered as Jonna groaned. Arta sighed as a smile lit her lips.

Al-Uzza whispered. "Call the guards. I do not have the breath. Must--" She sucked in air. "--must warn the others."

Jonna rose slowly as he shook off the hit and helped Arta to rise. "There is no need. I will not be staying."

Her voice became stronger as Lokke did not obey. "Guard. Guards!"

In desperation, Jonna called upon one of the only two spells he knew in this world. If the principles he had learned in the Otherworld held true universally, then his thoughts could modify the spell's purpose within certain parameters. *"Ba-ru-ya."*

Arta's face brightened. She reached out one hand into the air, closed her eyes, and felt the buildup coming.

A vortex of electrical blue light formed around Al-Uzza. He focused on exactly what he wished it to do. She gasped, each time sharper, until her eyes bulged. Her chest heaved as she sucked in air. "What-are-you-doing-to-me?" With a single exhale, her body released its tension, and her head rolled gently to the side. The blue vortex decreased until the crackles faded from view. For a long moment, she just lay there, staring at nothing.

Lokke touched her hesitantly with one finger. "You didn't kill her, did you?" He placed an ear to her chest. "I hear something beating inside." She giggled, and Lokke leaned back in surprise. "Are you okay?"

In a slow stretch, she moaned, "Ohhh." A hiccup left her lips, and her eyes opened in surprise. "Excuse me." She giggled again. "That was incredible. Sister, I--"

"He's mine." Arta warned as she fought to keep her eyes open. Her head lolled toward Jonna. "No more sharing. I want you all to myself."

Jonna sighed. "I really need to learn a different spell."

"What's wrong with this one?" Lokke beamed. "I bet she'd even be more fun now."

Al-Uzza giggled again. "Fun sounds like fun to me." A pout crossed her face. "But I feel too weak to get up." A mischievous grin erupted as her eyes darted toward Jonna. "Maybe you should help me to the bed."

Jonna's eyebrows crossed. "Can you stand, Arta?"

Her lips formed a pout. "You're coming back?"

He nodded. "I'm just going to make your sister more comfortable. I promise."

Her face brightened. "Okay."

Lokke beamed. "Comfortable sounds good."

With Jonna on one side and Lokke on the other, they lifted Al-Uzza up.

"Not that kind of comfortable," Jonna warned. They walked her toward the bed.

"But if you have one, can't I have one?"

"Lokke, I do not *have one*; you make them sound like objects, and they are not. They are drunk on electricity."

"Elect-tric-ity? What is that?" They laid her down on the bed. Lokke adjusted the pillow beneath Al-Uzza's head. She stared up with loving eyes which gradually slid shut. Her breathing became light.

"It's a form a power. Like one of the elements."

"Like fire, water, earth and air?"

"Sort of like fire, but a different form and combined with air."

"Teach me that. Please!"

Jonna huffed. "I am trying to get to the bottom of why I am here."

"Mahdi, I think--" Arta leaned sideways. Jonna raced over and caught her. "Grab the other side!"

"But I want to stay with Al-Uzza," the half-demon whined.

"Lokke, focus! Why are you here?" They headed toward the exit.

"To help you, of course. But--"

"Say the first three words again."

"To help you, of course."

"The first *three* words." They came within two feet of the door.

Lokke rubbed his chin. "To help you?"

Jonna grabbed the door handle and pulled it back. Two guards peered in. Their eyes recognized Arta and spotted Al-Uzza on the bed. "Is everything alright in here?" Each had a hand on an ornate dagger. The daggers protruded from sashes around their waists.

"Everything's just fine," Jonna nodded as he kept careful watch on the grip by which they held the daggers. "We are helping Arta back to her room." He gave a solemn smile. "A little too much to drink."

Their eyes narrowed.

A gentle shake woke Arta. "Arta, darling, please let the guards in on what we're doing?"

"Hmm?" Her eyes opened to look around. "Are we back at the room?" Her head rolled toward his shoulder, and she snuggled in.

"Not yet, love." He grinned at the guards. "We really need to go."

The faces didn't change expression, but they backed up. Lokke reached behind and closed Al-Uzza's door. He tapped one of the guards on the shoulder. "Thanks guys!" The three strode past.

Once the guards were out of sight, Jonna shifted promptly around a corner. He guided Lokke to support Arta's back against the wall. A stone ifrit head watched. "Artemis?" With his hand, he lifted her chin to face him. "Can you hear me?"

With eyes closed, she spoke, "Hmm?"

"Remember why we came? We need to find Deela."

"I want to return to the room." Footsteps caught their attention. The rune blade's hum rose. A man and woman turned a corner and walked past them casting curious looks. However, neither said a word. When the couple reached the next corner, they turned another way.

"After we find Deela."

Her voice whined, "You said after we found Lokke!"

"Artemis, can you help me?"

She nodded as she tried to snuggle closer. "Call me Arta."

"Arta?"

"Okay," her eyes fluttered open, "but this is the last time."

Voices echoed from the right but faded away just as fast.

"Arta?"

"Alright, already." She hiccupped and giggled. Her hand wavered to the right. "First stairs down."

They steadied her down the hall. A doorway became visible to their right with a stone ifrit face above the header. Past that, an archway appeared. Curved stairs led down.

They worked their way from stair to stair. The light orbs were smaller here and hung just above their heads. Each time Jonna approached too near, the rune blade would hum. At the bottom, a forked hall appeared.

"Which way, Arta?"

Arta blinked and stared. Her hand pointed to the right. A few of the doors they passed stood agape to reveal jars of variable sizes. Most sat upon brick shelves or flat areas cut into the walls.

At one of the wooden doors, they stopped. Arta opened it with a touch to the handle and pointed to a corner. "Through here. *Na-jwa-am.*"

A section of the wall slipped back. It slid sideways to reveal a curved staircase going down. The smell of moisture wafted up.

They worked their way down. Before the entrance left their view, she murmured, "*Na-jwa-am.*" The wall slid closed.

The lights brightened. The rune blade's hum grew. They stepped into a twenty by twenty room whose ceiling blazed with light. A bed, a wooden table, and a wooden chest stood in one corner.

On the table was a jar decorated with palm trees and a blue lake. A large bowl with a cloth hanging on it sat beside the jar. Woven covers lay upon the bed. Rugs decorated the floor with a small, short table toward the center of the room. Pillows had been placed around the short table. To the right, a doorway led to another hall. From the hall came sounds of water.

They reached the next hall and found more jars stored inside other rooms. The floor slanted down at a slight tilt. At the end of the hall, a large, round room opened. In the middle of the room, steps descended until they came to a pool of water. The liquid sparkled in bright blue light.

The nix part of him flickered awake though he could no longer hear Aroha's call. It made sense. If he had shifted to a different reality, she might not even exist in this world.

A woman wearing a headscarf sat before them. A murmured song left her lips as she gazed down at a wrapped cloth. In the cloth lay a baby.

"Great things await for you to grow. A coming age will show you so. When you do rise so strong and stout, the world will change what it's about."

Jonna peered at the woman. Her voice stirred no memory. He had only met Deela once in the prison city of Chernobog--at least in his reality. "Deela?"

The woman's eyes sparkled as she twisted. "She said you would know her name." Her eyes locked with his. "She said I would know you by the child." She rose from the step and approached slowly, careful to keep the child held close. "I did as I was told, my lord. Do not hold this against me." Her feet paused as her eyes fell. In front of Arta, she dropped to her knees. "Forgive me, goddess, for at last I can tell the truth. Deela is dead. I have cared for her son as my own."

Arta struggled to stay awake. "What are you talking about?" Her eyelids struggled but closed. "I need to go to sleep." Jonna and Lokke fought to keep her upright. They carried her back to the room with the bed.

The woman trailed after with a wrinkled brow. "Is she sick, my lord?"

"In a way." He glanced behind him. None of this made any sense. "She will be fine after some rest, hopefully."

"Hopefully?" She pulled back. "Should I be concerned for the baby? I've never known the gods to get sick."

"I don't think it's catching." They placed Arta on the bed.

"Catching?"

"It's not contagious."

She shook her head. "I don't understand."

From the day he had entered Elfleda's world, the magic he connected with automatically translated his language for those that listened and vice versa--for the most part. However, upon occasion, it seemed to hiccup. "Uh, the baby won't get sick."

She nodded but stayed back as she sat down cross-legged beside the short table. The baby had opened its eyes but so far had not made a sound. Those eyes focused on Jonna, and Jonna felt a connection.

"How--" He stopped and centered his thoughts. "What happened?"

Her lips trembled.

Jonna moved to sit across from her; Lokke followed his lead. "What are you afraid of? What is your name?"

She bit her lip. "I am called Salma."

Jonna nodded. "Thank you, Salma. And the first question?"

She gave a reluctant nod. "We found her on the road. Her body suffered from exposure and a lack of water. Wrapped in a blanket and held to her bosom was the child. Though the others of our group saw it as an ill omen, she pleaded with me to keep the baby safe. Her eyes--" She looked off at nothing. "They cut to my heart. She told me one would come to seek her. That I must protect the baby until that one came. She made me swear to use her name as a sign for the one who was to find her."

"They brought you to this city?"

Her head nodded. Her words slowed. "There were those that sought her life--" A tear started down one cheek. "--for being married to you."

Jonna kept his facial expression neutral, but his mind raced. After he had tricked the demon Azazel and gone into the dark mage's lair, in his reality, he had never seen her again.

Lokke leaned toward Jonna. "You crafty dog! I didn't know you had--"

Jonna's voice remained calm. "Lokke, let Salma finish her story."

"But I thought you were married to--"

"Lokke, please." He nodded to the woman. "Continue."

Her eyes darted to Lokke before returning to Jonna. "Once here, I prayed for guidance. Arta heard my plea."

"So she brought you here for protection?"

Her head bobbed quickly. "Babies do not exist here, my lord. They are prevented by the gods. Once I entered the outer walls, they would have killed me had they known I hid a child. He is your son, my lord."

Lokke huffed. "Whoa! How do you know it's Jonna's, hmm?"

"She swore, my lord." Her eyes stayed locked with Jonna's. "Do you not remember your pledge to her beneath the moons after Azazel died?" Fear crept into her eyes.

He nodded though he did not recall the moons. "I remember the death of Azazel."

"Then you know the truth. Why, then, do you not embrace the child?" She broke eye contact. "The way she spoke, you would never betray her trust."

Jonna cringed. With a step around the table, he moved to her side and peered at the baby. What could have happened to make him be with Deela when his heart belonged to Elfleda?

A distant baby's cry caught his ears. However, neither Lokke nor Salma reacted. The irises of Deela's baby expanded. Had Deela's baby heard the cry, too?

It made sense. If this was his son, a magical connection could easily be with the child. A network of beings unified by his common DNA? A shiver started at his head and traveled down to his toes.

"You are cold, my lord?"

"No," he whispered. "No, there's something more to this."

"To what?"

"Salma, I--" He thought carefully over his words. "You must not call me, my lord. I am not your lord; we are equals."

Salma's face flushed. "It is not the way of my people, my--"

140

"Call me Jonna, please. After all--" He looked down at the child in her hands. "Surely, that is the least you deserve." His heart smote him. How could he have a child with a woman he barely knew?

Lokke listened closely. Jonna could see him from the corner of his eye.

Jonna's gaze dropped to the baby. His heart melted as its tiny eyes stared up into his. This was his son; he could feel it. Despite the shifting of reality, this child was very real. He touched the baby's tiny hand.

A sparkle ignited between them. Not the blue electricity called by the spell, but a tiny burst of sunlight. Warmth swept his body, and he could hear other baby cries, too. Not here, not in this reality, but in others. How? His magic reached out to them. A connection did exist.

Arta stirred. As she rose, her eyes blinked. They narrowed at the scene before her. "I felt it was true, but could not confirm it. You may be the one."

The sparkle between him and the baby faded as Jonna removed his hand. "I am the one for what?"

Salma pulled the baby closer to hide his face. Lokke rotated toward the goddess as Jonna turned to face Arta.

Arta eyed Lokke, Salma, and the baby. She shook her head as if waking from a dream. "*Sta-sha-ta.*"

Lokke and Salma halted. The cover in Salma's arms did not stir. Jonna's eyes darted to them both. He checked Salma but felt no signs of life: not the beat of the heart or the expansion of the lungs. "What have you done?"

Arta breathed deeply. Her eyes focused on him. "It is a spell to keep them out of the moment so that they will not know what takes place next."

"You suspended them in time?"

She nodded, closed her eyes tightly, and gradually opened them again. Her left hand massaged her neck. "I'm glad that's over. Come here."

"Why?"

She rubbed the corner of her eyes. "I must know the truth."

Jonna rose slowly and moved toward Arta. "How?"

A smirk struck her lips. "You're afraid of me? After all we've done?"

"Done?"

"You joined with a goddess."

Jonna stopped. His voice became hard. "I did no such thing!"

"A merging of magic? A filling with energy? What do you think?"

"You absorbed the spell's energy." Jonna stepped back. "You fed upon me."

"Your magic is strong, Mahdi." She paused. "No, you told Salma to call you Jonna. That is your true name." A wisp of excitement glowed in her eyes. "I had to see if you had the potential. I had to know if you can hold up to the backlash that will follow."

"Backlash? What backlash?"

With a wave, the Zaman Dar appeared in her hand. As the cover turned back, the letters shimmered on the page. She rotated the book to face him. "Read."

His eyes narrowed. "I cannot understand the language."

"I did not say comprehend. I said, *read*."

He stared at the words.

She huffed. "If you are the one, it may be your only hope."

His wary eyes studied her face. "You speak in riddles."

"No, you understand in riddles. I am speaking *very* clearly. Do you think I would wait till now to hurt you?" She flicked one hand as if to throw the thought away. "I could have destroyed you at any time, but I chose to discover who you are. As you said, you are no god." Her head nodded toward the book. "Read."

CHAPTER 12

The letters moved and spun before him like lines and curves cast upon the page. A sparkle on the upper right caught his attention as the first word formed. The text read right to left.

"Nan."

Quiet dropped; even the lapping of the pool could not be heard. Though he did not understand the word, he 'felt' its meaning as a picture of the end of a railroad track dropped into his mind. It meant finality, the end of something. It meant the end of a declaration of fact. The air emitted a presence; the hairs on his arm stood up. He started again.

"Nan ac'vayu--"

A gentle breeze swept from the hall that led to the pool. It danced upon the floor and ruffled the edges of the book. Arta's eyes were closed, and her chin stayed lifted toward the ceiling. As he stared at the first words, the ones to their left continued to form.

"--nahwaena eka ava ac'el--"

He felt a strong presence. It consumed the room in which they stood. The air became thicker. It weaved into all. A distortion formed everywhere he turned except when he looked at the book.

"--ac'ava yish."

The sentence leaped from the page. It spun into a spiral in front of his eyes and flowed into the distortion.

A voice boomed around him. "Hear me, young one. The task you take is not a light thing. The path you choose will bring sorrow. Ask, if you will."

Jonna stared at the distortion. "Who are you?"

"I exist. That is all you can comprehend."

The creature's words struck his soul. His jaw dropped as immense power emanated from all directions. He fought to get his voice above a whisper. "I do not want to hurt anyone. I choose no path."

The voice of the being held confidence. "Every creature chooses through action or inaction. Every path has a consequence to all those in creation."

Jonna bit his lip. His own *consequences* had changed everything. Sweat trickled down his temples. His lungs labored in the thick air as the heat rose. "Whose creation? Yours?"

The voice chuckled. "Would that surprise you?"

At least the being had a sense of humor. "Quite the opposite," Jonna managed in a parched throat. "It would relieve me to know that the choices I made did not destroy the ones I loved."

The air to his left shimmered and sparkles took on a definite humanoid shape. "Of course, because you blame yourself for the death of your wife. You blame yourself for the world you cannot find. I know you, Jonna. I can see every decision, every choice, that brought you to the place you are. Your future is written just as any other."

The prophecy of the fates in the Otherworld came to mind, especially that of the fate Tlyme:

"Though the task you take will come to end, your quest for knowledge will not be so. Though the gods would use you as a tool, they will find you gone before you go."

Jonna gasped and tried to clear his throat. "I make my own choices. No one controls my fate."

"Indeed."

He swallowed as the loss of his wife stabbed his soul. His voice whispered, "Then it is my fault." His lungs wheezed. "I can't handle that."

Fists formed as his body shook. His knees slowly bent. With eyes on the ceiling above, he stared up. "What have I done?" Tears poured down his face. "It's my fault. It's all my fault!"

The words rebounded in his mind. His soul ripped in all directions at once. He existed nowhere, held together by fibers he could not understand--a mind separate from the body he wore.

The pain lessened, but with the loss of emotion, nothing felt real. All his memories, desires, and the love he had experienced faded into nothingness. There was no choice. He could not stay here and continue to exist.

The fibers pulled him back together. The pieces of his soul returned. Anguish filled his heart, but it opened the door so that he could live. Reality jarred back as his knees felt the floor.

"Be of good cheer, Jonna. All is not lost." The form beside him glowed with light, but he could not see it well through his tears. It touched him on the shoulder. "I give you a token of that promise. Learn to read its signs."

Something flared beneath the being's hand. The heat on Jonna's left shoulder increased and then faded.

"All creatures make choices. No one choice makes a decision come to pass. Your actions were part of the conclusion, not the cause."

"How--" He struggled to find his voice. "How do you know?"

The creature expanded in brightness. Shadows washed from the room.

Jonna's eyes clenched tightly shut.

"Because, I exist."

As seconds ticked away, the brilliance gained illumination until Jonna threw an arm over his face.

"Any last questions?"

A million questions hit Jonna's mind, but only one stood out. "What do I do now?"

The entity laughed. "You already know the answer. You choose."

A billion suns went off at the same time, and Jonna felt himself falling. He tumbled down a well of light with voices calling from all directions. Center. Focus. With blinded eyes, his hands reached out but could not touch anything. A single voice drew him near, and fingers touched his face.

Arta's voice became dominant. "You are the one. You will fulfill the prophecy just as I was instructed."

In a blink, the well of light vanished. He lay upon the bed with Arta on his left side. Lokke and Salma remained frozen exactly the way he remembered. "What happened?"

"You collapsed after reading the first sentence." She smirked. "But you *read* it."

"An entity came." Jonna's eyes tapered as he focused on the memories. "He. She." His head shook. "Whatever it was, it knows all about me."

"And that surprises you?"

In one swift movement, Jonna twisted, grasped her wrist, and pinned her down. His body hovered over hers. "What do you want from me?"

A smile lit her lips as blue crackles of energy erupted from her skin. She inhaled through her nose and let air slowly out through her mouth. "We are very good together."

"Arta!"

"Patience, young human." Her eyes became dark pools and focused on his. "While I don't mind a little roughness, I will not tolerate disrespect."

A prickling touched his skin. His fingers loosened one by one. His body rose to hover a foot above hers. "I told you I had the control, but you didn't believe me. Perhaps a demonstration?" With a turn of her wrist, he spun around and faced the hall that led to the pool. "Maybe a refreshing swim will make you more agreeable?"

With wide eyes, his body launched down the hall, reached the room with the pool, and plummeted toward it. He stopped only inches from its surface and hung suspended. Panic filled him. Had she been playing cat and mouse from the beginning? This didn't make sense.

His shoulder grew warm. The light-being's voice entered his head, "You have the power resist, but you must choose to use it."

146

How? He thought he was resisting!

Arta casually strolled into the room. "Then again, I do relent. No need to carry through with what I could obviously do." She waved back toward herself. His body shifted from above the pool, righted, and came to rest on one of the steps. The prickling sensation left, and her hold released. "There now, isn't that better?"

"So, I'm to be used as a puppet?"

"Puppet?" Arta laughed. "By no means. You are to free the people of this kingdom. That is foretold. That is what Mumin sought."

"Why would you want me to do that and chance losing your place in the kingdom?"

Her eyes shifted away. "You must ready yourself. What I do next, you will not like." She walked into the hall.

Frustration entered his voice. "Shouldn't I know what to prepare for?"

They passed into the bedroom.

"Why do that when it will be obvious when the time comes?"

He matched step with her. "Humor me."

She huffed. "Very well, but it will change nothing. The secret door by which we came will be revealed shortly. When it is, they will come for you." She bit her lip and looked toward Salma.

"And?" His hand grasped her arm firmly. "Arta, I must know."

Her eyes became sad. "The baby will die."

"No!"

The cover stirred. The baby stretched an arm up and touched Salma on the chest. A tiny yawn left its lips.

Bewilderment filled Arta's face. "How?"

Jonna whipped around the table and gently moved the cover back. The bright-eyed baby gazed up at him with a smile. The light-being's words rolled back. If Jonna could resist, so could his son, and his son did it by instinct. "Because, your spell didn't work on him." His eyes darted toward Arta. "Free the others, now."

Her eyebrows furrowed. "I told you, it will not matter."

From above, the grating of stone resonated down the stairs. "Free them!"

Her eyes briefly flashed fire before dipping to the baby. "I'm sorry. I cannot."

His shoulder warmed. "If you won't, I will. *Sta-sha-ta.*"

The baby touched Salma's chest as her eyes darted. "What happened?"

Lokke blinked and gawked at an empty bed. He twisted to see Arta beside him and jumped.

Footsteps hurried down the stairs. More than one set echoed.

Arta's sorrowful eyes took in Jonna. "I told you, it does not matter."

"You also thought they were all three frozen. You were wrong."

Doubt flickered across Arta's face, but her head shook. "It will not change the outcome."

"Want to bet?" Jonna drew the rune blade. The hum from the blade took on a life of its own. If he had to fight, he would. Although, he realized, the odds were not in his favor.

The footsteps came closer as he rapidly went over the spells he had learned in this land. Only those would be safe for him to say. Surely one of them offered a way to escape? What if it wasn't enough?

His eyes swept the room. On the bed lay the Zaman Dar. In one smooth motion, he sheathed the rune blade and stepped toward it.

Arta's voice strained, "What are you doing?"

"You told me to read the book."

Her steps matched his as she quickened to intercept him. "That was to show you the truth. You cannot read the book without preparation."

Jonna lifted it from the bed and flipped back the cover. The moving lines and curves on the page immediately appeared. His shoulder, where the light-being had touched him, became warmer.

Her hands lay on top of his. "Jonna, do not do this. Not now!"

His eyes narrowed upon her. "Then help them!"

Her jaw clenched as her eyes flashed flame. "Very well." She spun to view the three behind her. "I will make it painless. *Sva-mot-*"

Before she could finish, Jonna slammed into her from behind. She gasped as his weight knocked her forward toward the short table. Lokke dodged. Salma held the baby tight and slipped the opposite way. Arta mashed into the short table and went limp.

From the stairs, the footsteps reached the bottom. One of the two guards they had seen at Al-Uzza's quarters marched in first. His eyes darted to Arta, and he leaped in with drawn weapon. Behind him strode Mot.

Jonna dodged back, glared at them, and spoke, "*Sta-sha-ta.*"

Mot's eyes widened as he froze in place. The guard jerked to a stop with one foot on the floor, the other foot in mid-flight, and the dagger held before him. A second and third guard peered out.

Jonna's focus shifted to them. "*Sta-sha-ta.*"

Both froze in the entrance as they stood on the bottom steps. Other echoes came, but he could not see those that made them. Someone slammed into the unmoving guards, but the guards would not budge.

Lokke stepped closer to the guard with the dagger outstretched. "What did you do?" He backed up from the dagger and studied the man's arm from the side. With a finger, he pressed upon the bicep. The skin stayed flexible but the arm refused to move. "Okay, you really have to teach me this!" An arrow launched from the dimness of the stairwell. It sliced through the air and stabbed into the room's wall.

"Later." Jonna closed the book and slipped it under one arm. His right hand grasped Salma's free one, and he guided her down the hall toward the room with the pool. "I have an idea. Naida, the water sprite, helped me once in a pool to breathe underwater. If I can duplicate what she did--" A second arrow slammed into the wall beside them.

Lokke ducked. "Hey, wait for me!"

As they entered the round room, the illuminated water of the pool cast moving reflections on the ceiling.

Lokke raced up behind him. "How long will they be that way?"

"I have no clue." The room had one entrance and exit. Jonna stared at the water. The angle of the reflected light had altered from when he had first been there. "Get in."

Lokke stared. "Uh, Jonna, I don't know if you've noticed, but I have no magic in this world." He sheepishly grinned. "How am I to change into a frog?"

Jonna helped Salma into the pool. "You won't need to. You'll swim the old fashioned way by using your hands and feet." A frown dropped as his eyes centered on Salma. She had the baby in one arm and held the side of the pool with the other.

She gazed up at him. "How can this work?"

Lokke jumped in. A splash shot into the air and dowsed the others. The baby cried. Struck by water, Jonna gasped as he fell backwards while magic rainbow sparkles ignited around his legs. A fin formed as the book slipped from his grasp.

Salma jerked back from him, started to sink, and grabbed for the side; she missed. Down she plunged while fighting to keep the baby's head up.

With a roll, Jonna slipped off the steps and dropped beneath the water. His lungs breathed easily. He could see her gawking at him with wide eyes as she struggled to reach the surface. "It's okay, Salma. It's just a spell."

With a smooth stroke, he swam toward her. Air bubbles pushed from her mouth as she struggled to flee. He reached out and touched her.

She gasped as the water became like air, and her clothes became dry. With his free hand, he brought the baby down into the water. A smile lit its tiny lips. Terror gipped her face, "How?"

"We need to escape before the explanations."

Her head nodded quickly. She brought the baby in close.

The undistorted light beneath the surface lit the pool's walls and showed two caves: one sat dark with small flickers of orange, and the other glowed with outside light. He motioned toward the bright-lit cave, careful not to pull his touch from Salma and the babe. "We need to move quickly."

She stabilized the baby with one hand and used the other to hold his firmly. Jonna's fin turned them. All three caught sight of Lokke. His cheeks were puffed out with all the air he tried to keep in. His face turned a deeper red as his lips quivered with the effort to stay shut.

Jonna pointed to the surface. "Retrieve the book. I'll be back."

Lokke's head bobbed as he clawed his way up.

Jonna guided Salma through the bright-lit cave. The path twisted a little, but the cave stayed basically straight. Smaller passages led off as they swam through.

Fish flipped toward them, circled a few times, and dispersed. Plants that grew from the bottom of the cave waved in the slight current.

The cave ceiling vanished. A mirror-like reflection cast by the bottom of the water's surface replaced it.

Jonna's tail surged them upward. They broke through the mirror and stared at a rough, rocky outcropping. The cave roof rose above the water before it opened up to a large stretch of lake. He fought to shade his eyes as the day's setting sun glowed from just above the horizon.

To their right, steps ascended from the waves. Jonna helped Salma out of the water. "I'll be right back."

Down he dove, flipped around, and sped toward the pool. As he dodged a rock formation, his body circled wide. He caught the distorted image of Lokke with the book in his hands. Jonna's head burst through the surface. "Ready?"

Lokke jumped. "Don't sneak up on a half-demon like that!"

A groan echoed from the hall.

"Come on. Arta's starting to wake." He took the book from Lokke's grasp. As it slid down into the water, he noticed the book did exactly like the others' clothes; the water did not touch it.

Lokke's body slipped into the pool without splashing. He started to inhale, but before he could, Jonna grabbed his arm and pulled him under.

"Wait!" Lokke's eyes enlarged. "You may be used to this, but I'm not!"

Jonna chuckled. "Just relax, I'll guide you." He headed to the outside light but his attention was caught by a flicker of orange. The warmth on his arm grew. Was the light-being drawing him to the darker cave? He flipped his tail and turned.

"Hold it, don't tell me we're exploring? We need to get out, now!"

Jonna's tail flipped and sent them into the cave's darkness. "It will only take a moment." The light dimmed. His fingers touched the wall as he moved further in. Some parts felt smooth like glass; others felt fine-grained. It reminded him of the Ape Cave in the state of Washington. He and Stephanie had visited there and learned about its history. Could this city be built on volcanic rock?

Periodic flashes lit the dark. Jonna's pixie sight kicked in when the flashes vanished as well as a strange in-between vision. They changed direction around several rock formations until a hole appeared above them.

No steps led out as they broke the surface. The hole had worn over time. The air smelled dank and musky.

Jonna lifted himself up on the drier rocks and flipped his tail out of the water. Water drops flew in all directions.

"Hey, watch it!" Lokke climbed up beside him. "We are both trying to get up, you know."

As the fin dried, the scales fell off, and his legs returned. His stomach grumbled but he ignored it. Another flash of light from above brought his eyes to a rough cave entrance. A third flash showed part of a tall column.

He climbed toward the steep entrance, and Lokke followed. The closer they moved toward it, the warmer the air became.

Inside the second cavern, large, metal columns stood. They alternated in color. Between each pair stretched a thick metallic beam at least three hundred feet across. The columns stood in rows repeated until they reached the far side of the cave.

Above the columns, iron posts jutted down from the ceiling. When a spark of yellow lightning leaped between a pair of columns, it danced down the rows and bounced from one location to the next. Upon occasion, the lightning touched one of the iron posts and shot upward. Continuous streams of power would last from a few seconds to a minute or more.

Lokke grabbed Jonna's arm as Jonna stepped into the larger cavern. The half-demon's hand slipped off. "I don't like this."

Jonna stopped a few feet past the entrance. "This is how the gods create their power. It's similar to the old telegraphs which generated electricity from the earth."

The half-demon's head shook slowly. "That doesn't sound good, whatever a telegraph is. But it's not just that. I know that smell."

Jonna inhaled through his nose. Though at first he smelled nothing, a faint rotten-egg odor soon caught his attention. "Hold this." He handed the book to Lokke and crept nearer. The smell became stronger. The closer to the columns, the warmer the rocks felt when he touched them.

Within forty feet of the first column, he spotted small fissures in the floor. The rotten egg smell came from them. It made sense. That was how they generated power. They had harnessed the might of a volcano.

Movement caught his attention. Between two ridges lay a broad twisted gap that dropped deeper into the earth. Orange-red light reflected against the gap's walls. He shifted closer avoiding the fissures.

A flicker of fire caught his eye, but vanished before he could focus. Jonna heard the sizzle of something very hot.

A burst of warm air struck him. He leaned toward the edge of the gap and peered over its edge.

The orange-red glow of magma ambled its way through small streams as it vanished into dark corners. As the molten rock touched the gap's walls, the rocks that composed them would sometimes shift. Pieces crumbled to plunge into the lava. In return, super-heated rock shot up from the liquid to start its track back down toward the stream.

The ground beneath him shifted. He lurched back from the edge as cracks formed beneath his feet. The crackle of yellow electricity bounced across the columns and beams supported above his head.

A burning flicker caught his eye. The outline of a humanoid creature with wings burst into flame and vanished. Where the creature had been, a small flicker returned. It lifted up a rock and flew to a crumbling wall.

Jonna gaped as he settled a few feet from the edge. With only a visible blazing fist to grip the handle, a bucket floated through the air. As it approached the crumbling wall, a second flaming hand formed. While the first held the bucket, the second pulled out a trowel, dipped the trowel into the bucket, and came out with mortar.

The trowel spread the mortar over the rocks. Other flaming hands stacked rocks into place. Periodic humanoid outlines of flame ignited as the work continued. Once finished, the bucket turned toward his location.

As Jonna glanced at the entrance, Lokke waved franticly. Careful to avoid the fissures, Jonna worked his way back. A spark of flame burst beside him, and he felt a presence. Other flickers drifted in his direction. Whatever they were, he had caught their attention.

He hurried toward the half-demon and called, "We need to find Salma."

Lokke exhaled. "Thank the gods!" He scrambled after Jonna

as they headed for the small water opening. "I thought you'd never leave!"

"You don't like the smell?" Jonna chuckled as he sat down beside the pool. When his feet touched the water, colors swirled. The scales of his fin took shape as his feet, pants, and legs merged into one.

Lokke shook his head. "I know that smell too well."

As the fin completed, Jonna pushed off into the pool. "It reminds you too much of the Otherworld?"

"I don't mind certain places in the Otherworld," Lokke declared. "It's the lower depths I'd rather stay away from." The half-demon shivered.

Jonna treaded water. "They had stuff like this in the lower depths?"

With vigor, Lokke's head nodded as he slid in. "They weren't very nice either. Fabius' location was Paradise compared to what lay further down."

The flickers of flame assembled at the cave entrance above them. As a group, they headed toward the pool.

Jonna grabbed Lokke's arm without taking his eyes from the flickers. "Come on, we need to get back."

"I'm not the one--"

Lokke gasped as Jonna pulled him below the surface. He pointed a warning finger. "At least let me finish my sentence before you do that!"

With a laugh, Jonna dodged the formations and worked toward the main pool. As they slipped into the lighted water, a rainbow flash caught his eye.

He dove down until they skated just above the sandy bottom. His speed slowed to a crawl even though the lighted cave loomed before them.

"What are you waiting for?" Lokke pointed. "Let's go."

As they floated slowly near the lighted cave's entrance, Jonna pulled up short. Over the entry, a distortion of clear lines danced in horizontal and vertical interlaces just like a net. At the right angle, rainbow colors glowed.

"Trap," Jonna whispered. His finger traced the interlace but did not touch it. It lay on the walls of pool, as well as, the bottom. Only the light of the sun had given it away. With strong strokes, he followed the curvature of the pool back toward the darker cave. The interlace lay there, too.

His pulse quickened. "We can pass into the energy net but not out."

Lokke bit his tongue. "If they found us, Salma could be in trouble."

"I know, and so could my son." Jonna flipped over and stared up. A light glowed above the pool held by the hand of Mot. His nix hearing made out the words, "Feeling trapped, are we?"

Jonna shot toward the surface. Mot laughed. More humanoid shapes could be seen. Their knives were in their belts with hands on the handles.

Lokke reached over and grabbed Jonna's forearm. "Jonna, don't!"

"They only want me. That's why they were willing to kill everyone else. Take a deep breath and swim like crazy when I let go. You know the way to Salma. Protect her and the baby. Keep the book safe." He studied the interlace as he surged up. It covered everything. A foot from the surface, he twisted away.

Lokke's eyebrows rose. "Book? I don't have a book."

Jonna slowed. "In the cavern, remember? I gave you it to you?"

A smile crossed Lokke's face. "Oh, that book! Gotcha! I hid it behind some rocks."

"Lokke!" Jonna plunged toward the bright-lit cave. "There is no time for this. We'll have to find it later. Ready?"

Lokke nodded.

"One, two, three." He shoved Lokke away and touched the interlace.

Yellow rivulets of fire danced across his body as the net encircled him. His eyelids blinked out of control. His muscles spasmed, his fin stopped moving, and he gradually spun in a spiral. The interlace tightened around him as the water current carried him into the bright-lit cave. The net jerked his body to a stop, and Mot's men started to reel him in.

He tried to cry out, but the spasms would not let him. His nix lungs refused to breathe as his eyes lost focus.

Lokke swam unaffected about three feet ahead. The half-demon stopped and turned back.

Jonna's mind screamed. "Don't touch me! Go!" However, the words would not leave his throat. He tried to thrash against the interlace, but he had no control over his body.

Lokke grabbed Jonna's arm. Sparks of light shot out. Jonna's muscle spasms decreased, but only a little. The half-demon tried to pull him along.

The drag of the net increased. Lokke placed a second hand on Jonna's other arm, planted his feet on a rock formation, and heaved. He gained advantage, but not by much.

As the muscle spasms lessened, Jonna managed between rapid breaths, "Let-me-go!"

Lokke shook his head and grunted. By touching Jonna, the water breathing spell kicked back in. "Hold on! I can get you there!"

"Lokke, please!"

The half-demon stared at him and refused to loosen his grasp.

"If-they-have-me, they-may-leave-you-alone!" His eyes pleaded. "Save-Salma-and-the-baby!"

The net heaved back. Lokke's legs shook but held. Splashes hit the water behind Jonna.

Jonna spoke through clenched teeth, "Go! Quickly!" His body jerked out of Lokke's grasp.

Lokke snagged Jonna's shirt but it slipped from his fingers. "Go!"

Jonna heaved backwards as two guards swam up beside him.

They each grabbed an arm and forced him to the surface of the pool.

As Jonna's head broke into air, transparent lines hoisted him from the water fin first. He hung over the pool, and though the rivulets of fire decreased, he could not break free.

"Well now," Mot smiled smugly. "Who would have known this pool had fish?" The magical net spun slowly. Upside down, Jonna counted the guards at the pool's edge.

Footsteps sounded from the hall, and Arta came. Her eyes shot darts. "Where are they?"

Jonna felt the blood rushing to his head. "Where-are-who?"

"It is of no matter, sister," Mot grinned. "He's the one father wants, not the others. Besides, they can't possibly be far."

Doubt crossed Arta's face. "You don't know him."

"Bah," Mot shook his head. "You act as if he's a god. He's not. And if he's mortal, then he can die." He turned to a guard. "Father did not require him alive. Gut him like the fish he's become."

CHAPTER 13

The transparent net shifted. Jonna swung toward the side of the pool and shook his fin. Water drops fell to douse those below.

The guards attempted to dodge the drops. The man Mot had spoken to scowled as he pulled a dagger from his sash.

With the falling of the water drops, Jonna noticed the net's effect on him became less. As his fin changed into legs, he spoke clearly, "*Sta-*"

With matching pitch, Arta finished, "*sha-ta.*"

Mot and his guards froze. Jonna gawked. This was the first world he had encountered where a spell could be finished by a second person. Then again, she had done it earlier when she had redirected his destination.

Arta huffed, reached out a hand, and took Jonna's. "*Lys-ise-cho.*"

The net vanished. Her touch held him as he slowly rotated his feet to the down position. When level, his feet drifted to the floor. "I thought you wanted to kill us. Now you're helping me escape?"

"You being killed is not the plan." She glowered at him. "Now we both have to run." She spun toward the hallway. "Come on!"

His feet kept up with her. "I don't understand."

They reached the bedroom and dashed for the stairs. She took a deep breath. "Your understanding is not required."

Jonna jerked back. "I don't like the way you're talking to me. Either you explain, or we will part our ways."

Her body twisted toward him. "Are you blind? Can't you see the bigger picture?" Her fists formed tightly, her eyes squinted shut, and she gritted her teeth with a growl. "Your wife and child are going to die. Your friend is going to die. It is not a matter of if; it is a matter of how much pain they will suffer." Her eyes opened. "How many times do I have to say this? I tried to kill them mercifully, but you took that option away. Now, if we don't get moving, it may all be for nothing. Is that not clear enough?"

Jonna folded his arms. "No." His eyes scowled. "And until you explain what's behind this, I'm staying right here."

"Jonna, now is not the time and place!" She grunted. "Look, I know this can seem overwhelming."

"Not overwhelming, cryptic. I will not be manipulated, and I refuse to believe you know what will happen to my family and friends. You cannot know for sure, and I won't let you kill them."

A small stone bounced down the steps to land at their feet. "They're coming! We've used up too much time. If you don't trust me, fine. Just follow my lead until we get to a place where you can leave." She turned toward the stairs. "I wasn't supposed to be involved *like this* to begin with!"

He followed close. "If you broke your own prophecy, why can't I?"

They reached the first steps. The feet of others could be heard. "I did not break the prophecy. Though the details may vary, the outcome will be the same." Her eyes darted up the circular stairs. "We can't get past them like this." She pulled him into an isolated corner. "*Tvr-kor-ish.*"

The footsteps grew louder.

"We can't just stand here." Jonna reached for his rune blade, but she stayed his hand and placed a finger to his lips.

Three soldiers, with daggers in the front of their sashes and swords at their hips, hurried down the stairs. The last in line glanced toward the dim corner, but averted his attention immediately toward the bedroom.

Arta led the way up the stairs. Her steps were careful. Their sound was light. Her progress continued slowly until the secret door came into view. The dance of an electrical light shifted in the room beyond. Two guards stood with their backs toward the stairs.

"Carefully," Arta whispered.

One of the guards looked in their direction, but his eyes drifted to another part of the room.

Arta pointed to the doorway and walked carefully toward it. She continued in plain view, but neither of the two guards noticed. When she stepped into the hallway, she turned back and waved Jonna to follow.

Neither guard paid attention. As he walked, he studied his hand. It appeared perfectly solid, yet no one else noticed.

As they passed the other rooms, Jonna reached out and tapped her on the shoulder. In a whisper, he insisted, "I need that explanation."

Her voice remained calm though he could see her neck muscles tighten. "Now is not the time." They reached another set of stairs. Arta listened closely before she started up. At the top, she peered both directions, stepped out, and walked toward her room. "We need a place to talk. This spell is designed to redirect the attention. If they focus on our voices and are convinced we are there, they can see us."

"I have to know what you expect next before we continue."

"Don't you realize what's happened? There are three-hundred and sixty gods in this city, not to mention the humans, and we have just become the enemy." Her eyes went up to the ifrit head on the side of the wall. "A manhunt has not been declared. That's good for us. If it had, the stone ifrit's' eyes would have turned red. Once that happens, the runes embedded on them will attune to our bodies, and they will track us."

"Arta, just tell me."

Her voice rose despite the attempt to hide in a dark corner. "Look at us. You are a threat to all the gods, and they know it. I have helped you escape, and the punishment will be severe. If I tell you anything else--"

A strange calmness dropped over him. "You don't think I'll succeed."

"I don't--" She exhaled and took a deep breath. "I don't know any more." Her eyes kept watch. "I have to get to my room so I can think."

"That's the first place they will check. You're off script." His eyes brightened. "The prophecy is not going the way you thought."

They reached another corner, and she glanced back at him. "Ever since I absorbed the blue light, I just don't know."

"My magic." He nodded slowly. "My magic confuses the gods."

"Don't be so smug." She glared. "By not knowing, anything can occur."

"You can't remember?"

Her face flushed. "I--I can remember. It's just not--clear." She bit her lip. "Why can't I remember? I was taught its teachings my whole life."

Jonna listened to the hall in front of them but heard nothing. It felt too quiet. "What if what you were told was wrong?"

"One god would never lie to another. What would it profit?"

Jonna reached out and kept her still. "Unless it was in the prophecy."

She stopped and looked slowly back at him. "No."

"Why not? You were told the prophecy. You said it yourself." He leaned toward her. "Did you ever read it?"

"Of course not. It is forbidden--" Her eyebrows rose at the thought. "Forbidden for all but--Dagda." Her eyes looked far away. "Dagda always read from the scroll."

Feet marched into hearing from the hall they faced. Guards at the front of a line stepped into view. Mumin turned the corner. Jonna struggled to get his attention without the guards knowing. However, each time he stepped in front, Mumin looked the other way. He whispered, "Mumin?"

Mumin halted with a start. The spell redirected his gaze from them, but his head kept twisting back. He stared intently at the spot they stood. "You must be there." His body relaxed, and Jonna knew Mumin could now see him. Though the man's voice remained calm, his eyes showed pain. "You are well, I hope?"

Arta threw up her hands. "I warned you about breaking the spell."

Jonna ignored her and gave a nod to Mumin. "What's going on?"

"I fear your presence is required in the amphitheater." He bit his lip and averted his eyes. "Forgive your servant, goddess. You are both expected."

Arta stiffened her back. "On whose authority?"

Mot's irritated voice came from around the corner, "Our father's." He strode around into the corridor to face them. "You have done well, Mumin; our bargain will be kept." With a sneer, his eyes diverted to Arta. "Father knew what you would do. We were waiting for you to prove it."

Jonna's eyes bore into Mot's. "Then, it's time I met your father."

"No fear?" Mot scoffed. "This will be fun."

With a sober nod, Mumin pointed. "If you would come this way?"

The guards shifted formation to stand on both sides of Jonna and Arta as the two strolled into the main hall. Mot stayed in the back. Jonna felt the man's eyes on him. Mumin stayed in the front. The ifrit heads watched.

The corridor emptied out into a larger hall. The right wall curved. The left cut ninety degrees and then shifted straight forward again. On the left, doors and windows could be seen with signs carved onto hanging wooden planks. On the right, Mumin directed them to a curved wall with archways.

The archways had no joints or mortar. It reminded Jonna of the Roman Colosseum rather than a Greek amphitheater." Jonna's gaze caught the natural color of the walls. "It appears carved from the rock."

A long corridor stood out in front of them. Additional ifrit heads came into view. As Mot moved to the front, he pointed to someone hidden in the shadows. Shuffling could be heard. The bright light behind them cut off, and a dull glow replaced it. The glow dwindled as they walked. Periodically, closed entrances watched them pass. They stopped at two tall stone doors.

"Not carved." Arta shook her head. "Poured--Poured from the liquid fire that powers this great city."

"Silence," Mot's voice demanded. "Be pious before our father."

Jonna's eyebrows rose. On the dual stone doors before them a picture had been carved. It showed a lush spring with trees and grass. In the distant hills, a great palace stood with bulky columns and several floors. In front of the palace, a single man knelt with his head bowed as an glowing orb rose above the horizon.

The stone doors creaked as both pushed inward. Bright light replaced the dim, and the group marched into an arena.

Row upon row of bench-like seats surrounded them, but no one sat upon them. Thirty feet tall, a curved wall with small statues of ifrits placed on top, separated them from the seats.

They headed toward the opposite end where the curved walls extruded from a gigantic, uncut rock. In front of the rock lay a rectangular covered porch with ornate chairs placed under it on a dais. The dais, too, sat thirty feet up. However, stairs rose to meet the dais from the arena. A troop of guards stood at attention around its base. In the center throne of the dais sat a single man. A second man knelt in front of the first.

The seated man wore a purple cape trimmed in gold over a red robe decorated with intricate designs and symbols. A glitter of gold light bounced from a medallion that hung around his neck. The man's eyes watched them as they approached until they stopped at the base of the stairs.

The man who knelt rose quickly and waved to others unseen. Guards filed down the stairs to make a pathway between them. As the man who had kneeled reached the bottom stair, the guards in front of him parted.

With a tremor, Mumin bowed. "I have brought them, Muhammad."

Muhammad gave a nod. He turned toward Jonna and Arta. "Dagda wishes to see the stranger who has come to visit his great kingdom." His narrowed eyes took in Arta. "Along with those who invited him in."

The men guarding Arta and Jonna formed a half-circle to contain them. Jonna and Arta remained in the center. Dagda never rose from the throne. Mot slipped back toward the diameter of the circle. Muhammad stepped closer and paced around the goddess and the human.

Jonna's shoulder grew warm. His eyes watched Muhammad until the man moved from his peripheral vision. His gaze shifted to Dagda. "If you would like to meet me, why let your lackey do it?" Though the distance was great, Dagda chuckled.

Muhammad moved quickly in front. "How dare you! You only speak to Dagda at Dagda's request and with my permission." He threw a glance at the guards. "Take him to the pit. Leave him there until he is called for."

Two guards shifted from the circle and stood beside Jonna.

Arta looked up at her father. In a loud voice, she called out, "Father, I need to speak with you."

"And he will speak with you." Muhammad looked at Arta in disdain. "After which, you too, will be taken to a pit. You have betrayed Dagda."

Her shoulders rose as she glared back. "I have not betrayed him, and you will not speak to me in that way."

"Guards!" Two sentries moved beside her. "Escort Arta to the dais."

With a huff, she started up the stairs followed by her escorts. Muhammad swung back to view to Jonna. "Take him, now."

Anger flared in Jonna's mind. He spoke, "*Sta-sha-ta.*"

Nothing happened. Muhammad laughed and slowly turned toward him. "Magic is warded from here, or did you not know?"

The words 'their magic' burst into his mind. The idea teased him. It would be so easy to call upon his own magic from another reality. Wards or not, he knew it would work. He had done it in the land of the frost giants.

The loss of Elfleda and the world he knew stabbed into his heart. If he continued to break the majik partitions, all he knew could be lost forever.

The guards moved closer. The rune blade hummed on his back. That strange warmth rose on his shoulder. His frustration grew. The sneer on Muhammad's face burned within him as the prophet turned toward Dagda.

Azure energy crackled behind him. The rune blade's hum amplified. His feelings over the situation merged with the ability of the sword. From the blade's handle, blue electricity lashed out to strike the ground beside his escorts. The guards leaped away and tumbled into their companions.

"What is wrong with you?" Muhammad twisted toward them. "Take him!" The sword's hum grew. The prophet jerked back as blue lightning extended its floating fingertips. He stammered, "What is this?"

"Stop," Dagda's voice boomed. The guards moved back further, and Muhammad halted. "Invite the stranger to visit me."

Muhammad's jaw dropped, and his eyes narrowed. Though his voice stayed compliant, his eyes held scorn. "Mahdi Huri--" The tone became an insult. "Dagda requests to meet with you."

The rune blade's hum cut as Jonna`s anger abated. He nodded.

"Escort him," Muhammad scowled.

The guard`s eyes darted toward Jonna. They followed him up the stairs at a distance. The prophet brought up the rear. Dagda rose as Jonna advanced. Arta stood on Dagda's left.

"Come." Dagda motioned toward the back of the dais. "We

have much to talk about." His gaze centered on a part of the wall. "*Na-jwa-am.*"

Jonna frowned as the spell worked. He studied the area, but saw nothing different from down below. Muhammad had said that spells did not work here, and indeed, his had not. So how had Dagda done it?

A door slid back to reveal a hidden room with the strange glowing lights. No ifrit heads stared from the walls. Pillows sat on the floor around a long low table. Dagda motioned for them to pass through.

Jonna and Arta entered and turned to wait. When Muhammad, the last in line, approached, Dagda stopped him and whispered quietly. Muhammad's face gave nothing away. He simply nodded and turned back.

As Dagda joined them, he faced his daughter and Jonna. "Muhammad will wait for our return. *Na-jwa-am.*" The door closed behind them.

"Father," Arta's voice rose, "you cannot trust him."

Dagda smiled. "As I cannot trust you?"

Arta's face flushed.

Dagda's hand rose. "It is of no matter. Right now, I need to know about your friend." He turned to Jonna as he lowered his hand. "You seem to know about us. Why do we know nothing of you?"

"Why do you call yourself gods?"

The corners of Dagda's mouth lifted.

Arta's eyes narrowed. "We are gods. We--"

Dagda started to touch her lightly on the shoulder; azure lightning flashed out and crackled between them. His eyebrows rose as he jerked away his hand. "Hush, child." He waved toward an archway at the other end of the room. "Walk with me, both of you."

Jonna and Arta followed behind him as he led the way.

"Centuries ago, before the time that most remember, a single man stumbled in the desert." At the archway, he turned to the left. The glowing lights continued to show their path. "He was dying. For you see, his village had been raided. He had been severely wounded and was forced to flee."

A second room appeared decorated with gems mounted into the walls. Murals of cities had been painted on every wall's flat surface. Soft music played. A small chest sat nearby. Metal bicycle handles stood in one corner connected to the floor.

A pool of water, with steps going down, decorated part of the room with a lattice of flowers on one side. It fit Arta's description of the Najwa Miraj. In the center, water danced from a fountain portraying three women whose bodily shapes allured the eye.

"It was then he found a jar." Dagda pointed to a jar supported by the top of the fountain. The fountain's water shot up beside it. The water gradually travelled down the women's curves until it flowed into the pool.

"You see, the jar contained a marid, one of the most powerful jinn of our world. The jinn granted the man a wish in exchange for its freedom."

Arta walked slowly to the fountain. "I've never heard this story, but it--"

Dagda nodded. "The words of truth resonate in you. You feel it."

She nodded.

He turned back to Jonna, and a sad smile formed. "It would have been better had I died that day."

Arta turned toward him with shock on her face. "Father?"

Dagda took a deep breath. "We are not gods, my daughter, though many see us as such. The magic we have is a curse, not a blessing. It is a trap that we cannot escape on our own. It must come to an end."

"I know the prophecy." She strode to him. "I know what will happen."

A faraway look entered Dagda's eyes. "Do you?"

"Yes. You spoke of it when you read--" She glanced at Jonna before turning back to Dagda. "You didn't tell us everything, did you?"

Dagda shook his head. "When the end comes here, we will go to another. Do you remember?"

She nodded. "We will follow our future names."

His eyes focused on something else. "And another."

Her brow wrinkled. "We only have one future name."

His voice drifted further away. "And another."

"Father?" As her hand drew near his, blue electricity leaped from her. She jerked it back. Dagda smiled as his eyes followed the azure tendrils.

"The curse is forever, my daughter. We shall never know the sleep of death unless some other should grant us aid." His eyes turned to Jonna. "Will you help us break the cycle?"

Jonna swallowed. "You want me to help you *die*?"

Dagda nodded slowly.

"Father, no!"

"We were never meant to be gods, Arta. If the cycle is not broken, we will continue forever in a fate worse than death. Our kind will become more cruel and evil. We will destroy all we meet."

"But I don't want to die."

He started to touch her on the face, but the crackle of blue energy held him back. "You are young, Arta. Another lifetime will exist before our time to go, but go we must. If we are ever to find comfort in death, the cycle must be broken here."

Arta stared at the floor. "But I thought--"

"You know it is right, just as you knew the story was true. You are the part I did not speak of while reading the prophecy. You are the key to stopping the madness of what we have become. The knowledge of what and who you are flows through your veins. Immortality breeds boredom and evil. But to know your life is limited, to know that your time can be used up: that is the force that causes one to live, to love, to feel, and to be."

169

His body turned toward the small chest. With the twist of something out of sight, the top rose.

Glitters of light sparkled as Dagda reached in. A gold chain emerged. At its end, a medallion hung with a sun design that matched Lord Aubron's. Dagda turned to Arta. "Wear this as a symbol of my trust."

Arta shifted her long hair and tilted her head. Dagda laid it gently upon her, careful of the blue tendrils. She bowed.

He turned back to Jonna. "Will you help us?"

"I--" Jonna breathed out and studied both. "I don't know what to say."

"You will know," Dagda assured with downcast eyes. "When the time is right, you will know though it will not be easy." He looked to his daughter. "Take him to the pit."

"Hold it." Jonna stepped away. "One moment you are begging for my help and in the next want to lock me up? Don't I get a vote?"

"A vote to do what? You are a just person, Mahdi. I saw that in the amphitheater. You cannot kill another creature without provocation. You will not help us unless we show how ruthless we can be. I have asked for your aid. How else can you judge our actions and be honest?"

"But if you are not evil now, why would I do that before the time?"

"Amoral is just as depraved as evil itself. When any creature sees no difference between good and bad, it condemns itself."

Arta came forward and took his hand. "He's right. You are too good a person to help without just cause. You must understand what will happen if you don't." She gently pulled him to follow. His feet walked behind her into the previous hall.

"I don't get it. Why me?" He threw her a glance. "Why you?"

"It is the prophecy. Father already knows the outcome."

They reached the first room and headed toward the secret entrance. Jonna pursed his lips. "I want to read it for myself."

She stopped at the secret door. "Can you?"

"I read the first few sentences of Zaman Dar, didn't I?"

Her head bobbed slightly. "Unfortunately, we don't have time."

"Then make time. Let me see it. What if Dagda is only seeing what he thinks is true?"

"My father is a god."

"No," Jonna shook his head. "He is not. He said it himself. He was a man given god-like powers by a marid." Jonna's own mistakes came to mind, and his voice lowered. "Fallibility is a part of the human existence."

Doubt crossed her face, but her jaw clenched.

"You said it yourself, you don't want to die."

She slowly turned toward the hidden door. "*Na-jwa-am.*"

"Arta, listen to me!"

The door slid back, and a startled Muhammad turned to face them. Muhammad glared at both. "Take them to the pits."

The guards came forward with weapons drawn. The rune blade hummed, and they stopped. Arta pulled him forward onto the dais. "This is the way it must be. Come."

"You said that about my family." His hand jerked back, and in one smooth motion, his other hand slipped the rune blade from its holder. The blade glowed before him. Blue lightning pinged along its surface. "I don't believe you. Unlike you, I will not accept that fate."

Muhammad pointed and roared, "Imbeciles, stop him!"

Jonna backed toward the edge of the dais and glanced down as more guards reached the stairs. Thirty feet was a long way to drop. The alternative was to make a horizontal leap from the dais to the wall that protected the seats. The two were separated by twenty feet.

Arta strode slowly toward him. "Though my heart is heavy, I cannot let you do this." At the same time, Muhammad moved closer.

His shoulder grew warm. In slow motion, she raised her hand toward him and closed it slowly. An invisible hand grasped him around his waist. Its steel grip tightened. His lungs fought for air. He gasped, "Arta, no!"

A tear started down her cheek. "I am sorry."

Shallow breaths were all that would come as he struggled against the unseen foe. The idea that Dagda had used a spell on the dais floated into his thoughts, and his daughter did the same now, but he could not breathe enough to try it. His sight wavered. His arms felt weak. The warmth on his arm turned into a burn, and azure lightning lashed out.

Eyes wide, Arta buckled as her knees gave way. Muhammad struggled backwards through his men. The guards in front were shoved forward as those behind pushed.

Tendrils of blue energy whipped out to strike those too close. The smell of scorched hair and burnt flesh rose from the ranks of the troops. They scattered. A few raced across the arena.

A whisper entered his head as the shoulder warmth grew, "Do not leave her."

"Why?"

No answer came, but he knew his fate was tied to hers. With the rune blade in front, he pushed forward. The blue lightning thrashed out. His right hand held the sword while his left encircled the crumpled Arta. He lifted her up and hauled her to the edge of the dais closest to the seats.

It would never work. He could not hold his weapon, hold her, and leap the gap. Even if he sheathed his sword, to jump the gap would be impossible.

A dark opening about twenty feet square caught his attention. Its lip jutted out from the rock wall about nine feet down and offered enough of a ledge to balance on. If he could get to that first, a twenty foot drop to the arena floor would be much more palatable.

Voices from below caught his attention. A group of the guards assembled in the arena, but he could not see what they did.

A few of the dais' guards moved toward him. Wherever his eyes darted, the blue energy lashed like a whip. As they leaped back, Jonna sheathed his blade, secured the girl, and dropped over the side.

One foot landed on the lip of the dark opening; the other slipped. His leg trembled as his knee tried to buckle but held. Peripheral vision caught a pair of guards that raced into the arena with bags over their shoulders.

Jonna's free hand clawed for something to grab but found only the smooth surface of the dais' wall behind him. A clatter of metal and stone in the arena met his ears.

Beneath him, a guard's voice roared from just out of sight, "Ready!"

He shoved away from the dais side. As it propelled him, his second foot found its place on the horizontal lip. With quick steps, he started across like walking an I-beam. At the edge of his vision, he spotted a group of guards shifting into position. In their hands were bows and arrows.

"Aim!"

His feet raced toward the other side.

"Fire!"

Arrows shot toward him. The first ones struck the walls behind or bounced in front. A piercing pain wracked one shoulder, and his grip on the girl slipped. He shifted arms, but she tumbled to the right.

CHAPTER 14

Jonna fell into the dark opening. Bursts of flame lit around him and vanished. Glimpses of faces, not quite human, came and went. Arms grasped both sides of his body and held him floating in the air. His pixie sight tried to kick in, but it struggled against the flicker of the flames and the darkness that surrounded him. As his eyes adjusted to the variance, he realized how crowded this space really was.

The creatures were all around them. Not counting the two that held them up, ten others appeared, briefly, that is. For when the flames flickered out, he saw no creatures at all.

They lowered Jonna and Arta onto a rocky floor with three cave entrances. One led further into the rock while the other two went left and right. A burst of hot air came from the right and pushed past to the left. In that brief encounter, sweat trickled down the sides of his face, and his lungs labored to breathe.

A groan left his lips as the arrow that had pierced his arm grated against the bone. Arta lay upon the ground. He sank to his knees beside her. His head tilted forward as his lungs gulped air. Her eyes remained closed.

"Thank you." His voice echoed in the room and down the three caves.

The reply sounded like sizzling flames. "Shh."

He raised his head slowly to follow the sound. Next to his wounded shoulder, a humanoid creature with wings bent toward him. Fire danced across its body in brief starts and stops.

"Will you trust me?" In a brief glimpse, the fire rolled from its

174

shoulder, down the chest, and faded at the stomach. The rolling of the flames revealed female breasts.

He breathed as he fought back the discomfort in his shoulder. "Yes."

"Do not cry out, or the destroyer will come. Do you understand?"

Jonna gritted his teeth and nodded.

"Very well." She touched the shaft of the arrow.

His body clenched against the sharp pain, but he suppressed the groan.

"Very good." A black obsidian knife slipped from the darkness as she moved closer to wound. A flame erupted from her hand as the knife slit the shirt. Strangely, the flame did not burn his skin. She touched the area gently. "It is deep. Prepare yourself."

In the middle of a nod, a searing pain ripped through him. His muscles spasmed, his eyes widened, and his torso shot backwards. He collided with another who kept him from striking the rocks beneath him. Warm liquid flowed down his chest to mix with the sweat. He gasped out, "Thanks."

The creature shook her head. "It is not over; we must seal the wound."

One of her companions glanced at the center cave. He held out a thick, rolled up material and trembled, "Hurry, he may come at any moment."

Jonna stared at the roll.

"Take it."

With his good arm, he took it. It felt soft, yet rough and thick.

"Place it in your mouth."

Jonna had seen people bite on wood when no painkiller was available. "Why now?"

"Do it."

As his tongue touched it, a bitter-sweet taste emerged to fill his mouth. His nose tried to run, and his head felt light. A cool feeling drifted over his body. It filled every joint. Like a massage, his muscles relaxed.

"He is ready."

The creature that caught him held him still. The first leaned forward, pushed the skin tightly together, and breathed. A fiery mist enveloped the wound. Pinpricks danced as they penetrated the tissue. His breathing became shallow, and he drifted off to sleep.

~

The material beneath Jonna's right ear tickled. As his head turned to the left, his cheek touched a hand. His eyes blinked as the pixie sight kicked in.

First, the pulsing of a heart thumped methodically. The heat of the other organs faded into view in various shades of color. The skin rose to cover the organs. The chest lifted in shallow breaths. The clothes materialized in a duller glow. His mind clicked; Arta lay beside him.

The cool air crackled. His head rotated right as a blaze of fire ignited.

"For a human, you are very hardy."

He knew the voice. The being that watched was the one that had removed the arrow. She stared with black eyes encircled by flame.

"Why can I not see you except for the fires?"

"We can only be seen if we wish. Our bodies shift between planes."

He rubbed his eyes and then stopped. His arm ached but did not hurt. Warily, he extended the arm and rotated it. "You fade in and out of this reality?"

She inquired cautiously. "How is it that you understand?"

His throat felt parched. Though the cool air made it easier to breathe, it did not alleviate his thirst. A tiny drip met his ears. The source of it lay somewhere behind him. "Where I'm from, we research many things by theory."

"Theory?"

He bent his elbow and practiced moving the shoulder left and right. "Wow." He grinned. "Oh, sorry." His gaze turned back to her. "Yes, theory. We call it *science*. It is the way we learn how things work."

Flames ignited briefly as she nodded. "We use knowledge to maintain the foundation under the city. It provides the gods with their life force."

"I saw your technology. It uses the natural forces of the land to provide an electrical charge. It is quite impressive."

"Technology?"

"Constructions: the things you built down below."

"And electrical?"

"The fire generated from the earth that feeds the gods."

She focused on him, intently. As she did, flames traced a wing behind her. Her head tilted. "You have journeyed to the heart of the city?"

He nodded and yawned at the same time while he attempted to cover his mouth. "Yes. Who are you?"

"Shall I show you? Is it time?" The question was not directed to him, but to herself. "Yes." Her eyes focused upon him. "Please, do not be afraid. As you have seen, we only wish to help."

In a burst of flame, her entire body ignited. Jonna focused on her outline as she clothed it in fire. He noted the attachment of the wings at the back as well as the shapely form. She had no hair, but the feminine features were obvious. In the midst of it all, he spotted a glow lower than a human's heart inside her body. It pulsed with light.

"I am called Sitara."

He knew that face. Though not exact, it had similarity to the ifrit heads that warded the city. "That is a beautiful name."

Wonder entered her voice. "You are not afraid?"

He sat up with a slightly stiff back and smiled at her. Despite the material the creatures had given Arta and him for a bed, he had felt the rocky surface. Then again, it could be all the activity that been thrust upon him. "Should I be?"

"No." She pursed her lips. "Not of us. Only the Destroyer."

"And who is this Destroyer?"

"The great one. The one to whom the gods give sacrifice."

The Sight hit him. If she existed on multiple planes, could there be a link between his lost world and her other planes of existence? His voice offered, "I am called Mahdi in this world." He remembered the nixie, who had almost claimed him, but he had to take a chance. He had to prove he trusted her as she had trusted him. "But Jonna McCambel in my own."

A sense of recognition reached out to Jonna. She floated toward him speaking to herself. "And trust is returned." Her body descended to kneel beside him as she looked into his face. "I know that name."

His voice dropped lower. "How?"

"I know your world."

Hope flared. "I can go home." His eyes met hers. "My world exists!"

A slow, sad nod responded. "Perhaps, but not as you remember."

His heart fell. "Then I have truly changed reality." A tear formed in the corner of his eye and started down one cheek. Dagda's words rolled back into his mind. Was magic a curse? Was man intended to have such power?

Sitara whispered in a faraway voice. "Her name was Stephanie."

"Yes." Jonna wiped the tear from his face.

Her gaze became fixed. "Her name was Elfleda."

The pulse of the ifrit's heart grew faster. The illumination of the pulse became brighter. He leaned forward with furrowed brow. "Yes."

"Jonna," the ifrit touched his hand, "I am her."

The tingle of those long lost days flowed between them. It struck his heart to the core as shock filled his face. "No, this can't be real."

Her head turned to look up and away. "I remember a palace in the trees, a gateway by a well, a little boy--" Her gaze dropped to meet his.

He swallowed, and his voice fell. "Called home by his mother."

Her form became solid as the fire ignited. The glow of flames filled the room. She extended her hand to help him rise. "Do you believe me?"

The image startled him. How could this be her?

Flames of hope ignited in her eyes. "Tell me. I must hear the words."

His heart beat like a drum. It was impossible and yet-- His brow wrinkled, and he whispered, "I believe you."

A smile showed across her face. The flames in her eyes grew brighter. Her arms found his in a tight embrace, and their lips touched.

Sparks of light burst in all directions. Yellow clashed against blue wherever their bodies touched. Memories, not just of them, flowed into his head. In this life, in this world, she had an ifrit son. The boy had been chosen to be the next Destroyer.

Her body pressed harder against him. The longing to be one gripped his soul. She was really her. Though the body may be different, the spirit stayed the same. Elfleda, Stephanie, or Sitara, it did not matter by which name she went; it was her. He knew it, and he missed her with all his heart.

She reluctantly pushed him away. "But it cannot be."

He released as agony tore inside. "In this reality, we are not together."

Her head shook slowly. "We are of two different domains in this world. For us to stay together would bring great destruction."

"Why?"

Hot air wafted in. Her head jerked toward the right exit, and she shrank back. "You must stay here. I will return shortly." The flames went out.

Emotions tore at him. To come so far and yet be denied was more than he could bear. The ache in his arm felt worse, and the parched throat returned. To redirect his anguish, he sought to find the water.

With the pixie sight, he spotted the location of the drops. They distorted the energy signature of the rock wall behind it. A single palm caught the drops as they fell. The cool water soothed his dry throat but wouldn't wash away the inner conflict.

Arta moaned and shifted. When he turned around, she peered about with eyes wide open. He cleared his throat. "How are you feeling?"

She almost jumped out of her skin. "Mahdi?"

His body eased toward her. "I am right here." His hand touched hers.

She grabbed on tight. "Where is here?"

Leaning near, he asked, "You can't see?"

"No."

"At the moment," he frowned. "We are the guests of the ifrits."

Her body shook as she rose quickly. "We are in the abyss of the arena?"

"If you call that dark opening near the dais an abyss, sure. I find the creatures here--" His thoughts went to Sitara. "--friendly."

"They are not our friends, Mahdi. They are our slaves, and we are in their domain. We must flee at once; that is our agreement. *Jan-ros-shan.*" A ball of light formed in one corner of the room.

The warning Sitara had given rolled back into Jonna's mind. "Arta, I don't think that's wise. Sitara told me--"

She turned on him as her face went pale. "You know their names?" Her hand released his. "You have spoken with them?"

His head tilted with furrowed brow. "They are not here to hurt us."

Arta's eyes glared at him. "Then we have most definitely broken the covenant and you most of all."

180

With back straight, his voice became adamant. "I made no covenant."

She paced back and forth. "There will have to be a sacrifice. Three, maybe more. They may elect to make us witness the agony that unfolds."

His arms stopped her. "What are you taking about?"

Fear danced in her eyes. "We coexist by a treaty. The conditions are simple. We sacrifice one human once a year; they perform the duties to feed us our power. The arena is neutral ground. We are never to enter their domain, and they agree not to enter ours."

A roar echoed into the room. She whispered, "He knows we're here."

"Who is he?"

"Talumr, the Destroyer."

"And Talumr is?"

"A huge ifrit who jealously guards his people." Her hand latched onto his. "Come on, we have to get out of here!"

She dragged him toward the left exit and plunged into the dark. "*Jan-ros-shan.*" Light sprang up at the next turn. "I recall these tunnels. We are taught to study their layout as a child."

"Arta, if we keep leaving lights, he is bound to pick up our trail."

The roar moved closer. Hot air buffeted from behind. "He's coming!" She jerked to a stop at the tunnel's fork. "One way leads to the prison--there is a hidden passage we can open. He cannot break through. The other is a dead end." Her eyes grew larger. "And I can't remember which is which." She spread the fingers on her hand and watched the crackle of azure energy. "You have changed me, Mahdi. I am the same, and yet--"

Realization kicked in. "You are freed."

"What?"

"You are no longer bound to this city or the ifrit's energy."

Slack-jawed, she spoke, "If the connection to my father has been broken--" She swallowed. "I can die." Her eyes focused at her upheld hand. Her feet stayed frozen. The tunnel shook as something jarred its sides.

He pushed her to the right. "Move!"

The cave jagged, opened to an oval cutout, and showed a flat stone wall at the back. "Is this the dead-end?" In the middle of the room stood a huge stalactite suspended from the roof. Jonna cast, "*Jan-ros-shan.*"

Light flooded the room in a dazzling display of color. Minerals that had seeped down from above glowed in crystals of translucent hue.

She stared with narrowed eyes. "I--I don't know."

"Try it!"

Arta moved toward the stone wall. Runes decorated its surface.

"Try it!"

Her feet stepped back, and she spoke in a clear voice, "*Na-jwa-am.*"

Nothing happened. Eyes wide in fear, she turned toward him. Hot air burst into the room. Slowly, she dropped to her knees and pulled her arms around her. "It doesn't work."

Jonna stood by the entrance. Sweat ran in trickles down the sides of his face from the bursts of hot air. "What are you doing?"

"There is no hope."

"There is always hope. You can fight!"

"I am mortal."

He glared at her. "What do you think I am?"

Her brow wrinkled, and she whispered, "Yes, of course. How silly of me." Her eyes shifted to stare at the door. "If I die, I will simply be reborn as my future name--for the last time. The cycle has been broken." Her chin rose as she stood to her feet. "I am ready."

Jonna exhaled loudly. "That's not what I meant. Can't you cast a magic spell to free us while I distract him?"

"Distract who?"

He pointed down the tunnel as his eyebrows rose. "The ifrit, Talumr. Remember?"

"It will do no good."

"Fine." He reached behind and pulled out the rune blade as he marched past her toward the stone wall. Blue lightning crackled. "You want a hidden passage? I'll give you one!"

Both hands gripped the handle tightly as he swung back and heaved forward. The thought flashed through mind: what in the world am I doing? Metal struck stone; the vibration ripped backwards and tore through every muscle in his body. His head rang as the sound echoed in the room. He fell backwards and struck the ground. Blue crackles of power danced all around him. As the magic cleared, he stared up at the solid stone wall.

She kneeled down beside him. "I told you, it's a dead-end. It's protected by magic."

Jonna's head dropped back. "You didn't say magic."

"Didn't I?" She stood back up. "My mistake." Her eyes went to the door. "He's almost here. I can feel it."

With a shake of his head, Jonna rolled to his feet. A headache throbbed behind his temples. "How close?"

"Thirty feet, more or less."

He stepped toward the entrance of the cave and readied the rune blade with a two-handed grip. "Tell me when it's five."

"Twenty, fifteen, ten, now!"

Jonna leaped around the corner. The rune blade arced forward as his muscles became one with the weapon. A woman's scream met his ears. He jerked it to a stop. The backlash shot pain through his arms, and he tumbled against the side of the cave.

Sitara darted back. "I know that blade. Please, put it away."

He gasped in pain, "Arta!" A turn of his head showed the room empty. However, a slot had opened in the stone wall. "I am sorry, Sitara. We thought--"

"I have sent Talumr another direction, but he will know of the deception soon. I am afraid we only delay what must come."

The rune blade slid back into its sheath. Jonna caught his breath. "He knows the treaty has been broken?"

Sitara nodded slowly. "I am sorry. I tried to keep it from him but--" Her eyes narrowed. "--he knew."

"He is your husband."

"You knew?"

"I saw it when we touched."

She descended toward him and caressed his face. "He has blood lust, Jonna. He will not rest until you die. The treaty has been broken."

Jonna looked into her eyes. "I've lost you. What more can he take?"

Arta's voice called, "Mahdi, I found the passage!"

He turned to see Arta's head lean from the slot in the cave wall.

"It opened, not by magic, but by pressure placed in a pattern upon the runes. I remembered as you turned to strike. The way out is down here." She waved him to follow. "Hurry!"

"Sitara, I--" As his body swung back, the ifrit vanished. With a heavy heart, he walked toward the slot and stepped inside.

Lights had been placed to reveal rows of dark lines etched horizontally into the walls. Assorted weapons littered the floor. Bones in various degrees of decay lay upon the ground. Arta touched some of the runes just inside the slot, and the door sealed as if it had never been. When she started forward, he reached out and grabbed her arm.

She glanced back with a smirk. "Don't worry, it's safe. I've already been to the other end."

"I thought you said no one came into the ifrit domain?"

"No one from our city."

"Then how would they know of the runes and the hidden passage? If they were left to die, I assume sealed in, there has to be a reason."

Doubt crossed her face. "They--wouldn't know of the passage. Only we gods know."

"Exactly. Something was covered up."

She shook her head. "It makes no difference. We have a way out."

Her stride hastened, and he matched it. A glint of gold caught his eye. In what was left of rotten leather armor, he lifted up a gold pendant that matched Arta's. He palmed it and hurried to catch her. At the far end, Arta ran her fingers over another set of runes, and the wall slid open.

They stepped into a dim-lit room that smelled of old hay, mildew, sweat, and urine. Bars partitioned off both sides with chains rooted into the walls. Chamber pots sat in some corners while pieces of dried bone lay in others.

"This way." She pointed to a door past the last cage on their right. The echo of their steps bounced from wall to wall as they reached it. An ornate door ring pulled back the door without a hitch. As the door clanged shut behind them, barred windows revealed an inside view of the arena.

Voices called from outside the windows. Guards were positioned at every exit door. Jonna's eyes looked for an alternative route, but he finally sighed, "All roads lead to Rome."

Her eyebrows rose.

"In this case, it means everything goes through the arena."

She nodded and headed for the door. "Come on."

"What are you doing?"

"Father needs to be told what has happened. My people must prepare."

He grabbed her arm. "I didn't survive the ifrits to turn myself in."

Arta blinked. "Now I see it--that drive to survive against all odds. That's what father meant. That's why he wants to be mortal. That is--his gift to me." Her eyes softened. She kissed him firmly on the lips. "Thank you!" Arta pushed him away, opened the door, and strolled into the arena.

Jonna gaped. Guards hurried toward her, but she paid them no mind.

185

"Arta!" He rushed out to catch her as his right hand reached back and drew the rune blade from its sheath.

With a raised hand and head held high, she spoke, "*Sta-sha-ta.*" Their bodies froze in midstride.

Slack-jawed, Jonna glanced at the medallion in his grasp and focused on a troop of guards. "*Sta-sha-ta.*" The whole troop stopped suspended on one leg. Jonna grinned and hurried up the stairs.

Arta opened the hidden door and disappeared inside. He raced in behind her, turned down the hall, and skidded to a stop inside the Najwa Miraj. He heard the words, "Father, take my hands."

Jonna shouted out, "No, wait!"

Azure lightning leaped. Yellow clashed with blue. An aura of orange glowed as their hands touched. Vines of jagged light shot out.

Arta cringed against the pain. Her father gasped as the azure overcame the yellow with such force, his knees buckled under him. As the energy crackled away, Dagda leaned back against the wall. The man's lungs labored with every breath. Sweat trickled at his temples. His hand grasped his chest over his heart. "I'm fine. Give me minute."

Arta's hands shook as she turned toward Jonna. Her body slouched, yet her eyes glowed with delight. "I am the key. I am part of the prophecy." Her body fell toward him. The rune blade clattered to the floor as he caught her in mid-fall and lowered her carefully. He twisted toward Dagda. "How is she the key?"

"It is by her that the spell is broken."

Jonna's voice turned hard. "No, the spell was broken by me."

"You are the catalyst. She is the action."

"Look at her."

Dagda continued to focus on him.

"Look at your daughter!"

The man's eyes gradually dropped to view the unconscious Arta.

Jonna's face filled with fury. "Does it look like she can handle this?"

Dagda closed his eyes and shook his head. "She will be fine."

"She will be dead if she does that again. You have not succeeded in just gaining freedom. You have also hastened her death."

"If that is what must happen--" Dagda opened his eyes. "--so be it."

Jonna's jaw dropped. "You do want to die!"

The man's head slowly nodded. "Our time is over. We must pass on to our next existence without the bonds of eternity."

"You are insane." In one smooth motion, Jonna rose and caught the handle of the rune blade. It slipped easily into the sheath on his back. "And I will not be a part of it." He turned toward the exit and hurried down the hall. The sound of many voices met his ears as he stepped onto the dais. In the arena, Muhammad clapped his hands.

"You have done well, Mahdi. It is time for the final show."

CHAPTER 15

Jonna's voice became hard. "I do nothing for your entertainment."

"Ah--" A grin crossed Muhammad's face. "But you will. Bring them!"

To the right of the dais, guards emerged through an entrance. Mumin, Lokke, and Salma pushed forward at spear points. Salma held the baby's wrappings close to her chest.

Mot strode from a second entry and took a stance by Muhammad. With shoulders back and a sneer decorating his face, he stared at Jonna. "In another life, we might have been brothers."

"Never. Your whole family is insane."

A roar erupted from beside the dais. The arena guards backed toward the exits. Muhammad raised one eyebrow. "You broke the treaty, Mahdi. You entered the ifrits' domain. You will now pay the price with your life."

Jonna's eyes jerked toward the ifrit's abyss. Wisps of fire rose from the darkness. Hot air swished. Sweat formed upon his skin. The bursts grew in strength with each whoosh from the shaft. He rushed to the edge of the dais and hollered toward his friends and family, "Run! Flee!"

With no guards, they turned quickly. Mot shouted. *"Sta-sha-ta!"*

All three froze. The baby cried out. Muhammad's eyes narrowed as he listened. "What is this?" The man strode toward Salma.

A fiery claw reached up and grabbed the lip of the shaft. Burning eyes of coal looked up at Jonna with a face filled with hate.

Jonna glanced toward Muhammad. *"Sta-sha--"* Something slammed into his back. The spell did not complete. His body plunged forward, and his left hand released. The medallion plummeted into the arena.

A gasp escaped as his forearms struck the floor of the dais. The voice of Dagda called behind him. "You think we're insane? What will you be when you watch those you love die?" He stepped to the right of Jonna and nodded toward Talumr. "Take them."

"No!" Jonna shoved off the floor and twisted toward Dagda. One leg swept out to knock Dagda's legs from beneath him. The man fell face-forward toward the edge, but he caught a pillar to stop his fall. Jonna's left arm swung back and met the force of Dagda's left.

"Did you think I would be so easy? I, too, know fighting skills." He thrust Jonna back into a pillar as he pulled the dagger from his belt. The point touched Jonna's stomach. "Look at them."

Jonna's eyes remained on Dagda's face. His jaw clenched.

The king bared his teeth. "Look at them!" He forced Jonna's head to view his family and spoke directly at Jonna. *"Sta-sha-ta."*

Dagda's lips curled as he pulled back the knife. "I have made sure you will see and be unable to help. You will know what it's like to be immortal and feel your own soul die." The dagger slipped into its sash, and he pointed toward the arena.

Talumr dropped to the arena floor. The creature roared. His feet sent sand in all directions. Flames engulfed his body.

Muhammad moved beside Salma. "Wait." His hand shot up and stopped the ifrit. "There is something I must check." He stared with raised eyebrows as the baby's arm waved above the wrapping. "No!" He twisted toward the dais. "Dagda!"

The image of Jonna bursting forth from the womb after Esti's shoulder bite flickered in front of Jonna's eyes. With animalistic rage he did not understand, Jonna struck Dagda in the solar plexus.

Dagda's lungs halted in mid-breath as his body shot backwards. The pillar stopped him. His eyes were wide as his head whipped back and hit the pillar with a thud. The king sank to the floor.

Without a pause, Jonna leaped off the dais and struck the top of the ifrit's head with a hammer-like fist. Talumr bellowed, and the flames which Jonna had not felt before abruptly became hot.

He shoved away as Talumr twisted. His body launched to land mere inches from the dais' wall. His hands, where he had touched the ifrit, radiated throbbing heat. Despite the pain, he reached behind his back and pulled the rune blade. A glint of gold caught his eye. The medallion he had dropped lay half-buried in the sand. His left hand grasped it.

Flashes leaped upon the sword as Jonna rose to his feet. Thin tendrils of light sparked upon the ground. "There is only one way this will end, Talumr. Ask yourself if it's worth it."

Talumr's hands changed. Longer claws grew from the flames that encircled them. The ifrit stepped toward him and swiped. The rune blade rang against one of its claws.

The air around Jonna became hot as he labored to breathe. The wall of the dais became an oven reflecting the heat. Sweat ran down his face. The great shaft that led to the ifrit domain stood behind him. In a burst of inspiration, Jonna whispered, "*Tvr-kor-ish.*"

Talumr sliced the air above Jonna's head and grated his claws across the shaft's wall. Great gouges were ripped out as the stones complained. A fury of debris struck the ground.

Jonna dodged and edged closer. The hair on his arms gave off a terrible stench as it burned. Despite gasping for breath, he stepped forward and drove the rune blade into Talumr's foot.

The ifrit howled. As his foot rose off the ground, Jonna dove under, rolled, and stood up behind him. He threw the medallion over his head, grasped the rune blade with both hands, and sliced across the back of the ifrit's right leg.

Talumr twisted, roared, and slashed. The ifrit's fiery claws passed within inches of Jonna's skull. The heat of its body intensified. The sand that touched it turned to glass. Jonna fell backwards as the heat zapped his strength.

Muhammad shouted behind him and moved further from Jonna's group. "Where is he? Guards! Find him!"

The ifrit rose into the air, unable to stand without pain. As the air cooled around Jonna, Jonna's eyes looked up.

The Destroyer scanned the arena. As he did, bursts of flame from other ifrits materialized in splashes across the sky. The other ifrits were watching.

Jonna crawled toward his friends along the base of the arena's wall. His lungs labored to breathe the cool air. His skin radiated heat and agony. The ends of his hair smelled burnt.

The gritty sand of the arena floor, though hard-packed along the wall, stuck to his sweaty skin. His eyes spotted Muhammad clutching the baby. With a concerted effort, he rose to his feet beside Lokke and whispered, "*Sta-sha-ta*. Hold still, my friends."

Lokke blinked but did not move. Mumin did the same. Salma inhaled quickly as she realized no weight lay in her arms.

"Do not move until I give the word. Muhammad has the baby."

Salma's eyes narrowed though she did not turn her head.

"Have no fear, Salma. I am going to get him back."

Lokke shook his head slightly. "No, Jonna. Let us."

Mumin mouthed quietly. "I agree. If you try that, you'll have guards and an ifrit to deal with. Maybe even Mot as well."

Jonna's eyes darted to his son, held in the arms of his enemy. His muscles clenched. "I trust you all."

With quiet steps, he walked slowly toward the center of the arena. His path bypassed Muhammad, and he felt his shoulder warm. When he was ten feet in front of the man, he whispered, "I am here, Muhammad."

Muhammad jumped. "Where?" His head turned this way and that as he walked backwards.

Jonna followed, forcing him toward Mumin, Lokke, and Salma. "Where do you want me to be?"

Muhammad's hand slipped to his belt and withdrew his dagger. "Show yourself, or I will kill the child. The sacrifice must be made."

They neared Jonna's friends. "But not today."

Mumin snatched the dagger from Muhammad's hand. Lokke grabbed his throat and pinned his arms. Salma took the baby and drew him close. With a wrinkled brow, she checked the child. It cooed up at her.

The edge in Jonna's voice could not be missed. "If you say one word, if you draw any attention at all, my friends will kill you. Do you understand?"

A whimper escaped Muhammad's throat.

"Good. I have an ifrit to deal with." His gaze drifted up.

Each time Talumr circled, his irritation grew. His wings beat hot air down in furnace blasts. His eyes darted to every corner. His deep, otherworldly voice boomed, "Where is he?" His gaze enveloped Mot. "In the absence of your father, show him to me or take his place."

Mot's eyes narrowed. "How dare you threaten me! I am the son of a god!" His face flushed, and he jabbed a finger at the sky. "*Sva-mot-uka!*"

Great winds whipped into the arena. From all four directions they came. Bits of sand buffeted the walls.

Salma turned to protect the baby. Muhammad struggled, but Lokke tightened his grip. Mumin threw his arm up to protect his eyes. Jonna felt the sting across his skin. Mot laughed.

The four winds became one as the torrents of air spun together. With a wave of Mot's hand, the wind launched itself toward Talumr.

The ifrit snorted. "Your magic is no match for mine, god. We are the ones who give you your power by marid decree." In a mighty clap, the spinning vortex vanished. "Now, it is my turn."

Talumr dove as Mot twisted to run. The god slammed into a stone door. His fist beat upon it as he shouted for the guards, but it did not open. With eyes bulging, he turned to face the ifrit. He spat at the ground. "I curse you and all your kind!"

The ifrit dropped lightly to the sand, though it kept its right leg suspended. A smile creased its face. "So be it."

In a burst of fire, Mot screamed. His hair burned, and his skin blackened as the heat became tenfold. The flesh turned to ash and floated to the sky as the bones fell upon the sand.

Talumr inhaled deeply, savoring the aroma of ashen flesh. "It is done."

Jonna's voice came from behind the ifrit. "Not quite."

The ifrit spun to face the voice. "Where are you, coward? Why do you hide instead of face me?" His gaze switched to Jonna's loved ones. A cruel grin spread across his face. "Yes, perhaps the offense is so grievous that more than one sacrifice is required." It flapped its wings in anticipation.

The image of Sitara floated in Jonna's mind. He had seen the source of the light that beat within her. However, how could that help him here?

His pixie sight did not work in bright light, yet from the dark recess of power he had used to attack Dagda, another sight came.

He focused and ignored all but the flames. He had to concentrate; he had to believe. His shoulder burned. The rune blade hummed. The tendrils of azure light leaped around him. Vulkodlak and pixie sight merged.

"What is this?" Talumr gazed at a glowing spot on the sand. "Has the little bird finally revealed himself?"

Talumr's insides formed in front of Jonna's eyes. From soft and dim the image grew darker like a photographic negative. Internal organs shaped. The reproductive and digestive systems became separate parts. Each organ shimmered into view. The stomach churned, the lungs moved, and the heart beat. Yes, the sparkling pulse of life beat exactly like Sitara's, and he knew where to strike. With both hands on the rune blade, Jonna jumped and thrust.

Blue electricity sparkled as the sword plunged through the outer hide. Talumr gasped as Jonna's weight slammed into his chest. Rage filled the ifrit's face.

Jonna felt great fiery claws rip across his back. His clothes tore, and nails pierced his lungs.

Talumr staggered backwards and slammed into the stone doors.

A rumble hit the arena. The very foundations shook. The burn in Jonna's shoulder glowed with a bright azure light.

Yellow met blue in a radiance that made the sun look pale. The crackle of energy tore into the ifrit's body.

In rage, Talumr slurred his words as liquid fire rolled from the corners of his mouth. "Your widow will morn this day--human."

The air heated around them. Sweat stung where the skin bled. Unable to breathe deeply, Jonna struggled to answer back. "So--be--it."

Two arms clasped tightly to him, and the voice of Sitara whispered, "I am here, my love."

The heat no longer touched him. A bubble of comfort eased his pain despite the slowing of his heart. The coolness of a fresh spring day flooded into his veins. Air found his lungs. How was she protecting him?

The electricity from the sword continued to build, eating into Talumr. "Flee," he begged. "You must flee while you can!"

She gripped him tighter. "I will not leave you to die."

The azure tendrils raced along Talumr's body. They swallowed the fire of his essence. Jonna's hand gripped the rune blade tighter. "Love, if you stay, my magic will destroy you, too."

A fiery tear fell down her cheek as she whispered with loving embrace, "So be it."

The warmth in his shoulder grew. The Zaman Dar's words stirred his mind. His lips mumbled, "Nan ac'vayu nahwaena eka ava ac'el ac'ava yish."

A gentle breeze circled the arena, and he felt a presence. It consumed heat and cold, light and dark, until nothing else existed.

Strength coursed through his veins. His heart steadied. As the air thickened, it distorted the view of all but the rune blade stabbed into Talumr's burning heart.

A voice boomed. "You knew this sorrow would come."

"She will die," Jonna pleaded. Tears rolled down his cheeks. "I can't see her destroyed again. I can't lose her a second time." Sympathy flowed to him, but he knew the end would be the same.

"The body is fleeting, but the spirit lives on. You can't save her Jonna; she will not release you."

"Why?"

"Must you truly ask?"

Agony tore through his heart as he fought the growing lump in his throat. "No." His voice dropped. "But it doesn't stop the pain."

"Nor should it. That is true love."

Jonna laid back his head and screamed. The sound tore through the nothingness until his eyes dropped to the rune blade again. Life pulsed through it. The blue tendrils that had taken Talumr's body inched their way toward Sitara. He could breathe easily. The weakness had vanished. He turned under her limp body and looked into her eyes. Life still existed there.

"Sitara, look at me!"

A smile curled her lips as a fading glow lit her eyes. Her voice rose in excitement. "You live?"

"And so must you!"

Her head shook almost too slowly to see. "My life for yours, love. My death for your healing."

"No!"

Her eyes slowly closed as her voice dropped to a whisper, "If you find your way home, you may see me again." Her body turned translucent.

"No, God no!"

In the tiniest flicker of an orange flame, she faded away.

Voices caught his ear, and Jonna rolled from off the ifrit. Mumin, Lokke, and Salma raced toward him. Lokke got there first.

"I told them!" Lokke cried out. "I told them you would make it!" His hand clapped Jonna on the back. "That's how the game is played! Yeah! But uh--" He caught sight of Jonna's ripped shirt and leaned near him. "Do you have to play it so close next time?"

Jonna's eyebrows rose. "Next time?"

"Yeah, well, you know. If I know you're going to win, I might just lay down some wagers." Lokke grinned.

Jonna's face fell. "Lokke, I didn't make it."

Lokke stared with one eye closed. "Say that again?"

Mumin pulled up beside him followed by Salma and the baby. Sorrow showed upon his face. "I'm sorry, Mahdi. Muhammad got away."

Jonna's brow wrinkled. "Was any one hurt?"

"No, but--"

Lokke elbowed Mumin and pointed at the baby. Jonna's fingers adjusted the baby's wrap, and he gazed into the eyes of his son.

The tiny hand reached up for his. Jonna touched it with his finger. The brightness of the sparkle cast colors all around. The baby cooed.

Stillness dropped. Time refused to move forward. The cry of a child met his ears, and the baby's irises enlarged. Jonna caught the flicker of flames just beyond the feet of Talumr. He broke the connection to the baby.

One by one they appeared--ifrits standing with lowered heads. Salma pulled closer to Jonna and secured the baby in her arms. The arena filled to capacity. The ifrits' flames littered the sky. Lokke's eyes darted several directions at once. A single ifrit stepped forward. "Why?"

The ifrit appeared young. He stood short in stature with thin arms and legs. Jonna inhaled and could not meet his eyes. "I'm sorry."

Lokke elbowed him. "Don't say that! He was going to kill us all!"

The ifrit glanced at Lokke and shook his head. "Not him. Why her?"

Jonna focused on his face. "You saw what happened?"

The boy nodded as his eyes looked down with sorrow.

"She gave herself so that I could live."

Mumin glanced curiously at him. Lokke's eyebrows rose. Salma touched the slashes on his shirt. Her eyes opened in wonder.

Murmurs traveled in a wave through the ifrits. The boy stepped closer. "If you are to honor her memory, you must complete the task."

Jonna blinked. "What task?"

"You must free us. You must destroy the gods."

Jonna's mouth set in a grim line. In a hard voice, he spoke, "Show me."

The crowd of ifrits parted to open a way to the dais. Jonna leaned back and pulled the rune blade from Talumr's body. The body shimmered, the tiniest flame erupted, and it vanished.

He turned away. The boy walked beside him as those with Jonna followed. Jonna asked, "Can I know your name?"

The sideways look the boy gave reminded Jonna of Sitara. "As she believed in you, I will trust you, too. I am called Devamilu."

Jonna chuckled. "That's funny."

The young boy's brow wrinkled. "Funny, why?"

"If I remember the words correctly, it means *god is gracious* though from two different language roots."

Devamilu squinted. "Roots?"

"Sources."

Though the boy nodded, Jonna knew he didn't get it. He still couldn't help but grin. "My name means that, too."

They reached the steps of the dais. No guards appeared to stop them.

"This way." The ifrit flew to the top and waited for them to climb. Dagda's body had vanished, but the hidden door lay open. They followed the boy in, down the hall, and stopped in the room called Najwa Miraj.

197

Drops of blood were visible around the room. They originated next to the fountain. A wet footprint pointed toward the lattice.

Arta still lay where he had placed her. He reached down but found no physical damage. Her pulse remained steady and slow. His gaze came up to the others. "She lives, but is weak."

He rose and inspected the lattice. The blood trail rounded the corner. If Jonna remembered Arta's description correctly, there were stairs hidden behind it.

"Here." Devamilu pointed to the jar that sat on top of the fountain. "That is the home of the marid, and we must get him back inside."

Jonna turned from the lattice to the fountain. "If he's not there, then where is he?"

A tiny flame erupted in the boy's eyes. Jonna rubbed his own shoulder as it grew warmer. The boy extended his hand. "If you trust me, come."

His hand grasped the boy's. The room's air shimmered. Lokke seized Jonna's left shoulder. "You don't think you're going without us, do you?"

Mumin grabbed Lokke, and Salma grasped Jonna's right arm. A red flame leaped from the boy.

Fire danced upon them. Though it did not burn, they could feel the heat. Where it touched Jonna, the blue energy met it to create an orange glow. Devamilu watched the phenomena closely. As the flames completed their purpose, the boy's wings beat the air.

They descended through the floor. Rock, stone, or mortar, it did not matter. Their bodies passed into dungeon cells, caught strange looks from the prisoners, and dropped into the caverns beneath.

They emerged on a ledge overlooking the strange columns of metal which supported the large beams that connected them. Yellow electricity raced from one to another, jumped pairs, and zapped the iron bars which stabbed down from the roof. The glow of magma lit the large crevice that cut down the center of the cavern between the pairs.

Devamilu pointed to the magma as the spell ended. "He is here."

All released Jonna except Salma. "The magma is a marid?" His brow rose as the liquid frothed. "You want that in a small jar?"

"Not the magma, the person."

Ifrits worked at repairing the channel. As Jonna looked closer, Devamilu adjusted the angle of his hand.

In the cavern's center, the crevice widened out. Magma flowed around a large, flat area on which stood a pyramid. A series of large rocks formed stepping-stones through the magma from both sides of the crevice. A man walked out, gazed up for a moment, and stepped back into the pyramid.

"So you want the man to fit into the jar?" Jonna shrugged. It was possible. In his world, genies lived in bottles--at least in myth.

"He is not a man," Devamilu warned. "He is a being of great magic. He will say and do anything to trick you."

"Why does he stay there?"

"The magma contains him. Only by a human can he be sent to his jar."

Lokke leaned near him. "I don't like this." His eyes darted nervously. "I didn't like it before."

Devamilu turned his head toward Jonna. The flames in his eyes burned a little brighter. "You have been here?"

Jonna nodded. "However, I never saw the building or the man."

Salma's hold tightened. "There is something not right about this."

Mumin shook his head. "Mahdi, I agree with the others. This feels wrong. Earlier, when Muhammad escaped--"

The ledge on which they stood shifted. They all scrambled back.

Devamilu floated a foot off the ground and hunched toward them. "You must descend to the building, touch the man, and speak the words: 'ein-dy-mon'. If this is not done, Sitara's death will be for nothing."

The words struck Jonna's heart. He closed his eyes, clenched his jaw, and took a deep breath as he recalled the fading of Sitara's life. "Alright."

Salma clung tighter. "You must not do this. There is great danger."

He met her eyes, and his will focused even more. "Don't you see? I must do this. If the baby is to be safe, I must stop this evil creature."

Devamilu pushed. "Hurry, before he knows what has happened."

Jonna nodded. "Keep them safe until I return."

The ifrit pursed its lips. "Of course. Sitara would do no less."

The ledge angled steeply. Jonna slid from Salma's clutch and descended down a narrow crevice. Rocks shifted and rolled. He slowed to test each step for stability.

The young ifrit appeared in the air before him. "Hurry." His eyes darted. "The Time of Change is coming!"

The words jabbed Jonna. "Do I look like I'm on a Sunday stroll?"

The ifrit's eyebrows rose.

"Never mind. If you're in a big hurry, why don't you fly me down?"

Devamilu's eyes cut toward the pyramid. "I cannot move too close. If he sees me helping you, the element of surprise will be lost."

Bursts of flames ignited as ifrits fixed another crumbling edge. Jonna continued his careful pace.

Devamilu huffed as he descended beside Jonna. "Very well, I will take you as far as I can." He reached out. "Take my hand."

Jonna's shoulder grew warmer. Red flames danced out as Jonna's hand took Devamilu's, but unlike the first time, the spell stung. The energy of the rune blade surged toward the boy. The moment they touched the ground, Devamilu jerked his hand away with lowered eyebrows.

"Are you okay?"

"Yes," the boy hissed though he quickly contained it. "Go, quickly."

Jonna glanced up. He could see the three from above watching intently.

"Go!" The boy rubbed his hands together and licked his lips. "I will take care of your friends. You have my word."

The heat wafted up in bursts as the magma shifted below. Jonna made his way along the edge. He passed the columns of metal and listened to the electricity crackle across the connections.

The first of the stepping-stone paths came into view. Sweat trickled down his face. His eyes spotted a narrow cut in the wall.

The rock pressed from both sides, but he squeezed through along the downward slope until at last he stood upon the first rock. At roughly six feet in diameter, it felt stable under his feet.

The hot air filled his lungs. The smell of rotten eggs almost overwhelmed him. He leaped from the first to the second rock.

From the magma, a bubble burst. Liquid fire shot into the air. A flame erupted. As the liquid descended toward him, an ifrit appeared with his wings outstretched. The liquid rolled harmlessly off its back.

"Thanks!" He wiped the sweat from his eyes.

The ifrit shifted to full flame. "You should not be here."

Jonna leaped to the next rock. The rotten egg smell grew worse. He coughed. "I have come to put the marid in his jar." His feet leaped again and landed on a third rock.

The ifrit followed and shook its head. "You have come to die. You will not escape once you enter."

Jonna leaped again. "I have to end this." His eyes studied the next landing. The distance was further than the others, but the rock was much larger. "Your people must be free."

With an extra step, he leaped. The front of his foot landed, but the back did not reach solid ground. He lunged forward and twisted to drop on the rough surface. On his back, he stared up at the ifrit as his elbow stung.

The ifrit hovered with unblinking eyes. "You have been warned." The flames faded, but the beating of the wings could still be heard. Jonna rose to his feet as other wings gathered toward him. A look back showed he had maneuvered quite a distance across the flow.

Other voices met his ears. "Leave while you can. Do not go onward." He leaped, landed well, and spotted the next rock. Only two jumps left.

Many voices assailed him. They were all at once and from different directions. He turned toward the next rock, focused, and leaped.

The rock shifted, and his balance failed. Magma rose over one edge as the rock changed position. His feet scrambled. He dropped too close to the edge. Two ifrit hands stopped him mere inches above the flowing magma. The heat stung the surface of his skin as his heart raced wildly. He prayed an air bubble did not burst. The wings of the ifrits lifted him up.

One ifrit gaped at him. "Why do you not heed our warnings?"

The fumes from the flow burned in his lungs. "I have no choice."

The ifrit nodded slowly. It pointed toward the last leap, and in a sorrowful voice announced, "Proceed."

The word's tone cut through his focus. The doom that laced it hit his heart. His thoughts went to Sitara who had died to save his life. How could he do less?

With narrowed eyes, he focused on the far edge. His fingers stretched and tightened in an effort to relax. Jonna stepped back as close as he could to the flow and tuned out the world.

No longer could he feel the heat. Only the edge existed. He took two steps and leaped.

The rock behind him shifted. Magma splattered up its surface as he soared into the air. His right foot touched while his left pulled toward him. The momentum carried him forward. His body rolled onto the center area to stop just short of the pyramid's wall. The rock he had leapt from slipped beneath the liquid fire.

The air here smelled sweeter. The rotten egg smell vanished. His lungs sucked in oxygen as his skin absorbed the cooler temperature. His eyes saw the magma, but it no longer seemed to matter. Jonna rolled over, stood up, and walked around the corner of the structure.

No windows adorned its exterior. He stepped lightly toward the front opening and felt a gentle breeze. His body slipped inside.

Light from a blue sky filtered down. A valley stretched into the distance. To one side, fruit trees grew. A path led through the trees to a small shrine. He looked back at the entrance. "It's not just a pyramid; it's a portal."

His feet carried him down the path until he approached the small shrine. Candles lit the interior. A small table covered with a cloth adorned the far wall. A copy of the Zaman Dar lay upon the table. In front of the table, bowed forward upon a rug, a man prayed. Jonna stepped quickly and reached to touch him.

CHAPTER 16

"I have been expecting you, Jonna McCambel. Go on, finish your task."

Jonna hesitated. In his mind, a little voice screamed at him but he could not tell what it said.

"The angel Gabriel informed me of your coming." A soft breeze entered the shrine as the man waited, but Jonna didn't move. "If you are not going to complete your task immediately, may I turn to face you?"

"Of--course." As his hand pulled back, the oddity of the shrine hit him. Why would a marid be worshipping in a shrine?

The face of Muhammad stared at him, but the countenance felt different. The voice sounded the same, and yet-- "You are not the same man." The wind filtered through his hair. Its presence felt familiar.

"No," a sad smile crossed the man's face. "I am Munis. The likeness of me who you met was the marid. When he takes other forms, he is limited to their abilities. He has altered my name to corrupt the message."

Jonna's brow furrowed. "He imprisoned you?"

"The marid has his own designs upon humanity. He cannot be entirely freed from his jar unless another takes his place. He cannot place one there until his agreement with the gods is broken. He cannot break the agreement until a stranger comes to do his bidding." Munis' eyes stayed calm. "You are that stranger." The image of a bright white figure appeared to the right of Munis though the wind continued to blow.

"Why are you here?"

Munis met his eyes. "I chose to enter here. The angel Gabriel prepared it as a sanctuary against the marid's evil. The marid cannot enter. Only the guardians who maintain its structure can come within its touch."

Jonna's eyes narrowed. "So the ifrits that maintain the crevice do it to protect this shrine, not the city?"

The man nodded.

"And the marid thinks--"

"You will place me in his jar. Only the stranger, one not from this world, can reach me."

"Why you and not another?"

"Only Allah would know that answer."

"I have met Allah and was not impressed."

Munis chuckled. "Perhaps you met the wrong one."

The Zaman Dar's words floated on the breeze. "Nan ac'vayu nahwaena eka ava ac'el ac'ava yish."

The air distorted. The shining light of a second image formed to stand beside the table at the wall. The image pointed. "Read."

Jonna rose slowly. Munis did not move. The strange form to Munis' right never stirred. Jonna circled around them to stand beside the table. At his touch, the book opened to the first page.

The letters swirled over the page, but as he focused at the top right, the second line took shape.

"Nan kar idi aiol chiena nyni prabhu duygu nyni avani meter menat."

Pictures shaped themselves in the distortion. A forest of immense trees filled the horizon. Branches swayed as a great wind swept through them.

"Somaiea ac'akshi yuae anku ja'nilaena ac'tirena."

Great geysers from the depths of the sea launched into the air.

"Ja'atmanemaha ac'walidi tarme ja'ravy ac'afrym avti."

A sun rose followed by a second smaller one. The light altered the water into vapor, and clouds were born. The clouds darkened, and drops rained down on the trees.

"Nan niya tindayeine fayrj ud."

In a whisper, Jonna's head rose from the pages and looked toward the image. "And so it begins." His eyes tried to focus on the image beside him. "The Time of Change is cyclic."

The being nodded. "Nothing is lost in my creation."

The name *I Am* stood out in Jonna's mind. "Who are you?"

"Why do you ask questions when you already know the answers?"

Jonna's eyes squinted to see more details of the image, but none would come. Insight flashed. "Because I can't comprehend the answers?" He looked down at the book while at the same time remembering Arta's response when he accused her of speaking in riddles. "We can't translate the answers unless we are shown the truth. We don't have the concepts to understand them."

The image nodded.

Jonna's studies at the university were triggered. In English, the word 'stuff' meant many things or just anything, but it did not translate to Russian well. That language addressed only specific items.

He whispered, "Only through commonality do we understand. If mutual concepts are not known, it is impossible to understand each other." He studied the brightness. "Even if I thought I understood the words I read, you would still have to show me the truth."

The brightness grew. "You have done well, Jonna. You must save these people. You must defeat the marid."

"Why not you? Why leave it to me?"

"Every creature has choice as to what he will serve."

The bright light waved a hand, and the image of a man appeared. No expression existed on its face. The lungs did not move. However, when Jonna touched the flesh, warmth met his fingers.

"Speak the words the ifrit gave you, and they will come to pass."

Understanding came. The marid's rise to power lay in Jonna's choice to break majik's laws. Without that, this world would not exist. He had to finish this. *"Ein-dy-mon."*

The man's image vanished. Harsh winds struck as leaves rushed into the shrine. "Go." The wind's howl rose.

"Is that it?"

The brightness smiled. "You have done what was requested."

Jonna stared at his hand. "No, there must be more."

"Defeat the marid."

"How?" Jonna's eyes turned to find the swirling letters in the Zaman Dar, but no more text appeared. The distortion around him faded. The bright image dimmed. "Guide me. Help me!" His thoughts went to Elfleda, and his abuse of majik. "I don't want to make a mistake again!"

Words whispered to him. "That is all you must know."

The book jumped as Jonna struck the table. "What good are my actions if I can't save the ones I love?" He trembled as the loss of Elfleda brought tears to his eyes. He fought them back and stared down at the book. "You ask me to do something without giving me a clue!"

Munis' voice cut through his thoughts. "I asked nothing of you."

As Jonna rotated, so Munis turned to face him. The man did not seem surprised that Jonna had moved, nor was he concerned that only the two of them remained in the shrine. "Not you. It was--" No more words would come as Jonna shook his head. "This cannot be real."

Munis smiled. "The ways of Allah are not futile. Do what must be done."

Jonna set his jaw. "I am." He started for the door. "I've enough to deal with without cryptic messages and phantom gods." A gasp left his lips as he seized the doorpost of the shrine and the spot on his shoulder grew hot.

As the pain abated, Munis' voice made him pause. "Do not doubt what you know. Doubt only what you do not."

Jonna looked back. "Confucius says, huh?" He raced down the path.

A strong wind howled toward him. Tree limbs bent over to the ground. Fruit from the trees bounced in all directions. His eyes narrowed at the wind's source. It poured through the portal.

Words escaped his lips. "The marid--he knows something has happened." A single thought hit his mind: the others.

The wind tore at his clothes. Bits of sand and dirt soared around him. A spiraling wind ripped up a tree and tossed it into the air.

He struggled to the rock sides barely able to breathe. Pebbles stung as they slapped against his skin. Inch by inch, his fingers felt the bite of sharp rocks as his hands heaved him forward.

At last, only a three foot gap lay between him and portal. His hand surged ahead and slapped against the nearest side jamb. Fingers slid closer until he could grip the outer edge. With a lurch, his body lunged onward.

The joints in his body ached. The sinews were stretched to breaking. Every muscle grew hot as the strength poured in. Against the strain, his second hand grasped part of the jamb.

In tiny increments, his feet lifted from the ground to wave like a flag in the wind. The pressure jerked at his fingertips though he refused to let go.

Heave. His fingers slipped a notch as his muscles trembled. With gritted teeth, his voice mumbled. "I will not let go!"

In the light of the magma from the other side, the face of Devamilu sneered. "Thank you. You have saved my people." He struck Jonna's fingers with his fist, and Jonna's grip broke.

The air's torrent whipped Jonna backwards. Branches slapped at every side. The portal door shrunk with each second.

Sitara's own son had done this to him, but why? Why? As he soared into the heavens, he howled in anger and screamed, "*Sta-sha-taa!*"

A power drain he had not felt since the dark mage arena

shook his body. Dizziness took him, and he fought to focus upon the view below.

The squall stopped. Thunder rolled across the sky. Blue streaks of lightning shot out, and he held suspended in the air.

The portal stared up at him no more than a tiny dot on the horizon. Below him, mountains stood in all their white peaks and glory. Though he could move, his body did not fall.

A slit in the air caught his attention, and the head of a unicorn poked through. After looking both ways, it stepped cautiously out. "Impressive." It tapped its hooves on an unseen barrier. "That's one of the few things that would show me where you are."

Though the dizziness had subsided, weakness settled in. Jonna took deep breaths. "What thing?"

"You stopped time for an entire world. You modified a spell."

A lump rose in Jonna's throat. When he thought back, he had changed it--not only the verbal component, but his intentions, too. He had not wanted to fall. He recalled Väinämö's warnings and prayed he had not made things worse. "Uh, yeah." His throat became dry. "How do we fix this?"

The unicorn neighed in laughter. "I didn't do it. You did."

The weakness grew. "So, uh." Jonna swallowed as he scanned the area around him. "Let me rephrase the question. What in all of magic do I do now?" He stared at the unicorn with wide eyes.

The creature shook its head. "You can either come with me and step back closer to your own world, or stay and release this one."

Jonna glanced down at the terrain below him. "And fall?"

"Well," the unicorn turned its head so one eye could get a better view. "It is possible. After all, if you stay, you must fulfill the natural laws." It neighed with a nod. "Unless you know of another spell?"

"So your advice is to get out while I can?"

"It is your magic that holds this world in its current state. Remove the magic, and the world will resume."

Jonna bit his lip. "And the marid will succeed."

"Quite possibly."

His eyes shifted to the unicorn. "You know about the marid?"

"Of course I do." The unicorn smiled at him.

Jonna's eyes swept the land below. "Yeah." He pursed his lips. "I'm going to figure out that one, too."

The unicorn eyed him. "What one?"

"There's a number of things that don't make sense right now. You're one of them."

The creature grinned. "I'm flattered. Perhaps--" It chewed its cud a moment. "Perhaps I could help without interfering."

"Aw, come on. Now you sound like Väinämö."

"Väinämö who?"

Jonna's eyebrows rose. "That's right. You wouldn't know who that is because you've never met him." A smile brightened on his face. Jonna tapped his temple. "I'm going to figure this out. However, your suggestion would be greatly appreciated."

"You're welcome." The unicorn paused. "I think." It shook its head. "The way I see it, you have three problems. One, you can't just run off or all your efforts to help these creatures will be for nothing. Two, if you turn time back on, your magic be useless. And three, by turning time back on, you will more than likely plummet to your death."

Jonna thought. "Sounds logical so far. You know I won't run." He frowned. "If we can avoid the plummeting, that would be a great start. Your suggestion?"

"Oh--" The unicorn strolled toward him as if not paying attention. "Perhaps--" The creature shook its head abruptly and ducked near Jonna.

Jonna jerked back as the unicorn's horn struck a line beneath him, and a gap opened up. When Jonna glanced into it, he saw nothing.

"Sorry about that. Sometimes the altitude gets to me." The unicorn winked. "Well, it's sad I couldn't help. Ta-ta for now." It strolled back to the slit it had come from.

"What a minute. Where are you going? What did you do?"

"Do?" The creature blinked. "I'm not allowed to interfere, remember?"

"I know, but--" Jonna nodded at the ground. "--when time resumes--"

"Look, just because I'm magical doesn't mean I am not answerable for my actions. You know that." The unicorn winked. "Bye." It stepped through the slit and poked its head back out. "Well?"

"Well what?"

"Resume time."

"Now?" He glanced down at the slit below him. "That's not big enough to catch a fly let alone me!"

"Shh!" The unicorn glared. "And please hold on before you do!"

"Hold on to what?" He looked at the slit, again.

The creature huffed. "Surely I don't have to spell it out?"

Jonna reached down and touched the area around the slit. Nothing existed but air. He placed a hand in the middle of it and felt expandable walls. "Are you sure?"

Mirth entered the unicorn's eyes.

"Okay, here it goes." He shifted his body to grasp it with both hands, pulled it apart, and slipped both feet inside. They touched nothing, but the nothing of the slit expanded easily to allow him in. At waist deep, he turned to the unicorn. "*Sta-sha-taa?*"

Wind tore at him, struck his upper body, and tried to rip him from the slit. Jonna gasped as much because he could not breathe as from the weakness that overwhelmed him. With both hands firmly gripped on the slit sides, he slid down into it.

The air whipped above him. It whistled across the opening. He released his grip and watched the slit close.

Darkness consumed him as he fell through a bottomless pit. The absence of sound confused him. His arms flailed out but found nothing. Seconds felt like eternity. As the sound had left, so it returned in a deafening pitch. He slammed back on something hard.

Waves of agony rippled along his spine, and for a moment, he could not move. Gasping, he gradually rolled over until he lay upon his side.

The pyramid doorway stood open. The ifrit boy could not be seen but the warmth on his shoulder had returned. Rising slowly, Jonna stood.

The coolness around the pyramid remained, but the magma rolled in waves to crash against the rock. Bits and pieces splattered around the edges. The path he had come across had disappeared beneath the waves. That left only the path to the opposite side. Jonna dropped to a runner's stance, despite the complaint of his back, bolted forward, and leaped away from the pyramid.

The smell of rotten eggs made him lose focus. Arms floundered as he passed over the first rock to land on the second. Knees buckled. Lungs labored. His abused body refused to go on as he squatted down to rest.

The bursts of small flames which indicted that ifrits were about had vanished. Pieces of rock dropped from the cavern roof to crash into the magma. Even the rock he stood on sent vibrations into his body. The foundation of the city had lost its stability.

A baby's cry filled the cavern. His eyes darted to where his friends had been. With a deep breath, Jonna sprung to the next rock and tumbled on shaky legs. Only four rocks now lay between him and the crevice wall.

The ground shifted. The magma drained down a few inches. The newly uncovered smoking rock sent odd smells his direction. A rapid cough hit as he struggled to hold his breath. He leaped for the next rock and missed.

Ifrit hands caught him on either side and surged upward away from the crevice. He rose to just below the bars that carried electricity across them.

One of the ifrits spoke, "We have you. We will take you to your friends."

A burst of energy passed them on the beam above. They rose between two of the pairs and turned toward the ledge.

The voice of Devamilu screamed, "No, he must die!"

Yellow electricity arced toward the ifrits. It stunned one and tapped the other. The tapped one struggled to hold them all but could not keep them up. It descended toward the nearest beam and crashed upon it. From the ifrit, words wheezed, "I'm sorry."

Jonna reached out a hand and grasped the ifrit's arm. "Go, my friend. You have done all you can." The ifrits faded from sight.

"Nothing can save you." Devamilu maniacal laughter filled his voice.

As Jonna's ear listened, he turned upon the beam. To the left, Devamilu hovered in the air.

"You think you're stronger and mightier than I simply because you're human?" The ifrit spat fire at him. It exploded upon the bar. Jonna leaped back and fought to keep his balance. "You are weak. Now that we have been freed, my kind will rule the world!"

Jonna heard an electrical spark. He had to get off this beam but to jump meant certain death. He recalled what Munis had said about the marid taking different forms and the warmth in his shoulder that came when it was near. "You are not an ifrit."

The creature sneered. "Have I been that transparent?"

A second electrical charge initiated somewhere to Jonna's left. "Not entirely. However, you are a shape-shifter, after all."

"You think you know my kind?" A devious smile crossed the marid's face. "That's better still." It descended slowly toward him, and Jonna's shoulder burned. "We make slaves of humans. We can bid you do our will." His hand twisted ever so slightly, and Jonna fought the urge to jump. Though he battled, the impulse did not go away.

"You see, we are the greatest of all spirits that roam the earth. We are the most feared and sought after. When Dagda found me in the desert and lay dying, it took nothing to convince him of what he could become. A plan formed, and though it took thousands of years, I knew it would come to this." The marid grinned thoughtfully. "Perhaps, I will spare you. You can serve me for a thousand years in his place." It landed upon the beam.

Jonna shook his head. "You're wrong." The electrical crackle grew closer. "You have no power we do not give you."

"I am free." It spat at him. "You have done it yourself. No power on earth can make me return to the jar."

The marid looked toward the ledge. Jonna followed its gaze. A group of people came forward to watch. "And I'll prove it by making you watch those you love die." The marid raised its hand.

Jonna leaped, collided with the marid, and grabbed it by the neck. The warmth on his arm increased.

A wicked laugh left its lips as he struggled to hold on. "Surely you learned your lesson with Talumr?"

"*Ein-dy*--ahhh!" Red flames touched his skin; blue energy leaped in response but could not hold. His muscles trembled. He fought to speak the spell, but could not gather the words.

"Fool of a mortal. You could have lived. Now you *must* die."

Jonna's cries filled the cavern joined by the wicked laugh of the marid. His strength waned. His grip lessened. The thoughts he held flew as if they had never been. The smell of charred flesh filled his nostrils. A distant voice called. "Believe."

"No!" The marid shrieked. It searched the air. "You cannot interfere!"

"Believe, Jonna. You know the words."

The words surfaced, the cries stopped, and his body shook. He mumbled. "Nan-ac'vayu-nahwaena-eka ava-ac'el-ac'ava-yish."

The air distorted. The presence floated beside him. "Believe."

His trembling vanished. As if staring into another world, the frozen features of the marid glared at Jonna whose hands still clung to the creature's neck. "I have no magic. I have nothing left."

The presence reached out. Strength flowed in his body. "Your magic is gone. You need to rely on another." The shoulder warmth grew. A tingle of power danced through his arm. "But to do that, you must believe."

"How?"

"Accept the gift I have given. Accept that I am real."

Jonna's face flushed. "I don't know who you are to believe!"

The presence faded before him. The distortion gradually changed. The marid gave a slight closed-lipped smile. "Victory is mine!" The marid's hands came up toward Jonna's neck. "I will enjoy this."

A strange pinpoint of light erupted inside of Jonna. He remembered the words spoken by Munis, "Believe what you know."

What did he know? He gripped the neck of a marid in a world far from his own. He held life by a thread, and the marid brought the scissors. He had believed in himself and had failed twice in one day. Could he believe in a being that had no verifiable reality? How?

Choose. With a single word, clarity came. The request to believe had been extended. The opportunity was real. No magical power was required, save the decision of a human soul. The words whispered from his lips. "I believe." A tingle of power flowed through him. "I believe!" Blue energy sparked. It surged toward the marid with growing force.

The marid's eyes widened. "No, no!" It fought to break Jonna's hold but could not peel his hands away. "NO!"

Deadly red flames erupted. The beam beneath them softened. Yellow electricity ripped toward them. Blue energy lashed out to encircle the pair.

Jonna's eyes cleared. His mind turned razor-sharp. He stared into the marid's face and spoke with all calm, "*Ein-dy-mon.* Return to your prison."

The marid screamed. Both its hands turned to claws and jabbed for Jonna's throat. "I will not go empty handed! I will not!"

Its nails touched him, but could not penetrate. The azure electricity whipped out in tendrils down its fingers. The marid shrieked. The screeches echoed around the cavern as the creature vanished.

The abrupt fading of the marid's body dropped Jonna down on the deformed bar. The heat of the bar wafted up, but it did not burn his skin. In slow motion, he studied his hands. The burnt flesh had turned soft and light. With the weakness gone, he rose to his feet.

Yellow electricity arced toward him. It struck the pole he stood on and rushed down it. "It's time to put an end to this."

His knees bent as he placed both hands on the bar. With head held straight ahead, he stared into the lightning. It hit.

His whole body shook as the power tried to flow by but could not pass. His hair stood on end. The tingle danced all over his skin.

Heat built up as waves changed the view around him. Like the distortion of a hot paved street, he radiated blue heat in all directions.

A concept hit his mind. "I'm a human capacitor, and at the same time, I'm can change the frequency."

Azure lightning leaped from him. It rushed along the beam until yellow struck it. The yellow washed from orange to blue. It traveled the rest of the pairs until it hit the last column and dove into the earth.

The presence whispered, "Leave." Part of the ceiling crashed to the floor. A large crack opened below him in the crevice. The glow of the magma lessened, and strange gurgling noises rose from its depths.

Jonna leaped to his feet and ran toward the nearest column. Huge rocks lay stacked beside it. He jumped, caught his balance, and scrambled down.

The ledge came closer. The shadows multiplied behind him. He rushed toward the way up while sensing that something followed behind.

Hands gripped stone; feet caught footholds. Flickering flames bounced light down to him. As he neared the ledge, Mumin and Lokke reached out and hauled him up. He breathed deeply to catch his breath.

Mumin's eyes kept watch on the crevice below. In both his and Lokke's hands were torches. The Zaman Dar lay under Lokke's arm. The half-demon had retrieved the book from where he hid it. Lokke grinned at Jonna, "Come on, we've found a tunnel!"

Jonna turned to stare at the crevice as the ground shook. The odd feeling that something followed would not let go. Lightning arced, danced the beams, and shot into the ceiling. A thumping sound beat its way toward them. The rocks vibrated in unison.

A chill went up Jonna's spine as he raced after Mumin along the cavern wall. A cave entrance appeared. Salma grabbed his arm as they entered. Her eyes darted unceasingly toward the shadows. "Come on!"

The jerking of the ground made it difficult to run. Pieces of rock clattered. A circular stair appeared as the thumping grew louder. They curved around its interior to rise higher into the city.

Screams echoed. Metal weapons clashed. Archways gave pitiful moanings that cut to the heart. Legs ached as they all stumbled on.

Arta stepped before them with an arrow nocked in a bow. A quiver of arrows hung on her back. Her eyes narrowed as she took careful stance. She raised the bow and fired.

Lokke ducked. Mumin went right. Jonna jerked Salma against the wall. The head of the arrow struck something in the shadows. It shrieked.

"This way."

They followed her through the next archway. Ifrit heads showed red glowing eyes as the shadows gathered from behind. After several turns, they came to a dead end. The city shifted.

"Wait." She hurried to the previous fork and searched. For every arrow she shot, a shriek cried out. Footsteps became louder, and Al-Uzza hurried around the corner. Both women rushed toward Jonna and his companions.

Al-Uzza's sober eyes took them in. "We must hurry. The nasnas are getting closer, and the ghouls will be behind them." She grasped her sister's hand, and in unison they each pointed a palm toward the end of the hall. "*Ba-ru-ya.*"

CHAPTER 17

Whirling blue energy ignited. A vortex formed at the end of the hall. The electrical tendrils sparked in random directions to lick at the walls.

The hall shook as the walls swayed. Cracks crept along the floor. Arta stood at the side of the vortex with bow ready while Al-Uzza stepped in. "Hurry! The city won't hold much longer!"

Mumin passed through and then Lokke. Jonna stayed with Salma and the baby. He shifted his body to act as a shield. Arta shook her head. "I told you, we intend them no harm. You have my word."

Salma held the baby close while they passed. As the vortex tendrils snaked around them, she tightened her grip on Jonna's arm.

The spinning energy tossed them through the vortex, and they landed on a cobblestone floor. Rugs decorated the floor beside a bed, a dresser, and a desk. Two large windows opened up to the water. They could see the city on the far shore as smoke billowed up.

"And now," Arta nodded toward them. "I go to seek my father." She stepped back through the vortex.

"Help her," Salma pleaded toward Jonna. "The baby will be fine. She will not in that city."

With a nod, he pushed into the vortex and found himself back in a crumbling hall. Blocks dropped from the ceiling and struck the floor. Arta reached the corner and turned right. Jonna quickly followed. Thuds echoed.

Her bow came up. She spun to face behind them, and fired

two arrows in rapid session. Shrieks filled the hall. "Their numbers are growing. Hurry! I will guard from behind."

He stepped to the lead and pulled the rune blade. Azure sparks leaped upon its surface. "What are they?"

"The spawn of the demon Shiqq."

The hall turned. Voices cried in agony, but Arta refused to go to their aid. The dead littered the halls. A woman lay sideways in a corner and reached up for help as they passed. Jonna extended his hand.

An arrow sliced by him to strike the woman in the chest. Her shriek mirrored the others as she heaved backwards. Jonna glared at Arta.

Arta's face shed no tear. "Nasnas." With the tip of a prepped arrow, she rolled the body over. It had been split down the middle. Where the split had occurred, rough scar tissue covered it from head to foot. The creature had only one arm, one leg, half a body, and half a head. "Had it touched you, you would be dead." She checked the body. "Its other half could still be alive."

He moved away from the creature. "I bow to your wisdom."

Thuds echoed from the hall they headed toward. She touched his shoulder and whispered, "Not that way. We'll have to change course."

They dodged to a side archway. The smooth stone on the sides of the wall shifted as the city moved.

"Wouldn't it better to just transport over?" The thuds changed direction and entered the archway behind them.

"The more magic we use, the more it draws them. They smell it."

His eyes narrowed as they reached a fork. "What of the vortex?"

She nodded toward the right, and they started forward again. "Al-Uzza will have closed it by now."

Jonna glanced at the rune blade. "And magic weapons?"

Stairs appeared, and they started down. At the base, they

turned toward the right. The hall branched again, but Arta pointed toward the curve on the left. "Ours, yes. Yours, I don't know." The thuds became more distant. "We may be out-running them."

They passed storage rooms until a flight of stairs appeared. A door stood at the top. When they grabbed the handle, it would not budge. Arta struck the door several times.

Noise stirred behind it. Wood slid across wood. The door opened an inch as a single eye looked out. "Who's there?" The thuds grew closer.

"I am the goddess Arta. Open it!"

The door swung back, and Senka, the man Jonna had seen at Mumin's store, bowed quickly. He eyed Jonna. "Goddess, I am sorry, but with all the shaking of the city, I was fearful."

While Senka spoke, Jonna and Arta stepped in. Jonna closed the door and replaced the bar.

Arta scanned the room. "I can see that, but fearful of what?" Coins sat in small boxes all over a counter. "Shouldn't you be more fearful of losing your life?"

His eyes gawked at her. "What is life if I have no money to sustain me? Please--" He waved toward the front door. "--I must finish." His hands unbarred the door and pulled the door ring. As it opened, a man stared in. He reached forward and touched Senka's arm.

Senka screamed. His eyes rolled back in his head, and he collapsed to the floor. His body began to slowly split into two halves.

The creature who had touched Senka turned to face them as it hopped on one leg. With its only arm, it shoved back at the half-open door. The door slammed into Senka's body and opened wider.

An arrow sliced the air to pierce the creature's chest. The nasnas crashed backwards as Jonna and Arta spotted the arena entry directly across the way. Two arrows sank into Senka's body; one in each half.

Jonna hurried to the doorway and listened while Arta held her bow at ready. Nothing else moved. "Come on." With rune blade out, he looked both ways and hurried to stand beside the arena's outer wall.

Parts of the wall had already crumbled. Stones half-filled the entrance. Arta maintained watch while Jonna moved the debris. Unstable stones slid dangerously as he cleared a narrow path.

They stepped into darkness. Whatever light spell had been used, it no longer existed. Jonna reached back and took her hand. "Follow me."

Echoes bounced upon the walls. Thuds came from behind. As the great stone doors to the arena drew near, a dim light glowed.

A wisp of smoke hit their noses. The bar to secure the doors lay in place. Two ropes dangled near it. The heat generated when Mot had died had caused the ropes to burn.

Together, they tried to lift the bar but it would not budge. Arta pointed toward a side door. "We must to go up."

The side door pushed back easily to reveal a room. Broken furniture lay scattered. Rubble sat at the wall's base. A small staircase led up.

The stairs emerged in the seating area. Fumes from fires that had caught in the city blew in. A wealth of cries met their ears as people fled.

The two raced along the lower seats until they approached the dais. Between them and the dais lay the dark abyss that led to the domain of the ifrits. Jonna nodded toward the lip of the abyss. "Follow me."

He sheathed the rune blade, grabbed the wall, and lowered himself down. His fingers released, and he dropped. As his feet touched the lip that contained the darkness, he twisted to face the other way and walked to the dais' wall. "It's a whole lot simpler when archers aren't shooting at you."

A smirk hit her face. "Really?" Her hand flicked back and attached her bow to the quiver. Without a blink, she dropped off the side and landed on the lip. She turned and waited. "Ready?"

He leaned back against the wall and positioned his hands as a cup. "When you are."

She raced forward, placed a foot in his hands, and leaped. Her body went up, turned in the air, and landed smoothly to sit upon the wall over his head. Jonna chuckled. "Not bad."

"It was perfect." She looked down and extended her hands. "I'm stronger than I look, you know."

He laughed. "And I weigh more than you think." He gazed down at the arena floor. Debris littered the area, but one place lay clear. He turned around to face the lip's wall, slipped down until he hung by his hands, and dropped. Even with sand, the hit hurt. His hands dusted himself off as he rose and walked up the steps of the dais.

She pointed a finger. "You don't trust me. We must trust each other."

"If you want my complete trust, you will have to earn it back."

The secret room lay open. They stepped in quietly but heard no sound. The hall was clear too. At the Najwa Miraj, they stopped.

The fountain still flowed but the jar on top had vanished. The blood trail from before still led around the lattice though the blood had dried to almost black. Smoke billowed in small wisps from the water. As they passed around the lattice to the stairs, the smell of rotten eggs prevailed.

At the top of the stairs, an entry opened to a room covered in gold. Two windows looked toward the east. Carvings of pleasurable things decorated the walls. People drank, swam, and loved. The runes which decorated the carvings matched those Jonna had seen in the Zaman Dar.

Two large pillars showed the cycles of the year with the falling and rising of a star. Two suns dominated the pictorial skies of each with a horizontal crescent moon presiding over them. Huge pillows in the shape of a shoreline took up one quarter of the room. Silks of many colors caught the light and sparkled in all directions.

On one side of the room lay Arta's father. His arm clutched

the jar from the fountain. On the other side lay an ifrit boy still flaming upon the golden floor.

Arta dropped to her knees beside her father. Red stains decorated the front of his shirt. Tiny yellow sparks of energy jumped across his body. As the shirt shifted, claw marks were visible across his chest though his lungs still moved in shallow breaths.

The blue sparks of her energy clashed against the yellow. She turned toward Jonna. "Who would have done this?"

Her eyes darted to the ifrit boy. Though no blood lay upon his claws, red drops of liquid adorned the floor. "Why?" She rose quickly and pulled the bow from the back of her quiver. An arrow nocked. "Wake him."

"Wait." Jonna's eyes danced over the evidence. He remembered the marid taking the boy's shape. He placed himself between her and the boy. "We don't know what happened here."

"We know." Her eyes burned. "I want to see his face when he dies."

He walked toward her. His hand touched the bow and gradually pointed it down. "Besides, I don't want to be in front in case you miss."

Her words were firm. "I don't miss." Her hand lessened the pull of the string. "Usually." She huffed. "Wake him, please!"

"As you wish."

He reached the boy and kneeled down. The ifrit still breathed. A light touch upon the flames revealed they did not burn. From what he had learned of ifrits, if they were in battle, they could burn very well.

The boy's eyelids stirred. The tiny flames stared up at him, noted his position, and caught Arta across the room. "Are you my mother's friend?"

"If Sitara was your mother," Jonna's voice dropped, "Yes."

The boy inhaled sharply and whispered, "Then she *is* dead."

Jonna nodded. "Along with Talumr."

"How?" The boy's face contorted as he stared up at him.

A lump formed in Jonna's throat. "She gave her life for me."

Arta strode forward with angry eyes. "Why?" Her hand drew the bow to its maximum length. The arrow tip aimed at the boy. "Why?"

The boy's eyes drifted to Dagda. "It was not I."

"Liar." Her bow tip pointed at the floor. "His blood cries up from the surface you lie upon--the drips that fell from your fingers. Why?"

"It was not I, goddess."

She roared. "Then who was it?"

His voice stayed calm. "The marid."

"No." Jonna slowly shook his head. "That is impossible. Using the spell, I sent him back to his jar." He rose from the floor and stared at the body of Dagda. As he turned one hand over, a lid tumbled out. "No!" His eyes grew large. "We have to find him--right now."

Thuds echoed up the stairs. The ifrit rolled to his feet.

Arta's nocked arrow targeted the boy. "How do we know he's telling the truth?"

"Arta." Jonna slipped his rune blade from the sheath and turned to face the door. Blue energy sparked along the metal. "We need that vortex."

Frustration filled her voice. "I know." Her eyes stayed steady on the ifrit. "But I can't do it."

He moved to the door. "Forget the ifrit. We have worse problems."

With a thud, the body of a nasnas jumped into view. Its hand extended toward him. "Help me."

The rune blade sliced through the hand and along the torso. The parts fell to bounce upon the floor. Jonna leaped back. Other thuds echoed from below. "The vortex, now!"

Arta spun toward the doorway and loosed two arrows as more nasnas jumped upon the landing. The arrows stabbed into their chests. They tumbled backwards shrieking.

"I can't!" She nocked another arrow. "Spells don't work in this room even with medallions!"

Jonna glanced to the walls but saw no ifrit heads. "Why?"

"How should I know? It is my father's private quarters."

"Watch the door." As his feet moved backwards next to Dagda, he kicked the god.

"Watch it, that's my father!"

Dagda groaned.

"That's more like it. Wake up." Jonna glared down as the man's eyes slowly drew toward him. "Yeah, look at me. You opened the jar, why?"

Two thuds hit the landing. The bow twanged. One nasnas dropped dead, fell into the other, and both tumbled down the stairs.

The man spotted the rune blade that hovered over him. He coughed out, "You were--supposed--to change--the energy, not trap--the marid." The man's eyes closed

Jonna kicked him again. "Why?"

A thud hit the landing.

Dagda's eyes reopened as he attempted to focus. "Your energy--released us--from his control--yet gave--us access to--his magic. In the jar--his magic--doesn't work."

The bow twanged. Shrieks filled the room.

Jonna's face flushed as he remembered what Arta had said about their future names. "Your future names?" Rage filled him. "You let that murderer out just so you wouldn't die this time around?"

"Not all of us want to die." Arta's eyes remained on the doorway, but tears ran down her cheeks. "As with all creatures, death is final, Mahdi. He was protecting the family." She glanced in his direction. "But I wish--"

Three thuds hit the landing. The last bumped into the others and knocked them into the room. A fourth landed behind them as the two creatures that were knocked forward stabilized their feet and spread out.

Jonna leaped toward one, but with more space, the nasnas leaped back. It dodged left and lunged forward. The rune blade scored, but just barely. An ugly slice appeared across its half-chest. It pulled back and roared.

Arta's arrows struck time and again, but the nasnas had a foothold, and they used it for all they could. More pushed in. Arrows flew, the rune blade sliced, and the young ifrit focused his flame.

Searing flames of heat lashed out. They scored, but it did not deter the nasnas. The three were forced back further into the room.

Dagda cried out, still unable to rise. The nasnas leaped toward him. Arta swung in his direction and fired. The closest nasnas to Dagda dropped dead, but one near her lunged.

The ifrit latched onto her shoulders and pulled her back. The hand of the nasnas swiped and missed her bow hand. The next arrow flew with such force it stabbed through one and into the other. Both slammed back into the attacking horde and dropped dead.

Jonna felt the rune blade collide as it carved through another. "Out the window. We can't hold them!"

"My father!"

The rage of what Dagda had done had not dissipated from Jonna. He glared at the king as the man's gaze swept toward him.

"Devamilu, help him!"

The ifrit jerked his head toward Jonna. "How do you know my name?"

"Help him!"

Devamilu swooped from behind Arta and lifted Dagda's shoulders off the ground. The man groaned and snatched for the jar's lid but missed. He clung to the jar as the ifrit carried him toward the window.

"Arta, now you."

"I can't fly." Arta clenched her jaw. "I'll cover. You go."

The rune blade sliced wide to catch a nasnas who leaped into the air while in the same swipe, it cut through the arm of a second. Jonna slipped behind a pillar as a third lashed out to hit him. Its hand slapped loudly against the stone.

"I said move!" He spun toward her, and his free hand grabbed her waist. The arrow she nocked went high, but scored in the half-head of a foe.

"You can't do this!"

Glancing out a window, his eyes spotted the buildings far below. "Would you rather be dead?" His foot stepped upon the bottom of the windowsill, and he leaped out the window.

She screamed, "Here or there?"

The location of the room became startling clear. It towered above all the others. They plunged toward the city below.

The idea of the slit the unicorn had created surfaced in his mind. The vortex was his only hope. As the ground rushed up, he cried out, "*Ba-ru-ya!*"

Agony tore through his insides. Jonna's magic had not fully renewed. His muscles clenched. He refused to breathe in an effort to fight the pain.

The blue energy vortex opened below them. The electrical tendrils whipped out. His arm with the blade extended in an effort to slow their descent. A burst of wind struck them from the side, and they missed.

The laugh of the marid met their ears. "Oh, this will be fun!"

Two claws lashed out and bit into Jonna's shoulders. Blood trickled down his shirt. The rune blade hummed as his arms shook in agony.

Arta held him tightly by one arm, looked into his eyes, and gave a nod. "It's okay. I know what to do." Her lips touched his gently.

The marid goaded, "How sweet." Its wings beat the air as it rose higher. "True love at last. That is rare for a goddess."

Her free hand traced Jonna's arm in loving caress. It touched the wrist that held the rune blade and shoved it into an upward arc.

The marid gasped. Azure energy leaped from the blade as it plunged into the creature's side. The wings slowed. Their upward thrust stopped. Its claws released from Jonna's shoulders. Still held firmly in Jonna's hand, the rune blade slipped from the marid's body, and they plummeted from the sky.

Arta glanced at Jonna and swung out her free arm. Their descent slowed. She tested various positions. They dropped toward the spinning vortex.

Blue electricity lashed out to encircle them. It coursed through their bodies. She wrapped her arms around him. "You may never be mine," she spoke softly, "But you do have my heart."

The vortex remained as she added power of her own and kept them suspended in its grasp. His wounds healed. Their magic merged.

"It would be so easy, you know." She leaned against his chest. "We could go anywhere, any place. All you must do is say the word."

The agony lessened, and his lungs took in air. The taunt muscles relaxed though his hand refused to let go of the rune blade.

"Are you better?" She stared into his eyes as hers glowed brightly. "Then it is time." Her lips touched his once more.

They bumped down upon pillows. Details of the room with the cobblestone floor came into view. The windows stared at the city where smoke billowed in great dark clouds.

The pressure of Arta upon of his chest redirected his attention. Her eyes were closed, her arms were around him, but her hands were lax. Her lungs barely moved.

He laid the rune blade beside him, and all the energy vanished. Gently, he rolled her off upon the pillows.

He felt different but could not tell how. If she had healed his wounds, what had it cost her?

Devamilu swooped in through the window and dropped to the floor. "I'm--sorry. I tried to get back, and when I found you gone--" Words failed as his face tore between relief and regret. "I wish I had known!"

Jonna blinked. "Sorry for what?"

The ifrit swallowed. "The marid took the baby."

A baby's cry called to him. It echoed as if down a great well, and the sound of waves bounced near it. Jonna's brow wrinkled. "When?"

"Just minutes before you arrived."

"But--" His eyes looked to the blade beside him. Its magic had certainly pierced the creature; it had to be dead. His body rose as his left hand lifted the hilt of the rune blade. The energy crackled to life as he slipped it into its sheath. "Is Salma okay?" At the mere idea that the marid still lived, anger swelled within him.

The ifrit boy gave a single nod. "I can show you."

The building's hallway turned right and left. The ifrit headed left. Decorative swirls embellished the doors that faced the water.

A set of stairs led to a large living room. Past the living room, a door led to a patio. The ifrit shied away with downcast eyes to let him pass.

Jonna's jaw clenched. His eyes darted to the arms of Salma. She had wrapped them around herself in a tight embrace. The anger rose until his skin radiated heat.

Salma shook with sobs as Jonna draw near. The rune blade hummed. His shoulder prickled as his whole body burned with anger. Her tears dropped into the water.

"It took him," she wailed. "Only for a moment did I set him down."

He reached up and touched her shoulder. The shaking grew worse.

"I have failed you, my lord."

Jonna stared at the water. His face contorted between fear and anger. He whispered, "Do we know where he went?"

Her head nodded, and she pointed back toward the city. "There. That is the direction he flew."

"I'll get him back, don't worry." His eyes narrowed as they watched the waves bounce against the shore.

"If you had only left the marid alone, none of this would have happened."

His brow creased. "This is not my fault."

"You chose to help the ifrits. You chose to disrupt the magic. You chose--" In rage, she swung at him.

Eyes wide, he blocked the blow with his forearm.

Her voice dropped to whimper. "You chose for all of us."

The words bit deep. It had always been the same. He had elected to use magic without the proper learning. He had selected to stay in a world that made him a terrible weapon. Almundena flashed into his mind and the dreadful power that had threatened to consume him with the Eye of Aldrick. Had he become the thing he dreaded most? His hands trembled.

Salma grimaced. Her hand brushed her side and a red spot appeared.

The memory of Arta as she thrust the rune blade over Jonna's head stirred his mind. He squinted, drew the rune blade, and listened as the hum soared. Munis' words echoed. The marid could take many forms.

Salma's eyebrows rose. She took a step back.

Jonna's brow creased though his voice stayed calm. "What's my name?"

A puzzled look crossed her face. "What do you mean, Mahdi?" Her eyes darted to the sword. She stepped back as he pushed toward her.

Mumin strode to the patio. "Mahdi, what are you doing?"

Jonna's free hand came up. "Stay back, Mumin. This is between Salma and me." His grip tightened on the weapon. "Tell me, or by God, I will run you through!"

Mumin's jaw dropped. Lokke swung past the door and collided with Mumin. As he bounced back, he gawked. "Jonna! What are you doing?"

Jonna stepped forward.

Tears ran down Salma's cheeks. "Jonna!" She screamed out. "I call you Jonna!"

His voice turned hard. "Too late."

CHAPTER 18

Jonna thrust. The blade bit deeply as it curved upward to pierce her heart. Shock struck across her face as the light brightened briefly in her eyes. With the hilt firmly grasped, he twisted the sword. A sharp inhale followed as her body slumped toward the floor.

The blade pulled smoothly away. Blood flowed freely from the wound. His eyes stared down unbelieving as the words whispered from his lips, "You are not Salma. You didn't know my name."

Lokke rushed toward him, thought twice, and backed up. "Have you gone mad?" He knelt down beside her and looked up at Jonna. "You just murdered her!"

Mumin stepped to the side but did not approach. "He has been taken. He is possessed." The man dropped to his knees and chanted.

Jonna turned toward them. He felt numb all over as the anger drained away. The rune blade clattered to the patio. The crackle of energy faded. His knees bent slowly until he sat and leaned back against the stone railing. "It's not her. It can't be." His eyes stayed riveted directly in front.

Lokke edged toward the rune blade. "The baby had just been stolen." He shook his head. "She was hysterical. What did you expect of her?"

"I--" Jonna pressed both palms against his eyes. "I thought--" A cold ripple went through him. "All the signs were there: the rune blade, as well as the shoulder." He removed his palms. "What have I become?"

Lokke inched closer to the sword.

Mumin's chant stopped. He gasped. "You thought she was the marid?"

Lokke reached out to knock the sword away.

Jonna nodded and spoke without a glance, "Don't touch it, Lokke."

The half-demon froze. "I--er--"

"Jonna," Mumin's voice rose. "Look!"

Jonna's brow creased as he turned. A light waved over Salma's body. A flame moved down the center of the corpse from head to toe. The image of Salma vanished. In its place lay a fiery, winged creature. It matched the one that dug its claws into his shoulders.

Relief flooded through him. At the same time, his heart beat wildly.

Lokke's eyes opened wide as he spoke what was in all their minds. "If that's the marid, where is Salma?"

Jonna snatched up the sword. Energy crackled across it. "Did she leave the house?"

"No, but--" Lokke swallowed with a glance at Mumin. "--we didn't see the marid enter either."

The baby's cry echoed back to him. "Waves, water, a tunnel of some sort." His eyes swept toward the city. "If the marid told the truth about the baby, it has to be a trap."

Devamilu stepped up behind him. "Nothing can live in the city now. All have fled. Most of my people have left. The nasnas have killed many, and the ghouls have come in behind. To go back--" The ifrit shook his head. "--would not be wise."

A whisper escaped Jonna's lips. "But it is imperative."

A dim picture formed. For a moment, he thought he saw through the infant's eyes. "The child lies upon a mound of skulls surround by the water." He turned to the ifrit. "Do you know this place?"

The ifrit boy looked down. "It is not good for an ifrit to enter there. When the gods of the city send people to enter, they never come back."

"I need you to take me, if only to the entrance." A foreboding shook him. "Time is of the essence."

"I--will." Devamilu swallowed. "In honor of my mother." His brow creased. "Why did she give her life to protect you?"

"I am Jonna McCambel from a world you do not know. In another place, she was my wife."

The last name rolled awkwardly off the boy's tongue. He nodded slowly and extended his hand. "Come."

"Not without me." Lokke stepped forward. Mumin did the same.

Jonna eyed them both. The nasnas' attack lay vivid in his mind. "Have you weapons?"

Mumin spoke quietly. "Not everything is about might, my friend. Sometimes, it is about faith."

"You remind me of another." Jonna sighed. "Come then."

"Wait!" Lokke dashed back into the house and returned with his backpack fuller. "I almost forgot!"

Mumin grabbed hold of Jonna's arm; Lokke did the same.

Lokke's eyebrows rose. The flame that did not burn leaped out to encircle them. "This is way too familiar."

Devamilu gave him a sideways glance. "Do you know this spell?"

They floated off the ground as the ifrit's fiery wings beat, rotated toward the city, and swung out over the water. Their speed gradually increased until the waves beneath them became a blur.

As they reached the far shore, the ifrit's speed slowed. He rose about forty feet and arced around a great tower.

Creatures stirred in the shadows. Eyes watched from windows. The thuds of the nasnas met their ears. The city had truly been taken.

They followed several cross streets until they came to an outside courtyard. In the middle of the courtyard stood a gazebo with words carved into the stone header: Agokera Atma Aterekiit.

Devamilu landed before the gazebo's steps. The flame

dissipated as their hands released. "The way is here. I should not go beyond this point."

Jonna nodded. "Thank you."

"I will wait for your return." His wings struck the air and lifted him from the ground. His body rose to settle upon the top of the gazebo.

Jonna read the words in the header. He had no idea what the words meant, and yet, an image of a wandering star drawn toward a black hole drifted into his mind. His feet entered the gazebo.

A three-foot wall stood in the center. It encircled a hole. Above the hole, a round, wooden basket hung suspended by four ropes. The four ropes connected to a metal ring. The ring attached to two thicker, dual ropes with a self-controlled pulley and handle. This was so the person who used the basket could manipulate its movement up and down. Jonna waved. "Our chariot waits."

The three crowded in although the basket's design fitted two comfortably. Jonna studied the pulley, released the block, and kept the handle from turning too fast. The dimness grew as the daylight faded. The coolness of the earth wafted up to send chills along their spine. Below, oil lamps danced with flame.

The sides of the hole fell away to reveal a wooden dock set on a small shoreline beside the wall of the cave. Curiously, a lion's pelt had been tacked to the cave wall by great nails. Fog hung over the water beyond the dock. Three small wooden boats, four feet wide each and tied off, bobbed softly as the waves struck their bows. They climbed out of the basket.

The picture of the mound of skulls surfaced into Jonna's mind. The soft pat of waves against land echoed in the distance. "It must be in the center of the lake."

The boats had no oars. Long poles lay across the wooden boards that made up their seats. A series of wooden posts stood out in the water every three feet until they vanished into the fog. As Jonna and Lokke climbed into one of the boats, Mumin untied the rope that held it and stepped toward the front. Vibrations shot in all directions disturbing the waves.

Jonna placed the pole into the water and pushed. The boat went smoothly forward to glide into the fog. The cold fog struck their face and hands. Lokke rubbed his hands together and placed them under his thighs.

An eerie calm met their ears. A creature splashed to their right. The wooden posts shifted slightly as if something beneath the waves pushed against them. Extra posts surfaced from the fog, but the distance between them varied.

A diffused brightness grew ahead as the fog distorted their vision. A splash hit the water again, this time closer to the boat.

As the fog thinned, a small island appeared with a dock. On its shore, there were trees and steps that rose to a central shrine but the details were obscured. A man sat on a plain stone throne beneath the shade of one of the trees. Over his shoulders lay two great snakes. Their tails could not be seen, and their tongues licked the air. The man's eyes brightened as a smile crossed his face.

The boat pulled up to the wooden dock. Mumin threw the mooring rope over one of the dock's posts.

"Welcome," a jovial voice laughed. "I am Zahhak, ruler of this island." His focus settled on Jonna, and he held up his hand. "However," his tone became nonchalant, "I must warn you. Whoever steps upon my shore must join me for dinner." His grin widened. "After all, I get so few visitors."

Lokke's eyebrows rose as his head bobbed. "Dinner sounds nice."

Jonna tapped him on the arm. "Lokke."

"I'm just saying."

A frown descended on Jonna's face. "Sir, I seek a woman and a child."

"Indeed?" The man's head shook. "I am the only one on the island. No one ever lasts long." His eyes darted between the three. Whenever he looked at one of them, the two snakes watched the others. "Although, my invitation for dinner is still open." He smiled again.

"That would be--" Jonna glanced back at Mumin who shook his head. "--nice. Mumin, would you stay with the boat?"

Mumin gave a single nod and accepted the pole from Jonna's hand.

Zahhak's eyebrows crossed as his voice dropped. "Two? Only two?" The snakes waved nervously on his shoulders. "No, not two. Four." The smile returned and his voice became louder. "Quickly, this way." He rose from his throne and hurried up the stairs.

Mumin's voice stayed low. "Jonna, we should leave this place; it is evil. This is Zahhak. He is a Deev. He is a demon."

"I must find them, Mumin. I cannot leave." A splash echoed from behind them. "However, there is no reason for either of you to chance this. Both of you should stay in the boat."

Lokke laughed. "Oh come on, Mumin. I'm a half-demon, and you don't see people running from me."

"Deevs are demons who have chosen evil; they were created by it. You have chosen good."

Lokke dismissed Mumin's words with a wave of his hand and climbed out onto the dock. "Come Jonna, let's get this over with. We might be missing dinner." He stepped from the dock to the shore. The island rumbled. Maniacal laughter issued from up the steps. He stopped and stared, but Zahhak could not be seen.

"Yeah," Jonna chuckled. "Nothing evil in that, but we're committed now." As he joined Lokke, a second rumble sounded. The rune blade hummed as a crackle of energy zapped the ground next to Lokke.

Lokke jumped. "Watch where you shoot that thing!"

Mumin called from the boat. "And don't go into the shadows. His minions are everywhere!"

The words shook Jonna, but a touch of the baby's mind made him more determined. His eyes narrowed at the stairs, but his feet raced up them. "They're here. I know they are!"

The stairs led under an umbrella of trees. Shadows dominated the sides. Branches cracked, leaves shifted, and flickers moved just out of sight. A chill went up his spine.

The stairs curved as they rose until they opened to a marble floor with a checkered pattern of red and black. To their right lay a portico. A stone table with stone chairs had been set up. Fruits of various trees sat in bowls around the table but the center remained bare.

"Please--" Zahhak stepped from an archway dressed in a flowing white robe. "Be seated. The main course has," he grinned, "yet to arrive."

Lokke gave a broad smile. "Don't mind if I do."

Jonna caught his elbow and whispered, "You distract him while I hunt."

"Certainly." He turned toward the king and reached to clap him on the shoulder but thought better of it when a snake hissed. "Er-um, you know, we have a lot in common."

The king's eyebrows rose and a strange smile crossed his face. "Do we?"

"We certainly do. You have snakes attached to your shoulders. I have a horn."

As the two headed away, Jonna moved to the left. Where the marble floor ended, a three-foot wall rose. It looked out over the down sloping hill. Splintered bones decorated the landscape all the way to the water. The skulls had been cracked.

His feet leaped over the wall. Old bones snapped under them. Nothing looked fresh, thankfully, or the smell would have been overwhelming.

A trail weaved its way toward the water. It led away from the skulls onto a rocky outcropping. A coo caught his attention. As his gaze scanned above him, a wave of cloth fluttered.

His hands grasped the rocks, found handholds, and worked their way up. A flat plateau appeared with a cave that vanished into the dark.

Salma lay unmoving. The baby was beside her. Jonna scrambled up the last edge and looked them over. The baby stared up at him with large round eyes. A smile crossed its lips.

"Why is it that I never hear you cry in person?" Jonna chuckled. "Not that I'm complaining." He knelt beside Salma and took her pulse. She breathed. When his hand touched the side of her face, her eyes fluttered.

"J--Jonna?"

He nodded.

"Jonna, the marid--"

His voice became hard. "He's dead."

Her eyes met his. "He knew he was going to die. He told me he knew. He wanted to hurt you through me and the baby."

His voice softened. "I know. It will be fine."

A tear started down her cheek. "You don't understand. By coming here, you can never leave, just as we cannot. By being here, we are trapped until our natural lives end."

Zahhak laughed behind them. "Which may be sooner than you think."

Jonna stood up as Zahhak stepped from the darkness of the cave. Behind Zahhak walked Lokke. An ox-headed mace lay in Lokke's right hand.

"Lokke--" Zahhak nodded. "--you know what to do."

Lokke's sober face held no hope. "I'm--sorry." He trembled from an unseen force. "All of you must come with me." Flickers of shadows moved around him. Whispers called from the depths of the cave.

Jonna placed himself between his family and Zahhak. "We will not."

A smug smile struck Zahhak's face. "Even for friend?"

The shadows danced around Lokke. Lokke howled. He seized his right wrist with his left as he dropped to his knees unable to let go of the mace.

"You see, the longer you refuse to obey, the more I will increase Lokke's pain."

The half-demon shrieked. His knuckles turned white as his fist squeezed against the handle of the weapon. One by one, his knuckles popped.

"How much pressure does it take before Lokke's hand breaks?"

The shadows danced. Their whispers became louder.

"Or not." Zahhak waved his hand, and the shadows pulled back.

Lokke sobbed as his lungs heaved. His eyes implored Jonna.

"Perhaps this is the best place." Zahhak smiled. "Kill them."

The half-demon's iron mace lunged forward and dragged Lokke to his feet. Jonna's right hand reached back, pulled the rune blade, and parried the strike in the air. Fire sparked at impact. Jonna's muscles strained.

"You see, my friend." Evil danced in Zahhak's eyes. "This is the Gorz-e Mehr. The very weapon used to subdue me and cast me into this accursed place. Can yours be any stronger?"

The mace skated halfway up the blade's length, broke the pressure, and descended in a quick twirl, but the rune blade shoved it down to miss its target. Gorz-e Mehr circled up and back over Lokke's head to come in toward the left. Jonna clutched the rune blade's hilt with both hands and drove the mace back the other direction. Blinding light shot out as the vibrations ripped down both opponents' arms.

Lokke struggled to let go of the mace but could not release it. Sweat trickled down Jonna's face.

"You cannot win," Zahhak taunted. "Though you struggle, you only delay what will come."

"You are evil Zahhak. Your very use of the weapon corrupts its magic and makes it weak."

Jonna used his legs to push forward and drove Lokke back. The shadows lashed out teasing him to step within their reach.

Zahhak laughed. "There is only one way to end this match." Glee lit his eyes. "You must kill your friend." An evil grin passed over his face. "Either way, my snakes will feast on your brains tonight." The man licked his lips as the two snakes stuck out their tongues. "The meal will be delicious, and your son will be the last."

Jonna's jaw set. His eyes narrowed. The place of darkness brought by Esti's bite surged with new strength. The sword slowly pushed the mace back. "You will not kill my son or anyone else today!"

The word kill echoed in his mind. As his blade held the mace in place, his gaze looked into Lokke's eyes. Lightning formed upon the blade as it jumped from spot to spot. "You have been a good friend, Lokke."

The half-demon's eyes grew round. "No, Jonna! Don't do it!"

"Jan-ros-shan!"

An azure ball of light leaped from the blade. It rose above Lokke's head and crashed on the ground behind him. Blue electricity whipped out as its branches drove back the shadows of darkness.

Two bolts struck: one toward Lokke and the other toward Zahhak. Zahhak flew backwards as the bolt slammed into his chest. The shadow voices screamed. The cave shook. Rocks dropped to the rugged cave floor.

Lokke gasped as the bolt struck his back. He arched forward as his heart stopped. His grip released, and the weapon collapsed to the floor.

Jonna sheathed his blade and rushed to Lokke. "Help me. Quickly!"

Salma and Jonna flipped Lokke on his back. "Breathe into his mouth when I say." Jonna positioned his palms over Lokke's breastbone. He looked into Salma's eyes. "Ready."

Her eyes narrowed as she gazed down at Lokke. "He is dead."

"Call it magic, but do as I request."

She nodded nervously.

"Breathe!"

She pressed her mouth to Lokke's and blew.

Jonna watched her carefully. "Let the air come out; that's it. Now breathe again."

Lokke's lungs expanded and released. Jonna counted as he compressed the half-demon's chest multiple times. "Again."

240

Salma obeyed and watched as the lungs expanded and contracted.

"Again!"

Jonna felt his muscles tense. If the heart didn't start soon--

"Again!"

As Salma neared Lokke to blow, the half-demon coughed. Her eyes opened wide as she watched him blink. She jerked back.

"W--What happened?" His lungs heaved. "I thought I was--"

"Dead?" Jonna gave a nervous chuckle. "You were, my friend. It was the only way."

Water lapped against wood as something plunged into the water. As Jonna and Salma turned toward the lake, Lokke struggled to rise. Mumin floated from the fog toward the rocky shore.

Jonna helped Lokke to his feet. "Hurry! Grab the mace."

Lokke shook his head in rapid strokes. "No way! Never again!" He wiggled his fingers. "I like my hand too much!"

Salma pulled the mace closer. She had to use both hands to lift it. "Here, my lord."

The shadow voices moaned weakly from the dark.

"Take it to the boat with Lokke. I'll get the baby."

Her eyes darted to the child. "But my lord?"

"Go."

His gaze swept toward Zahhak. The demon stirred. Jonna darted toward the baby, picked him up, and hurried down the rocky path.

Lokke and Salma reached the boat first and slipped toward the back with Mumin. The boat rocked as Mumin steadied it with his pole. The vibration sent waves in all directions.

A maniacal laugh echoed from above them. "Try all you want. You cannot flee! Your son will be the last!"

Jonna dropped into the boat as Mumin pushed off. The fog cloaked them. A splash sounded very close. Water drops fell upon their heads. A guttural cry pierced the fog as the boat shifted back and forth.

A wooden post passed them. They turned right as Mumin pushed the boat back the way he had come. The island's diffused light faded. The pole became shorter as Mumin plunged it into the water. His eyes shot to Jonna. "We must move closer to the island before it is too deep."

Thuds on wood caught their ears. The sound approached from Jonna's left until it passed them in the fog and vanished. A splash sent drops into the air as the end of the boat was shoved. Cold fog touched their skin as chills went through them. They shot further out.

"That way," Jonna pointed.

The pole sank until it could not be seen. Something grabbed the other end, and Mumin quickly jerked it back.

The boat dipped sharply sideways. The pole slipped out of Mumin's hand. Water spilled into the boat's bottom. Jonna scrambled to keep his feet dry.

As Mumin plunged his hand after it, the pole shot up from the dark depths. He dodged as it smacked the wood. The boat heaved and began to tip as something struck it under the water.

Jonna threw his weight the other direction. Webbed hands reached out for the baby. He jerked back as the webbed hands grabbed the side of the boat. His free hand came down in a fist.

A wail rose as the hands released. The boat rocked sharply back and forth as something struck its bottom. A guttural cry rose from the depths as a black shape emerged to leap into the air. It swiped at Mumin and Lokke as it soared above them.

Salma thrust the mace up. A screech met their ears as the horns of the ox head raked across the creature's belly. It tumbled out of control and splashed down on the other side of the boat. A murky liquid rose to the water's surface.

Guttural cries echoed. Splashes landed in several places at once.

Jonna looked in the direction they needed to go. "Quickly!"

Instead of trying to reach the bottom, Mumin placed the pole on a nearby post and shoved. The boat launched forward. Lokke reached and grabbed the next. Salma did the same. The splashes grew closer. The guttural cries shrieked in rage as the boat glided swiftly through the fog.

A steady speed built as they ploughed ahead. The line of wooden posts appeared. They turned right and followed the posts.

The cries, though close, did not come nearer. The splashes dropped off one by one. Silence met their ears as they pulled up beside the other boats and glided into the dock.

Lokke leaped out without waiting for the others. He shivered against the cold. Salma followed him, laid the Gorz-e Mehr upon the dock, and turned with outstretched arms for the baby.

Jonna placed him gently in her arms as his heart ached. It was the first time he had held his son. His eyes met hers. "We're almost there."

A rustle drew their attention. On the shore beyond the dock, Zahhak glared. He stood in front of the wooden lift. "You think you've beaten me, but you haven't." Victory shone in his eyes.

Jonna hefted the mace and walked calmly to stand in front of the others while Mumin climbed out of the boat. "Your games are over, Zahhak. You cannot hold us here. Move away from the lift."

A grin spread across his face. "By all means, my friends." A maniacal laugh left his lips as he slipped back.

Jonna eyed him closely. He waved to the others as he refused to let the man out of his sight. "Go."

Mumin moved to the lift, joined by Lokke and Salma. They climbed on as Salma anxiously called, "Come!"

His feet walked backwards toward them. The grin on Zahhak's face grew. The lift creaked. Jonna threw it a glance. "There's no room for all five of us, and he knows it. Go on. When you get to the top, Lokke, you bring it back. I'll watch Zahhak."

"No," Salma pleaded. "You cannot stay here."

Mumin touched her shoulder. "We must get you to safety. We must protect you and the baby."

Lokke shifted uncomfortably as his eyes went to Zahhak. "Jonna, I should stay, too." He gazed at the Deev. "I know his tricks, now."

"Then who will bring it back?"

The half-demon sighed. He used the crank to start the climb up.

The lift rose slowly. When the platform reached the ceiling, the lift stopped and would go no further.

Zahhak chanted. "He who comes to see the land, with foot that's placed on island grand, does step upon the shore that's there, and forever stays within my lair." A grin crossed his face.

A shiver went through Jonna. He remembered the ground as it shook with his first step upon the shore. The lift started down.

"You see, my friends," Zahhak's smile broadened. "There is no escape."

As the lift stopped, Lokke slid off. "He's right. We can't go back."

Jonna thought carefully about the chant. "Tell Mumin to head up."

Zahhak gloated. "It will do you no good."

Lokke blinked. "But we're trapped."

Jonna's voice rose. "Mumin, attempt it anyway."

A slow nod answered, and the lift rose.

Amazement crossed Zahhak's face. "And yet, you still try. Why?"

The lift almost reached the ceiling.

Jonna's eyes narrowed. "They did not step upon your shore. Lokke and I did. Mumin stayed in the boat, and Salma and the baby were carried in through the air."

The lift passed through.

Zahhak's faced turned red with anger; his jaw clenched. "No. No! I will have all of you!" He rushed toward Jonna. The snakes attached to his shoulders hissed and curled. Their bodies elongated and struck at the pair.

Lokke ducked. Jonna dodged. Snake teeth lashed out to bite the air. Zahhak's hands grabbed at Lokke's neck.

The mace slammed into a snake head. Blood oozed from the cracked skull. As the light vanished in its eyes, from Zahhak's shoulders, another grew to take its place.

Lokke punched as he dodged the other snake. Its teeth snapped next to his head. He jabbed with his horn. The snake whipped back.

Zahhak screamed a war cry and lunged. The mace's horns ripped across his stomach twice. The Deev pitched backwards. The wounds bled as he staggered, and an entire third and fourth snake tumbled from them.

Lokke and Jonna leapt away. Zahhak's left shoulder finished its replacement, but the snake on his right shoulder writhed in pain where Lokke's horn had struck its body.

"I don't think this is working." Jonna brought the mace down and crushed the nearest ground snake. The other struck at him but missed. "At least these die." He nailed the second reptile.

Lokke's eyebrows rose. "At least."

The staggering Zahhak slowed. His eyes focused once again as an evil smile curled his lips. He lunged toward them, heedless of the mace. Jonna took aim and swung for the man's human head.

Zahhak slammed into him. The snakes snapped the air. The mace tumbled from Jonna's hands. Lokke jumped, snatched up the mace, and scored on the back of Zahhak's head. The man jerked, his eyes grew, and all three heads collapsed.

Jonna pushed the body from off of him.

Lokke's lungs heaved. "Is he dead?"

Jonna's fingers checked Zahhak's pulse. "Something still beats though I wouldn't call it a heart." He picked up the mace. "I want to make sure he never wakes up."

The voice of Devamilu shouted down from above the ceiling. "Do not kill him!"

"Devamilu?" Jonna looked up slowly. "What are you doing here?"

"Mumin and Salma told me of your plight. I know how to free you."

CHAPTER 19

"Regardless--" Jonna stared down in disgust. "--this menace needs to die." Energy leaped from the handle of his sword. It struck the end of the mace, danced around its handle, and ricocheted between the two sharp horns. He raised the weapon above his head.

"No!" The ifrit descended into the cave though his eyes darted nervously about. "To do so will bring a greater foe upon the world." He pointed to the lion skin nailed to the cavern wall. "And not even the talisman will contain it."

The mace slowly lowered. "What do you suggest?"

"We will leave him here, and I will take you to your proper place." Devamilu extended his hand. "Are you ready?"

A wind stirred through the fog. It spun in twirls of two and three.

Jonna gazed up at the hole. Mumin, Salma, and the baby were there. He whispered as his eyebrows crossed, "Are they safe from the nasnas?"

The ifrit gave a sympathetic nod. "They are safe."

The twirls grew stronger. Liquid leaped from the lake to form waterspouts. Dark shapes with webbed appendages dove for the depths.

Devamilu's voice grew anxious. "We must go, now."

Water creatures with wings rose from the waterspouts and hovered.

Jonna and Lokke grasped the ifrit's hand.

The water creatures boomed, "Ifrits are forbidden to enter the abode of Zahhak. You shall die." A wave of water washed toward them.

The ifrit's flames flared with a golden red light. "Hang on!"

The wave struck. They tumbled toward the cavern wall. Jonna's legs pulled together as his tail formed.

Devamilu's body sizzled as it collided with the water. Steam erupted to block their vision. The liquid spun in a surge that tore at their limbs.

The grip Lokke and Jonna held loosened. The mace slipped from Jonna's grasp to tumble into the torrent. Their fingers stretched as they pulled apart. In a last desperate attempt, Jonna spoke in the water, "*Ba-ru-ya!*"

The azure vortex exploded around them. The walls of the cavern shook. Their bodies hung suspended above the swirling energy as water washed over an invisible bubble. The three spun slowly with Devamilu's hand as the axis.

Devamilu's flames flared brightly with a golden red light as they rotated in-between the void. He turned to Jonna. "You cannot reenter this world, but you have given me respite to take you to your own."

His body simmered. Stars twinkled as darkness claimed all before them. The vision Jonna had seen, reading the words of the gazebo, abruptly made sense. Devamilu carried them across realms of creation. They saw stars that had never been born. They passed through planes of existence that humanity had never imagined nor could find the words to describe.

Their fingers slipped further until they barely touched. The ifrit gave a knowing nod. "I will remember, Jonna. I will remember the evil that my father, the Destroyer, did. I will remember the love that my mother gave. I will remember your sacrifice--Farewell." Their fingers slipped apart.

~

Jonna felt solid ground beneath him. Grass touched the side of his head. As he opened his eyes, a forest rose above him with its gigantic trees. His voice whispered, "Is this home, or--"

A tiny winged creature floated into sight. The light sparkled from its wings, and it laughed in delight. "It is our home, but I don't know if it's yours." Its giggle was joined by others. Jonna pushed up from the ground to see a sparkling miniature palace set in the trees.

Familiarity struck his nose. The scent of the forest smelled the same. "Do you know me?"

The winged creature bowed. "But of course, Lord Jonna. Your exploits are known throughout the realm, despite your somewhat--" She flew to his shoulder and waved to the others. "--disheveled appearance."

A sparkling thread whipped through the air as multiple faeries maneuvered it into place. One punched a hole into the end of a pine needle, threaded it, and stitched pieces of his shirt together. As the stitch on one rip finished, the two pieces merged leaving no evidence of a seam. The faeries worked until the shirt became whole.

"There now. Isn't that better?" The faery bowed before him. It rose to meet his gaze with sober eyes. "Are you lost, my lord?"

He nodded slowly. "Somewhat. Can you point me toward my home?"

"Of course. We faeries know every part of the forest." She winked at him. "It is our domain after all. You may call me Zimola." She turned toward another faery. "Unile, call Xaymin at once. Send word that Lord Jonna has been found. Timplemay and Offsemar, you will journey with Lord Jonna and Unile to his abode."

A sparkling faery raised her hand. Her wings glittered in rainbow colors. "Can I go? A flower needs aid, and I would love the company."

Zimola nodded with a smile. "Of course, Poetestay." Her eyes swept the trees. "Are there others?"

Hands went up all around her; she laughed. "We can't all go. We can't neglect our chores." Her finger pointed. "Zetta and

Zephan, you better go, too, just in case. The rest of us back to work." She bowed to Jonna. "I shall report to Questar at once."

The faeries flittered in excitement as they dashed about. Their wings caught the light in sparkles as rays of sunlight bounced.

"If you are ready, my lord." Timplemay curtsied as she hung in the air. She pointed toward the right. "We should go this way."

As Jonna rose, Unile, Offsemar, Poetestay, Zetta, and Zephan flew behind Timplemay. Another faery appeared but fluttered into some flora.

Jonna turned toward the direction Timplemay pointed and bowed. "After you." The faeries giggled as Timplemay started forward.

A breeze floated through the trees. It brought the pleasant fragrance of flowers. Never had Jonna smelled aromas so vivid. Red, pink, and purple azaleas glowed beneath the trees. White, bell-shaped flowers hung from evergreen shrubs. The fragrance of nutmeg struck his nose. Red berries lay to one side. Heart-shaped leaves cast a faint spicy aroma. To his surprise, his nose separated each with unusual clarity. "This is not fall?"

Timplemay smiled. "It is spring, my lord."

"I left as fall started." His lips pursed. "This makes no sense."

Several faeries joined to lift a branch that had fallen across the trail. It rose as he approached and gently dropped to lie among the trees.

Timplemay turned to Offsemar. "Please make a note to clean that up. Questar will check that the trails are clear."

With bright eyes, Offsemar nodded. He produced a tiny piece of the parchment, pulled out a quill, and made a mark. As Jonna walked by him, the faery hurried to catch up with the others.

A tree stump bordered by gigantic tree trunks came into view. Though the trail continued, Timplemay led him toward the trunk. She waved her hand, and her face broke into a broad smile. "Your transport, my lord."

Jonna touched one of the trees and cautiously passed between them. The old charred stump had jagged spires on one side though the rest lay relatively flat. He glanced back at her with eyes wide open.

Her tiny voice prompted, "Please, step up."

The wind stilled. With feet on the stump, he turned to Timplemay.

The faeries spread out around him, each equidistant from the others. Their tiny voices joined to sing.

"Sparkles of a magic held

By forest trees and distant dells,

We bid thee bring a spark to bear

This human to his abode so fair."

Glimmers of sparkles dropped toward him from the trees. The branches moved though no wind blew. A twirl of glowing lights appeared to descend toward the stump. A small creature leaped into the faery ring.

Prickles of static electricity touched him on every side. The faeries rose above his head and clasped hands. They fluttered as they circled in dance.

"Sparkles of a magic held

By forest trees and distant dells,

We bid thee bring a spark to bear

This human to his abode so fair."

The glowing lights twirled faster. The wings of the faeries increased their movement. The outside view of the world beyond the circle of trees waved. The distortion grew until it could not be seen.

The singing dropped. The dancing stopped. As the faeries released their hands, the outside world formed again.

A different forest waved in a gentle wind. The wind passed through the circle of trees and blew upon his face. The smell of horse manure assaulted his nose. The stump he stood on had been shaped and flattened.

"We are here!" Timplemay glowed. He followed her through

the gigantic trees that created the second faery ring and found another path.

The trail continued though the forest vanished. As they strode from the trees, a barley field sprouted to his right and a wheat field to his left.

Timplemay led Jonna toward a curve in the road. Mountains rose beyond the wheat field, and he could hear the sound of a river. He could smell the scent of moving water. It stirred his nix connection. *The Sight* hit. In the vision that appeared, sometime soon, three armed people would travel with him toward a river.

The curve went right. The road wove along the edge of the forest. The laughter of children met his ears. At a junction in the road, a signpost pointed three directions. The sign that pointed directly ahead had been newly refreshed with paint. Jonna read the words. "Castle McCambel." He stood stunned. The last he knew, they lived in the elves' tree city.

Timplemay spotted his shocked expression. "Are you ill, my lord?"

His lungs breathed in deeply and let the air out slowly as his eyes caught hers. "No, no, continue, please." The group moved forward.

Dread surged up in him. The ifrit had not been able to return to him to his home. Each step he took grew heavier as he marched down the road. He decided to ask, "Timplemay, how long have I lived in the castle?"

The faery tilted her head. "Time is so relative, especially between humans and those of magic." Her cheeks dimpled. "Excluding you, I mean, my lord." She tapped her lips. "Perhaps, twenty cycles?"

Jonna's eyebrows rose. "Twenty years?"

"I would have to consult Questar to be exact. You had it built after you defeated Lord Tanyl when he tried to take the elvish throne." She smiled broadly. "You brought peace to our land."

The trees thickened on each side of the road as the border of the field to their left curved toward them. The road narrowed.

Lord Tanyl's name boomed back. The elf had been at the ceremony when Jonna had signed the scroll along with Lord Tanyl's betrothed, Lady Mylaela. The two had not bowed.

They walked deeper into the forest. The vibration of a spider-thread rope whistled from above. His gaze focused up. From the trees, a basket descended. It touched the forest floor so softly, no sound occurred.

The door opened. Two elvish guards appeared from the trees as Sir Verity stepped from the basket.

"You're alive!" The elf sighed with relief. "We thought you were dead!"

The basket stirred. With a glowing smile, Lady Mylaela stepped into the forest light. Her curled, auburn hair bounced lightly upon her shoulders.

At her side, a beautiful young woman gazed at him with bright eyes. The woman rushed toward him and threw her arms around him. "Father!"

With wide eyes, he whispered, "Elpis? You're all grown up!"

Her laugh came like a pleasing song. "Dad, you were only missing a week." Her grip tightened as he hugged her. She released him with a bright smile and pushed back gently. "But thank you for the compliment." The fae caught her eye, and she grinned. "You found new companions."

Poetestay came forward. "A pleasure to meet you. This is so exciting!"

Unile sniffed to keep back tears. "You're so big now. The stories we heard were of a little girl found in Diggory!"

Zephan and Zetta sprinkled faery dust in a quick circle. It dropped over Jonna and Elpis' heads. Offsemar shied back. Timplemay grinned.

Mylaela stepped to his side and slipped her arm around him. She whispered into his ear, "And she's not the only one who missed you."

Jonna's eyes closed. It was all wrong, and yet, Elpis was his same little girl all grown up. "Is everyone okay?"

"For the moment," Sir Verity's weighty voice interrupted.

Jonna opened his eyes and stared at the elf.

"My lord, we should return to the palace immediately. I have grave news which must be dealt with."

Mylaela gave him a slight squeeze. "Your return could not have come at a better time though the celebration may have to wait." She lightly touched her lips to his and whispered, "Tonight is not that far away."

Leaves crunched from their left. The guards swung toward the sound and drew their weapons. A single elf scout raced toward them. The sound of another creature sprinted in pursuit. The creature stopped, and a thud sounded. The elf scout staggered past the closest tree and dropped to the ground at the guards' feet. A human arrow extended from his back.

Sir Verity waved toward the woods. "Find the assassin!" Elvish guards materialized from beside trees and tall shrubs. He turned to Jonna. "We must get you safely inside."

Jonna broke Mylaela's hold while she drew her weapon. He dropped to his knees beside the fallen elf and rolled him over.

The elf's eyes met his as words mumbled from his lips. "Lord Tanyl by the Enaid River." The elf's lips quivered. "They mass at the river."

Jonna looked up at the others. "Tend him. Do not let him die!" Tears struck the corners of his eyes as the word *die* roared through him. Too many had died to save his life.

Two elves approached from his right. They lifted the runner and made their way to the basket. The basket ascended.

Jonna rose as his jaw clenched. "Which direction did he scout?"

Sir Verity touched his arm. "My lord, we need a plan."

"We must attack before their scout returns. How many elves are ready?"

"Four legions can descend at any moment. Others are on patrol."

"I want three of the best warriors."

Sir Verity leaned near. "My lord, I caution you against this."

"Three," Jonna's words remained firm.

Mylaela stepped up. "I will be one." Her elvish blade shone in the light.

He stared into the eyes of a woman he did not know, and yet, he trusted her; after all, Elpis seemed at ease. "We need two more."

She turned to Sir Verity. "Call Peredur and Agtoa."

As an elf hurried to enter another descending basket, Elpis caught him and whispered something out of Jonna's hearing. He nodded, stepped in, and rose into the trees. Jonna watched the basket go and then shifted his gaze toward the forest.

Several armed elves returned. They carried a body among them. With hands and feet bound, it was tersely dropped on the same spot where the scout had fallen. It was human, and from it, words spat up. "If you're going to kill me, do it now. I will tell you nothing."

A basket descended from the city. As it touched, the door opened and two elves clad in leather armor stepped out. Each held a sword and a bow. They stopped beside Elpis and handed her a sword, two quivers, and two bows. They moved next to Jonna. "We were called, my lord?

A faint skunk odor struck Jonna's nose as he knelt near the man. His nix knowledge kicked in. He remembered how vivid the smells of the forest were when he had first walked with the fae. The odor reminded him of skunk cabbage. The shrub covered the sides of some forest streams.

Other things stood out as well. A mix of sand and clay lay moist on the edges of the man's boots. Based on the information he had learned in the nix's pool, the scent of the river water and the mix of the soil matched a crossing about a quarter mile away. He looked the man in the eyes. "You've told me all I need to know."

Timplemay dropped near Jonna's face.

With wide eyes, the bound man tried to pull away.

She curtsied to Jonna. "My lord, we would like to help." The other faeries nodded.

"Very well."

Giggles of delight erupted.

"But we must keep silent."

They all covered their mouths and continued to nod.

As he stood up, they rose with him. Jonna turned to the others. "The man we want is Lord Tanyl. No other should suffer. However, if our mission is at risk, do not hesitate to do what must be done."

Timplemay nodded with round eyes. "We can help scout."

Elpis stepped forward and held out a bow with quiver to Mylaela. Mylaela accepted and dropped the quiver over her shoulder. As Elpis prepared her own, she spoke, "I want to come, too."

"No."

"But, Dad."

His voice rose. "You have no knowledge of war. These have already experienced it."

Her voice hardened. "I saw Tanyl kill Elfleda with the Dagger of Dilysmer. I have the right to be there."

The words stung Jonna. So that was how Elfleda died in this world?

Anger lit its fire within him. "I don't--" The thought brought a lump to his throat. "You are not ready."

"But--"

Mylaela placed a hand on her shoulder. "Your father is right. After more training, perhaps." She turned toward Elpis and shook her head. "Once you step across, you can never go back."

Elpis narrowed her eyes, but said nothing.

Jonna turned toward the forest. "Move out."

The fae divided their forces. Timplemay and Offsemar stayed with Jonna, Poetestay hung by Mylaela, Zetta floated by Peredur, and Zephan kept to Agtoa.

The trees swept by as Jonna weaved left and forward. The knowledge that Tanyl had killed Elfleda ate into his human soul.

The rushing of mighty waters touched his ears. Huge rocks adorned the crossing and blocked their view of the other side. Jonna climbed halfway up the nearest rock and turned to Timplemay. "What do you see?"

She fluttered above the rock and peered. "No one is here. No one crosses the ford. Wait! There are two eyes. Yes, I see them! Two eyes in the shadows!"

Jonna nodded. "Where there's one pair, there may be more." He dropped from the rock to land lightly on some barren soil. "Who knows the other side of the river?"

Peredur raised a finger. "I do, my lord."

"Can you get to the other side without being seen?"

The elf nodded.

"I need to know where their camp is." He turned to Offsemar. "Would you go with him, as well as Zetta, to bring back word?"

Offsemar's tiny head nodded. His voice squeaked, "I will, my lord."

"Thank you." He swung back to Peredur. "If you find him, wait for us. I want no mistakes."

Peredur shifted right, wove around rocks, and slipped from sight.

Jonna turned as a tiny creature ducked behind a tree. Timplemay twisted to face the river and motioned with her thumb to Poetestay and Zephan. The two spread out right and left to vanish in the flora. Jonna positioned himself so that he could watch the spot from his left peripheral.

A tiny head peeked out. A flutter of wings beat the air. The bodies of Poetestay and Zephan slowly approached from behind. Poetestay placed her hands on her waist and called out sharply, "Uphren, how could you?"

The tiny faery bolted to the right, but Zephan snagged him. "Not so fast! Does Zimola know you're gone?"

A sheepish smile crossed Uphren's face.

"I thought not." Zephan huffed. "She's not going to be happy."

"I had to come!" Uphren pleaded. "You found Lord Jonna, and--"

Poetestay pointed. "You go home right now and--"

Timplemay raised a hand. "Shh." A noise stirred from the other side of the river. She rose above the rock.

"Three are on horseback: two men and one elf. The elf is in the lead. Crossbows--the two men carry crossbows." She ducked toward Jonna. "They're coming!"

Jonna turned to the others. "Do nothing unless I say. Follow when word has come from Peredur." Mylaela and Agtoa nodded.

Poetestay pointed to Uphren. "Hide right here! Got it?"

Uphren nodded quickly.

She dashed to float beside Mylaela.

Mylaela slipped back into the foliage, and emerged on the opposite side of the trail. Zephan joined Agtoa. They pressed closer to the rocks as they shifted away from Jonna. Jonna moved back down the trail with Timplemay. He found an easy spot to hide and stepped out of sight. Timplemay kept watch around a tree.

Water splashed louder as those who approached from the far side reached the center of the ford. One of the horses grunted, another neighed, but the riders forced them on. As their hooves touched the near bank, both Mylaela and Agtoa slipped deeper into the brush.

The horses trod past the large rocks and into the trees on the marked trail. The elf pulled back and the horse stopped. "I know you're there. Come out and this will be much easier."

Jonna stepped onto the trail. "Who are you?"

"That depends," the elf grinned, "on who you are."

"I am Jonna McCambel of the woodland elves."

The elf leaned back on the horse. "Well, Jonna. I am Aldyth, and I have been contracted by Lord Tanyl to find you."

"Then I have made your job easy." Jonna walked nonchalantly toward them. "Shall we go to see Tanyl?"

"Hm." The elf shook his head and glanced at the two men with him. "I should have charged double just for the profit." A chuckle came from both. "Very well." The horses walked backwards from the center of the trail as they let Jonna pass. "And in elvish tradition, since you are a lord, I'll even let you keep your weapon. However, try nothing, or you will die."

Jonna nodded. "Thank you." Past the rocks, the bank angled toward the river. The thought of walking through the stream brought him up short. "Might I ask for a ride?" He motioned toward the elf's horse.

"Afraid of a little water?" The elf laughed. "Unfortunately, we only have three, and though you amiably come with us, I do not trust you."

A chuckle escaped Jonna's lips. "As well you shouldn't. But remember, if I walk across, you bring the consequences upon yourself." He waved toward the water. "Shall I proceed?"

The elf's horse moved beside him as the elf watched. "By all means."

Jonna walked into the river; colors rose in swirls around his legs. The cool liquid flowed over his feet. He knew what would happen, but he had never tried to halt the transition before. His skin responded to the water's touch, yet his will fought against it. The rune blade gave a slight hum as he focused on staying human.

Aldyth traced the river with his eyes. They returned to stare at Jonna as he slipped back behind.

No change occurred as Jonna reached the center of the ford, but his lungs heaved. Every moment he fought to resist, the nix part became stronger. The rune blade's hum grew.

As he cocked his head, the elf's voice rose. "Halt! Do not move!"

The noching of crossbows met Jonna's ears. Unable to fight anymore, he threw himself into the river. Crossbow bolts plunged into the water.

"Reload!" The elf spurred his horse after Jonna. It jumped out of the ford to sink deeper. As the horse's head submerged, the elf leaped from it.

Jonna released his will as he dropped beneath the surface. His nix tail flashed into existence. He flipped further down as another splash struck above him, and the head of Aldyth appeared. Air bubbles rose from the elf's face as he searched with open eyes. They grew large as Jonna reached up and pulled him deeper still.

The current pushed them downstream. Fish scattered at their approached. Jonna's tail spun them around to dodge sharp rocks. As Aldyth struggled against Jonna's hold, the elf's right hand reached toward a dagger at his waist.

Jonna caught the hand. They flipped back and forth in the water. The elf brought his knees up and pushed. Jonna's hold slipped as his body shoved downward to strike against the bottom of the river. The elf rose upward, pulled his dagger, and dove.

A flip of Jonna's tail shot him out of the way as the dagger struck. It bit deeply into the bottom. Clouds of sediment billowed.

Jonna spun but could not see the elf. His nix senses stirred. He dodged as a blade flashed. He pulled the sheathed rune blade.

Blue energy crackled to cast eerie shadows in all directions. The elf's eyes narrowed as he darted back.

Jonna's voice traveled clearly through the water. "Tell Lord Tanyl, I am coming to find him."

The elf sheathed his dagger and climbed toward the surface.

The current caught Jonna. He floated downstream, still under the water, until the elf could no longer be seen. The rune blade slid into its sheath. The river deepened.

Currents stirred beneath him as he tried to think about his next move. A transparent face with flowing hair formed in the water beside him. "Jonna," its high-pitched voice whispered.

He floated to his side to see it better.

"Jonna, this is not your destiny."

He knew the words were true, but had no idea how to change it. "I--know. Nothing is right."

"To continue this course will only bring your death. It will stop what was meant to be. Do you not feel the current's call? There is but one path for you to take before the gods choose otherwise."

Jonna reached with his nix senses. The river responded. A path lay through a stream that ended at a lake. The raven's words echoed back. "Find the hill that mountain-borne, lies past lakes and snakes the thorn. When you seek what you will find, then you'll know the right of mind."

An image appeared in the water. The path led past a shore whose bank held a thicket of dense thorns. They spread away from the water as far as the eye could see.

He nodded slowly. "I will heed your words."

"You must tell the keeper of the lake that Cyhiraeth gave you pass. Do you understand?"

His head nodded again. "Thank you."

"Go, before the fate that you created finds you, and you hear my cry of death."

With a great swish of his tail, Jonna sped with the currents. He swept toward a cavity in the river that opened to a cave. The current became faster. It curved under the forest to pass into the depths of the dark.

The knowledge to travel this world lay in his mind. The pool of Aroha's knowledge showed him the way. Though he could not see it, he knew the land above raced by. As the darkness faded, a light appeared ahead.

The current merged into a lake. As his head broke the surface of the water, he saw trees, much smaller than those of the elves, standing upon islands. Among the islands stood three tall towers. To his right, a thicket of thorns formed a barrier that vanished into the distance away from the water's edge.

Ravens landed in the trees on the islands. Their cries filled the valley around the lake. Cooking fires on a shore between the thicket and the islands wafted smells of fish in his direction.

His stomach grumbled. The exertion of his nix form had used up a lot of energy. His tail swished forward.

"Well now," a deep voice boomed. "Who be ya' now? Nix don't often live long in these waters."

With a flip of the tail, Jonna followed the voice. On the nearest island, a tall, stocky man watched him. He sat before a fire as fish turned upon a spit. A small boat bobbed near the shore.

From a fish in his hand, the man cut off small chunks and tossed them to the ravens. A glowing net lay to his left. Jonna's amulet hung from a corner of the man's table.

Jonna approached slowly. "I seek the keeper of the lake."

"Well ya' found him. And now that ya' have, what are you going to do?" His eyes peered into Jonna's. Without breaking eye contact, he placed the fish down and raised a mighty hammer. The handle held a twisted star just above the grip. "This lake and the fish belong to the Clan Raven Smith dwarfs. If ya' want to hunt here, you'll have to go through me."

Jonna shifted back and kept his eyes from straying toward the amulet. "I don't want to hunt at all." He ignored the hunger in his stomach. "Cyhiraeth sent me."

The man closed one eye and narrowed the other. "Prove it. Where's the gem?"

Jonna's head shook. "She never mentioned a gem."

The man's muscles bulged as he sat the hammer down beside the seat and opened his closed eye. "Just like her. Send a nix in without a clue. Then again, most nix don't know what clues are to have. You're different."

He crossed his arms and leaned back in his chair. "Where the river flows from this lake, a small alcove lies under the water. Your price to be here is to retrieve one gem. One, and bring it to me. If ya' so much as eat a fish, or do anything else I deem as unnecessary, I will net ya', cook ya', and feed ya' to the ravens. Do ya' understand?"

Jonna's eyes narrowed. "Those are stout words, especially from a thief."

261

"Thief?" The man gave a hearty laugh. "I've stole nothing of yours."

"You have my amulet."

"A raven gave it me." The man grinned. "Ya' want it back, find the gem."

CHAPTER 20

Jonna and the lake keeper locked eyes. The ravens fell silent. As if sensing the encounter, others by the fires on the shore pointed toward the island. A few moved toward their boats.

A hearty flicker danced behind the dwarf's expression. "Try me, I dare ya'. Do ya' think I've been the keeper this long without some way of enforcing it?"

The Sight hit. Jonna looked up and to the right. Images flickered in his mind of the alcove beneath the water, long dark tentacles, a tiny faery named Uphren, and Elpis' face.

The man's voice speculated, "There's a *Sight* you don't usually see in a nix."

Jonna's voice hardened. "I'll get your gem. You keep your word."

As Jonna dropped beneath the water's surface, the ravens resumed their calls, and a hearty laugh echoed across the lake.

The sound muffled. He drifted away from the island, felt the current through his hair, and adjusted his path toward the river's headwaters.

Fish separated at his approach. The hunger in his stomach grew. The nix part of him had no qualms about biting into a fresh one, but the human part fought against it.

A stone marker appeared on the lake floor. The Elvish symbol of eternity stared up at the surface of the water. Beyond it, the ground dropped sharply as a whirlpool spun in a column.

The current sucked at him though his fin kept it at bay. Beneath the spinning whirlpool, light glistened from an assortment of gems, silver and gold weapons, yellowish shields, and four-pronged hooks.

The vision of the long, dark tentacles made him wary. He tracked along the edge of the drop-off till it curved into a stone wall. The wall consisted of large, cut rock stacked uniformly. Elvish markings decorated the stones though the majority lay buried in the silt of the lake.

Elvish? Here? Why?

A flick of his tail pushed him closer to the wall. Where the silt touched, the edges of a set of stairs led down into the drop-off.

He counted as he went. Based upon the size of the stones, the stairs stopped at thirty feet.

Dark entrances met his eyes. Their wooden doors lay crumbled in heaps upon the ground. Metal latches, hinges, and large rings of gold glittered up in the stray rays of light.

No gems glowed from the entrances. The idea that they originated here did not make sense. The tilt of the gem pile and its position gave clue that they were carried by the current and dropped into the alcove from above. If this was not their origin, what was this place?

He swam closer to the first entrance. His pixie sight kicked in. Corners of the room beyond lit up as the edges of the blocks showed different depths of color. Holes stood out in stone walls about the height of-- His tail gave a half-curve as his body floated in. More holes, not just in the walls, but also in the floor. His body turned slowly. If he didn't know better, this felt like a dungeon. A dungeon in the lake? Items washed into an alcove? None it made sense unless it used to be a city.

Water jetted out. He could hear the noise separate from the whirlpool column. His fin swept him toward the entrance to scan the area.

Nothing else moved, and the noise had vanished. He drifted toward the gems. His hand brushed the weapons upon the floor; the exquisite craftsmanship showed not only elvish designs but others as well.

TWISTED FATES

The gems sparkled. Red, blue, yellow, and clear were dominant, but purple and green also lay scattered throughout. He picked up a clear stone and turned it over in his hand. The facets caught the light from above and created a mirror of the things behind. In its reflection, something long and dark slipped toward him.

He dropped the gem, flipped, and pulled away. A long tentacle with suction cups whipped by. His nix sense felt another, and he dodged. Two more came from the sides as a second jet of water met his nix senses.

The creature shifted to contain him between the stone wall and the whirlpool. His hands reached down and grabbed the first thing they touched: one of the four-pronged hooks. He swung it at a tentacle. The tentacle whipped back as another came from a different direction. The hook scored. The tentacle thrashed. It jerked Jonna toward the others. An almost transparent tail snaked after the hook. Its design reminded Jonna of the spider-woven ropes used to lift the elvish baskets.

One of the creature's appendages smacked against his body. A mild sting rippled through him. He dodged back, but his reflexes were slowed. Light slaps hit him on every side.

Dizziness struck him. He could not tell up from down. Twelve tentacles, six on each side reached to pull him in.

His eyes cleared enough to see a single way out directly beneath the creature. His tail flipped, his body shot forward, and the creature snagged him with a thirteenth tentacle under its belly.

He inhaled sharply as a strange feeling of euphoria filled his mind. His struggle stopped, and the stings vanished. His eyes slowly closed. The raven's words entered his mind, but they no longer seemed to matter. He drifted on a gentle cloud suspended in the air.

A jet of water struck his face as the creature tightened its grip. Jonna's eyelids struggled to open. Through the slits, the transparent face of Cyhiraeth appeared before him. "Wake. The gods cannot have you yet." She touched him on the shoulder.

The euphoria lessened. The disorientation passed. Though the grip of the tentacle held his body, his hands were not bound.

The rune blade flashed as he drew it and sliced through the thirteenth tentacle. The appendage unraveled to sink toward the bottom.

The creature expanded. Its tentacles elongated and lashed. A dark ichor poured from the wound to block out the light from above.

The rune blade's power rose around Jonna as he drove straight up into the beast's belly. A wail rose from its lips as the elvish blade bit deep.

It tried to jet from Jonna, but its body wouldn't respond. The movement of the tentacles slowed, its four eyes slowly closed, and it went silent. As its body turned sideways to float toward the surface of the water, it struck the wall that contained the lake.

Jonna sheathed the rune blade, but the exertion caused the nix in him to rise. His eyes spotted a school of fish. With a swish of his tail, he shot forward and snatched one from the group.

His mouth salivated at the thought. It squirmed in his grasp. The dwarf's warning rolled through his mind. On the verge of exhaustion, he thrust it away.

The force drove him back. The touch of something behind him made him spin around. The spin entangled his lower fin and cast him into the whirlpool's edge.

The current shot him upward. He rose above the alcove where it slammed him against the wall. The higher he went, the stronger the push until he broke the surface.

The flowing lake held him firmly to the edge as he struggled to free his lower fin from a spider-woven rope. Debris from the lake rolled toward him and knocked him into a waterfall's torrent.

His nix body slid over a flat surface until it tumbled down an immense waterfall. In twists and turns, his fin came free, but he plummeted toward the river's headwaters.

As he struck the water, air bubbles rose all around him. The roar of the falls deafened his ears. Sticks and branches poked him in a relentless mass of broken ends.

Gradually, the water calmed. Able to move only weakly, he floated with the current. Hunger tore at his insides.

Rocks swept by. Currents swung him about. Gurgling sounds met his ears. At long last, a log bumped his body.

As his hands dipped down, he felt the ground beneath him. Slowly, he broke the surface, flipped over, and dragged himself to the bank.

The thicket of thorns had vanished. In its place lay trees of various fruits. The water upon his fin dried as the sun bore down.

His legs reformed, and with them, the appetite of the nix lessened. His thoughts drifted from the idea of raw fish to the fruits that caught his attention on the ground.

He ate hungrily though what kind of fruit it was, he could not tell. A tiny creature dropped near him and zipped away at lightning speed. The voice of Elpis met his ears. "Father!"

His gaze rose. With bow in hand, she hurried down the hill. A quiver lay upon her back. Around her waist, a belt held a leather-tied pouch, a dagger, and a sword.

The fruit restored his strength, but the weakness left in stages. He whispered, "I told you--"

"Hush." She put a finger to his lips as she kneeled beside him. "Whether you like it not, I'm here, and I'm going to help."

A slight chuckle escaped his lips. "You remind me of--" A tear struck his eye, but he pushed it away. "How did you find me?"

"I waited long enough for you not to see me and tagged behind. Peredur's fae did not come, so the others started to search along the river for you. Uphren told me what happened and joined me." A smug smile hit her lips. "Apparently, we found you first."

Uphren grinned. "It was the wail of the scycalite. I know its cry. You defeated it, my lord!" The fae's chest rose in pride. "It was a bane to all magical creatures as it sucked the magic from them until their physical bodies failed. Shall I tell the others?"

"No." Jonna's voice hardened as he looked up into his daughter's face. "Our path is another way."

Her eyebrows crossed. "But your plan?"

By dragging his body back, he leaned against a tree. His strength continued to return. "Up this river is a lake guarded by a protector. I must gain entry."

"Why?"

"It is the only way to restore what should be."

Elpis wrinkled her brow. "I don't understand."

They rose together. Jonna extended his hand. "Trust me." As her hand touched his, he felt the warmth of her love.

"Always, father."

He grinned. "Just not enough to stay home?"

"Don't even go there. I'm over twenty, you know."

"I can't disagree."

They followed the river until the thicket of thorns appeared. The clusters blocked their path. Though Elpis cut them with her elvish sword, they immediately grew back.

Jonna nodded. "Magic protected." He stretched. The walk had helped to revive him. "I thought as much. Between the protector, the scycalite in the water, the mountains, and the thickets at the sides, this place is like a fortress." The idea made him think of the city beneath the lake. "They are protecting something, but what I do not know. Yet, it has to do with what I must find."

Elpis watched the waterfall. The rush of water roared as it struck, producing great, white foam at the bottom. Just above the foam, rocks jutted out in steps reaching almost halfway up until it met a smooth stone surface. "How are we going to reach it if we can't cut through the thicket?"

Jonna remembered his fin being tangled and scanned the top of the waterfall. A thin, almost transparent, thread bounced periodically from the falling water. "There, an elven rope. It has dropped over the edge." He pointed with his finger. "That's the fastest way in."

They followed the edge of the thicket down to the water. Waves frothed against the shore.

"Can you climb?"

"Dad, we live in a tree."

They stepped from stone to stone along the shore. Mist shot toward them. Sprays leaped above to descend again. Each time they hit, Jonna could feel the nix call though he resisted. Sweat trickled down as he struggled to hold off the transformation.

At the right side of the great falling water, gaps between rock ledges could be seen. He slipped between two and worked his way up toward the rope. Splashes tested his willpower. He gritted his teeth to keep from turning. The pattern of the water shifted to give a visual guide of the rope's location.

As a human, the coolness of the lake water numbed his hands. His eye kept watch on Elpis though she never complained. Uphren dodged back and forth to avoid the falling liquid.

When Jonna's hands grasped the spider-woven rope, he gave two quick tugs. The rope gave slightly but held. "Are you sure?"

Elpis' gaze remained steadfast. Her hands gave a slight quiver, but she nodded. Her teeth chattered, "You just have a plan for when we get to the top. That's all I ask." Her eyes met his.

What to do at the end of their climb had never occurred to Jonna. He planned to pull himself with the rope across the top of the stone wall and flip his transformed body into the lake on the other side. With tail not entangled, he should have no problem battling the torrent. Elpis presented a different problem. She could freeze or drown while trying to move across the top of the stones.

He climbed until he stood upon the tallest rock. Behind him stood the flat stone wall. "Come beside me."

She started toward him. "What are you going to do?"

"I'll go first." He wrapped the end of the rope around her and secured it with a double knot. "When I get on the other side, I'll give a tug. Take a deep breath before dowsing yourself in the water. It will chill you to the bone. Don't stop. If you stop, you'll freeze. Can you handle that?"

Her head nodded slowly.

He grinned. "Alright, let's do this."

With one hand on the rope, he reached up with the other and pulled himself hand over hand toward the top of the stone wall. Water poured over him as gravity aided the descending flood. A glance back showed Elpis as she clung to the rocks to keep the rope steady while her own body served as an anchor for them both.

The pouring liquid struck his face and drenched his body. He shook his head to keep it out of his eyes and fought to stay in control of his will.

His hands numbed, but he could not change. He needed his feet to help control the rope. His lungs labored against the chill.

Jonna's hand touched the top of the wall. The water poured down in a mass. His willpower slipped. His feet tried to turn. In a last great effort, he heaved up to splash down into the torrent.

The chill of the water stopped as his tail formed. Still with his hands on the rope, he used his tail to push against the torrent. Despite the increased strength, he breathed heavily as he dropped into the lake contained by the thick stone wall.

He tugged twice. The rope vibrated back and forth as he felt Elpis climb. The seconds passed. The vibrations stopped. He rose to look above the water's surface as his tail used great strokes to hold his body still.

His daughter's hand stretched up from the other side briefly but vanished. Uphren searched from above the water but did not drop in. When the rope didn't move, Jonna heaved.

Every muscle bulged. His arms shook. The water held Elpis back like a huge whale on a string. By inches, she lifted over the far side and pulled toward him. His fin felt the strain. When he ducked beneath the water to check her progress, she had only made it halfway. At this rate, she would die. He knotted a loop in the spider-woven rope to take up the slack.

With a grasp upon it, he flipped his tail back on top of the stone wall and worked his way toward her. Her eyes saw but did not blink though the irises did expand. Her lips had turned blue though her jaws remained tightly clenched. Her body shook.

His right hand gripped tightly as his fingers reached out. At his touch, her eyes blinked, and he watched the blue lips turn red. "Hold onto my arm. When I swing around, climb onto my back."

She nodded with eyes wide open. As she grasped his arm tightly with both hands, he shifted the direction of his body to point toward the lake and took firm hold on the rope.

Under the water, Jonna's nix tail waved above the flat stone surface as the current shoved against him. He felt Elpis' hands adjust until her arms encircled his neck.

A grunt left his lips at he moved hand over hand toward the lake. His fingers twitched with the strain. His tail thrust forward to relieve the pressure but with her weight bearing down upon him, it did little good.

With trembling arms, he lowered them both down into the lake's alcove. The four-pronged hook shifted as the tentacle it had pierced bobbed in the water. They slipped past the scycalite, dodged the whirlpool, and skimmed the floor. Jonna picked up the diamond he had dropped and handed it to Elpis. "Will you carry this?"

Still with wide eyes, she nodded, undid the leather wrap of her pouch, and placed the clear stone securely inside. They drifted up.

Elpis' grasp around his neck relaxed in stages. She adjusted to a single handhold and raised the other like a flag through the water.

The drag increased, but not much. The fact that she recovered quickly pleased him. The fact that she did not freak out about his tail pleased him even more. Perhaps *The Sight* had prepared her?

At the top of the underwater stairs, his nix senses said to head slightly right to reach the islands, but he chose to swing out in a wide circle and check the bottom of the lake.

The depth rarely dropped less than ten feet, and in many occasions it deepened even beyond the depth of the alcove. They passed over stairs, pits, and rooms. Some rooms had four walls, but the roof was gone. A few had stone roofs. The peaked pitch of the stone roofs showed carvings of forests at both ends along with letters. The idea that the elves had lived there, not in the trees, intrigued Jonna.

A particularly tall building, with a sharp, angular stone roof, lay in one of the strongest lake currents. Sparkles flashed out from it.

He stopped at its door, but it would not budge. Through a single crack, gems would occasionally tumble out, the current would catch them, and they would work their way toward the alcove.

He swung back toward the islands. Above him, a few boat bottoms headed in that same direction. Thin pieces of wood broke the surface from above, pulled back, and pushed the boats forward. His tail flipped quickly to leave the boats behind him.

Images glimmered through Jonna's mind: a room of gold, Elpis in danger, and a shadowy door. Was it possible *The Sight* was improving the closer he came to his goal?

As the floor of the lake changed, Elpis pointed. The land curved and rose to the right. His nix body arched enough to follow the curve. Unusual stone steps rose from the water. The water's surface bounced up and down upon the stone distorting the light. He stopped beside the steps.

Elpis floated away from his back though she still maintained a hold. As her body became vertical, he reached a hand back. She grasped it tightly, released her hold around his neck, and touched the steps with her feet.

His tail swished so he could stay near her. His mind remembered the chill the lake had caused.

Her head broke the surface first, followed by her shoulders. As her waist reached the air, his own head poked above the waves.

Ravens called. Wings fluttered from tree to tree. A massive tower rose before them. The smell of a wood fire wafted from the right, and Jonna caught sight of the man's camp.

With his free hand, he climbed up onto the bank as his other kept hold of Elpis until she stood completely out of the water.

When his hand released hers, her eyes rose in amazement as she stared down at her clothes. "I'm--dry."

Her gaze went toward him as he flipped his tail out of the water to land upon the shore. The sunlight dried the water drops, and his pants and shoes reformed.

He chuckled. "Yeah, it seems to be a side effect." His stomach grumbled, but not as much as before his nix body changed.

Her eyes sparkled with a grin. "Dad, I saw this with *The Sight*, but in person it is so incredible!"

"Comes in handy, doesn't it? There are a few side effects I am trying to overcome, namely the desire to eat raw fish, but it may be a matter of practice." His grin matched hers. "I hope."

A tiny bullet darted toward them and flopped to the ground near Jonna. Uphren stared up as his tiny lungs heaved. "Found you!"

Elpis grinned down at him with a laugh. "You did."

The faery got his feet under him and slowly rose into the air. "Well, what did I miss?" He shivered. "That lake water was cold!"

"Well now," the man's voice rose from the direction of the fire. "It seems ya' made it after all. On top of that, ya' multiplied." The man picked up his hammer, laid it over his shoulder, and walked toward them.

Jonna rolled over and stood up. "Elpis, this is--" He waited for the man's introduction.

The man eyed him carefully. "Keeper will suffice."

Jonna shrugged. "The Keeper of the lake."

The man's hand gripped the hammer's handle tighter. "Did ya' get the stone?"

"Please, hand him the stone."

She reached to her side, undid the leather wrap, and pulled out the clear stone. It caught the light in its multiple facets. The ravens above them lowered their voices to almost a whisper.

The man's eyes sparkled. "That ya' did." His hand extended. "I'll take that."

"Wait." Jonna stepped between them. "I've done as you asked. I want my amulet."

One of the man's eyes rose toward him. "Ya' don't get it, do ya'? I make the rules here, not you." The hammer on his shoulder took on a glow. The rune blade on Jonna's back hummed as azure electricity crackled around Jonna.

A grin spread across the man's face. "I knew something was different about ya'. Ya' don't belong here. Only he who can save majik can retrieve a gem."

Elpis glanced up toward the right as her eyes grew larger, and *The Sight* kicked in. She turned slowly to her father. "He's right."

The man snapped his fingers. A raven dropped from the trees and snatched the amulet from the man's table. It leaped into the air, swerved, and dropped it onto the man's open palm.

"Come on, both of ya'."

As all three started forward, the Keeper turned to gaze at the faery. "Not you. Only the other two."

The fae's smile dropped.

"Uphren--" Images of the others battling Lord Tanyl's men flashed through Jonna's mind, but he could not get a clear vision. "Find the others. Let them know where we are." Uphren nodded quickly and zipped off.

"It will do them no good. They cannot get to you." The man approached one of the large towers and stopped before a door. "My name is Steredenn Ord. You can call me Ord. It is the least I can do before what happens next." The star on the handle of his hammer sparkled as he passed through the door. It cast a glow in all directions to light the dark interior.

"What do you mean?"

Stairs went up and down. The man did not answer as he led them lower. After about twenty feet, repeated groans could be heard. The splash of water struck their ears as Ord stepped down into a dark hall. Glimmers of light reflected off the top of a thin layer of liquid.

"The old spells are failing. We've rigged pumps to keep the water out."

Jonna nodded. "So, this is a flooded city. What did you mean by, it's the least you can do?"

Ord touched a wall and ignored his questions. "At one time, this city existed as the capital of an empire; a name spoken in awe. Now, I keep the others out."

"Others?"

The man threw a grin. "Who wouldn't want to sack this city? And not just for its wealth. There is magic here greater than any can imagine."

The Sight hit Jonna. "And the reason Cyhiraeth sent me to you."

"She's a smart one, alright." He chuckled. "But I can't trust just anyone who mentions her name."

"So you sent to me to the scycalite as a test?"

"I had to know if you were the one."

"Dad," Elpis dropped back and took his hand. Her hand felt cold as she grasped his. "The one for what?"

Words caught in his throat as he whispered, "The--the one to make everything right."

They reached a second set of stairs and rose. Doors branched off to various hallways, but the climb continued up. Jonna's legs felt it, Elpis pushed to keep up, but Ord kept walking up the steps as if none of this made a difference.

A golden door appeared. The elvish symbol of eternity glistened in the glow of the hammer's light. Ord pulled a golden key from his pocket, inserted it into a lock, and turned it. Massive clicks resonated through the hall. The stairs rumbled. The sound of metal against metal met their ears. When the man's finger tapped the door, it swung silently out.

The room shone in gold and silver. The floor held marble tiles of circular shapes, squares, and intersecting lines of different colors. As they stepped in, two massive bars of a silvery material sat on either side of the door. These must have produced the metallic sliding sound as they pulled apart to let the door open.

A great anvil stood in the center of the room. A bellows attached to a long, open forge lay beside it. The forge's glow lit the room while fire descended brightening the coal. A dragon's toe pumped the bellows.

The glowing eyes of the dragon stared down as its breath struck the forge once more. Its golden shape lay almost transparent against the rest of the room. Its high, deep voice bellowed, "At last, you have come to release me from my burden."

Jonna and Elpis gawked. Ord grinned.

The wings of the dragon had extended to press against the curved ceiling. Made of clear crystal, the ceiling contained delicate silver threads woven into its surface to create sections.

Cracks lay across it; pieces had dropped to the floor. The pieces sparkled in the light from the glow of the forge's fire.

Ord bowed politely to the dragon and glanced back at the others. "In my own language, this place is known as Mor Tigh. In the ancient Elvish, they called it Mare Ty."

"And in Draconic?" The dragon raised her eyebrows. "Tai Hwt."

The Sight flickered across Jonna's mind. "Great House?"

"Greater than all houses," Ord nodded. "It is the room of all existence. It is the place that worlds divide."

Jonna stared up slack-jawed and pointed at the delicate lines that wove throughout the ceiling. "It holds the partitions that separate all majik."

A ping sounded above their heads. The dragon's eyes grew large. "We must hurry. The time is near."

Ord rushed to the anvil, sat down his hammer, and lifted a smaller one from beside the forge. He held out a hand to Elpis. "Give me the gem."

A foreboding swept through Jonna. As Elpis started forward, he caught her hand. "No, let me."

The dragon's voice called softly from above. "You cannot stop this Jonna. You have ventured beyond the realm you should know. Let the girl complete her task."

"No." His eyes caught Elpis' eyes. "My wife has been taken. You cannot have my daughter."

Elpis stared back. "Father, I feel--" Jonna watched as the *The Sight* hit her. Her eyes narrowed as her mouth dropped open. Her hand let the gem fall into his open palm. Her voice whispered as it filled with fright, "I will do as you ask."

The room rumbled. A crack ripped across the ceiling. Crystal shards rained down.

Ord's voice rose. "Quickly man, there is little time!"

The dragon's head shook. "Oh mortal men who so desire to change what now must be. A million places of desire swept endless toward the sea. Quickly, Jonna, before you miss the time." A tear formed in the dragon's eye. It grew in size.

"Quickly!" Ord raised the hammer. "I must have it now!"

Jonna turned toward the man and slammed into an invisible barrier. The tear upon the dragon's cheek rolled slowly down. He shoved the hand with the gem forward, but it would not pass.

His empty hand struck at the barrier, and it sank slowly through. His eyes narrowed. His will pushed harder. With gritted teeth and legs straining, he fought against the unseen shield.

His body pierced though sluggishly. As his right arm pulled along from behind, the movement slowed down. The elbow passed, the forearm, the wrist, but it stopped tight as he reached the fist with the diamond.

The dragon shook her head. "It cannot be without her doing. Alas, all is lost."

CHAPTER 21

The tear rolled to the edge of the dragon's cheek.

Elpis leaped forward and grasped her father's hand. "Let me do it." Her eyes pleaded. "It must be."

"No."

"Daddy, please!"

Jonna's eyebrows rose. "Throw it."

"What?"

"There is no time. Throw it to Ord."

She grasped the gem as he dropped it. The dragon's tear fell toward the floor. The gem flew from her hand, passed over his head, and landed in Ord's palm.

"Got it!"

The man held up the diamond as the tear reached him. The two touched. Magic sparkled in all directions as the gem took on a golden glow. He lowered the gem to the amulet, sat it on top of its surface, and struck down with the hammer.

The gem melted into the amulet's surface like butter in the hot sun. Steam rose. A slit and iris formed. The glow of magic crackled across its surface. "I dub thee, Anryulong, after your great namesake." He smiled up at the dragon. "Do ya' mind?"

The dragon shook its head. "It is fitting, indeed."

Sharp, piercing pains struck Jonna's body. His arms and legs jerked from the jolts, yet he somehow maintained his stance. The invisible barrier vanished.

The dragon released its pressure against the crystal ceiling as it began to mend. "Quickly, hand me all the crystal shards. As many as you can find!"

They all scrambled: Ord, Jonna, and Elpis. As they placed the shards into the dragon's palm, she put them into the ceiling. With each piece, additional cracks healed as if they had never been broken.

When the last few were laid on the dragon's palm, a shadowy door formed behind her. "Go, quickly. You will return when the time is right."

Ord snatched up his great hammer. "Come on!"

Elpis and Jonna rushed behind him, stepped through the doorway, and emerged in a forest clearing. Tents stood throughout the trees. Camp fires burned as men and elves stared in surprise. Warriors rose to their feet with weapons drawn. A call went out through the camp.

A circle of weapons formed around them, but not too close. The visage of Lord Tanyl gawked from outside the circle. "Move!" He pushed apart two of the warriors that made up the ring. "How? Call Aldyth. Now!"

A tent stirred. As the flap came back, Aldyth rubbed sleepy eyes, caught sight of the circle, and grinned.

"Aldyth, explain this!"

His voice held no surprise. "I told you he got away. He said he was coming."

"In the center of my camp! What are you going to do?"

"Nothing." Aldyth leaned back against a tent support. "He's here as I told you. I've done my part. Now, he's all yours."

Lord Tanyl's eyes narrowed as he caught the looks of those around him. He drew his elvish sword. "Perhaps, he is."

Ord stepped forward as he laid the huge hammer on his shoulder. "Sorry, friend. This is not your battle, and he is not your foe." He pointed up at the trees behind Tanyl.

As the warriors followed his arm, a slit appeared in the sky. From it, a unicorn's horn appeared. The unicorn neighed as it stepped through the slit and walked on thin air to the ground.

Elves and men scrambled in all directions. Gods and

goddesses, demons and devils, emerged one by one to create their own circle around the trio. Jonna recognized a few: Cyhiraeth from the river; Zahhak from the northwest kingdom; Lokke his friend; Lucasta from the dark elf forest; Tlyme, Wisuiboeo, and Yses of the Norse three fates; Mulo, Lokke's relative; Dunner; and Dagda, King of the Otherworld.

The unicorn blinked at Jonna. "Are you surprised?"

"No." Jonna's eyes swept around the circle. "I expected this."

"How did you know?"

"Magic," Jonna's voice sounded far away. He remembered Tlyme's words when she prophesied his fate, "Though the gods would use you as a tool, they will find you gone before you go." His gaze stopped on Tlyme, and she nodded with a slight smile. He turned back to the unicorn. "What do you want from me?"

"You have proven yourself a worthy opponent, Jonna. You have taken what was given and used it ways we did not foresee. We cannot let you control us, or all would cease. You must make a choice, will you be a god with a god's limitations or die a mortal."

Jonna shook his head. "I do not want to control anyone."

"But you do. Even now, in a world in which you do not belong, in a world created by the very choices you did with magic, you struggle to save a daughter you were not meant to meet."

Elpis hand touched his shoulder. Her voice shook. "He's right, Dad. I love you for trying, but we are both out of place."

A tear touched the corner of Jonna's eye. "I--I can only operate in the now. I cannot change what has already happened."

"No, you can't. Nor can we. Nor will you as a god."

Jonna glared at them. "Then what good is magic?"

The unicorn looked to the others.

"You've heard his question. Who would dare to answer?"

Cyhiraeth stepped forward. "You know me." She turned her gaze upon all. "You know my cry is for those who must cease to be. But it was not always so." A smile crossed her lips. "I was the goddess of the rivers and streams, and my home was filled joy until my lot was changed forever." A frown washed away the smile. "Do not let them change you, Jonna. You still have a choice."

The unicorn inhaled sharply. "Silence."

Cyhiraeth bowed and stepped back to her place in line.

The unicorn stared at Jonna with his dark eyes. "What is done cannot be undone. What has happened cannot be reversed. It is a known fact for all gods." His eyes swept the others. "Who will speak? Be warned, do not confuse desires for facts."

Lokke stepped forward. His wide eyes scanned the others. "I-- I really don't know why I'm here. Sure, I'm a half-demon, I mean, I can't help what I am. But I can't let you force this god-thing on Jonna. He proved to me that I can change things if I wish. I can be anything I want despite what others say. I, for one--"

"Silence!"

Lokke leaped back in line.

"Is there no one who will confirm the truth? Have all of you gone mad?" His icy glare narrowed at each. "You have seen the damage Jonna has done, yet you applaud him as he suffers from the choices he has made. Is that what you want? All of you?"

Dagda, King of the Otherworld, stepped forward. "I tried to keep him bound." He narrowed his eyes at the benevolent gods and goddess. His finger thrust at them. "But you let him go free."

Tlyme leaned forward and whispered, "He brings hope where there is none. He makes men greater than the gods."

Murmurs broke out among them. Voices rose. The men and elves slipped further back into the shadows, all except one.

Lord Tanyl's voice rose from behind. "He brings death, not hope. He defiles what is pure." His voice shook with anger. "I want my revenge!"

Dagda turned to the unicorn. "And even his own turn against him. Why not let them decide?"

The unicorn stepped backwards to open a path.

The elf lord walked past though his eyes kept vigilance on the gods. He jabbed a finger a Jonna. "You destroyed our kingdom by removing the dark mages." He unsheathed his sword. "It is time to pay."

"Wait." A sneer crossed Dagda's face. "Let's be fair about this."

From the ground in front of Tanyl, yellow lightning lashed out. It struck the elf's sword and danced along its blade. As the tingles touched Tanyl's skin, a wicked smile creased his face. "Well, now. This is so much better." He whipped the sword from side to side. Lightning struck against the air. His gazed turned to Jonna as he pointed the sword in Jonna's direction. "I want you dead."

Lightning leaped out as Tanyl's laugh filled the camp. It arced toward Jonna but stopped mere inches from his body. The huge hammer that Ord held drew the power in.

"Not so fast, Dagda." The dwarf chuckled with a cocky smile. "You said this was a fair fight." He turned to Jonna. "You may draw your weapon."

The rune blade lifted from Jonna's sheath. The hum it gave rippled through his body. "Rules?"

Tanyl laughed. "What rules?"

As Ord pulled back his hammer, it laid calmly on his shoulder. "Now."

Lightning shot from the elf's sword. The rune blade caught and absorbed it. The two opponents circled.

Jonna watched Tanyl's eyes. "You were behind it. You helped the dark mages establish power."

"What of it?" Tanyl feinted with his sword. Jonna stepped back. Ord moved out of the way. "If it weren't for your meddling, the elvish throne would be mine."

"You are evil, Tanyl. You bring darkness upon the land."

Tanyl lashed out. The two blades collided with a ring and slid sideways from each other. "I keep the balance of what must be. Without balance, there is only chaos." His sword struck low and then whipped up at a curved angle to slice in front of Jonna's neck.

Jonna's feet jumped back. He caught the blade from behind,

and forced it toward the ground. In a lunge, Jonna leaned in to jab an elbow into the elf's throat.

Tanyl stumbled backwards toward Elpis as he gasped. His throat muscles tightened. His lungs labored to suck in air as his eyes darted wildly.

Jonna's face flushed with foreboding anger. "You want to know how it feels, Tanyl?" He advanced toward the man. "You want to know what it feels like to sense your own life ebbing away?"

Tanyl stepped forward despite the lack of breath. His blade plunged for Jonna's heart but at the last moment with a twist of the wrist, slipped upward.

Jonna's head dodged back. The rune blade arced in front of him. It caught the elf's blade but not before a sting registered on the tip of his chin. Liquid oozed down.

The air came back into Tanyl's lungs. "You may be stronger than me, but I am still more agile." The sword arced. The rune blade caught it.

Jonna eyes narrowed as he focused on Tanyl. Tanyl's sword darted to the right. The rune blade hit it dead on. The elf thrust toward the left. The Rune Blade of Knowledge parried.

A third time the elf slashed, and the rune blade struck above the hilt. The vibration ripped up the elf's blade almost jerking it from Tanyl's hands. Jonna shifted from both hands to his left, kept pressure on the opponent's blade, and shoved toward Tanyl.

As Jonna extended a right punch toward Tanyl's jaw, their bodies collided. The fist connected. Tanyl jerked from the punch. Jonna's right hand circled back toward his own body, bent his arm at the elbow, and stabbed into the elf's solar plexus.

Tanyl tried to suck in air but his lungs refused to work. He lifted his blade despite the lack of breath. The rune blade knocked it away. It rose again, only to have it knocked back.

Jonna glared at him. "You prey on those that are weaker and claim some great spoil. Yours is not a victory. You're a bully and a fraud." With a front snap kick, he tagged the elf between the legs.

Tanyl groaned. The elf buckled, dropped his sword, and tumbled to the ground.

Jonna turned to the Dagda. "Can an evil god bleed?" He stepped toward the god and froze. Only from the neck up could he move.

Eyes bulging, Dagda stepped back into the circle of the gods.

Merriment lit the unicorn's face. "Choose, Jonna. Will you be a god and have the revenge you desire on Dagda, or will you remain human and die?"

The look on Dagda's face had not faded. Fear trembled the corners of his mouth. Jonna's eyes narrowed, "You will leave me and mine alone."

Dagda's body shook, but his voice remained strong, "I am the god of the underworld. You cannot give me orders!" He flicked his hand toward Tanyl.

Elpis' voice screamed, "Jonna!"

Blue crackles of power leapt from the rune blade. Jonna broke the magic that held him and spun around.

Tanyl charged with sword extended. Lightning lashed out.

The rune blade caught it, but not before the tendrils of power reached Jonna's shoulder. His arm went numb. He shifted the blade to his other hand as the swords collided.

Though the elf's sword rebounded away, Jonna fell backwards and landed upon the ground. The elbow that held Jonna's sword struck first, and the rune blade flew from his hand.

The triumphant voice of Tanyl called out, "If I prey upon the weak, what are you?" He raised his sword.

Elpis screamed a war cry. An arrow met her bow, nocked, and fired.

A thud sounded as it struck Tanyl's back to protrude out his chest. In slow motion, he turned to face her.

Her eyes bore into him. "That was for Elfleda whom you slew."

His words roared. "How dare you!" His face sneered as he

staggered in her direction. Jonna groaned, rolled to his feet, and snagged his rune blade with his working hand.

She let a second arrow fly. "That is for my father."

Tanyl jerked back but forced his body forward as the sword he carried dropped lower. The tingle left Jonna's other arm as he flexed his fingers and gained speed. He caught Elpis' face and shook his head.

A third arrow nocked; the bow twanged. A razor sharp point of death leaped toward Tanyl.

Tanyl screamed and lunged forward again. The arrow stabbed through his heart. He staggered a step and dropped to his knees.

"And that is for me."

The elf lord wavered side to side. Blood trickled from the sides of his mouth. The hilt of his sword touched the ground as he lost the strength to raise it. A mocking laugh escaped his lips as he whispered. "I'll see you in the Otherworld."

Lightning built on Tanyl's blade. The metal shook as it vibrated. The electrical energy gained momentum and worked its way toward the top.

It leaped just after Jonna slammed into Tanyl. The elf tumbled forward, and the blade sliced through his own body. In a dazzling display, the energy released by the elf shot toward the cosmos.

The unicorn smirked. "Until next we meet, Jonna."

The gods faded. Ord slipped into the forest. Only the camp personnel remained. Silence fell upon all until an elf of rank cautiously stepped forward and knelt beside Tanyl. He raised his sword in the air. "Our Lord is wounded! Take them!"

Arrows shot from the underbrush to stab into trees and slash through ropes. Tents collapsed, and men scattered. The elf who had spoken staggered sideways as an arrow pierced his arm, and his sword tumbled to the ground.

Timplemay flew to Jonna's side followed by Uphren. "Come on!" She waved her hand, and a mist rose to hide them. "It won't last long!"

They crawled away within the mist. The mist hovered only three feet above the ground. The faeries guided them around the brush and trees until at last they slipped into the shadows.

Shouts rose in confusion. Mylaela slipped in beside them with Poetestay by her side. Her eyebrows narrowed, "You're hurt!'

"A scratch only." His lips smiled but his eyes stayed on Elpis. A faraway look had taken her.

Peredur slid in to their left. "They don't have a clue how many we are. They are dropping into defensive mode."

Agtoa came from their right. "A party is searching the mist. I suggest we leave now." His eyes caught Elpis, and his voice dropped. "Is Tanyl dead?"

Jonna nodded. "He's dead. Once their army realizes what's happened, I don't anticipate they'll follow very long."

Agtoa sighed. "But if Tanyl's lieutenant keeps control--"

Peredur grinned. "I wouldn't worry about that." His gaze caught Elpis' expression, and his brow wrinkled. "Did she--"

Jonna nodded. "Yes, and now she'll have to deal with the consequences."

A shadowy doorway came into view, and Jonna knew exactly what it was for. He took them all in. "Peredur, can you get them back across the river safely?"

The warrior nodded.

Jonna turned to Mylaela. "Guard them. I will met you--" Would he? He had no idea what was about to happen, but he had to keep up hope. "--there." A smile lit his face. "There is one last thing I must do."

Mylaela kissed him though a curious glance crossed her face. "I will do as you ask."

"Thank you."

He rose toward the shadowy doorway, took one last look behind, and stepped through. Jonna heard a baby cry.

The room called Mor Tigh appeared. The golden dragon stared at her palm in dismay. "They will not fit. I can't make them go back."

Jonna approached slowly. "You sent the doorway?" The sound of light footsteps came behind him, but he did not turn.

The dragon held her palm in his direction; five tiny specs of light reflected from her hand. "I told you she had to fulfil her task. She should have died before the battle. Now, all is changed."

A lump formed in Jonna's throat. "What do you mean by all?"

"If a piece of the crystal cannot be replaced, it will heal over to create its own reality." She pointed up. "It has already begun."

The silver strands which separated majik sparkled in the light. On sections with no cracks, a bright glow would form on one end and rush to meet the other. Those realms were alive with living creatures whose lives had been renewed. Only five areas did not sparkle at the edges. In each, a tiny piece had not been replaced.

He took the pieces from her hand. "Lift me up. I will help you."

"There is danger in what you attempt. You must place the pieces with no thoughts other than to return them. Do not influence their purpose with your own desires."

His eyes narrowed. "If you cannot place them, which is worse? Letting them heal, or letting me return them?"

The dragon gave a nod. "Letting them heal on their own would be the worse of the two. Perhaps, this was meant to be." Her claw wrapped around his waist and lifted him toward the ceiling. The heat from her body made him sweat. He could feel the beating of her heart.

Near the ceiling, he studied the first section. Almundena floated into his mind and the joy that had filled her face. The shard slipped in. It vanished as the section became whole.

The second piece rose. It drew him toward the right. The dark elf city formed in his thoughts and the last words of Queen Siardna. A cold shiver hit him as the shard fit into place.

The third sparkled in his hand. He remembered the touch of his son, and his heart beat faster. His eyes were drawn to the area of a grand spiral. There, at the end, a single piece had fallen. As it rose into place, a far off giggle met his ears.

Two left. He could feel the worlds they went to. The shape of an S formed one reality. The other curved with a snake-like tail.

The piece he chose shifted, but he could not get a location fix. The name Esti came to mind and the darkness of rebirth when he had lost his memory. The shard vanished into the crystal.

And lastly? Though he lifted the piece toward the ceiling, he could not make it fit. Each time he turned to adjust its angle, the hole to which it belonged moved.

"Father, let me try."

His gaze dropped to the floor. Elpis stood beneath him. All her weapons had been removed and lay upon the ground around her. Tears stained her face. He turned to the dragon. "Can she help?"

The dragon nodded. "If you wish." It reached down with its free hand and picked Elpis up. She rose to hover by his side.

His finger pointed. "There."

She took the small shard and stared as it sparkled in the light. "Dad--" Her voice broke. "Dad, you were right. I should have listened. I should have known. I just--I couldn't let him--"

"I know why you did it though it will still be hard. To take another life rips at your soul. I wanted to spare you." He took her hand. "Never think it will change the love I have for you. Never think that it will make you less than what you are."

Tears started down her face as she nodded. With a lift of her finger, she raised the shard up to its place. The shard slid in.

"Dad," her voice rose as her body faded. "Dad, I love you!" Her grip on his lessened though the fingers never moved. As her body vanished, her voice echoed until it, too, drifted away.

Loneliness hit his heart. The dragon opened the fist Elpis had been in and stared at her empty palm. "Fascinating."

Jonna swallowed. "Did she go home?"

The dragon lowered him to the ground. "Perhaps, if that home still exists."

His eyes drifted around the room. "How do I get home?"

288

"How do you know you aren't?"

"You mean--" He turned toward the golden door. The great silvery bars held it securely closed. "The room was unlocked before."

The dragon nodded.

He walked toward it and then turned around. The bright yellow of the lighted room had changed to an orange-red. The dragon faded from sight. "But I don't have a key."

"Farewell, Jonna. The time has come to accept your fate. The world you've changed will call and bait. Step upon the threshold given, and all will be explained. When the doorway comes for you, waiting is a dead man's game." The shadowy door appeared; it waved beside the lighted forge.

A sparkle on the anvil caught his eye; his amulet glistened in the reddish glow. He stepped toward it, picked up the amulet, and dropped it over his head. A metallic thud sounded against his chest. With a last glance up, he passed through the doorway.

~

Bright light assailed his eyes. The murmur of voices caught his ears. Smells he had never noticed came from every direction. He stood in the palace of the woodland elves before Queen Freya.

As his fingers reached for the quill, his eyes blurred. The sleeve of the shirt he wore matched the one given to him in the desert, yet no one noticed. The rune blade hung on his back, as well as two medallions: the dragon eye amulet and the one from Arta's world.

The world took on a rainbow tint as the colors around him swirled. The Queen's eyes widened. Elfleda's eyebrows rose. Bob shot away from Jonna as if thrown by an unseen force.

Elves on all sides stepped back from the couple as dancing glitters of light spun away. The elven sign of infinity on the floor glowed with bright, white light.

The quill touched the scroll. He watched his own hand sign his name. As the date filled in, relief coursed through him. *No ping!*

A broad smile crossed his face as he released the quill to float in the air. It rose above the scroll to hover and gradually faded away.

The scroll closed of its own accord and slowly dropped toward the elf page that had brought it. The page placed it in its leather cover.

Elfleda whispered to him and sent tingles up his spine. "Turn."

His heart beat wildly as he whispered back, "You're alive!"

"What?"

He took her hand and gripped it tightly. His thumb rubbed her index finger as they turned toward those behind them. In quick glances, he looked in her direction as a silly grin took his face.

The corner of her eyes caught him, and she blushed.

Bob the pixie slid in beside them, and grumped, "What was that?" He rubbed a spot on his backside. "Slammed into the archway, I did. Ouch!"

Elfleda threw him a nod. "Shh."

Clapping rose around them, and cheers reached their ears. The grin on Jonna's face never wavered. His eyes tore from Elfleda to briefly scan the crowd.

Toward the back, Lord Ilbryn and Lady Lyeecia stood. Though they did clap, their expressions were not so cheery. Lord Tanyl and Lady Mylaela could not be seen. Tanyl he had better watch, although Lady Mylaela could be a boon.

His search caught the elf with the silver eyes, and he remembered Prince Conall. The elf sniffed the air in Jonna's direction. Were the elf and the prince the same person? Only time could prove that true.

Jonna and Elfleda stepped from the dais and stopped. Jonna's heart leapt. Elpis, his wonderful little girl, approached from the right wearing a beautiful elvish gown. The weave of the cloth held embedded jewels that glittered in the room's glow.

In her hands, a small pillow held a single ring along with six cords. The cords were woven of different colors and laid out in straight lines.

She walked to the center between the couple and turned to face both. A glow lit her face as she spoke the words, "In the tradition of the woodland elves, blessed and kept by majik, we bind together this couple true by ring and cords of fabric." She stifled a giggle.

Elfleda winked at her as she lifted her hand that held Jonna's to a horizontal position. Jonna went with it. He didn't remember practicing this for the ceremony, but just to hold her hand brought warmth to his heart.

A page stepped near. He reached for one of the six cords. "In the cord of silver, wealth is found. Prosperity will be yours. Wrapped around the wrists of two, reflected moonlight bathes its hue. The powers they draw will focus and sway, warning the leprechauns true. May greed shy away from you."

He laid the silver cord upon their wrists, wrapped it around once, and tied an elvish knot. As he bowed back, a second page approached. The second one picked up a gold cord.

"Power, strength, and perfection: may they come to all your days. Held within affection, the love you hold will not fade. Cling to one another, never let each go, and the bond you hold together will grow stronger forever more."

The page laid the gold cord next to the silver, wrapped it once, and tied it. The loop it formed slipped under the first. He stepped back as a third page approached to lift up the color white.

"In the wholeness of beauty, perfection unmeasured, pure, undefiled, and held in esteem. The wonder of nature, in all adaptation, opens the pathway to heart's love unseen."

The third page did the same. The cord dropped over their wrists. It was wrapped and tied. The loop slipped through the gold to bind all three cords together.

A fourth page appeared, followed by a fifth and a sixth. Their colors were red, blue, and green. As they finished, Queen Freya descended from the dais. She lifted the single ring and held it up for all to see.

"This ring of one to one is bound, though separate they will be. The love within both reaches out so all can then now see. Against the foe who challenges, against the swell of doubt, the magic of this ring will strive to keep their union free without."

A ray of light descended and struck ring. The middle glowed yellow and white. When the glow faded, the ring separated into two equal halves. "Extend your fingers."

Without breaking the interlaced cords, their fingers separated. On to each hand, Queen Freya slid one ring. "The union is complete. The crown princess and prince have been bound. Let no one outside the union interfere with this eternal renown." A smile lit the queen's face as she whispered, "Go--find the tree."

A path opened before them. Elfleda cast a mischievous glance at Jonna. "Run!" As they raced between the elves, colorful lights burst above them. They passed through unscathed, though some of the threads of light lingered on their clothes.

Sir Verity met them at the dual doors. "This way, Your Highnesses." He pointed toward a waiting basket. Two elf warriors guarded the door. His voice spoke quickly, "All you need is inside. Hurry!" He winked and opened the basket door. As their feet settled, the basket dropped.

With one hand still bound to his, Elfleda drew his hand close to her heart and gazed into his eyes. "Were you surprised?" She kissed his fingers, and his heart beat wildly.

His eyebrows rose. "I don't know what happened. Did--did we just get married?"

Her eyes glowed as she nodded.

"It's okay with me," he grinned. "I'm all for two honeymoons. But we were already married."

Her words were like a wondrous song. "In your world, not in mine. When mother found out I was pregnant, she insisted it be done in the elvish way on the symbol of eternity."

"So, she really does like me?"

"Of course." Her laughter sent tingles up his spine. "Why would you doubt it?"

"Well, I mean, being sent to the Otherworld with Dagda, and--"

She placed a finger to his lips. He ached to hold her closer. "Politics, love, only kingdom politics. They have nothing to do with personal feelings."

The basket touched the ground, and the door swung open. After undoing the cords, she placed them in one hand, and hurried out with laughter. "Bring the bag with you!"

Jonna looked around and spotted a large leather bag. He picked it up by the handle and poked his head out. "This?"

A silent forest answered.

"Elfleda?" He stepped out of the basket and listened. Small footsteps approached from behind, and he caught a wisp of Elpis' long hair from the corner of his eye. In a dash, the footsteps raced toward him. The bag slipped from his hand. He turned, snatched her up, and spun her around. "Gotcha!" He blinked back tears.

"Daddy!" She squealed and pushed upon him to let her down. "We have to find mom!"

Jonna wiped the corners of his eyes. "What's this about?"

As her feet touched the ground, she pointed. "Come on, I'm supposed to lead you to her just like the pixies who married the first elf king and queen." Her hand grabbed his, and she tugged.

He held her in place while her feet struggled to move him. "Why haven't I heard this story?"

"Daddy, come on! We have to find the eternal tree." She squealed, "Hurry!"

He let her go and matched pace behind her. They wove to the left away from the tree city, curved through a trail in the underbrush, and crossed a stream over a giant log. On the far side of the log, they slid down its curve to reach the forest floor, and then raced along an edge of green until a large tree came into view.

Many trees in the forest were ages old, well over thirty feet in diameter. Yet, this tree dwarfed them all with its massive trunk of no less than sixty feet.

As their eyes followed its trunk into the sky, a spiral of hidden, covered stairs bordered by handrails emerged. The bark camouflaged the spiral well. Every so many steps up, a small plateau with three outer walls and a window showed.

A glimmer of light caught their attention. Someone hurried from plateau to plateau igniting a sparkle of light.

"Come on!" Elpis pulled his hand.

He kept pace with her. As they reached the tree's base, Bob soared up beside them. "Hey, you guys left so quickly!"

Jonna's eyes took in the spiral steps as they rose into the clouds. It was a long way up. "Why are we doing this again?"

Elpis giggled. "Not us, you. You have to climb to the top and follow the sparkles of elvish magic. It's part of the celebration."

The scent of apple blossoms struck his nose. *The Sight* hit; it was the honeymoon suite. That sounded like fun.

His feet took two steps at a time for the first three hundred. At each plateau, a faery bowed holding an enchanted branch. The tip of the branch glowed. With each branch, a new fragrance would float toward him.

His agility surprised him though his lungs labored as he reached higher up the trunk. Above the other trees, when the clouds parted, the scenery went on for miles in one direction and stopped at the mountains in the other. Gaps appeared in the forest as rivers ambled through. Across the mountains, a desert showed.

The stairs opened up to a wondrous carved building, set within the top of the branches without hindering the tree's growth. Column supports created a porch in which two chairs and a table had been set. Through an archway lay a living room and a bedroom. As he hurried toward the bedroom, a noise caught his attention, and he dodged quickly forward.

A mace arced down, missed his shoulder, and struck the wooden floor. As Jonna ducked out of reach and drew the rune blade, a hum filled the structure. He gawked at the face of a person he knew. "Aldyth?"

The elf raised the mace and prepared to attack. "Do I know you?" He swung a blow toward Jonna's body. The rune blade parried and bit into the handle with an unusually strong strike.

The elf jerked his weapon back. "That's a sharp blade, but I know how to deal with swords." The mace arced in a loop before Jonna could turn his edge. Aldyth grinned as he slammed his mace into the side of the blade. The rune blade rippled, absorbed the impact, and the mace shattered.

Aldyth leaped away as the mace handle tore from his hands. "That is some blade!" He reached for his elvish sword, but as it left its sheath, Jonna slapped it way with the tip of his own. It clattered to the floor.

"Lord Tanyl didn't tell you what you were up against, did he?" He drove the elf into a wall.

The elf's eyes darted to his own sword. The edge danced in the light.

"I wouldn't," Jonna dared. "I won't be so nice, this time."

The elf's eyebrows rose. "This time? You act like I've met you before."

"Where is Lord Tanyl? Where is Elfleda?"

"Look," Aldyth extended his open palms. "I don't know anything about a female elf. My job was to knock you out and bring you in. A few busted bones didn't matter to him. I was warned it might not be easy." His gaze dropped to the shattered mace. "That was an understatement."

Jonna growled. "Tell me where he is, and I'll be there."

The elf considered as he watched the light play upon the rune blade. "Alright, say I believe you. What stops you from showing up with a hundred elves at your back?"

"Not a thing. What stops you from ambushing me?"

Aldyth grinned. "Nothing. Except the fact that I don't care how you arrive. As long as you show up, I get paid." His grin widened. "Shi Me River. Head due east. You can't miss it." He raised his hands. "We've reached an agreement. May I have my sword?"

Remembering the same person from the other reality, Jonna nodded.

With slow, easy movements, the elf leaned over, placed his right hand on the hilt, kept it low across the floor, and raised it only enough to drop it into the sheath at his side. "Guess I should have started with this, then the outcome might have been different. However, I'm good either way." He stepped outside and glanced back. "By the way, there are two guards near the entrance of the camp. They're buddies of mine. I'll tell them you're coming, and they will see you safely through the other checkpoints."

"That will make it easier."

"Anything to make the transition smooth." As the elf strolled out the door, he laughed.

CHAPTER 22

Due east--that would take him into Conall's hunting ground if this reality mirrored the other. The wind billowed his shirt, shifted the dragon eye amulet, and tapped it against the golden medallion of Arta's reality. Was he really back in his own world? If the shirt and medallion had carried over, what else might be different, too?

He stared over the edge of the building. It was a long way down. Yeah, the stairs would work, but there had to be a faster way.

The pixie spell to float rolled through his mind. It could work, if he had returned to the correct reality. If not--he cringed at the repercussion. The majik partitions could shatter again. No, this had to be home. It had to!

With focused eyes, he stirred up the memory. "*Atalante.*"

His body rose from the wooden floor and hovered above it. With great relief, no ping sounded. Now what? A wind stirred. Like a feather, he blew over the handrail.

His hands grabbed branches. They shoved him east as he pulled forward and down. A gust of wind struck. He held tightly to the tree branches as the wind whipped him about.

The breeze lightened, and he thrust further east. His mind buzzed over past events. Elpis--he had forgotten Elpis at the tree's base!

As his right hand snagged a branch, his body whipped around it until the friction of his grip slowed him down. His legs pushed against the side of a tree and sent him toward the forest floor.

A tiny humanoid rose to intercept his path. "Jonna, what is going on? Where's Elfleda?" Bob made a circle around him. "And why are you using pixie magic to float?"

"Lord Tanyl has taken Elfleda. Is Elpis safe?" As they floated closer to the ground, Jonna searched the base of the tree. His eyes narrowed, and his jaw clenched.

"Elpis? Of course she's okay. I left her--" Bob's gaze raked the forest floor, and his head darted about as he pointed. "--right there." He swallowed. "She's gone!"

Doom fell across Jonna. "It's Aldyth's insurance that I keep my word."

"Word? What word? Who's Aldyth?"

He focused on Bob. "How quickly can you get to the Shi Me River?"

"With you that light?" Bob the Pixie grinned. "Quick as a whistle. But uh, the cross currents may be a little tricky."

"Do it."

Bob grabbed hold of his collar with a mischievous smile. "Hang on!"

Jonna's body darted forward. He whipped through the trees. They soared over rolling hills, undergrowth, and small streams. As Jonna focused on nothing, the smells around him became sharper. A strong, wet-dog smell came from in front.

A lower valley appeared. A stream branched into three to run across the vale in snake-like directions. Round huts with wooden sticks and grass dotted the basin as the huge trees loomed up from the valley floor. "Stop!"

Bob stopped. Jonna whipped around him. The pixie lost his grip, and Jonna sailed by. "Wait!" He zipped to the other side and pushed to halt Jonna's movement. The speed abated, and Jonna stabilized in the air.

Jonna's right hand pointed. "I need to go there, first."

Bob's eyes grew. "In the middle of the Vulkodlaks? Are you crazy?"

A sweet aroma wafted toward Jonna, but he could not comprehend what it was. "We need help. Shove me toward the center of their camp. I'll be right back."

The pixie rolled his eyes. "If you say so, but if they eat you, it's not my fault!" He shook his head.

"Noted. Now, push!"

Bob rose above him and shoved. Jonna's body shot down toward a group of huts. The scent grew sweet and delightful. Drawn by aroma, he used his arms to glide toward it. At the top of a hut, he rotated so that his feet were below him. "*Ne Atalante.*"

His body fell, hit the top of the hut, hesitated, and plunged through. A support post snapped. He tumbled to land upon something soft. Hay from the roof showered down upon his head as he waited for the avalanche to cease. The smell of straw mixed with the scintillating aroma. It filled his nostrils and threatened to steal his reason.

As the dust from the hay cleared, a creature shifted in the debris. It coughed several times, pushed back straw, and stared at him. A woman, clearly not dressed, glared at him. "By whose right do you--" Her breath inhaled quickly, and she sniffed the air. "You are one of my clan; you have answered my call. And yet, you are not. Who are you?"

Her face jogged Jonna's memory. "Esti?"

Curiosity added to the surprised look. "How do you know my--name?" Her hand shook as she reached toward his face. When her fingers touched his cheek, she whispered, "This cannot be." The sweetness became intoxicating. His head spun. She pulled her fingers quickly back.

A deep voice rose from outside the hut. "Esti? Are you okay?"

Her voice faltered as she forced her eyes from Jonna. Exerting great control, she found it. "I'm fine, Limbik. Just a--branch. I'll be out shortly."

Jonna squinted in an effort to focus. Elfleda came to mind, and it helped to clear his thoughts. His voice filled with urgency. "Esti, I need your help. I need to find Prince Conall." The strange desire for the sweetness rushed back, but he shook it away. "Trust me, please. It is a matter of life and death."

She shook against the attraction and forced herself from him. Her hands found a robe, pulled it around, and cinched it tightly closed. The robe adhered to her body to outline alluring curves. "I don't know why, but I do believe you. I--I will find him." She dusted off the hay, stepped to the leather door covering, and passed swiftly through.

A rumble of voices gathered outside the hut. As she left, the sweetness abated a little, and his mind could focus more easily.

What was he doing here? Why was he drawn to Esti? He considered leaving before she returned. Though the scent had lessened, the madness of the sweet aroma lay vivid in his mind.

It would be much easier to cast the float spell, launch upward, and head into the trees. However, it would also stop the plan he had in mind.

The leather door covering shifted. Esti entered, and the scent grew powerful. Her chest heaved as she drew nearer. An elf followed with silver eyes. Was this the elf at the palace?

The elf peered at him as the shadow and light played across Jonna's face. His voice demanded, "I am Prince Conall. Who are--" The elf's eyes tapered as he sniffed the air. His tone changed warily, "You are heir apparent to the Elvish throne." His eyes narrowed further. "It is true; he is one of us, and yet--" He threw a look at Esti. "How can this be?"

Her lungs heaved as she inhaled deeply. Her face turned a light crimson. "I don't know. A spell, maybe, but, it's so strong, I find it hard to resist." She shook her head. "It doesn't make sense. Only I can turn--"

Worry crossed Jonna's face. "What doesn't make sense? What are you talking about?" His eyes darted from one to the other though they went to Esti more often. "What is wrong with me?" He massaged his eyebrows with both palms.

Conall examined him intently. "Why are you here?"

The urgency returned to Jonna's voice as he focused. "I need your aid. Lord Tanyl has taken my wife and child. I need your help to save them."

Conall's eyes narrowed. "Why didn't you go the elves?"

"There is no time." Jonna remembered what the older Elpis had told him, and the scent that drew him lost more of its power as his will hardened. "If I don't move soon, he could kill them."

Conall pursed his lips. His head nodded slowly. "Alright, as a courtesy to the Elvish nation, I will summon my forces." His voice took on an edge. "You will owe me a favor." A wolfish grin barely emerged. "Are you sure you're willing to pay the price?" His sly eyes turned to Esti.

Jonna nodded. "You have my word."

The wolfish grin finished forming. "What do you ask of me?"

"Due east of here is Lord Tanyl's camp. I need a distraction."

The prince nodded. "You will have it." His voice rose. "Limbik, call Jasna, Vytautas, and Gerulf. We have a mission." He turned to Esti. "You will see to Prince Jonna's needs, and then report when you are done." Conall rose, strode through the door, and vanished as the flap closed.

Jonna's eyes riveted to Esti. Every sniff threatened to steal his mind. "Needs?" The sweetness he smelt oozed from around her and intensified; his pulse grew faster. What was wrong with him? "I must leave at once."

"You must drink from the Cup of Arnulf, first." As she ogled him, sweat ran down her neck, and she panted faster. "We both must. After that, it will be easier. To endure in our present state could be disastrous to both of our missions."

His eyes would not leave her as she slipped toward a small, wooden chest. At her touch, it opened. Inside, various jars and bottles stood.

She studied a line of chalices and chose one with a wolf upon its side. Brownish powder sprinkled into the chalice. A liquid was added and an herb before she turned to face him. "This will help control the symptoms."

Her eyes closed as she slipped some of the liquid. "That's better. Not quite so strong. Tolerable. We must be careful until you fully understand." She extended the chalice toward him. The closer her hand loomed, the more jittery she became.

His heart beat wildly. Sweat dripped down his brow. "Why do I feel this way?"

"You have Vulkodlak blood in your veins, my clan's Vulkodlak blood, and I am--in heat. You are awakening."

The words cut through his emotions and gave back a measure of control. "How? When? You mean, in heat like--dogs?"

"You have the blood of wolves, not dogs." She tried to slow her breathing. "Please, you must drink. The drink's calming effect will only last for a short time. It will help subdue the scent your body generates in response to mine."

He reached forward to take the chalice. As he did, his bottom two fingers touched hers. Desire swelled in him.

Her eyes shot open. She reached out with her free hand. It shook as she fought to stay in control.

They pulled closer together. Her body pressed against him. "Drink--" She pleaded weakly as her eyes grew larger. "--before I cannot resist." With a trembling hand, she kept the chalice in front as a slim barricade to what might come.

The desire to push the chalice away roared through him, but Elfleda's plight called. His wife was Elfleda. Elfleda was his wife. He focused on the words until his hands tipped the cup, and the liquid poured into his mouth.

He gagged. How Esti had done it so easily made no sense at all. The sweetness of the aroma drifted from him, and his breathing slowed.

She turned her back toward him as her body shook. "Go, now, before it's too late."

"Thank you, Esti."

"Go, please!"

"Atalante."

Jonna rose a foot from the floor and hovered. He grabbed the wall and shoved upward.

Her scent still filled his nostrils, but the strength had greatly diminished. Had it not been for the Cup of Arnulf, he may not have left that hut. As he soared upward, one thing remained certain; it would not be wise to be near Esti until whatever she went through finished.

His body rose quickly to the right. Bob dropped to his shoulder. "Well? Will they help us?"

"Prince Conall is mounting a distraction." A slight wind started to blow.

Bob rubbed his hands together. "Great! So, what's next?"

Jonna drifted to the left before he could grab another branch. "Bob!"

"Oh, yeah! Sorry!" He tagged Jonna's collar and moved east. "How do we find them?"

The word *vulkodlak* popped into Jonna's mind. What advantages did they have? "I think I know." His eyes closed as he thought back to the palace right after he appeared. He remembered the touch of Elfleda's skin, the tingle, the--smell. Yes, she did have a scent he hadn't noticed before. Even now, when he focused, so did Bob and himself. A heightened sense of smell? Perhaps this vulkodlak's curse wasn't so bad after all.

His thoughts focused on Elfleda's scent. With a slow inhale, he searched the air. A faint odor touched his nose, and he pointed. "That way."

Bob looked around but saw nothing. "How do you know?"

"Are you going to doubt me or help me?"

"Gotcha!" Bob dodged the tree in front and wove through the forest. The aroma of Elfleda grew stronger, and a whiff of Elpis met his nose. The more he focused on the ability, the easier it came.

Everything, every tree, every plant around them gave off a unique smell. A whole new world opened until it threatened to overwhelm him. He focused on just Elfleda.

They rose over a knoll. A clearing opened on the other side. A palisade fence stood at the base of the next hill. At the top of the hill, a second fence stood. The wooden poles that made it up had been narrowed at the top and capped with metal spikes.

Two gates stood out: one in each of the fences. Guard towers rose on each side of the gates. Lookouts patrolled the interior of the walls with slits cut so they could peer through.

Barracks had been set up within the second fence along with two large buildings. The largest building stood taller with a waist high wall around the top. The wall surrounded a flat roof that worked as a floor with a trap door.

"Hold here, Bob."

The pixie slowed and held them steady against the wind. His grip shifted to Jonna's sleeve so he could turn around and look at him.

Jonna gave a single nod. "Keep a firm hold. I'm going to vanish until we land on that tallest building. Ready?"

Bob nodded.

"Unum-Clastor-Fillum."

Bob's eyebrows rose as he started to fly backwards. "This is just a little bit strange." His grip tightened on the sleeve. "Okay, here it goes." He focused on the landing spot below them, spun around, and slammed into a tree. The pixie released his grip, fell backwards, and tumbled down.

Jonna caught the side of the tree and shoved down after him. The sound of the wind snaked toward him through the trees. His hand reached out to snag the pixie right before the gale struck.

Caught in the gust, he shot away from the tree to tumble end over end. A downdraft grabbed him. It whipped him toward the top of the first palisade within inches of the sharp, metal spikes, and rolled him like a bowling ball up the side of the hill.

His right hand cushioned the blow for Bob as his left shoulder slammed into the second wooden fence. Despite his reduced weight, the fence shook. Voices on the other side called. Archers came near with arrows nocked in their bows.

He remained still. As long as he did not speak, no one could see him. He tucked Bob into some high grass.

The words "strong wind" hit his ears as the warriors standing guard inside the second wooden fence slowly drifted away. He exhaled, heard the noise, and swallowed. His body appeared in the visible world.

Lungs stopped as he held his breath. When he was sure no one looked in his direction, he breathed in slowly and whispered, "*Unum-Clastor-Fillum.*" His body faded from view once more.

He stifled a sigh, picked up Bob, and crept toward the gate in the second fence. It lay open, but two guards stood in front. His fingers found a rock and tossed it along the fence.

One of guards turned toward the noise and stepped forward.

When neither looked his direction, Jonna slipped quickly through the gap between them only to discover more warriors lined the sides of the path beyond. He dropped into the shadows and hid Bob. So far, so good.

A distraction was called for, but how? His mind noted he stood behind two of the guards, so he snagged a guard's foot with his own and jerked. The guard crashed to the ground. The second turned toward his fellow. In the commotion, others came to investigate, and Jonna weaved behind them.

The path he took led by the barracks first. Toward the center, men and elves relaxed although not together. The elves assembled on the west side; the men were on the east. Jonna stayed behind the men as Elfleda's scent led past two other buildings. The scent came from the largest tower.

Shouts rose from the perimeter of the fort. His nose caught the hint of wolves, hundreds of them, on all sides of the camp. Prince Conall had kept his word. His head darted toward the east. Esti approached from there.

A huge bell rang in alarm. Elves and men from the barracks rose quickly. He ducked back as several warriors hurried out of the largest building. Before the door closed, he slipped in.

The desks and chairs were empty. Muffled voices floated down some stairs. A slap echoed. He rushed up.

At the next floor, he turned. A curved hall went past three doors. As he neared the first, Bob groggily asked, "Who turned out the lights?"

A man walked out of a doorway with a red palm mark across his cheek. He growled, "I'll let Lord Tanyl know you have declined his invitation."

Elfleda's voice sneered, "You do that. And next time, tell him to have the guts to do it himself!"

The man stopped and stared at the pixie Jonna held in his hand. Of course, since Jonna could not be seen, it appeared the pixie hovered.

"What do we have here?" The man leaned closer.

Bob blinked. "Did anyone see the tree that ran over me?"

The man's hand reached forward. Jonna thrust-kicked to his stomach, stepped in, and uppercut to his jaw. The man's body slammed backwards into the wall and slid slowly down. Jonna strode into the open doorway.

A beautiful elvish room met his eyes. The silk bed covers glistened in the light of lamps. Elfleda paced across the center of the room.

"Bob? Bob!" She hurried toward him.

Bob blinked wide-eyed. "Elfleda?"

"Bob, where's Jonna? We have to find Jonna!"

Bob reached a hand out to tap the empty air. "He was right with me until--" His head shook. "Sorry. Do trees hit back?"

"Bob!"

His tiny hand lifted. "Give me a minute. I'm still getting my bearings."

"How did you find me?"

"He didn't. I did." Jonna shimmered into view.

Elfleda leaped toward him and gripped him tight. "I thought you were dead. They told you were dead!"

"Then why didn't you leave?"

"The room is warded. It blocks magic and will not let me step out."

His eyebrows crossed as he glanced at the exit. "Can I get out?"

"It is only designed to keep me in."

His face fell. "They have Elpis, too."

Her brow creased. "No." She pushed him toward the doorway. "Go, find her now. I will be here when you return."

"Let me get you out, first. I don't want you trapped here." The words the older Elpis had spoken cut through him. In her reality, Tanyl had killed Elfleda. "I don't like what he has planned."

"I can handle Tanyl. Elpis can't."

He set his feet as an odd strength flowed through him. She grunted but could not budge him toward the exit. "Listen to me, Elfleda. Listen, please!" His body turned, and his eyes looked into hers. "I will not leave you in peril." He lifted the dragon eye amulet from his neck and slipped it over her head.

The moment it touched her chest, she glanced down. "It is altered. I sense a different magic."

"It has restored the balance of the majik partitions. Ord called it the Eye of Anryulong because of the great golden dragon who helped us. Go to the elvish city. Let the queen know what has happened."

Her head shook. "You don't understand. Tanyl has the Dagger of Dilysmer. I cannot leave you."

"You can do no good trapped in this room." His eyes took on a faraway look as *The Sight* kicked in. "I will not have you defenseless." His jaw dropped in horror. "If you stay, I already see the outcome."

"Jonna!"

He touched the amulet. "Take her home."

"Jonna, no!"

Elfleda vanished.

The scene changed. The room around him faded from sight. He stood beside the Well of Urd in Ethese and gazed into its waters. The words, "*What do you see?*" flowed to his ears. In an

307

instant, he found himself back at Tanyl's camp. No ping had sounded; the partitions were still in balance. Something else had happened. When he touched his neck, the golden medallion from Arta's reality was warm to the touch. Did the medallion have power here, too? If so, what was it? He heard Elpis cry out.

His body flew past the doorway, his nose smelled the air, and he swept to the left. He sniffed at the third room; she had just been there.

The scent, almost as strong, led up the steps to the story above. He spun the corner in time to see a flicker of her dress as someone carried her.

With heaving lungs, Bob pulled beside him. "When did you get so fast?"

Jonna raced down the corridor with all his senses multiplied a hundredfold. Rooms and stairs shot past. His eyes caught every flicker. His ears picked up the tiniest sounds. His head throbbed as he tried to focus on only those he chased.

Bob shouted from a turn behind. "Jonna, wait for me!"

Muffled screams rose outside the building. Voices yelled as troops formed regiments. The twang of crossbow bolts met his ears. The cry of wolves tore at his heart.

He rounded the corner and found another set of stairs. They were steeper and ended at a flat square in the ceiling.

His legs leaped four steps at a time. At the top, he slammed against the square. Both hands pressed it as his legs strained. The stairs bowed and cracked. The door bent upward.

As daylight cracked the edges, he saw a metal bolt twisted in a curve. The bolt snapped. The square launched back to slam against wood. His lungs heaved as he walked the last few stairs and turned to face Elpis with her kidnapper.

Aldyth held a knife to the child's throat. A nervous smile crossed his lips. "You made it. We only have to wait for Lord Tanyl, and my transaction is complete."

Jonna's eyes burned as his voice deepened. "Let the girl go."

"Not till I have my money."

Jonna took a step forward.

"Not so close." Aldyth nodded at the girl. "This knife might slip."

A savage anger burned in Jonna. His eyes shifted. The world took on a strange red tint. "*Perun.*"

Lightning burst from a bright clear sky and struck the floor around Aldyth and Elpis.

The man jerked but held his stance. "Impressive, but you and I both know, you wouldn't dare chance hurting this sweet child."

Footsteps creaked from the stairs below. Jonna shifted to watch Aldyth and Elpis as well as who came up next.

Lord Tanyl sneered at Jonna as he stepped upon the landing. "No hugs for a fellow noble? That's not very friendly, especially since I'll be comforting your widowed wife." A grin spread across his face. "You did a great job rescuing her. Her sweet mother forbade her to come to your aid, so now I have her and the amulet." He drew an odd shaped dagger. Instead of a single blade, a second blade cut the first in the middle at a ninety degree angle. The dual shape of the dagger's blades formed an x. It tapered from the handle to a very sharp point. "Only one thing remains."

Jonna reached for the rune blade, but his hand stopped at Tanyl's words.

"I wouldn't do that. Aldyth might slip."

Jonna's enhanced ears listened. He could hear Elpis' shallow breaths. The ones next to her were Aldyth's. If he could do that--his eyes stared into Tanyl's as he brought his right hand down from the rune blade. His voice became very calm. "Alright, let's play it your way."

Tanyl's irises enlarged. Though his facial expression did not change, sweat formed on the sides of his face. He advanced cautiously toward Jonna. "This will only take a moment."

A sweet aroma caught Jonna's nose. His hands relaxed more.

"Remember," Tanyl taunted. "Any unexpected moves and the girl dies."

Jonna's voice remained casual. "Aldyth, I'll double what Tanyl is paying you if you'll simply walk away."

Tanyl stopped and threw a nervous glance at Aldyth. "Don't listen to him. A dead man can't pay anything."

Esti's scent grew stronger.

Bob shot up through the square hole in the floor. "Jonna, Lord Tanyl is--" His eyes grew large. "--here." He swallowed. "Uh, er, sorry."

Tanyl stepped back to keep both in sight. "Call the pixie to come beside you, now!"

As Bob flew toward him, Jonna nodded slightly in the pixie's direction. "Aldyth, what if I can prove my ability to pay. Right here, right now. Would that be enough?

Aldyth's eyes studied him. "How?"

The voice of Tanyl growled. "That's enough. Don't you see he is playing you for a fool? Does he look like he has any money hidden on him?" Tanyl spat at Jonna. "You're time is up."

Jonna held up a closed fist. "Shall I pay the man, Bob?"

A sparkle gleamed in Bob's eye. "Of course, Your Highness." As he passed near Jonna, small sparkles fell from the side of Bob's body. The sparkles dropped over Jonna's hand. It was the same magic Bob had used at a bar in the city of Diggory when Jonna had sought to find his wife.

Aldyth's hand tightened on the dagger. His eyes narrowed at Bob. "No tricks."

As Jonna's palm opened, a gold coin lay upon it. Bob gave a smug smile. A sparkle caught in Aldyth's eye.

"If I can do this, how much more do think I can supply?" Esti's fragrance lay beneath them on the floor below. His blood raced at its presence, but he kept control. His hand flipped the coin toward Aldyth.

Aldyth relaxed the dagger as he reached with his free hand to catch the coin in the air. Something hit the stairs at a run. A large she-wolf turned at the landing and leaped for Aldyth's throat.

TWISTED FATES

The dagger in Aldyth's hand turned toward the she-wolf. His feet slid back as he shoved Elpis into the wolf's path.

A vicious growl erupted. With a twist of her head, the wolf's jaws clamped down onto the elf's wrist. The dagger clattered to the ground, and the she-wolf dragged Aldyth toward the edge of the building.

Aldyth shrieked as Elpis dashed toward Jonna. Tanyl lunged to swipe, not at Jonna, but at the little girl.

With a burst of speed, Jonna smashed into Lord Tanyl with his right shoulder. He snatched hold of the elf's wrist with his left hand, pulled down, and slammed upward with his right forearm against the elf's elbow.

Tanyl screamed out as the elbow shattered. The dagger clattered to the landing. Jonna elbowed a shot to the throat as he released the elf's right wrist and sent the lord flying back. Tanyl crashed against the deck. The elf did not get up.

The sweet fragrance faded. Aldyth had vanished. Jonna turned back to Elpis and threw his arms around her. She grabbed hold with great sobs.

An enraged roar came from behind him. He spun to see Tanyl charging toward him with the dagger glistening in the light.

A portal flash behind the elf. Elfleda stepped out, raised her hand, and spoke harshly, "*Rhewbodol!*"

Lord Tanyl froze in mid-charge. She walked around the frozen lord and glared. "You will pay for your deception and lies. I swear it!" She reached up and removed the Dagger of Dilysmer from his hand, and then turned to Jonna and Elpis. Her gaze softened. "Quickly, the portal will close soon."

The battle around them had lessened. No more cries met their ears. Jonna looked down over the fort beneath. Some wolves dragged off bodies while others ripped the bodies apart.

Footsteps sounded upon the wooden stairs, and Prince Conall strode onto the landing. A wolfish grin crossed his face. "We have done as bargained, Your Highness." The prince bowed. "It will be

311

our reward to clean up the mess. After all, my troops are hungry." His eyes darted to Lord Tanyl. "And him, as well, if you wish."

Elfleda's head turned toward Jonna with a questioning glance.

Jonna knew her intent. "I believe Lord Tanyl is to stand trial before the queen for his crimes." His voice turned hard. "The rest are yours."

The prince gave a smug smile. "You are gracious, Your Highness, thank you. We will meet again." Conall laughed as he stepped down the stairs. The echoes of his laughter bounced up until he passed too far away to hear.

Guards came through the portal, stepped to each side of Tanyl, and lifted him up. They carried him through.

"We should go." Elfleda shivered as the stench of the dead grew stronger. "This is no place for a little girl."

He shifted Elpis to one arm and placed the other around Elfleda. "It's time to go home."

CHAPTER 23

Jonna stirred. The silk sheets lay upon him, and Elfleda snuggled at his side. The bedroom in the eternal tree felt comfortable and pleasant. All had been forbidden to disturb their honeymoon, thus said the queen.

His head tilted toward his wife. Her breath rose and fell. The rustle of leaves around them announced the gentle breeze outside. Without a noise, he moved away, slipped his feet from the covers, and sat up. His feet touched the wooden floor.

Despite the coolness, the wood remained warm. Silently, he picked up a robe, donned it, and steered through the living room onto the porch outside. The stairs down the great tree were to his left. This time, the queen had set guards to protect the staircase.

Moonbeams dropped to shine upon the floor. He sat down to think.

Tomorrow at noon, he would receive his official title as Protector of the Realm. After the recent saving of his family, and the defeat of Lord Tanyl, all disputers of his right to be named had gone silent.

The wind whipped in a quick blast. His robe fluttered.

A dark image sailed his way, and a song floated on the wind. "Wake, my hero. Come to me in a time of flight and fancy-free. Open up the gates that swing, and know that you have begot four kings."

A baby's cry met his ears, but its voice lay far off in the distance. A raven fluttered past, stared at him, and took off.

"Your message is old, raven. There is only one heir to the Elvish throne, and that lies within Elfleda."

The raven cawed as it swerved away.

Jonna added as he watched the raven vanish into the darkness, "Give my regards to Ord."

He touched the Eye of Anryulong around his neck. The slit of the dragon eye could be seen even in this light. However, there was another. The golden medallion from Arta's reality had also been transferred to his. Had things truly returned to the way the world should be, or had he altered them forever?

His thoughts drifted to Ord's city beneath the lake, to Almundena, Princess Alfgia, and Deela, wherever, however, they were now. And somewhere faraway, the fragrance of Esti drifted on the wind.

ABOUT THE AUTHOR

J.W. Peercy spent his early years in California, (fifteen minutes from Disneyland!). As to the effect of this experience, we can only guess, but imagination seems to make the top of the list. During his later years in Texas, he received a BA in Computer Science with a minor in Math. Although analytical, the creative side has to find a way out. To ease the pain, he designs websites, programs code, and writes. If you like the book, drop him a line. If you don't like the book, drop him a line anyway. He will appreciate the feedback. As in the words of J.R.R. Tolkien, 'May the hair on your toes never fall out!'

OTHER BOOKS BY LINE BY LION

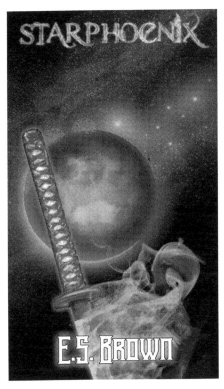

A galaxy teeters on the brink of war over dwindling energy reserves. An act of terror on a distant planet leaves half a million people dead. A world leader is murdered by a mysterious cyborg assassin. Maxim Starphoenix is the one person who can bring those responsible to justice. If his own government doesn't kill him first.

Action. Adventure. Fantasy. Heroes. Corruption. Conspiracy theories. Spirituality.

It's 9/11 meets "Star Wars" in the debut novel from E. S. Brown.

Circuits & Steam is an anthology featuring bold tales of man meets machine. Encounter eight exciting stories from authors K.A. DaVur, Sara Marian, Brick Marlin, Thomas Lamkin, Jr., Marian Allen, Katina French, James W. Peercy and Dani J. Caile, told in a cyberpunk or steampunk style. What makes you human? In the dystopian near-future, a desperate young woman makes a stunning decision, a cybernetically-enhanced waitress discovers her true nature, a white collar worker learns the true cost of her latest technological enhancement and a streetwise urchin makes desperate a bid for freedom. What defines your destiny? We journey to a 19th century that never was for a humorous tale of airship adventure, a town under attack by mechanical monsters, a case of alchemy and mistaken identity, and a gritty adventurer faced with a telling choice. Cyberpunk and steampunk explore our often toxic relationship with technology. Do our gadgets make us more than human, or just more human? Step inside our time machine and find out....

Be Careful What You Wish For, Some Dreams Take On A Life Of Their Own... It was just a matter of time... quantum leaps in technology, mind over matter, wars fought with thought, reality as malleable as clay. The Earth they knew was ravaged. Mankind finally had to face his darkest fears... and his own extinction. Their only hope was to fight fantasy with fantasy. Still guilt-ridden years after the death of his friend, Ayin has drifted most of his life bound to no man's rules. When he awakens without memory in a mysterious realm not on any map, a mythic guardian unloads the weight of all worlds on his shoulders. Aided by a nobleman, a musician, and a scholar, he must save the Tree of Dreams from a living nightmare before it unravels all of creation.

DREAMTIME

A True Story That Hasn't Happened Yet

ALAN J MARTIN

318

Made in the USA
Charleston, SC
23 September 2015